William Faulkner
FLAGS IN THE DUST

William Cuthbert Faulkner was born in 1897 in New Albany, Mississippi, the first of four sons of Murry and Maud Butler Falkner (he
later added the "u" to the family name himself). In 1904 the family
moved to the university town of Oxford, Mississippi, where Faulkner
was to spend most of his life. He was named for his great-grandfather
"The Old Colonel," a Civil War veteran who built a railroad, wrote a
bestselling romantic novel called *The White Rose of Memphis*,
became a Mississippi state legislator, and was eventually killed in
what may or may not have been a duel with a disgruntled business
partner. Faulkner identified with this robust and energetic ancestor
and often said that he inherited the "ink stain" from him.

Never fond of school, Faulkner left at the end of football season
his senior year of high school, and began working at his grandfather's
bank. In 1918, after his plans to marry his sweetheart Estelle Oldham
were squashed by their families, he tried to enlist as a pilot in the U.S.
Army but was rejected because he did not meet the height and
weight requirements. He went to Canada, where he pretended to be
an Englishman and joined the RAF training program there.
Although he did not complete his training until after the war ended
and never saw combat, he returned to his hometown in uniform,
boasting of war wounds. He briefly attended the University of Mississippi, where he began to publish his poetry.

After spending a short time living in New York, he again returned
to Oxford, where he worked at the university post office. His first book,
a collection of poetry, *The Marble Faun*, was published at Faulkner's
own expense in 1924. The writer Sherwood Anderson, whom he met
in New Orleans in 1925, encouraged him to try writing fiction, and
his first novel, *Soldier's Pay*, was published in 1926. It was followed by
Mosquitoes. His next novel, which he titled *Flags in the Dust*, was
rejected by his publisher and twelve others to whom he submitted it.
It was eventually published in drastically edited form as *Sartoris* (the
original version was not issued until after his death). Meanwhile, he
was writing *The Sound and the Fury*, which, after being rejected by

one publisher, came out in 1929 and received many ecstatic reviews, although it sold poorly. Yet again, a new novel, *Sanctuary*, was initially rejected by his publisher, this time as "too shocking." While working on the night shift at a power plant, Faulkner wrote what he was determined would be his masterpiece, *As I Lay Dying*. He finished it in about seven weeks, and it was published in 1930, again to generally good reviews and mediocre sales.

In 1929 Faulkner had finally married his childhood sweetheart, Estelle, after her divorce from her first husband. They had a premature daughter, Alabama, who died ten days after birth in 1931; a second daughter, Jill, was born in 1933.

With the eventual publication of his most sensational and violent (as well as, up till then, most successful) novel, *Sanctuary* (1931), Faulkner was invited to write scripts for MGM and Warner Brothers, where he was responsible for much of the dialogue in the film versions of Hemingway's *To Have and Have Not* and Chandler's *The Big Sleep*, and many other films. He continued to write novels and published many stories in the popular magazines. *Light in August* (1932) was his first attempt to address the racial issues of the South, an effort continued in *Absalom, Absalom!* (1936), and *Go Down, Moses* (1942). By 1946, most of Faulkner's novels were out of print in the United States (although they remained well-regarded in Europe), and he was seen as a minor, regional writer. But then the influential editor and critic Malcolm Cowley, who had earlier championed Hemingway and Fitzgerald and others of their generation, put together the *Portable Faulkner*, and once again Faulkner's genius was recognized, this time for good. He received the 1949 Nobel Prize for Literature as well as many other awards and accolades, including the National Book Award and the Gold Medal from the American Academy of Arts and Letters and France's Legion of Honor.

In addition to several collections of short fiction, his other novels include *Pylon* (1935), *The Unvanquished* (1938), *The Wild Palms* (1939), *The Hamlet* (1940), *Intruder in the Dust* (1948), *A Fable* (1954), *The Town* (1957), *The Mansion* (1959), and *The Reivers* (1962).

William Faulkner died of a heart attack on July 6, 1962, in Oxford, Mississippi, where he is buried.

FLAGS IN THE DUST

BOOKS BY WILLIAM FAULKNER

The Marble Faun (1924)

Soldier's Pay (1926)

Mosquitoes (1927)

Sartoris (1929) [*Flags in the Dust* (1973)]

The Sound and the Fury (1929)

As I Lay Dying (1930)

Sanctuary (1931)

These 13 (1931)

Light in August (1932)

A Green Bough (1933)

Doctor Martino and Other Stories (1934)

Pylon (1935)

Absalom, Absalom! (1936)

The Unvanquished (1938)

The Wild Palms [*If I Forget Thee, Jerusalem*] (1939)

The Hamlet (1940)

Go Down, Moses (1942)

Intruder in the Dust (1948)

Knight's Gambit (1949)

Collected Stories of William Faulkner (1950)

Notes on a Horsethief (1951)

Requiem for a Nun (1954)

A Fable (1954)

Big Woods (1955)

The Town (1957)

The Mansion (1959)

The Reivers (1962)

Uncollected Stories of William Faulkner (1979, Posthumous)

William Faulkner

FLAGS IN
THE DUST

VINTAGE INTERNATIONAL

Vintage Books

A Division of Random House, Inc.

New York

FIRST VINTAGE INTERNATIONAL EDITION, JANUARY 2012

Library of Congress Cataloging-in-Publication Data
Faulkner, William, 1897–1962.
Flags in the dust.
An uncut version of the work published in 1929 under title: Sartoris.
I. Title.
[PZ3.F272F 4] [PS3511.A86] 813'.5'2
74-3315

Vintage ISBN: 978-0-307-94676-8

www.vintagebooks.com

146028962

PUBLISHER'S NOTE

This edition follows the text of *Flags in the Dust* as corrected in 2006 by Noel Polk. An editors' note on the corrections by Noel Polk follows the text; the line and page notes were prepared by Joseph Blotner.

FLAGS IN THE DUST

One

1

As usual old man Falls had brought John Sartoris into the room with him, had walked the three miles in from the county Poor Farm, fetching, like an odor, like the clean dusty smell of his faded overalls, the spirit of the dead man into that room where the dead man's son sat and where the two of them, pauper and banker, would sit for a half an hour in the company of him who had passed beyond death and then returned.

Freed as he was of time and flesh, he was a far more palpable presence than either of the two old men who sat shouting periodically into one another's deafness while the business of the bank went forward in the next room and people in the adjoining stores on either side listened to the indistinguishable uproar of their voices coming through the walls. He was far more palpable than the two old men cemented by a common deafness to a dead period and so drawn thin by the slow attenuation of days; even now, although old man Falls had departed to tramp the three miles back to that which he now called home, John Sartoris seemed to loom still in the room, above and about his son, with his bearded, hawklike face, so that as old Bayard sat with his crossed feet propped against the corner of the cold hearth, holding the pipe in his hand, it seemed to him that he could hear his father's breathing even, as though that other were so much more palpable than mere transiently articulated clay as to even penetrate into the uttermost citadel of silence in which his son lived.

The bowl of the pipe was ornately carved and it was charred with much usage, and on the bit were the prints of his father's teeth, where he had left the very print of his ineradicable bones as though in enduring stone, like the creatures of that prehistoric day that were too grandly conceived and executed either to exist very long or to vanish utterly when dead from an earth shaped and furnished for punier things. Old Bayard sat holding the pipe in his hand.

"What are you giving it to me for, after all this time?" he had asked, fingering the pipe, and old man Falls answered.

"Well, I reckon I've kept it long as Cunnel aimed for me to," old man Falls answered. "A po' house aint no fitten place for anything of his'n, Bayard. And I'm goin' on ninety-fo' year old."

Later he gathered up his small parcels and left, but still old Bayard sat for some time, the pipe in his hand, rubbing the bowl slowly with his thumb. After a while John Sartoris departed also, withdrawn rather to that place where the peaceful dead contemplate their glamorous frustrations, and old Bayard rose and thrust the pipe into his pocket and took a cigar from the humidor on the mantel. As he struck the match the door across the room opened and a man wearing a green eyeshade entered and approached.

"Simon's here, Colonel," he said in a voice utterly without inflection.

"What?" Old Bayard said across the match.

"Simon's come."

"Oh. All right."

The other turned and went out. Old Bayard flung the match into the grate and put the cigar in his pocket and closed his desk and took his black felt hat from the top of it and followed the other from the room. The man in the eyeshade and the cashier were busy beyond the grille. Old Bayard stalked on through the lobby and passed through the door with its drawn green shade and emerged upon the street, where Simon in a linen duster and an ancient top-hat held the matched geldings glittering in the spring afternoon, at the curb.

There was a hitching-post there, which old Bayard retained with a testy disregard of industrial progress, but Simon never used it. Until the door opened and Bayard emerged from behind the drawn shades bearing the words "Bank Closed" in cracked gold leaf, Simon retained his seat, the reins in his left hand and the thong of the whip caught smartly back in his right and usually the unvarying and seemingly incombustible fragment of a cigar at a swaggering angle in his black face, talking to the shining team in a steady, lover-like flow. He spoiled horses. He admired Sartorises and he had for them a warmly protective tenderness, but he loved horses, and beneath his hands the sorriest beast bloomed and acquired comeliness like a caressed woman, temperament like an opera star.

Old Bayard closed the door behind him and crossed to the carriage with that stiff erectness which, as a countryman once remarked, if he ever stumbled, would meet itself falling down. One or two passers and a merchant or so in the adjacent doorways saluted him with a sort of florid servility, and behind him the shade on one window drew aside upon the disembodied face of the man in the green eye-shade. The book-keeper was a hillman of indeterminate age, a silent man who performed his duties with tedious slow care and who watched Bayard constantly and covertly all the while he was in view.

Nor did Simon dismount even then. With his race's fine feeling for potential theatrics he drew himself up and arranged the limp folds of the duster, communicating by some means the histrionic moment to the horses so that they too flicked their glittering coats and tossed their leashed heads, and into Simon's wizened black face there came an expression indescribably majestical as he touched his whiphand to his hatbrim. Bayard got into the carriage and Simon clucked to the horses, and the onlookers, halted to admire the momentary drama of the departure, fell behind.

There was something different in Simon's air today, in the very shape of his back and the angle of his hat: he appeared to be bursting with something momentous and ill-contained. But he withheld it for the time being, and at a dashing, restrained pace he drove among the tethered wagons about the square and swung into a broad street where what Bayard called paupers sped back and forth in automobiles, and withheld it until the town was behind them and they trotted on across burgeoning countryside cluttered still with gasoline-propelled paupers but at greater intervals, and his employer had settled back for the changing and peaceful monotony of the four-mile drive. Then Simon checked the team to a more sedate pace and turned his head.

His voice was not particularly robust nor resonant, yet somehow he could talk to old Bayard without difficulty. Others must shout in order to penetrate that wall of deafness beyond which Bayard lived; yet Simon could and did hold long, rambling conversations with him in that monotonous, rather high sing-song of his, particularly while in the carriage, the vibration of which helped Bayard's hearing a little.

"Mist' Bayard done got home," Simon remarked in a conversational tone.

Old Bayard sat perfectly and furiously still for a moment while his heart went on, a little too fast and a little too lightly, cursing his grandson for a furious moment; sat so still that Simon looked back and found him gazing quietly out across the land. Simon raised his voice a little.

"He got offen de two oclock train," he continued. "Jumped off de wrong side and lit out th'ough de woods. Section hand seed 'im. Only he aint never come out home yit when I lef'. I thought he wuz wid you, maybe." Dust spun from beneath the horses' feet and moiled in a sluggish cloud behind them. Against the thickening hedgerows their shadow rushed in failing surges, with twinkling spokes and high-stepping legs in a futility of motion without progress. "Wouldn't even git off at de dee-po," Simon continued, with a kind of fretful exasperation. "De dee-po his own folks built. Jumpin' offen de bline side like a hobo. He never even had on no sojer-clothes. Jes a suit, lak a drummer er somethin'. And when I 'members dem shiny boots and dem light yaller pants and dat 'ere double-jinted backin'-up strop he wo' home las' year. . . ." He turned and looked back again. "Cunnel, you reckon dem war folks is done somethin' ter him?"

"What do you mean?" Bayard demanded. "Is he lame?"

"I mean, him sneakin' into his own town. Sneakin' into town, on de ve'y railroad his own gran'pappy built, jes' like he wuz trash. Dem foreign folks done done somethin' ter him, er dey done sot dey po-lice atter him. I kep' a-tellin' him when he fust went off to dat 'ere foreign war him and Mr Johnny neither never had no business at——"

"Drive on," Bayard said. . . . . . . "Drive on, damn your black hide."

Simon clucked to the horses and shook them into a swifter gait. The road went on between hedgerows parallelling them with the senseless terrific antics of their shadow. Beyond the bordering gums and locusts and massed vines, fields new-broken or being broken spread on toward patches of woodland newly green and splashed with dogwood and judas trees. Behind laborious plows viscid shards of new-turned earth glinted damply in the sun.

This was upland country, lying in tilted slopes against the unbroken blue of the hills, but soon the road descended sheerly into a valley of good broad fields richly somnolent in the levelling afternoon, and presently they drove upon Bayard's own land, and from time to time a plowman lifted his hand to the passing carriage. Then the road approached the railroad and crossed it, and at last the house John Sartoris had built and rebuilt stood among locusts and oaks and Simon swung between iron gates and into a curving drive.

There was a bed of salvia where a Yankee patrol had halted on a day long ago. Simon brought up here with a flourish and Bayard descended and Simon clucked to the team again and rolled his cigar to a freer angle, and took the road back to town.

Bayard stood for a while before his house, but the white simplicity of it dreamed unbroken among ancient sunshot trees. Wistaria mounting one end of the veranda had bloomed and fallen, and a faint drift of shattered petals lay palely about the dark roots of it and about the roots of a rose trained onto the same frame. The rose was slowly but steadily choking the other vine, and it bloomed now thickly with buds no bigger than a thumbnail and blown flowers no larger than silver dollars, myriad, odorless and unpickable.

But the house itself was still and serenely benignant, and he mounted to the empty, colonnaded veranda and crossed it and entered the hall. The house was silent, richly desolate of motion or any sound.

"Bayard."

The stairway with its white spindles and red carpet mounted in a tall slender curve into upper gloom. From the center of the ceiling hung a chandelier of crystal prisms and shades, fitted originally for candles but since wired for electricity; to the right of the entrance, beside folding doors rolled back upon a dim room emanating an atmosphere of solemn

and seldom violated stateliness and known as the parlor, stood
a tall mirror filled with grave obscurity like a still pool of
evening water. At the opposite end of the hall checkered sunlight fell in a long slant across the door, and from somewhere
beyond the bar of sunlight a voice rose and fell in a steady preoccupied minor, like a chant. The words were not distinguish-
able, but Bayard could not hear them at all. He raised his voice
again.

"Bayard."

The chanting ceased, and as he turned toward the stairs a
tall mulatto woman appeared in the slanting sunlight without
the back door and came sibilantly into the house. Her faded
blue garment was pinned up about her knees and it was darkly
and irregularly blotched. Beneath it her shanks were straight
and lean as the legs of a tall bird, and her bare feet were pale
coffee-splashes on the dark polished floor.

"Wuz you callin' somebody, Cunnel?" she said, raising her
voice to penetrate his deafness. Bayard paused with his hand
on the walnut newel post and looked down at the woman's
pleasant yellow face.

"Has anybody come in this afternoon?" he asked.

"Why, naw, suh," Elnora answered. "Dey aint nobody here
a-tall, dat I knows about. Miss Jenny done gone to huh club-
meetin' in town dis evenin'," she added. Bayard stood with his
foot raised to the step, glowering at her.

"Why in hell cant you niggers tell me the truth about
things?" he raged suddenly. "Or not tell me anything at all?"

"Lawd, Cunnel, who'd be comin' out here, lessen you er
Miss Jenny sont 'um?" But he had gone on, tramping furiously
up the stairs. The woman looked after him, then she raised her
voice: "Does you want Isom, er anything?" He did not look
back. Perhaps he had not heard her, and she stood and
watched him out of sight. "He's gittin' old," she said to herself

quietly, and she turned on her sibilant bare feet and returned down the hall whence she had come.

Bayard stopped again in the upper hall. The western windows were closed with latticed blinds, through which sunlight seeped in yellow dissolving bars that but served to increase the gloom. At the opposite end a tall door opened upon a shallow grilled balcony which offered the valley and the cradling semicircle of the eastern hills in panorama. On either side of this door was a narrow window set with leaded panes of vari-colored glass that, with the bearer of them, constituted John Sartoris' mother's deathbed legacy to him, which his youngest sister had brought from Carolina in a straw-filled hamper in '69.

This was Virginia Du Pre, who came to them, two years a wife and seven years a widow at thirty—a slender woman with a delicate replica of the Sartoris nose and that expression of indomitable and utter weariness which all Southern women had learned to wear, bringing with her the clothing in which she stood and a wicker hamper filled with colored glass. It was she who told them of the manner of Bayard Sartoris' death prior to the second battle of Manassas. She had told the story many times since (at eighty she still told it, on occasions usually inopportune) and as she grew older the tale itself grew richer and richer, taking on a mellow splendor like wine; until what had been a hair-brained prank of two heedless and reckless boys wild with their own youth, was become a gallant and finely tragical focal-point to which the history of the race had been raised from out the old miasmic swamps of spiritual sloth by two angels valiantly fallen and strayed, altering the course of human events and purging the souls of men.

That Carolina Bayard had been rather a handful, even for Sartorises. Not so much a black sheep as a nuisance all of whose qualities were positive and unpredictable. His were merry blue eyes, and his rather long hair fell in tawny curls about his temples. His high-colored face wore that expression of frank and high-hearted dullness which you imagine Richard First as wearing before he went crusading, and once he hunted a pack of fox hounds through a rustic tabernacle in which a Methodist revival was being held; and thirty minutes later (having caught the fox) he returned alone and rode his horse into the ensuing indignation meeting. In a spirit of fun purely: he believed too firmly in Providence, as all his actions clearly showed, to have any religious convictions whatever. So when Fort Moultrie fell and the governor refused to surrender it, the Sartorises were privately a little glad, for now Bayard would have something to do.

In Virginia, as an A.D.C. of Jeb Stuart's, he found plenty to do. As the A.D.C. rather, for though Stuart had a large military family, they were soldiers trying to win a war and needing sleep occasionally: Bayard Sartoris alone was willing, nay eager, to defer sleep to that time when monotony should return to the world. But now was a holiday.

The war was also a godsend to Jeb Stuart, and shortly thereafter, against the dark and bloody obscurity of the northern Virginia campaigns, Jeb Stuart at thirty and Bayard Sartoris at twenty-three stood briefly like two flaming stars garlanded with Fame's burgeoning laurel and the myrtle and roses of Death, incalculable and sudden as meteors in General Pope's troubled military sky, thrusting upon him like an unwilling garment that notoriety which his skill as a soldier could never have won him. And still in a spirit of pure fun: neither Jeb Stuart nor Bayard Sartoris, as their actions clearly showed, had any political convictions involved at all.

Aunt Jenny told the story first shortly after she came to them. It was Christmas time and they sat before a hickory fire in the rebuilt library—Aunt Jenny with her sad resolute face and John Sartoris, bearded and hawklike, and his three children and a guest: a Scottish engineer whom John Sartoris had met in Mexico in '45 and who was now helping him to build his railway.

Work on the railroad had ceased for the holiday season and John Sartoris and his engineer had ridden in at dusk from the suspended railhead in the hills to the north, and they now sat after supper in the firelight. The sun had set ruddily, leaving the air brittle as thin glass with frost, and presently Joby came in with an armful of firewood. He put a fresh billet on the fire, and in the dry air the flames crackled and snapped, popping in fading embers outward upon the hearth.

"Chris'mus!" Joby exclaimed with the grave and simple pleasure of his race, prodding at the blazing logs with the Yankee musket-barrel which stood in the chimney corner until sparks swirled upward into the dark maw of the chimney like wild golden veils, "year dat, chilluns?" John Sartoris' eldest daughter was twenty-two and would be married in June, Bayard was twenty, and the younger girl seventeen; and so Aunt Jenny for all her widowhood was one of the chillen too, to Joby. Then he replaced the musket-barrel in its niche and fired a long pine sliver at the hearth in order to light the candles. But Aunt Jenny stayed him, and he was gone—a shambling figure in an old formal coat too large for him, stooped and gray with age; and Aunt Jenny, speaking always of Jeb Stuart as Mister Stuart, told her story.

It had to do with an April evening, and coffee. Or the lack of it, rather; and Stuart's military family sat in scented darkness beneath a new moon, talking of ladies and dead pleasures and thinking of home. Away in the darkness horses moved invisibly with restful sounds, and bivouac fires fell to glowing points like spent fireflies, and somewhere neither near nor far the General's body servant touched a guitar in lingering random chords. Thus they sat in the poignance of spring and youth's

immemorial sadness, forgetting travail and glory, remembering instead other Virginian evenings with fiddles above the
myriad candles and slender grave measures picked out with
light laughter and lighter feet, thinking *When will this be
again? Shall I make one?* until they had talked themselves into
a state of savage nostalgia and words grew shorter and shorter
and less and less frequent. Then the General roused himself
and brought them back by speaking of coffee, or its lack.

This talk of coffee began to end a short time later with a
ride along midnight roads and then through woods black as
pitch, where horses went at a walk and riders rode with sabre or
musket at arm's length before them lest they be swept from saddle by invisible boughs, and continued until the forest thinned
with dawn-ghosts and the party of twenty was well within the
Federal lines. Then dawn accomplished itself yet more and all
efforts toward concealment were discarded and they galloped
again and crashed through astonished picket-parties returning
placidly to camp, and fatigue parties setting forth with picks
and axes and shovels in the golden sunrise, and swept yelling
up the knoll where General Pope and his staff sat at breakfast al
fresco.

Two men captured a fat staff-major, others pursued the
fleeing breakfasters for a short distance into the sanctuary of
the woods, but most of them rushed on to the General's private
commissary tent and emerged presently from the cyclonic
demolition of it, bearing plunder. Stuart and the three officers
with him halted their dancing mounts at the table and one of
them swept up a huge blackened coffee-pot and tendered it to
the General, and while the enemy shouted and fired muskets
among the trees, they toasted each other in sugarless and
creamless scalding coffee, as with a loving cup.

"General Pope, Sir," Stuart said, bowing in his saddle to
the captured officer. He drank and extended the pot.

"I'll drink it, Sir," the major replied, "and thank God he is not here to respond in person."

"I had remarked that he appeared to leave hurriedly," Stuart said. "A prior engagement, perhaps?"

"Yes, Sir. With General Halleck," the major agreed drily. "I am sorry we have him for an opponent instead of Lee."

"So am I, Sir," Stuart answered. "I like General Pope in a war." Bugles were shrilling among the trees far and near, sending the alarm in flying echoes from brigade to brigade lying about the forest, and drums were beating wildly to arms and erratic bursts of musketry surged and trickled along the scattered outposts like the dry clatter of an opening fan, for the name 'Stuart' speeding from picket to picket had peopled the blossoming peaceful woods with gray phantoms.

Stuart turned in his saddle and his men came up and sat their horses and watched him alertly, their spare eager faces like mirrors reflecting their leader's constant consuming flame. Then from the flank there came something like a concerted volley, striking the coffee-pot from Bayard Sartoris' hand and clipping and snapping viciously among the dappled branches above their heads.

"Be pleased to mount, Sir," Stuart said to the captive major, and though his tone was exquisitely courteous all levity was gone from it. "Captain Wylie, you have the heaviest mount: will you——?" The captain freed his stirrup and hauled the prisoner up behind him. "Forward!" the General said and whirled rowelling his bay, and with the thunderous coordination of a single centaur they swept down the knoll and crashed into the forest at the point from which the volley had come before it could be repeated. Blue-clad pigmy shapes plunged scattering before and beneath them, and they rushed on among trees vicious with minies like wasps. Stuart now carried his plumed hat in his hand and his long tawny locks, tossing to the rhythm of his speed, appeared as gallant flames smoking with the wild and self-consuming splendor of his daring.

Behind them and on one flank muskets still banged and popped at their flashing phantoms, and from brigade to brigade lying spaced about the jocund forest bugles shrilled their importunate alarms. Stuart bore gradually to the left, bringing all the uproar into his rear. The country became more open and they swung into column at the gallop. The captured major bounced and jolted behind Captain Wylie and the General reined back beside the gallant black thundering along beneath its double load.

"I am distressed to inconvenience you thus, Sir," he began with his exquisite courtesy. "If you will indicate the general location of your nearest horse picket I shall be most happy to capture a mount for you."

"Thank you, General," the major replied, "but majors can be replaced much easier than horses. I shall not trouble you."

"Just as you wish, Sir," Stuart agreed stiffly. He spurred on to the head of the column again. They now galloped along a faint trace that was once a road. It wound on between vernal palisades of undergrowth and they followed it at a rapid controlled gait and debouched suddenly upon a glade, and a squadron of Yankee cavalry reined back with shocked amazement, then hurled forward again.

Without faltering Stuart whirled his party and plunged back into the forest. Pistol-balls were thinly about their heads and the flat tossing reports were trivial as snapping twigs above the converging thunder of hooves. Stuart swerved from the road and they crashed headlong through undergrowth. The Federal horsemen came yelling behind them and Stuart led his party in a tight circle and halted it panting in a dense swampy copse and they heard the pursuit sweep past.

They pushed on and regained the road and retraced their former course, silently and utterly alert. To the left the sound of the immediate pursuit crashed on, dying away. Then they cantered again. Presently the woods thickened and they were forced to slow to a trot, then to a walk. Although there was no more firing and the bugles too had ceased, into the silence, above the strong and rapid breathing of the horses and the sound of their own hearts in their ears, was a nameless something—a tenseness seeping from tree to tree like an invisible mist, filling the dewy morning woods with portent though birds flashed swooping from tree to tree, unaware or disregardful of it.

A gleam of white through the trees ahead; Stuart raised his hand and they halted and sat their horses, watching him quietly and holding their breaths with listening. Then the General advanced again and broke through the undergrowth into another glade and they followed, and before them rose the knoll with the deserted breakfast-table and the rifled commissary tent. They trotted warily across the glade and halted at the table while the General scribbled hastily upon a scrap of paper. The glade dreamed quiet and empty of threat beneath the mounting golden day; laked within it lay a deep and abiding peace like golden wine; yet beneath this solitude and permeating it was that nameless and waiting portent, patient and brooding and sinister.

"Your sword, Sir," Stuart commanded, and the prisoner removed his weapon and Stuart took it and pinned his scribbled note to the table-top with it. The note read:

"General Stuart's compliments to General Pope, and he is sorry to have missed him again. He will call again tomorrow."

Stuart gathered up his reins. "Forward," he said.

They descended the knoll and crossed the empty glade and at an easy canter they took the road they had traversed that dawn—the road that led toward home. Stuart glanced back at his captive, at the gallant black with its double burden. "If you will direct us to the nearest cavalry picket I will provide you with a proper mount," he offered again.

"Will General Stuart, cavalry leader and General Lee's eyes, jeopardise his safety and that of his men and his cause in order to provide for the temporary comfort of a minor prisoner of his sword? This is not bravery: it is the rashness of a heedless and headstrong boy. There are fifteen thousand men within a radius of two miles of this point; even General Stuart cannot conquer that many, though they are Yankees, single-handed."

"Not for the prisoner, Sir," Stuart replied haughtily, "but for the officer suffering the fortune of war. No gentleman would do less."

"No gentleman has any business in this war," the major retorted. "There is no place for him here. He is an anachronism, like anchovies. At least General Stuart did not capture our anchovies," he added tauntingly. "Perhaps he will send Lee for them in person?"

"Anchovies," repeated Bayard Sartoris who galloped nearby, and he whirled his horse. Stuart shouted at him, but he lifted his reckless stubborn hand and flashed on; and as the General would have turned to follow a Yankee picket fired his piece from the roadside and dashed into the woods, shouting the alarm. Immediately other muskets exploded on all sides and from the forest to the right came the sound of a considerable body put suddenly into motion, and behind them in the direction of the invisible knoll, a volley crashed. A third officer spurred up and caught Stuart's bridle.

"Sir, Sir," he exclaimed. "What would you do?"

Stuart held his mount rearing, and another volley rang behind them, dribbling off into single scattered reports, crashed focalized again, and the noise to the right swelled nearer. "Let go, Allan," Stuart said. "He is my friend."

But the other clung on. "It is too late," he said. "Sartoris can only be killed: you would be captured."

"Forward, Sir, I beg," the captive major added. "What is one man, to a paladin out of romance?"

"Think of Lee, for God's sake, General!" the aide implored. "Forward!" he shouted to the troop, spurring his own mount and dragging the General's onward as a body of Federal horse broke from the woods behind them.

"And so," Aunt Jenny finished, "Mister Stuart went on and Bayard rode back after those anchovies, with all Pope's army shooting at him. He rode yelling 'Yaaaiiiih, Yaaaiiiih, come on, boys!' right up the knoll and jumped his horse over the breakfast table and rode it into the wrecked commissary tent, and a cook who was hidden under the mess stuck his arm out and shot Bayard in the back with a derringer.

"Mister Stuart fought his way out and got back home without losing but two men. He always spoke well of Bayard. He said he was a good officer and a fine cavalryman, but that he was too reckless."

They sat quietly for a time, in the firelight. The flames leaped and popped on the hearth and sparks soared in wild swirling plumes up the chimney, and Bayard Sartoris' brief career swept like a shooting star across the dark plain of their mutual remembering and suffering, lighting it with a transient glare like a soundless thunder-clap, leaving a sort of radiance when it died. The guest, the Scottish engineer, had sat quietly, listening. After a time he spoke.

"When he rode back, he was no actually cer-rtain there wer-re anchovies, was he?"

"The Yankee major said there were," Aunt Jenny replied.

"Ay." The Scotsman pondered again. "And did Muster-r Stuart retur-rn next day, as he said in's note?"

"He went back that afternoon," Aunt Jenny answered,

"looking for Bayard." Ashes soft as rosy feathers shaled glowing onto the hearth, and faded to the softest gray. John Sartoris leaned forward into the firelight and punched at the blazing logs with the Yankee musket-barrel.

"That was the god-damdest army the world ever saw, I reckon," he said.

"Yes," Aunt Jenny agreed. "And Bayard was the god-damdest man in it."

"Yes," John Sartoris admitted soberly, "Bayard was wild." The Scotsman spoke again.

"This Musterr Stuart, who said your brother was reckless: Who was he?"

"He was the cavalry general Jeb Stuart," Aunt Jenny answered. She brooded for a while upon the fire; her pale indomitable face held for a moment a tranquil tenderness. "He had a strange sense of humor," she said. "Nothing ever seemed quite so diverting to him as General Pope in his night-shirt." She dreamed once more on some far away place beyond the rosy battlements of the embers. "Poor man," she said. Then she said quietly: "I danced a valse with him in Baltimore in '58," and her voice was proud and still as banners in the dust.

. . . . But the door was closed now, and what light passed through the colored panes was richly solemn. To his left was his grandsons' room, the room in which his grandson's wife and her child had died last October. He stood beside this door for a moment, then he opened it quietly. The blinds were closed and the room had that breathless tranquillity of unoccupation, and he closed the door and tramped on with that heavy-footed obliviousness of the deaf and entered his own bedroom and crashed the door behind him, as was his way of shutting doors.

He sat down and removed his shoes, the shoes that were

made to his measure twice a year by a Saint Louis house, then he rose and went in his stockings to the window and looked down upon his saddle-mare tethered to a mulberry tree in the back yard and a negro lad lean as a hound, richly static beside it. From the kitchen, invisible from this window, Elnora's endless minor ebbed and flowed unheard by him upon the lazy scene.

He crossed to his closet and drew out a pair of scarred riding-boots and stamped into them and took a cigar from the humidor on his night table, and he stood for a time with the cold cigar between his teeth, having forgotten to light it. Through the cloth of his pocket his hand touched the pipe there, and he took it out and looked at it again, and it seemed to him that he could still hear old man Falls' voice in roaring recapitulation: "Cunnel was settin' thar in a cheer, his sock feet propped on the po'ch railin', smokin' this hyer very pipe. Old Louvinia was settin' on the steps, shellin' a bowl of peas fer supper. And a feller was glad to git even peas sometimes, in them days. And you was settin' back agin' the post. They wa'nt nobody else thar 'cep' yo' aunt, the one 'fo' Miss Jenny come. Cunnel had sont them two gals to Memphis to yo' gran'pappy when he fust went to Virginny with that 'ere regiment that turnt right around and voted him outen the colonelcy. Voted 'im out because he wouldn't be Tom, Dick and Harry with ever' skulkin' camp-robber that come along with a salvaged muskit and claimed to be a sojer. You was about half-grown then, I reckon. How old was you then, Bayard?"

"Fourteen."

"Hey?"

"Fourteen. Do I have to tell you that everytime you tell me this damn story?"

"And thar you all was a-settin' when they turned in at the gate and come trottin' up the carriage drive.

"Old Louvinia drapped the bowl of peas and let out one squawk, but Cunnel shet her up and told her to run and git his boots and pistols and have 'em ready at the back do', and you lit out fer the barn to saddle that stallion. And when them Yankees rid up and stopped—they stopped right whar that flower bed is now—they wa'nt nobody in sight but Cunnel, a-settin' thar like he never even heerd tell of no Yankees.

"The Yankees they sot thar on the hosses, talkin' 'mongst theyselves if this was the right house or not, and Cunnel settin' thar with his sock feet on the railin', gawkin' at 'em like a hillbilly. The Yankee officer he tole one man to ride back to the barn and look fer that 'ere stallion, then he says to Cunnel:

" 'Say, Johnny, whar do the rebel, John Sartoris, live?'

" 'Lives down the road a piece,' Cunnel says, not battin' a eye even. ''Bout two mile,' he says. 'But you wont find 'im now. He's away fightin' the Yanks agin.'

" 'Well, I reckon you better come and show us the way, anyhow,' the Yankee officer says.

"So Cunnel he got up slow and tole 'em to let 'im git his shoes and walkin' stick, and limped into the house, leavin' 'em a-settin' thar waitin'.

"Soon's he was out of sight he run. Old Louvinia was waitin' at the back do' with his coat and boots and pistols and a snack of cawn bread. That 'ere other Yankee had rid into the barn, and Cunnel taken the things from Louvinia and wropped 'em up in the coat and started acrost the back yard like he was jest takin' a walk. 'Bout that time the Yankee come to the barn do'.

" 'They aint no stock hyer a-tall,' the Yank says.

" 'I reckon not,' Cunnel says. 'Cap'm says fer you to come on back,' he says, goin' on. He could feel that 'ere Yank a-watchin' 'im, lookin' right 'twixt his shoulder blades, whar the bullet would hit. Cunnel says that was the hardest thing he ever done in his life, walkin' on thar acrost that lot with his back to'ads that Yankee without breakin' into a run. He was aimin' to'ads the corner of the barn, whar he could git the house between 'em, and Cunnel says hit seemed like he'd been a-walkin' a year without gittin' no closer and not darin' to look back. Cunnel says he wa'nt even thinkin' of nothin' 'cep' he was glad the gals wa'nt at home. He says he never give a thought to yo' aunt back thar in the house, because he says she was a full-blood Sartoris and she was a match fer any jest a dozen Yankees.

"Then the Yank hollered at him, but Cunnel kep' right on, not lookin' back nor nothin'. Then the Yank hollered agin and Cunnel says he could hyear the hoss movin' and he decided hit was time to stir his shanks. He made the corner of the barn jest as the Yank shot the fust time, and by the time the Yank got to the corner, he was in the hawg-lot, a-tearin' through the jimson weeds to'ads the creek whar you was waitin' with the stallion hid in the willers.

"And thar you was a-standin', holdin' the hoss and that 'ere Yankee patrol yellin' up behind, until Cunnel got his boots on. And then he tole you to tell yo' aunt he wouldn't be home fer supper."

"But what are you giving it to me for, after all this time?" he had asked, fingering the pipe, and old man Falls had said a poorhouse was no fit place for it.

"A thing he toted in his pocket and got enjoyment outen, in them days. Hit 'ud be different, I reckon, while we was a-buildin' the railroad. He said often enough in them days we was all goin' to be in the po'house by Sat'd'y night. Only I beat him, thar. I got thar fo' he did. Or the cemetary he meant, mo' likely, him ridin' up and down the survey with a saddlebag of money night and day, keepin' jest one cross tie ahead of the po'house, like he said. That 'us when hit changed. When he

had to start killin' folks. Them two cyarpet baggers stirrin' up
niggers, that he walked right into the room whar they was a-
settin' behind a table with they pistols layin' on the table, and
that robber and that other feller he kilt, all with that same dang
der'nger. When a feller has to start killin' folks, he 'most always
has to keep on killin' 'em. And when he does, he's already dead
hisself."

It showed on John Sartoris' brow, the dark shadow of fatality and doom, that night when he sat beneath the candles in
the dining room and turned a wine glass in his fingers while he
talked to his son. The railroad was finished, and today he had
been elected to the state legislature after a hard and bitter fight,
and doom lay on his brow, and weariness.

"And so," he said, "Redlaw'll kill me tomorrow, for I shall be
unarmed. I'm tired of killing men. . . . Pass the wine, Bayard."

And the next day he was dead, whereupon, as though he
had but waited for that to release him of the clumsy cluttering
of bones and breath, by losing the frustration of his own flesh
he could now stiffen and shape that which sprang from him
into the fatal semblance of his dream; to be evoked like a genie
or a deity by an illiterate old man's tedious reminiscing or by a
charred pipe from which even the rank smell of burnt tobacco
had long since faded away.

Old Bayard roused himself and went and laid the pipe on
his chest of drawers. Then he quitted the room and tramped
heavily down the stairs and out through the back.

The negro lad waked easily and untethered the mare and
held the stirrup. Old Bayard mounted and remembered the
cigar at last and fired it. The negro opened the gate into the lot
and trotted on ahead and opened the second gate and let the
rider into the field beyond. Bayard rode on, trailing his pungent smoke. From somewhere a ticked setter came up and fell
in at the mare's heels.

Elnora stood barelegged on the kitchen floor and soused her mop into the pail and thumped it on the floor again.

> *"Sinner riz fum de moaner's bench,*
> *Sinner jump to de penance bench;*
> *When de preacher ax 'im whut de reason why,*
> *Says 'Preacher got de women jes' de same ez I'.*
>   *Oh, Lawd, Oh Lawd!*
> *Dat's whut de matter wid de church today."*

2

Simon's destination was a huge brick house set well up onto the street. The lot had been the site of a fine old colonial house which stood among magnolias and oaks and flowering shrubs. But the house had burned and some of the trees had been felled to make room for an architectural garbling so imposingly terrific as to possess a kind of majesty. It was a monument to the frugality (and the mausoleum of the social aspirations of his women) of a hillman who had moved in from a small settlement called Frenchman's Bend and who, as Miss Jenny Du Pre put it, had built the handsomest house in Frenchman's Bend on the most beautiful lot in Jefferson. The hillman had stuck it out for two years during which his women-folks sat about the veranda all morning in lace-trimmed "boudoir caps" and spent the afternoons in colored silk riding about town in a rubber-tired surrey; then the hillman sold his house to a new-comer to the town and took his women back to the country and doubtless set them to work again.

A number of motor-cars ranked along the street lent a formally festive air to the place, and Simon with his tilted cigar stub wheeled up and drew rein and indulged in a brief colorful altercation with a negro sitting behind the wheel of a car parked before the hitching-block. "Dont block off no Sartoris ca'iage, black boy," Simon concluded, when the other had moved the motor and permitted him access to the post. "Block off de commonality, ef you wants, but dont intervoke no equipage waitin' on Cunnel er Miss Jenny. Dey wont stan' fer it."

He descended and tethered the horses, and his spirit mollified by the rebuke administered and laved with the beatitude of having gained his own way, Simon paused and examined the motor-car with curiosity and no little superciliousness tinged faintly with respectful envy, and spoke affably with its conductor. But not for long, for Simon had sisters in the Lord in this kitchen, and presently he let himself into the yard and followed the gravel driveway around to the back. He could hear the party going on as he passed beneath the windows: that sustained unintelligible gabbling with which white ladies could surround themselves without effort and which they seemed to consider a necessary (or unavoidable) adjunct to having a good time. The fact that it was a card party would have seemed neither paradoxical nor astonishing to Simon, for time and much absorbing experience had taught him a fine tolerance of white folks' vagaries and for those of ladies of any color.

The hillman had built his house so close to the street that the greater part of the original lawn with its fine old trees lay behind it. There were once crepe-myrtle and syringa and lilac and jasmine bushes without order, and massed honeysuckle on fences and tree trunks; and after the first house had burned these had taken the place and made of its shaggy formality a mazed and scented jungle loved of mockingbirds and thrushes, where boys and girls lingered on spring and summer nights among drifting fireflies and quiring whip-poor-wills and usually the liquid tremolo of a screech owl. Then the hillman had bought it and cut some of the trees in order to build his house near the street after the country fashion, and chopped out the jungle and whitewashed the remaining trees and ran his barn- and hog- and chicken-lot fences between their ghostly trunks. He didn't remain long enough to learn of garages.

Some of the antiseptic desolation of his tenancy had faded now, and its present owner had set out more shrubbery— jasmine and mock-orange and verbena—with green iron tables and chairs beneath them and a pool and a tennis court; and Simon passed on with discreet assurance, and on a consonant- less drone of female voices he rode into the kitchen where a thin woman in a funereal purple turban and poising a beaten biscuit heaped with mayonnaise, and a mountainous one in the stained apron of her calling and drinking melted ice-cream from a saucer, rolled their eyes at him.

"I seed him on de street yistiddy and he looked bad; he jes' didn't favor hisself," the visitor was saying as Simon entered, but they dropped the theme of conversation and made him welcome.

"Ef it aint Brother Strother," they said in unison. "Come in, Brother Strother. How is you?"

"Po'ly, ladies; po'ly," Simon replied. He doffed his hat and unclamped his cigar stub and stowed it away in the hat-band. "I'se had a right smart mis'ry in de back. Is y'all kep' well?"

"Right well, I thank you, Brother Strother," the visitor replied. Simon drew a chair up to the table, as he was bidden.

"Whut you gwine eat, Brother Strother?" the cook demanded hospitably. "Dey's party fixin's, en dey's some col' greens en a little sof' ice-cream lef' fum dinner."

"I reckon I'll have a little ice-cream en some of dem greens, Sis' Rachel," Simon replied. "My teef aint much on party doin's no mo'." The cook rose with majestic deliberation and waddled across to a pantry and reached down a platter. She was one of the best cooks in Jefferson: no mistress dared protest against the social amenities of Rachel's kitchen.

"Ef you aint de beatin'es' man!" the first guest exclaimed. "Eatin' ice-cream at yo' age!"

"I been eatin' ice-cream sixty years," Simon said. "Whut reason I got fer quittin' now?"

"Dat's right, Brother Strother," the cook agreed, placing the dish before him. "Eat yo' ice-cream when you kin git it. Jes' a minute en I'll——Here, Meloney," she interrupted herself as a young light negress in a smart white apron and cap entered, bearing a tray of plates containing remnants of edible edifices copied from pictures in ladies' magazines and possessing neither volume nor nourishment, with which the party had been dulling its palates against supper, "git Brother Strother a bowl of dat 'ere ice-cream, honey."

The girl clashed the tray into the sink and rinsed a bowl at the water tap while Simon watched her with his still little eyes. She whipped the bowl through a towel with a fine show of derogatory carelessness, and with her chin at a supercilious angle she clattered on her high heels across the kitchen, still under Simon's unwinking regard, and slammed a door behind her. Then Simon turned his head.

"Yes, ma'am," he repeated, "I been eatin' ice-cream too long ter quit at my age."

"Dey wont no vittle hurt you ez long ez you kin stomach 'um," the cook agreed, raising her saucer to her lips again. The girl returned and with her head still averted she set the bowl of viscid liquid before Simon who, under cover of this movement, dropped his hand on her thigh. The girl smacked him sharply on the back of his gray head with her flat palm.

"Miss Rachel, cant you make him keep his hands to hisself?" she said.

"Aint you 'shamed," Rachel demanded, but without rancor. "A ole gray-head man like you, wid a fam'ly of grown chillen and one foot in de graveyard?"

"Hush yo' mouf, woman," Simon said placidly, spooning spinach into his melted ice-cream. "Aint dey erbout breakin' up in yonder yit?"

"I reckon dey's erbout to," the other guest answered, putting another laden biscuit into her mouth with a gesture of elegant gentility. "Seems like dey's talkin' louder."

"Den dey's started playin' again," Simon corrected. "Talkin' jes' eased off whiles dey et. Yes, suh, dey's started playin' again. Dat's white folks. Nigger aint got sense ernough ter play cards wid all dat racket gwine on."

But they were breaking up. Miss Jenny Du Pre had just finished a story which left the three players at her table avoiding one another's eyes a little self-consciously, as was her way. Miss Jenny travelled very little, and in Pullman smoke-rooms not at all, and people wondered where she got her stories; who had told them to her. And she repeated them anywhere and at any time, choosing the wrong moment and the wrong audience with a cold and cheerful audacity. Young people liked her, and she was much in demand as a chaperone for picnic parties.

She now spoke across the room to the hostess. "I'm going home, Belle," she stated. "I think we are all tired of your party. I know I am." The hostess was a plump, youngish woman and her cleverly-rouged face showed now an hysterical immersion that was almost repose, but when Miss Jenny broke into her consciousness with the imminence of departure this faded quickly, and her face resumed its familiar expression of strained and vague dissatisfaction and she protested conventionally but with a petulant sincerity, as a well-bred child might.

But Miss Jenny was adamant and she rose and her slender

wrinkled hand brushed invisible crumbs from the bosom of her black silk dress. "If I stay any longer I'll miss Bayard's toddy time," she explained with her usual forthrightness. "Come on, Narcissa, and I'll drive you home."

"I have my car, thank you, Miss Jenny," the young woman to whom she spoke replied in a grave contralto, rising also; and the others got up with sibilant gathering motions above the petulant modulation of the hostess' protestings, and they drifted slowly into the hall and clotted again before various mirrors, colorful and shrill. Miss Jenny pushed steadily on toward the door.

"Come along, come along," she repeated. "Harry Mitchell wont want to run into all this gabble when he comes home from work."

"Then he can sit in the car out in the garage," the hostess rejoined sharply. "I do wish you wouldn't go. Miss Jenny, I dont think I'll ask you again."

But Miss Jenny only said "Goodbye, goodbye" with cold affability, and with her delicate replica of the Sartoris nose and that straight grenadier's back of hers which gave the pas for erectness to only one back in town—that of her nephew Bayard—she stood at the steps, where Narcissa Benbow joined her, bringing with her like an odor that aura of grave and serene repose in which she dwelt. "Belle meant that, too," Miss Jenny said.

"Meant what, Miss Jenny?"

"About Harry. . . . . . . Now, where do you suppose that damn nigger went to?" They descended the steps and from the parked motors along the street came muffled starting explosions, and the two women traversed the brief flower-bordered walk to the street. "Did you see which way my driver went?" Miss Jenny asked of the negro in the nearest car.

"He went to'ds de back, ma'am." The negro opened the

door and slid his legs, clad in army o.d. and a pair of linoleum putties, to the ground. "I'll go git 'im."

"Thank you. Well, thank the Lord that's over," she added. "It's too bad folks haven't the sense or courage to send out invitations, then shut up the house and go away. All the fun of parties is in dressing up and getting there." Ladies came in steady shrill groups down the walk and got into cars or departed on foot with bright, not-quite-musical calls to one another. The sun was down behind Belle's house, and when the women passed from the shadow into the level bar of sunlight beyond they became delicately brilliant as paroquets. Narcissa Benbow wore gray and her eyes were violet, and in her face was that tranquil repose of lilies.

"Not children's parties," she protested.

"I'm talking about parties, not about having fun," Miss Jenny said. "Speaking of children: What's the news from Horace?"

"Oh, hadn't I told you?" the other said quickly. "I had a wire yesterday. He landed in New York Wednesday. It was such a mixed-up sort of message, I never could understand what he was trying to tell me, except that he would have to stay in New York for a week or so. It was over fifty words long."

"Was it a straight message?" Miss Jenny asked. The other said Yes, and she added: "Horace must have got rich, like the soldiers say all the Y.M.C.A. did. Well, if it has taught a man like Horace to make money, the war was a pretty good thing, after all."

"Miss Jenny! How can you talk that way, after John's —— after —— "

"Fiddlesticks," Miss Jenny said. "The war just gave John a good excuse to get himself killed. If it hadn't been that, it would have been some other way that would have been a bother to everybody around."

"Miss Jenny!"

"I know, my dear. I've lived with these bullheaded Sartorises for eighty years, and I'll never give a single ghost of 'em the satisfaction of shedding a tear over him. What did Horace's message say?"

"It was about something he was bringing home with him," the other answered, and her serene face filled with a sort of fond exasperation. "It was such an incoherent message. . . . . . . Horace never could say anything clearly from a distance." She mused again, gazing down the street with its tunnel of oaks and elms through which sunlight fell in spaced tiger bars. "Do you suppose he could have adopted a war-orphan?"

"War-orphan," Miss Jenny repeated. "More likely it's some war-orphan's mamma." Simon appeared at the corner of the house, wiping his mouth on the back of his hand, and crossed the lawn with shuffling celerity. His cigar was not visible.

"No," the other said quickly, with grave concern. "You dont believe he would have done that? No, no, he wouldn't have. Horace wouldn't have done that. He never does anything without telling me about it first. He would have written: I know he would. You really dont think that sounds like Horace, do you? A thing like that?"

"Hmph," Miss Jenny said through her high-bridged Norman nose. "An innocent like Horace straying with that trusting air of his among all those man-starved European women? He wouldn't know it himself, until it was too late; especially in a foreign language. I bet in every town he was in over seven days his landlady or somebody was keeping his supper on the stove when he was late, or holding sugar out on the other men to sweeten his coffee with. Some men are born to always have some woman making a doormat of herself for him, just as some men are born cuckolded. . . . . . . How old are you?"

"I'm still twenty-six, Miss Jenny," the younger woman replied equably. Simon unhitched the horses and he stood now beside the carriage in his Miss Jenny attitude. It differed from the bank one; there was now in it a gallant and protective deference. Miss Jenny examined the still serenity of the other's face.

"Why dont you get married, and let that baby look after himself for a while? Mark my words, it wont be six months before some other woman will be falling all over herself for the privilege of keeping his feet dry, and he wont even miss you."

"I promised mother," the other replied quietly and without offense. . . . . . . "I dont see why he couldn't have sent an intelligible message."

"Well. . . ." Miss Jenny turned to her carriage. "Maybe it's only an orphan, after all," she said with comfortless reassurance.

"I'll know soon, anyway," the other agreed, and she crossed to a small car at the curb and opened the door. Miss Jenny got in her carriage, and Simon mounted and gathered up the reins.

"Let me know when you hear again," she called as the carriage moved forward. "Drive out and get some more flowers when you want 'em."

"Thank you. Goodbye."

"All right, Simon." The carriage moved on again, and again Simon withheld his news until they were out of town.

"Mist' Bayard done got home," he remarked, in his former conversational tone.

"Where is he?" Miss Jenny demanded immediately.

"He aint come out to de place yit," Simon answered. "I 'speck he went to de graveyard."

"Nonsense," Miss Jenny snapped. "No Sartoris ever goes to the cemetery but once. . . . Does Colonel know he's home?"

"Yessum, I tole him, but he dont ack like he believed I wuz tellin' him de troof."

"You mean, nobody's seen him but you?"

"I aint seed 'im neither," Simon disclaimed. "Section han' seed 'im jump off de train and tole me——"

"You damn fool nigger!" Miss Jenny stormed. "And you went and blurted a fool thing like that to Bayard? Haven't you got any more sense than that?"

"Section han' seed 'im," Simon repeated stubbornly. "I reckon he knowed Mist' Bayard when he seed 'im."

"Well, where is he, then?"

"He mought have gone out to de graveyard," Simon suggested.

"Drive on!"

Miss Jenny found her nephew with two bird-dogs in his office. The room was lined with bookcases containing rows of heavy legal tomes bound in dun calf and emanating an atmosphere of dusty and undisturbed meditation, and a miscellany of fiction of the historical-romantic school (all Dumas was there, and the steady progression of the volumes now constituted Bayard's entire reading, and one volume lay always on the night-table beside his bed) and a collection of indiscriminate objects—small packets of seed, old rusted spurs and bits and harness buckles, brochures on animal and vegetable diseases, ornate tobacco containers which people had given him on various occasions and anniversaries and which he had never used, inexplicable bits of rock and desiccated roots and grain pods—all collected one at a time and for reasons which had long since escaped his memory, yet preserved just the same. The room contained an enormous closet with a padlocked door, and a big table littered with yet more casual objects, and a locked roll-top desk (keys and locks were an obsession with him) and a sofa and three big leather chairs. This room was always referred to as the office, and Bayard now sat here with his hat on and still in his riding boots, transferring bourbon whisky from a small rotund keg to a silver stoppered decanter while the two dogs watched him with majestic gravity.

One of the dogs was quite old and nearly blind. It spent most of the day lying in the sun in the back yard, or during the hot summer days, in the cool dusty obscurity beneath the kitchen. But toward the middle of the afternoon it went around to the front and waited there quietly and gravely until the carriage came up the drive, and when Bayard had descended and entered the house it returned to the back and waited again until Isom led the mare up and Bayard came out and mounted. Then together they spent the afternoon going quietly and unhurriedly about the meadows and fields and woods in their seasonal mutations—the man on his horse and the ticked setter gravely beside him, while the descending evening of their lives drew toward its peaceful close upon the kind land that had bred them both. The young dog was not yet two years old; his net was too hasty for the sedateness of their society overlong, and though at times he set forth with them or came quartering up, splashed and eager, from somewhere to join them in midfield, it was not for long and soon he must dash away with his tongue flapping and the tense delicate feathering of his tail in pursuit of the maddening elusive smells with which the world surrounded him and tempted him from every thicket and copse and ravine.

Bayard's boots were wet to the tops and the soles were caked with mud, and he bent with intense preoccupation above his keg and bottle under the sober curiosity of the dogs. The keg was propped bung-upward in a second chair and he was siphoning the rich brown liquor delicately into the decanter by means of a rubber tube. Miss Jenny entered with her black bonnet still perched on the exact top of her trim white head, and the dogs looked up at her, the older with grave dignity, the younger one more quickly, tapping his tail on the floor with fawning diffidence. But Bayard did not raise his head. Miss Jenny closed the door and stared coldly at his boots.

"Your feet are wet," she stated. Still he didn't look up, but held the tube delicately in the bottle-neck, while the liquor mounted steadily in the decanter. At times his deafness was very convenient, more convenient than actual, perhaps; but who could know certainly? "You go up stairs and get those boots off," Miss Jenny commanded, raising her voice. "I'll fill the decanter."

But within the walled serene tower of his deafness his imperturbability did not falter until the decanter was full and he pinched the tube and raised it and drained it back into the keg. The older dog had not moved, but the younger one had retreated beyond Bayard, where it lay motionless and alert, its head on its crossed forepaws, watching Miss Jenny with one melting unwinking eye. Bayard drew the tube from the keg and looked at her for the first time. "What did you say?"

But Miss Jenny returned to the door and opened it and shouted into the hall, eliciting an alarmed response from the kitchen, followed presently by Simon in the flesh. "Go up and get Colonel's slippers," she directed. When she turned into the room again neither Bayard nor the keg was visible, but from the open closet door there protruded the young dog's interested hind quarters and the tense feathering of his barometric tail; then Bayard thrust the dog out of the closet with his foot and emerged himself and locked the door behind him.

"Has Simon come in, yet?" he asked.

"He's coming now," she answered. "I just called him. Sit down and get those wet boots off." At that moment Simon entered, with the slippers, and Bayard sat obediently and Simon knelt and drew his boots off under Miss Jenny's martinet eye. "Are his socks dry?" she asked.

"No'm, dey aint wet," Simon answered. But she bent and felt them herself.

"Here," Bayard said testily, but Miss Jenny ran her hand over both his feet with brusque imperturbability.

"Precious little fault of his if they aint," she said across the topless wall of his deafness. "And then you have to come along with that fool yarn of yours."

"Section han' seed 'im," Simon repeated stubbornly, thrusting the slippers onto Bayard's feet. "I aint never said I seed him." He looked up and rubbed his hands on his thighs.

Bayard stamped into the slippers. "Bring the toddy fixings, Simon." Then to his aunt, in a tone which he contrived to make casual: "Simon says Bayard got off the train this afternoon." But Miss Jenny was storming at Simon again.

"Come back here and get these boots and set 'em behind the stove," she said. Simon returned and sidled swiftly to the hearth and gathered up the boots. "And take these dogs out of here, too," she added. "Thank the Lord he hasn't thought about bringing his horse in with him." Immediately the old dog came to his feet, and followed by the younger one's diffident alacrity, departed with that same assumed deliberation with which both Bayard and Simon obeyed Miss Jenny's brisk implacability.

"Simon says——" Bayard repeated.

"Simon says fiddlesticks," Miss Jenny snapped. "Have you lived with Simon sixty years without learning that he dont know the truth when he sees it?" And she followed Simon from the room and on to the kitchen, and while Simon's tall yellow daughter bent over her biscuit-board and Simon filled a glass pitcher with fresh water and sliced lemons and set them and a sugar bowl and two tall glasses on a tray, Miss Jenny stood in the doorway and curled Simon's grizzled remaining hair to tighter kinks yet. She had a fine command of language at all times, but when her ire was aroused she soared without effort to sublime heights. Hers was a forceful clarity and a colorful simplicity and a bold use of metaphor that Demosthenes would have envied and which even mules comprehended and of whose intent the most obtuse persons remained not long in doubt; and beneath it Simon's head bobbed lower and lower and the fine assumption of detached preoccupation moulted like feathers from about him, until he caught up the tray and ducked from the room. Miss Jenny's voice followed him, descending easily with a sweeping comprehensiveness that included a warning and a suggestion for future conduct for Simon and Elnora and all their descendants, actual and problematical, for some years.

"And the next time," she concluded, "you or any section hand or brakeman or delivery boy either sees or hears anything you think will be of interest to Colonel, you tell me about it first: I'll do all the telling after that." She gave Elnora another glare for good measure and returned to the office, where her nephew was stirring sugar and water carefully in the two glasses.

Simon in a white jacket officiated as butler—doubled in brass, you might say, only it was not brass, but silver so fine and soft that some of the spoons were worn now almost to paper thinness where fingers in their generations had held them; silver which Simon's grandfather Joby had buried on a time beneath the ammoniac barn floor while Simon, aged three in a single filthy garment, had looked on with a child's grave interest in the curious game.

An effluvium of his primary calling clung about him

always, however, even when he was swept and garnished for church and a little shapeless in a discarded Prince Albert coat of Bayard's; and his every advent into the dining room with dishes brought with him, and the easy attitudes into which he fell near the sideboard while answering Miss Jenny's abrupt questions or while pursuing some fragmentary conversation which he and Bayard had been engaged in earlier in the day, disseminated, and his exits left behind him a faint nostalgia of the stables. But tonight he brought dishes in and set them down and scuttled immediately back to the kitchen: Simon realized that again he had talked too much.

Miss Jenny with a shawl of white wool about her shoulders against the evening's coolness, was doing the talking tonight, immersing herself and her nephew in a wealth of trivialities— petty doings and sayings and gossip—a behavior which was not like Miss Jenny at all. She had opinions, and a pithy, savagely humorous way of stating them, but it was very seldom that she descended to gossip. Meanwhile Bayard had shut himself up in that walled tower of his deafness and raised the drawbridge and clashed the portcullis to, where you never knew whether he heard you or no, while his corporeal self ate its supper steadily. Presently they had done and Miss Jenny rang the little silver bell at her hand and Simon opened the pantry door and received again the cold broadside of her displeasure, and shut the door and lurked behind it until they had left the room.

Bayard lit his cigar in the office and Miss Jenny followed him there and drew her chair up to the table beneath the lamp and opened the daily Memphis newspaper. She enjoyed humanity in its more colorful mutations, preferring lively romance to the most impeccable of dun fact, so she took in the more lurid afternoon paper even though it was yesterday's when it reached her, and read with cold avidity accounts of arson and murder and violent dissolution and adultery; in good time and soon the American scene was to furnish her with diversion in the form of bootleggers' wars, but this was not yet. Her nephew sat without the mellow downward pool of the lamp, with his feet braced against the corner of the hearth from which his boot-soles and the boot-soles of John Sartoris before him had long since worn the varnish away, puffing his cigar. He was not reading, and at intervals Miss Jenny glanced above her glasses and across the top of the paper toward him. Then she read again, and there was no sound in the room save the sporadic rustling of the page.

After a time he rose, with one of his characteristic plunging movements, and she watched him as he crossed the room and passed through the door and banged it to behind him. She read on for a while longer, but her attention had followed the heavy tramp of his feet up the hall, and when this ceased she rose and laid the paper aside and followed him to the front door.

The moon had gotten up beyond the dark eastern wall of the hills and it lay without emphasis upon the valley, mounting like a child's balloon behind the oaks and locusts along the drive. Bayard sat with his feet on the veranda rail, in the moonlight. His cigar glowed at spaced intervals, and a shrill monotone of crickets rose from the immediate grass, and further away, from among the trees, a fairy-like piping of young frogs like endless silver small bubbles rising, and a thin sourceless odor of locust drifted up intangible as fading tobacco-wraiths, and from the rear of the house, up the dark hall, Elnora's voice floated in meaningless minor suspense.

Miss Jenny groped in the darkness beside the door and from beside the yawning lesser obscurity of the mirror she took Bayard's hat from the hook, and carried it out to him and put it in his hand. "Dont sit out here too long, now. It aint summer yet."

He grunted indistinguishably, but he put the hat on and

she turned and went back to the office and finished the paper and folded it and laid it on the table. She snapped the light off and mounted the dark stairs to her room. The moon shone above the trees at this height and it fell in broad silver bars through the eastern windows.

Before turning up the light she crossed to the southern wall and raised a window there, upon the crickets and frogs and somewhere a mockingbird. Outside the window was a magnolia tree, but it was not to bloom yet, nor had the honeysuckle massed along the garden fence flowered. But this would be soon, and from here she could overlook the garden, could look down upon cape jasmine and syringa and callacanthus where the moon lay upon their bronze and yet unflowered sleep, and upon those other shoots and graftings from the faraway Carolina gardens she had known as a girl.

Just beyond the corner from the invisible kitchen, Elnora's voice welled in mellow falling suspense. *All folks talkin' 'bout heaven aint gwine dar* Elnora sang, and presently she and Simon emerged into the moonlight and took the path to Simon's cabin below the barn. Simon had fired his cigar at last, and the evil smoke of it trailed behind him, fading; but when they had gone the rank pungency of it seemed still to linger within the sound of the crickets and of the frogs upon the silver air, mingled and blended inextricably with the dying fall of Elnora's voice.

All folks talkin' 'bout heaven aint gwine dar

His cigar was cold, and he moved and dug a match from his waistcoat and relit it and braced his feet again upon the railing, and again the drifting sharpness of tobacco lay along the windless currents of the silver air, straying and fading slowly amid locust-breaths and the ceaseless fairy reiteration of crickets and frogs. There was a mockingbird somewhere down the valley, and after a while another sang from the magnolia at the corner of the garden fence. An automobile passed along the smooth valley road, slowed for the railway crossing, then sped on. Before the sound of it had died away, the whistle of the nine-thirty train drifted down from the hills.

Two long blasts with dissolving echoes, two short following ones; but before it came in sight his cigar was cold again, and he sat holding it in his fingers and watched the locomotive drag its string of yellow windows up the valley and into the hills once more, where after a time it whistled again, arrogant and resonant and sad. John Sartoris had sat so on this veranda and watched his two daily trains emerge from the hills and cross the valley into the hills, with lights and smoke and a noisy simulation of speed. But now his railway belonged to a syndicate and there were more than two trains on it that ran from Chicago to the Gulf, completing his dream, while John Sartoris slept among martial cherubim and the useless vain-glory of whatever God he did not scorn to recognise.

Then old Bayard's cigar was cold again and he sat with it dead in his fingers and watched a tall shape emerge from the lilac bushes beside the garden fence and cross the patchy moonlight toward the veranda. His grandson wore no hat and he came on and mounted the steps and stood with the moonlight bringing the hawk-like planes of his face into high relief while his grandfather sat with his dead cigar and looked at him.

"Bayard, son?" old Bayard said. Young Bayard stood in the moonlight. His eyesockets were cavernous shadows.

"I tried to keep him from going up there on that goddam little popgun," he said at last with brooding savageness. Then he moved again and old Bayard lowered his feet, but his grandson only dragged a chair violently up beside him and flung himself into it. His motions were abrupt also, like his grandfather's, but controlled and flowing for all their violence.

"Why in hell didn't you let me know you were coming?" old Bayard demanded. "What do you mean, straggling in here like this?"

"I didn't let anybody know." Young Bayard dug a cigarette from his pocket and raked a match on his shoe.

"What?"

"I didn't tell anybody I was coming," he repeated above the cupped match, raising his voice.

"Simon knew it. Do you inform nigger servants of your movements instead of your own granddaddy?"

"Damn Simon, sir," young Bayard shouted. "Who set him to watching me?"

"Dont yell at me, boy," old Bayard shouted in turn. His grandson flung the match away and drew at the cigarette in deep troubled draughts. "Dont wake Jenny," old Bayard added more mildly, striking a match to his cold cigar. "All right, are you?"

"Here," young Bayard said, extending his hand. "Let me hold it. You're going to set your moustache on fire." But old Bayard repulsed him sharply and sucked stubbornly and impotently at the match in his unsteady fingers.

"I said, are you all right?" he repeated.

"Why not?" young Bayard snapped. "Takes damn near as big a fool to get hurt in a war as it does in peacetime. Damn fool, that's what it is." He drew at the cigarette again, then he hurled it not half consumed after the match. "There was one I had to lay for four days to catch him. Had to get Sibleigh in an old crate of an Ak. W. to suck him in for me. Wouldn't look at anything but cold meat, him and his skull and bones. Well, he got it. Stayed on him for six thousand feet, put a whole belt right into his cockpit. You could a covered 'em all with your hat. But the bastard just wouldn't burn." His voice rose again as he talked on. Locust drifted up in sweet gusts, and the crickets and frogs were clear and monotonous as pipes blown drowsily by an idiot boy. From her silver casement the moon looked down upon the valley dissolving in opaline tranquillity into the serene mysterious infinitude of the hills, and young Bayard's voice went on and on, recounting violence and speed and death.

"Hush," old Bayard said again. "You'll wake Jenny," and his grandson's voice sank obediently; but soon it rose again, and after a time Miss Jenny emerged with her white woolen shawl over her night-dress and came and kissed him.

"I reckon you're all right," she said, "or you wouldn't be in such a bad humor. Tell us about Johnny."

"He was drunk," young Bayard answered harshly. "Or a fool. I tried to keep him from going up there, on that damn Camel. You couldn't see your hand, that morning. Air all full of hunks of cloud and any fool could a known that on their side it'd be full of Fokkers that could reach twenty-five thousand, and him on a damn Camel. But he was hell-bent on going up there, damn near to Lille. I couldn't keep him from it. He shot at me," young Bayard said; "I tried to drive him back, but he gave me a burst. He was already high as he could get, but they must have been five thousand feet above us. They flew all over him. Hemmed him up like a damn calf in a pen while one of them sat right on his tail until he took fire and jumped. Then they streaked for home." Locust drifted and drifted on the still air, and the silver rippling of the tree frogs. In the magnolia at the corner of the house the mockingbird sang. Down the valley another one replied.

"Streaked for home, with the rest of his gang," young Bayard said. "Him and his skull and bones. It was Ploeckner," he added, and for the moment his voice was still and untroubled with vindicated pride. "He was one of the best they had. Pupil of Richthofen's."

"Well, that's something," Miss Jenny agreed, stroking his head.

"I tried to keep him from going up there on that goddam little popgun," he burst out again.

"What did you expect, after the way you raised him?" Miss Jenny asked. "You're the oldest. . . . . . . You've been to the cemetery, haven't you?"

"Yessum," he answered quietly.

"What's that?" old Bayard demanded.

"That old fool Simon said that's where you were. . . . You come on and eat your supper," she said briskly and firmly, entering his life again without a by-your-leave, taking up the snarled threads of it after her brisk and capable fashion, and he rose obediently.

"What's that?" old Bayard repeated.

"And you come on in, too." Miss Jenny swept him also into the orbit of her will as you gather a garment from a chair in passing. "Time you were in bed." They followed her to the kitchen and stood while she delved into the ice box and set food on the table, and a pitcher of milk, and drew up a chair.

"Fix him a toddy, Jenny," old Bayard suggested. But Miss Jenny vetoed this immediately.

"Milk's what he wants. I reckon he had to drink enough whisky during that war to last him for a while. Bayard used to never come home from his, without wanting to ride his horse up the front steps and into the house. Come on, now," and she drove old Bayard firmly out of the kitchen and up the stairs. "You go on to bed, you hear? Let him alone for a while." She saw his door shut and entered young Bayard's room and prepared his bed, and after a while from her own room she heard him mount the stairs.

His room was treacherously illumined by the moon, and without turning on the light he went and sat on the bed. Outside the windows the interminable crickets and frogs, as though the moon's rays were thin glass impacting among the trees and shrubs and shattering in brittle musical rain upon the ground, and above this and with a deep timbrous quality, the measured respirations of the pump in the electric plant beyond the barn.

He dug another cigarette from his pocket and lit it. But he took only two draughts before he flung it away. And then he sat quietly in the room which he and John had shared in the young masculine violence of their twinship, on the bed where he and his wife had lain the last night of his leave, the night before he went back to England and thence out to the Front again, where John already was. Beside him on the pillow the wild bronze swirling of her hair was hushed now in the darkness, and she lay holding his arm with both hands against her breast while they talked quietly, soberly at last.

He had not been thinking of her then. When he thought of her who lay rigid in the dark beside him, holding his arm tightly to her breasts, it was only to be a little savagely ashamed of the heedless thing he had done to her. He was thinking of his brother whom he had not seen in over a year, thinking that in a month they would see one another again.

Nor was he thinking of her now, although the walls held, like a withered flower in a casket, something of that magical chaos in which they had lived for two months, tragic and transient as a blooming of honeysuckle and sharp as the odor of mint. He was thinking of his dead brother; the spirit of their violent complementing days lay like a dust everywhere in the room, obliterating that other presence, stopping his breathing, and he went to the window and flung the sash crashing upward and leaned there, gulping air into his lungs like a man who has been submerged and who still cannot believe that he has reached the surface again.

Later, lying naked between the sheets, he waked himself

with his own groaning. The room was filled now with a gray light, sourceless and chill, and he turned his head and saw Miss Jenny, the woolen shawl about her shoulders, sitting in a chair beside the bed.

"What's the matter?" he said.

"That's what I want to know," Miss Jenny answered. "You make more noise than that water pump."

"I want a drink."

Miss Jenny leaned over and raised a glass from the floor beside her. Bayard had risen to his elbow and he took the glass. His hand stopped before the glass reached his mouth and he hunched on his elbow, the glass beneath his nose.

"Hell," he said. "I said a drink."

"You drink that milk, boy," Miss Jenny commanded. "You think I'm going to sit up all night just to feed you whisky? Drink it, now."

He emptied the glass obediently and lay back. Miss Jenny set the glass on the floor.

"What time is it?"

"Hush," she said. She laid her hand on his brow. "Go to sleep."

He rolled his head on the pillow, but he could not evade her hand.

"Get away," he said. "Let me alone."

"Hush," Miss Jenny said. "Go to sleep."

Two

1

Simon said: "You aint never yit planted nothin' whar hit ought ter be planted." He sat on the bottom step, whetting the blade of his hoe with a file. Miss Jenny stood with her caller at the edge of the veranda above him, in a man's felt hat and heavy gloves. A pair of shears dangled below her waist, glinting in the morning sunlight.

"And whose business is that?" she demanded. "Yours, or Colonel's? Either one of you can loaf on this porch and tell me where a plant will grow best or look best, but if either of you ever grew as much as a weed out of the ground yourselves, I'd like to see it. I dont give two whoops in the bad place where you or Colonel either thinks a flower ought to be planted; I plant my flowers just exactly where I want 'em to be planted."

"And den dares 'um not ter come up," Simon added. "Dat's de way you en Isom gyardens. Thank de Lawd Isom aint got to make his livin' wid de sort of gyardenin' he learns in dat place." Still whetting at the hoe blade he jerked his head toward the corner of the house.

He wore a disreputable hat, of a fabric these many years anonymous. Miss Jenny stared coldly down upon this hat.

"Isom made his living by being born black," Miss Jenny snapped. "Suppose you quit scraping at that hoe and see if you cant dare some of the grass in that salvia bed to come up."

"I got to git a aidge on dis curry-comb," Simon said. "You go'n out dar to yo' gyarden: I'll git dis bed cleaned up." He scraped steadily at the hoe-blade.

"You've been at that long enough to find out that you cant possibly wear that blade down to the handle with just a file. You've been at it ever since breakfast. I heard you. You get on out there where folks passing will think you're working, anyhow."

Simon groaned dismally and spent a half minute laying the file aside. He laid it on a step, then he picked it up and moved it to another step. Then he laid it against the step behind him. Then he ran his thumb along the blade, examining it with morose hopefulness.

"Hit mought do now," he said. "But hit'll be jes' like weedin' wid a curry-c——"

"You try it, anyway," Miss Jenny said. "Maybe the weeds'll think it's a hoe. You go give 'em a chance to, anyhow."

"Ise gwine, Ise gwine," Simon answered pettishly, rising and hobbling away. "You go'n see erbout dat place o' yo'n; I'll 'tend ter dis."

Miss Jenny and the caller descended the steps and went on around the corner of the house.

"Why he'd rather sit there and rasp at that new hoe with a file instead of grubbing up a dozen blades of grass in that salvia bed, I cant see," Miss Jenny said. "But he'll do it. He'd sit there and scrape at that hoe until it looked like a saw blade, if I'd let him. Bayard bought a lawn mower three or four years ago— God knows what for—and turned it over to Simon. The folks that made it guaranteed it for a year. They didn't know Simon, though. I often thought, reading about those devastations and things in the papers last year, what a good time Simon would have had in the war. He could have shown 'em things about devastation they never thought of. Isom!" she shouted.

They entered the garden and Miss Jenny paused at the gate. "You, Isom!"

This time there was a reply, and Miss Jenny went on with her caller and Isom lounged up from somewhere and clicked the gate after him.

"Why didn't you——" Miss Jenny looked back over her shoulder, then she stopped and regarded Isom's suddenly military figure with brief, cold astonishment. He now wore khaki, with a divisional emblem on his shoulder and a tarnished service stripe on his cuff. His lean sixteen-year-old neck rose from the slovenly collar's limp, overlarge embrace, and a surprising amount of wrist was visible below the cuffs. The breeches bagged hopelessly into the unskillful wrapping of the putties which, with either a fine sense for the unique or a bland disregard of military usage, he had donned prior to his shoes, and the soiled overseas cap came down regrettably on his bullet head.

"Where did you get those clothes?" The sunlight glinted on Miss Jenny's shears, and Miss Benbow in a white dress and a soft straw hat turned also and looked at him with a strange expression.

"Dey's Caspey's," Isom answered. "I jes' bor'd 'um."

"Caspey?" Miss Jenny repeated. "Is he home?"

"Yessum. He got in las' night on de nine-thirty."

"Last night, did he? Where is he now? Asleep, I reckon?"

"Yessum. Dat's whar he wuz when I lef' home."

"And I reckon that's how you borrowed his uniform," Miss Jenny said tartly. "Well, let him sleep this morning. Give him one day to get over the war. But if it made a fool out of him like it did Bayard, he'd better put that thing on again and go back to it. I'll declare, men cant seem to stand anything." She went on, the guest in her straight white dress following.

"You are awfully hard on men, not to have a husband to

bother with, Miss Jenny," she said. "Besides, you're judging all men by your Sartorises."

"They aint my Sartorises," Miss Jenny disclaimed promptly. "I just inherited 'em. But you just wait: you'll have one of your own to bother with soon; you just wait until Horace gets home, then see how long it takes him to get over it. Men cant stand anything," she repeated. "Cant even stand helling around with no worry and no responsibility and no limit to all of the meanness they can think about wanting to do. Do you think a man could sit day after day and month after month in a house miles from nowhere and spend the time between casualty lists tearing up bedclothes and window curtains and table linen to make lint and watching sugar and flour and meat dwindling away and using pine knots for light because there aren't any candles and no candlesticks to put 'em in, if there were, and hiding in nigger cabins while drunken Yankee generals set fire to the house your great-great-great-grandfather built and you and all your folks were born in? Dont talk to me about men suffering in war." Miss Jenny snipped larkspur savagely. "Just you wait until Horace comes home; then you'll see. Just a good excuse for 'em to make nuisances of themselves and stay in the way while the women-folks are trying to clean up the mess they left with their fighting. John at least had consideration enough, after he'd gone and gotten himself into something where he had no business, not to come back and worry everybody to distraction. But Bayard now, coming back in the middle of it and having everybody thinking he was settled down at last, teaching at that Memphis flying school, and then marrying that fool girl."

"Miss Jenny!"

"Well, I dont mean that, but she ought to've been spanked, hard. I know: didn't I do the same thing, myself? It was all that harness Bayard wore. Talk about men being taken in by a uniform!" She clipped larkspur. "Dragging me up there to the wedding, mind you, with a church full of rented swords and some of Bayard's pupils trying to drop roses on 'em when they came out. I reckon some of 'em were not his pupils, because one of 'em finally did drop a handful that missed everything and fell in the street." She snipped larkspur savagely. "I had dinner with 'em one night. Sat in the hotel an hour until they remembered to come for me. Then we stopped at a deli-catessen and Bayard and Caroline got out and went in and came back with about a bushel of packages and dumped 'em into the car where they leaked grease on my new stockings. That was the dinner I'd been invited to, mind you; there wasn't a sign of anything that looked or smelt like a stove in the whole place. I didn't offer to help 'em. I told Caroline I didn't know anything about that sort of house-keeping, because my folks were old-fashioned enough to cook food.

"Then the others came in—some of Bayard's soldier friends, and a drove of other folks' wives, near as I could gather. Young women that ought to've been at home, seeing about supper, gabbling and screeching in that silly way young mar-ried women have when they're doing something they hope their husbands won't like. They were all unwrapping bottles—about two dozen, I reckon, and Bayard and Caroline came in with that silver I gave 'em and monogrammed napkins and that delicatessen fodder that tasted like swamp grass, on paper plates. We ate it there, sitting on the floor or standing up or just wherever you happened to be.

"That was Caroline's idea of keeping house. She said they'd settle down when they got old, if the war was over by then. About thirty-five, I suppose she meant. Thin as a rail; there wouldn't have been much to spank. But she'd ought to've had it, just the same. Soon as she found out about the baby, she named it. Named it nine months before it was born and told everybody about it. Used to talk about it like it was her grand-father or something. Always saying Bayard wont let me do this or that or the other."

Miss Jenny continued to clip larkspur, the caller tall in a white dress beside her. The fine and huge simplicity of the house rose among thickening trees, the garden lay in sunlight bright with bloom, myriad with scent and with a drowsy hum-ming of bees—a steady golden sound, as of sunlight become audible—all the impalpable veil of the immediate, the famil-iar; just beyond it a girl with a bronze skirling of hair and a small, supple body in a constant epicene unrepose, a dynamic fixation like that of carven sexless figures caught in moments of action, striving, a mechanism all of whose members must move in performing the most trivial action, her wild hands not accusing but passionate still beyond the veil impalpable but sufficient.

Miss Jenny stooped over the flowerbed, her narrow back, though stooping, erect still, indomitable. A thrush flashed modestly across the bright air and into the magnolia tree in a dying parabola. "And then, when he had to go back to the war, of course he brought her out here and left her on my hands." The caller stood motionless in her white dress, and Miss Jenny said: "No, I dont mean that." She snipped larkspur.

"Poor women," she said. "I reckon we do have to take our revenge wherever and whenever we can get it. Only she ought to've taken it out on Bayard."

"When she died," Narcissa said, "and he couldn't know about it; couldn't have come to her if he had? And you can say that?"

"Bayard love anybody, that cold devil?" Miss Jenny clipped larkspur. "He never cared a snap of his fingers for anybody in his life except Johnny." She snipped larkspur savagely. "Swelling around here like it was our fault, like we made 'em go to that war. And now he's got to have an automobile, got to go all the way to Memphis to buy one. An automobile in Bayard Sartoris' barn, mind you; him that wont even lend the bank's money to a man that owns one. . . . . . . Do you want some sweet peas?"

"Yes, please," Narcissa answered. Miss Jenny straightened up, then she stopped utterly still.

"Just look yonder, will you?" she pointed with the shears. "That's how they suffer from war, poor things." Beyond a frame of sweet peas Isom in his khaki strode solemnly back and forth. Upon his right shoulder was a hoe and on his face an expression of rapt absorption, and as he reversed at the end of his beat, he murmured to himself in measured singsong. "You, Isom!" Miss Jenny shouted.

He halted in midstride, still at shoulder arms. "Ma'am?" he said mildly. Miss Jenny continued to glare at him, and his military bearing faded and he lowered his piece and executed a sort of effacing movement within his martial shroud.

"Put that hoe down and bring that basket over here. That's the first time in your life you ever picked up a garden tool of your own free will. I wish I could discover the kind of uniform that would make you dig in the ground with it; I'd certainly buy you one."

"Yessum."

"If you want to play soldier, you go off somewhere with Bayard and do it. I can raise flowers without any help from the army," she added, turning to the guest with her handful of larkspur. "And what are you laughing at?" she demanded.

"You both looked so funny," the younger woman explained. "You looked so much more like a soldier than poor Isom, for all his uniform." She touched her eyes with her fingertips. "I'm sorry: please forgive me for laughing."

"Hmph," Miss Jenny sniffed. She put the larkspur into the

basket and went on to the sweet pea frame and snipped again, viciously. The guest followed, as did Isom with the basket; and presently Miss Jenny was done with sweet peas and she moved on again with her train, pausing to cut a rose here and there, and stopped before a bed where tulips lifted their bright inverted bells. She and Isom had guessed happily, this time; the various colors formed an orderly pattern.

"When we dug 'em up last fall," she told her guest, "I'd put a red one in Isom's right hand and a yellow one in his left, and then I'd say 'All right, Isom, give me the red one.' He'd never fail to hold out his left hand, and if I just looked at him long enough, he'd hold out both hands. 'Didn't I tell you to hold that red one in your right hand?' I'd say. 'Yessum, here 'tis.' And out would come his left hand again. 'That aint your right hand, stupid,' I'd say. 'Dat's de one you said wuz my right hand a while ago,' Mr Isom says. Aint that so, nigger?" Miss Jenny glared at Isom, who again performed his deprecatory effacing movement behind the slow equanimity of his grin.

"Yessum, I 'speck it is."

"You'd better," Miss Jenny rejoined warningly. "Now, how can anybody have a decent garden, with a fool like that? I expect every spring to find corn or lespedeza coming up in the hyacinth beds or something." She examined the tulips again, weighing the balanced colors one against another in her mind. "No, you dont want any tulips," she decided, moving on.

"No, Miss Jenny," the guest agreed demurely. They went on to the gate, and Miss Jenny stopped and took the basket from Isom.

"And you go home and take that thing off, you hear?"

"Yessum."

"And I want to look out that window in a few minutes and see you in the garden with that hoe again," she added. "And I want to see both of your right hands on it and I want to see it moving, too. You hear me?"

"Yessum."

"And tell Caspey to be ready to go to work in the morning. Even niggers that eat here have got to work some." But Isom was gone, and they went on and mounted to the veranda. "Dont he sound like that's exactly what he's going to do?" she confided as they entered the hall. "He knows as well as I do that I wont dare look out that window, after what I said. Come in," she added, opening the parlor doors.

This room was opened but seldom now, though in John Sartoris' day it had been constantly in use. He was always giving dinners, and balls too on occasion, with the folding doors between it and the dining room thrown open and three negroes with stringed instruments on the stairway and all the candles burning, surrounding himself with a pageantry of color and scent and music against which he moved with his bluff and jovial arrogance. He lay also overnight in this room in his gray regimentals and so brought to a conclusion the colorful, if not always untarnished, pageant of his own career, contemplating for the last time his own apotheosis from the jocund mellowness of his generous hearth.

But during his son's time it fell less and less into use, and slowly and imperceptibly it lost its jovial but stately masculinity, becoming by mutual agreement a place for his wife and his son John's wife and Miss Jenny to clean thoroughly twice a year and in which, preceded by a ritualistic unswaddling of brown holland, they entertained their more formal callers. This was its status at the birth of his grandsons and it continued thus until the death of their parents, and later, to that of his wife. After that Miss Jenny bothered with formal callers but little and with the parlor not at all. She said it gave her the creeps.

And so it stayed closed nearly all the time and slowly acquired an atmosphere of solemn and macabre fustiness. Occasionally young Bayard or John would open the door and peer into the solemn obscurity in which the shrouded furniture loomed with a sort of ghostly benignance, like albino mastodons. But they did not enter; already in their minds the room was associated with death, an idea which even the holly and tinsel of Christmas tide could not completely obscure. They were away at school by the time they reached party age, but even during vacations, though they had filled the house with the polite bedlam of their contemporaries, the room would be opened only on Christmas eve, when the tree was set up and a fire lighted, and a bowl of eggnog on the table in the center of the hearth. And after they went to England in '16 it was opened twice a year to be cleaned after the ancient ritual that even Simon had inherited from his forefathers, and to have the piano tuned or when Miss Jenny and Narcissa spent a forenoon or afternoon there, and formally not at all.

The furniture loomed shapelessly in its dun shrouds; the piano alone was uncovered, and Narcissa drew the bench out and removed her hat and dropped it beside her. Miss Jenny set the basket down and from the gloom back of the instrument she drew a straight, hard chair, uncovered also, and sat down and removed her felt hat from her trim white head. Light came through the open door, but the windows were shuttered behind heavy maroon curtains, and it served only to enhance the obscurity and to render more shapeless the hooded anonymous furniture.

But behind these dun bulks and in all the corners of the room there waited, as actors stand within the wings beside the waiting stage, figures in crinoline and hooped muslin and silk; in stocks and flowing coats; in gray too, with crimson sashes and sabres in gallant sheathed repose; — Jeb Stuart himself perhaps, on his glittering garlanded bay or with his sunny hair falling upon fine broadcloth beneath the mistletoe and holly boughs of Baltimore in '58. Miss Jenny sat with her uncompromising grenadier's back and held her hat upon her knees and fixed herself to look on as her guest touched chords from the keyboard and wove them together and rolled the curtain back upon the scene.

In the kitchen Caspey was having breakfast while Simon his father, and Elnora his sister, and Isom his nephew (in uniform) watched him. He had been Simon's understudy in the stables and general handy-man about the place, doing all the work that Simon managed, through the specious excuse of decrepitude and filial gratitude, to slough off onto his shoulders and that Miss Jenny could devise for him and which he could not evade. Old Bayard also employed him in the fields occasionally. Then the draft had got him and bore him to France and the St Sulpice docks as one of a labor battalion, where he did what work corporals and sergeants managed to slough off onto his unmilitary shoulders and that white officers could devise for him and which he could not evade.

Thus all the labor about the place devolved upon Simon and Isom, but Miss Jenny kept Isom piddling about the house so much of the time that Simon was soon as bitter against the War Lords as any professional Democrat. Meanwhile Caspey was working a little and trifling with continental life in its martial phases rather to his future detriment, for at last the tumult died and the captains departed and left a vacuum filled with the usual bitter bickering of Armageddon's heirs-at-law; and Caspey returned to his native land a total loss, sociologically speaking, with a definite disinclination toward labor, honest or otherwise, and two honorable wounds incurred in a razor-hedged crap game. But return he did, to his father's querulous satisfaction and Elnora's and Isom's admiration, and he now sat in the kitchen, telling them about the war.

"I dont take nothin' fum no white folks no mo'," he was saying. "War done changed all dat. If us cullud folks is good enough ter save France fum de Germans, den us is good enough ter have de same rights de Germans is. French folks thinks so, anyhow, and ef America dont, dey's ways of learnin' 'um. Yes, suh, it wuz de cullud soldier saved France and America bofe. Black regiments kilt mo' Germans dan all de white armies put together, let 'lone unloadin' steamboats all day long fer a dollar a day."

"War aint hurt dat big mouf o' yo'n, anyhow," Simon said.

"War unloosed de black man's mouf," Caspey corrected. "Give him de right to talk. Kill Germans, den do yo' oratin', dey tole us. Well, us done it."

"How many you kilt, Unc' Caspey?" Isom asked deferentially.

"I aint never bothered to count 'um up. Been times I kilt mo in one mawnin' dan dey's folks on dis whole place. One time we wuz down in de cellar of a steamboat tied up to de bank, and one of dese submareems sailed up and stopped, and all de white officers run up on de bank and hid. Us boys downstairs didn't know dey wuz anything wrong 'twell folks started clambin' down de ladder. We never had no guns wid us at de time, so when we seed dem green legs comin' down de ladder we crope up behin' 'um, and ez dey come down one of de boys would hit 'um over de haid wid a piece of scantlin' and another would drag 'um outen de way and cut dey th'oat wid a meat-plow. Dey wuz about thirty of 'um. . . . . . . Elnora, is dey any mo' of dat coffee lef'?"

"Sho," Simon murmured. Isom's eyes popped quietly and Elnora lifted the coffee-pot from the stove and refilled Caspey's cup.

Caspey drank coffee for a while. "And another time me and a boy wuz gwine along a road. We got tired unloadin' dem steamboats all day long, so one day de Captain's dog-robber foun' whar he kep' dese here unloaded passes and he tuck a han'ful of 'um, and me and him wuz on de road to town when a truck come along and de boy axed us did us want a lif'. He wuz a school boy, so he writ on three of de passes whenever we come to a place dat mought be M.P. invested, and we got along fine, ridin' about de country on dat private truck, 'twell one mawnin' we looked out whar de truck wuz and dey wuz a M.P. settin' on it whilst de truck boy wuz tryin' to explain to him. So we turned de other way and lit out walkin'. After dat we had to dodge de M.P. towns, 'case me and de other boy couldn't write on de passes.

"One day we wuz gwine along a road. It wuz a busted-up road and it didn't look much like no M.P. country, but dey wuz some of 'em in de las' town we dodged, so we didn't know we wuz so close to whar de fightin' wuz gwine on 'twell we walked onto a bridge and come right onto a whole regiment of Germans, swimmin' in de river. Dey seed us about de same time we seed dem and div under de water, and me and de other boy grabbed up two machine guns settin' dar and we sot on de bridge rail, and ev'y time a German stuck his haid up fer a new breaf, us shot 'im. It wuz jes' like shootin' turkles in a slough. I reckon dey wuz clost to a hun'ed us kilt 'fo' de machine guns run dry. Dat's whut dey gimme dis fer." He drew from his pocket a florid plated medal of Porto Rican origin, and Isom came quietly up to see it.

"Umumuh," Simon said. He sat with his hands on his knees, watching his son with rapt astonishment. Elnora came up also, her arms daubed with flour.

"Whut does dey look like?" she asked. "Like folks?"

"Dey's big," Caspey answered. "Sort of pink lookin' and

about eight foot tall. Only folks in de whole American war dat could handle 'um wuz de cullud regiments." Isom returned to his corner beside the woodbox.

"Aint you got some gyardenin' to do, boy?" Simon asked him.

"Naw, suh," Isom answered, his enraptured gaze still on his uncle. "Miss Jenny say us done caught up dis mawnin'."

"Well, dont you come whinin' ter me when she jumps on you," Simon warned him. "Whar'd you kill de nex' lot?" he asked his son.

"Us didn't kill no mo' after dat," Caspey said. "We decided dat wuz enough and dat we better leave de rest of 'um fer de boys dat wuz gittin' paid fer killin' 'um. We went on 'twell de road played out in a field. Dey wuz some ditches and ole wire fences and holes in de field, wid folks livin' in 'um. De folks wuz white American soldiers and dey egvised us to pick us out a hole and stay dar fer a while, ef us wanted de peace and comfort of de war. So we picked us out a dry hole and moved in. Dey wasn't nothin' to do all day long but lay in de shade and watch de air balloons and listen to de shootin' about fo' miles up de road. De white boy wid me claimed it wuz rabbit hunters, but I knowed better. De white boys could write, so dey fixed up de passes and we tuck time about gwine up to whar de army wuz and gittin' grub. When de passes give out we foun' whar a French army wid some cannons wuz livin' over in de woods a ways, so we went over whar dey wuz and et.

"Dat went on fer a long time, 'twell one day de balloons wuz gone and de white boys says it wuz time to move again. But me and de other boy didn't see no use in gwine nowhar else, so we stayed. Dat evenin' we went over to whar de French army wuz fer some grub, but dey wuz gone too. De boy wid me says maybe de Germans done caught 'um, but we didn't know;

hadn't heard no big racket since yistiddy. So we went back to de cave. Dey wasn't no grub, so we crawled in and went to bed and slep' dat night, and early de nex' mawnin' somebody come into de hole and tromped on us and woke us up. It wuz one of dese army upliftin' ladies huntin' German bayonets and belt-buckles. She say 'Who dat in here?' and de other boy says 'Us shock troops'. So we got out, but we hadn't gone no piece 'fo' here come a wagon-load of M.P.s. And de passes had done give out."

"Whut you do den?" Simon asked. Isom's eyes bulged quietly in the gloom behind the woodbox.

"Dey tuck us and shut us up in de jail-house fer a while. But de war wuz mos' thu and dey needed us to load dem steam-boats back up, so dey sont us to a town name' Bres'.......
I dont take nothin' offen no white man, M.P. er not," Caspey stated again. "Us boys wuz in a room one night, shootin' dice. De bugle had done already played de lights out tune, but we wuz in de army, whar a man kin do whut he wants es long es dey'll let 'im, so when de M.P. come along and says 'Put out dat light', one of de boys says 'Come in here, and we'll put yo'n out'. Dey wuz two of de M.P.s and dey kicked de do' in and started shootin', and somebody knocked de light over and we run. Dey foun' one of de M.P.s de nex' mawnin' widout nothin' to hole his collar on, and two of de boys wuz daid, too. But dey couldn't fin' who de res' of us wuz. And den we come home."

Caspey emptied his cup. "I dont take nothin' offen no white man no mo', lootenant ner captain ner M.P. War showed de white folks dey cant git along widout de cullud man. Tromple him in de dus', but when de trouble bust loose, hit's 'Please, suh, Mr Cullud Man; right dis way whar de bugle blow-in', Mr Cullud Man; you is de savior of de country.' And now de cullud race gwine reap de benefits of de war, and dat soon."

"Sho," murmured Simon.

"Yes, suh. And de women, too. I got my white in France, and I'm gwine git it here, too."

"Lemme tell you somethin', nigger," Simon said. "De good Lawd done took keer of you fer a long time now, but He aint gwine bother wid you always."

"Den I reckon I'll git along widout Him," Caspey retorted. He rose and stretched. "Reckon I'll go down to de big road and ketch a ride into town. Gimme dem clothes, Isom."

Miss Jenny and her guest stood on the veranda when he passed along beside the house and crossed toward the drive.

"There goes your gardener," Narcissa said. Miss Jenny looked.

"That's Caspey," she corrected. "Now, where do you reckon he's headed? Town, I'll bet a dollar," she added, watching his lounging khaki back, by means of which he contrived to disseminate in some way a sort of lazy insolence. "You, Caspey!" she called.

He slowed in passing Narcissa's small car and examined it with a disparagement too lazy to sneer even, then he slouched on.

"You, Caspey!" Miss Jenny repeated, raising her voice. But he went steadily on down the drive, insolent and slouching and unhurried. "He heard me," she said ominously. "We'll see about this when he comes back. Who was the fool anyway, who thought of putting niggers into the same uniform with white men? Mr Vardaman knew better; he told those fools at Washington at the time that it wouldn't do. But politicians!" She invested the innocent word with an utter and blasting derogation. "If I ever get tired of associating with gentlefolks, I know what I'll do: I'll run for Congress. . . . Listen at me! tiradin' again. I declare, at times I believe these Sartorises and all their possessions just set out to plague and worry me. Thank the Lord, I wont have to associate with 'em after I'm dead. I dont know where they'll be, but no Sartoris is going to stay in heaven any longer than he can help."

The other laughed. "You seem very sure of your own destination, Miss Jenny."

"Why shouldn't I be? Haven't I been laying up crowns and harps for a long time?" She shaded her eyes with her hand and gazed down the drive. Caspey had reached the gate and he now stood beside the road, waiting for a wagon to pass. "Dont you stop for him, you hear?" she said suddenly. "Why wont you stay for dinner?"

"No," the other answered. "I must get on home. Aunt Sally's not well today. . . . . . " She stood for a moment in the sunlight, her hat and her basket of flowers on her arm, musing. Then with a sudden decision she drew a folded paper from the front of her dress.

"Got another one, did you?" Miss Jenny asked, watching her. "Lemme see it." She took the paper and opened it and stepped back out of the sun. Her nose glasses hung on a slender silk cord that rolled onto a spring in a small gold case pinned to her bosom. She snapped the cord out and set the glasses on her high-bridged nose, and behind them her gray eyes were cold and piercing as a surgeon's.

The paper was a single sheet of foolscap; it bore writing in a frank, open script that at first glance divulged no individuality whatever; a hand youthful yet at the same time so blandly and neatly unsecretive that presently you wondered a little.

"You did not answere mine of 25th. I did not expect you answer it yet. You will answer soon I can wait. I will not harm you I am square and honest you will lern when our ways come to gether. I do not expect you answer Yet. But you know where you make a sign."

Miss Jenny refolded the paper with a gesture of fine and

delicate distaste. "I'd burn this thing, if it wasn't the only thing we have to catch him with. I'll give it to Bayard tonight."

"No, no," the other protested quickly, extending her hand. "Please dont. Let me have it and tear it up."

"It's our only evidence, child—this and the other one. We'll get a detective."

"No, no; please! I dont want anybody else to know about it. Please, Miss Jenny." She reached her hand again.

"You want to keep it," Miss Jenny accused coldly. "Just like a young fool woman, to be flattered by a thing like this."

"I'll tear it up," the other repeated. "I would have sooner, but I wanted to tell someone. It—it—I thought I wouldn't feel so filthy, after I had shown it to someone else. Let me have it, please."

"Fiddlesticks. Why should you feel filthy? You haven't encouraged it, have you?"

"Please, Miss Jenny."

But Miss Jenny still held on to it. "Dont be a fool," she snapped. "How can this thing make you feel filthy? Any young woman is liable to get an anonymous letter. And a lot of 'em like it. We all are convinced that men feel that way about us, and we cant help but admire one that's got the courage to tell us, no matter who he is."

"If he'd just signed his name. I wouldn't mind who it was. But like this. . . . . . . Please, Miss Jenny."

"Dont be a fool," Miss Jenny repeated. "How can we find who it is, if you destroy the evidence?"

"I dont want to know." Miss Jenny released the paper and Narcissa tore it into bits and cast them over the rail and rubbed her hands on her dress. "I dont want to know. I want to forget all about it."

"Nonsense. You're dying to know, right now. I bet you look

at every man you pass and wonder if it's him. And as long as you dont do something about it, it'll go on. Get worse, probably. You better let me tell Bayard."

"No, no. I'd hate for him to know, to think that I would—— might have. . . . . . . It's all right: I'll just burn them up after this, without opening them. . . . I must really go."

"Of course: you'll throw 'em right into the stove," Miss Jenny agreed with cold irony. Narcissa descended the steps and Miss Jenny came forward into the sunlight again, letting her glasses whip back into the case. "It's your business, of course. But I'd not stand for it, if 'twas me. But then, I aint twenty-six years old. . . . Well, come out again when you get another one, or you want some more flowers."

"Yes, I will. Thank you for these."

"And let me know what you hear from Horace. Thank the Lord, it's just a glass-blowing machine, and not a war widow."

"Yes, I will. Goodbye." She went on through the dappled shade in her straight white dress and her basket of flowers stippled upon it, and got in her car. The top was back and she put her hat on and started the engine, and looked back again and waved her hand. "Goodbye."

The negro had moved down the road, slowly, and had stopped again, and he was watching her covertly as she approached. As she passed he looked full at her and she knew he was about to hail her. She opened the throttle and passed him with increasing speed and drove swiftly on to town, where she lived in a brick house among cedars on a hill.

She was arranging the larkspur in a dull lemon urn on the piano. Aunt Sally Wyatt rocked steadily in her chair beside the window, clapping her feet flatly on the floor at each stroke. Her work basket sat on the window ledge between the gentle billowing of the curtains, her ebony walking-stick leaned beside it.

"And you were out there two hours," she said, "and never saw him at all?"

"He wasn't there," Narcissa answered. "He's gone to Memphis."

Aunt Sally rocked steadily. "If I was them, I'd make him stay there. I wouldn't have that boy around me, blood or no blood. . . . . . . What did he go to Memphis for? I thought that aeroplane what-do-you-call-it was broke up."

"He went on business, I suppose."

"What business has he got in Memphis? Bayard Sartoris has got more sense than to turn over any business to that hairbrained fool."

"I dont know," Narcissa answered, arranging the larkspur. "He'll be back soon, I suppose. You can ask him then."

"Me ask him? I never said two words to him in his life. And I dont intend to. I been used to associating with gentlefolks."

Narcissa broke some of the stems, arranging the blooms in a pattern. "What's he done that a gentleman doesn't do, Aunt Sally?"

"Why, jumping off water tanks and going up in balloons just to scare folks. You think I'd have that boy around me? I'd have him locked up in the insane asylum, if I was Bayard and Jenny."

"He didn't jump off of the tank. He just swung off of it on a rope and dived into the swimming pool. And it was John that went up in the balloon."

"That wasn't what I heard. I heard he jumped off that tank, across a whole row of freight cars and lumber piles and didn't miss the edge of the pool an inch."

"No he didn't. He swung on a rope from the top of a house and then dived into the pool. The rope was tied to the tank."

"Well, didn't he have to jump over a lot of lumber and freight cars? And couldn't he have broken his neck just as easy that way as jumping off the tank?"

"Yes," Narcissa answered.

"There! What'd I tell you? And what was the use of it?"

"I dont know."

"Of course you dont. That was the reason he did it." Aunt Sally rocked triumphantly for a while. Narcissa put the last touches to the blue pattern of the larkspur. A tortoise-shell cat bunched suddenly and silently in the window beside the work basket, with an effect as of sleight-of-hand. Still crouching it blinked into the room for a moment, then it sank to its belly and with arched neck fell to grooming its shoulder with a narrow pink tongue. Narcissa moved to the window and laid her hand on the creature's sleek back.

"And then, going up in that balloon, when——"

"That wasn't Bayard," Narcissa repeated. "That was John."

"That wasn't what I heard. I heard it was the other one and that Bayard and Jenny were both begging him with tears in their eyes not to do it. I heard——"

"Neither one of them were there. Bayard wasn't even there. It was John did it. He did it because the man that came with the balloon got sick. John went up in it so the country people wouldn't be disappointed. I was there."

"Stood there and let him do it, did you, when you could a telephoned Jenny or walked across the square to the bank and got Bayard? You stood there and never opened your mouth, did you?"

"Yes," Narcissa answered. Stood there beside Horace in the slow, intent ring of country people, watching the globe swelling and tugging at its ropes, watched John Sartoris in a faded flannel shirt and corduroy breeches, while the carnival man explained the rip-cord and the parachute to him; stood there feeling her breath going out faster than she could draw it in again and watched the thing lurch into the air with John sitting on a frail trapeze bar swinging beneath it, with eyes she could not close, saw the balloon and people and all swirl slowly upward and then found herself clinging to Horace behind the shelter of a wagon, trying to get her breath.

He landed three miles away in a brier thicket and disengaged the parachute and regained the road and hailed a passing negro in a wagon. A mile from town they met old Bayard driving furiously in the carriage and the two vehicles stopped side to side in the road while old Bayard in the one exhausted the accumulate fury of his rage and in the other his grandson sat in his shredded clothes and on his scratched face that look of one who has gained for an instant a desire so fine that its escape was a purifaction, not a loss.

The next day, as she was passing a store, he emerged with that abrupt violence which he had in common with his brother, pulling short up to avoid a collision with her.

"Oh, ex—— Why, hello," he said. Beneath the crisscrosses of tape his face was merry and bold and wild, and he wore no hat. For a moment she gazed at him with wide, hopeless eyes, then she clapped her hand to her mouth and went swiftly on, almost running.

Then he was gone, with his brother, shut away by the war as two noisy dogs are penned in a kennel far away. Miss Jenny gave her news of them, of the dull, dutiful letters they sent home at sparse intervals; then he was dead. But away beyond seas, and there was no body to be returned clumsily to earth, and so to her he seemed still to be laughing at that word as he had laughed at all the other mouthsounds that stood for repose, who had not waited for Time and its furniture to teach him that the end of wisdom is to dream high enough not to lose the dream in the seeking of it.

Aunt Sally rocked steadily in her chair.

"Well, it dont matter which one it was. One's bad as the other. But I reckon it aint their fault, raised like they were. Rotten spoiled, both of 'em. Lucy Sartoris wouldn't let anybody control 'em while she lived. If they'd been mine, now. . . ." She rocked on. "Beat it out of 'em, I would. Raising two wild Indians like that. But those folks, thinking there wasn't anybody quite as good as a Sartoris. Even Lucy Cranston, come from as good people as there are in the state, acting like it was divine providence that let her marry one Sartoris and be the mother of two more. Pride, false pride."

She rocked steadily in her chair. Beneath Narcissa's hand the cat purred with lazy arrogance.

"It was a judgment on 'em, taking John instead of that other one. John at least tipped his hat to a lady on the street, but that other boy. . . . . . . " She rocked monotonously, clapping her feet flatly against the floor. "You better stay away from that boy. He'll be killing you same as he did that poor little wife of his."

"At least, give me benefit of clergy first, Aunt Sally," Narcissa said. Beneath her hand, beneath the cat's sleek hide, muscles flowed suddenly into tight knots, like wire, and the animal's body seemed to elongate like rubber as it whipped from beneath her hand and flashed out of sight across the veranda.

"Oh," Narcissa cried. Then she whirled and caught up Aunt Sally's stick and ran from the room.

"What—" Aunt Sally said. "You bring my stick back here," she said. She sat staring at the door, hearing the swift clatter of the other's heels in the hall and then on the veranda. She rose and leaned in the window. "You bring my stick back here," she shouted.

Narcissa sped on across the porch and to the ground. In

the canna bed beside the veranda the cat, crouching, jerked its head around and its yellow unwinking eyes. Narcissa rushed at it, the stick raised.

"Put it down!" she cried. "Drop it!" For another second the yellow eyes glared at her, then the animal ducked its head and leaped away in a long fluid bound, the bird between its jaws.

"Oh-h-h, damn you! Damn you! You——you Sartoris!" and she hurled the stick after the final tortoise flash as the cat flicked around the corner of the house.

"You get my stick and bring it right back this minute!" Aunt Sally shouted from the window.

She had seen Bayard once from a distance. He appeared as usual at the time—a lean figure in casual easy clothes unpressed and a little comfortably shabby, and with his air of smoldering abrupt violence. He and his brother had both had this, but Bayard's was a cold, arrogant sort of leashed violence, while in John it was a warmer thing, spontaneous and merry and wild. It was Bayard who had attached a rope to a ninety foot water tank and, from the roof of an adjoining building, swung himself across the intervening fifty yards of piled lumber and freight cars and released the rope and dived into a narrow concrete swimming pool while upturned faces gaped and screamed—a cold nicety of judgment and unnecessary cruel skill; John who, one County Fair day, made the balloon ascension, the aeronaut having been stricken with ptomaine poisoning, that the county people might not be disappointed, and landed three miles away in a brier thicket, losing most of his clothing and skin and returning to town cheerful and babbling in the wagon of a passing negro.

But both of these were utterly beyond her; it was not in her nature to differentiate between motives whose results were the same, and on occasions when she had seen them conducting themselves as civilized beings, had been in the same polite room with them, she found herself watching them with shrinking and fearful curiosity, as she might have looked upon wild beasts with a temporary semblance of men and engaged in human activities, morally acknowledging the security of the cage but spiritually unreassured.

But she had not seen them often. They were either away at school, or if at home they passed their headlong days in the country, coming into town at rare intervals and then on horseback, in stained corduroy and flannel shirts. Yet rumors of their doings came in to her from time to time, causing always in her that shrinking, fascinated distaste, that blending of curiosity and dread, as if a raw wind had blown into that garden wherein she dwelt. Then they would be gone again, and she would think of them only to remember Horace and his fine and electric delicacy, and to thank her gods he was not as they.

Then the war, and she learned without any surprise whatever that they had gone to it. That was exactly what they would do, and her nature drowsed again beneath the serene belief that they had been removed from her life for good and always; to her the war had been brought about for the sole purpose of removing them from her life as noisy dogs are shut up in a kennel afar off. Thus her days. Man became amphibious and lived in mud and filth and died and was buried in it; the world looked on in hysterical amazement. But she, within her walled and windless garden, thought of them only with a sober and pointless pity, like a flower's exhalation, and like the flower, uncaring if the scent be sensed or not. She gave clothing and money to funds, and she knitted things also, but she did not know where Saloniki was and was incurious as to how Rheims or Przemysl were pronounced.

Then Horace departed, with his Snopes, and the war became abruptly personal. But it was still not the same war to which the Sartoris boys had gone; and soon she was readjusted again, with Aunt Sally Wyatt in the house and the steady unemphasis of their feminine days. She joined the Red Cross and various other welfare organizations, and she knitted harsh wool with intense brooding skill and performed other labors while other women talked of their menfolks into her grave receptivity.

There was a family of country people moved recently to town—a young man and his pregnant wife and two infant children. They abode in a rejuvenated rented cabin on the edge of town, where the woman did her own housework, while the man was employed by the local distributor for an oil company, laboring all day with a sort of eager fury of willingness and a desire to get on. He was a steady, exemplary sort, willing and unfailingly goodnatured and reliable, so he was drafted immediately and denied exemption and ravished celeritously overseas. His family accompanied him to the station in an automobile supplied by the charity of an old lady of the town and they watched him out of their lives with that tearless uncomplaining gravity of primitive creatures. The Red Cross took charge of the family, but Narcissa Benbow adopted them. She was present when the baby was born two weeks later, she superintended the household—meals and clothing—until the woman was about again, and for the next twelve months she wrote a monthly letter to the husband and father who, having no particular aptitude for it save his unflagging even temper and a ready willingness to do as he was told, was now a company cook in the S.O.S.

This occupation too was just a grave centering of her days; there was no hysteria in it, no conviction that she was helping to slay the biblical Beast, or laying up treasure in heaven. Horace was away too; she was waiting for him to return, marking time, as it were. Then Bayard Sartoris had returned home, with a wife. She sensed the romantic glamor of this with interest and grave approval, as of a dramatic scene, but that was all; Bayard Sartoris went away again. Narcissa met his wife now and then, and always with a little curiosity, as though, voluntarily associating so intimately with a Sartoris, she too must be an animal with the temporary semblance of a human being. There was no common ground between them, between Narcissa with her constancy, her serenity which the other considered provincial and a little dull, and the other with her sexless vivid unrepose and the brittle daring of her speech and actions.

She had learned of John Sartoris' death without any emotion whatever except a faint sense of vindication, a sort of I-told-you-so feeling, which recurred (blended now with a sense of pitying outrage, blaming this too on Bayard) when Bayard's wife died in childbirth in October of the same year, even though she stood with old Bayard's deaf and arrogant back and Miss Jenny's trim indomitability amid sad trees and streaming marble shapes beneath a dissolving afternoon. Then November, and bells and whistles and revolvers. Horace would be coming home soon now, she thought at the time. Before Christmas, perhaps. But before he did so she had seen Bayard once on the street, and later, while she and Miss Jenny were sitting in Miss Jenny's dim parlor. The doors were ajar as usual, and young Bayard appeared suddenly between them and stood looking at her.

"It's Bayard," Miss Jenny said. "Come in here and speak to Narcissa, sonny."

He said Hello vaguely and she turned on the piano bench, and shrank a little against the instrument. "Who is it?" he said, and he came into the room, bringing with him that cold leashed violence which she remembered.

"It's Narcissa," Miss Jenny said testily. "Go on and speak to her and stop acting like you dont know who she is."

Narcissa gave him her hand and he stood holding it loosely, but he was not looking at her. She withdrew her hand, and he looked at her again, then away, and he loomed above them and stood rubbing his hand through his hair.

"I want a drink," he said. "I cant find the key to the desk."

"Stop and talk to us a few minutes, and you can have one."

He stood for a moment above them, then he moved abruptly and before Miss Jenny could speak he had dragged the holland envelope from another chair.

"Let that alone, you Indian!" Miss Jenny exclaimed. She rose. "Here, take my chair, if you're too weak to stand up. I'll be back in a minute," she added to Narcissa; "I'll have to get my keys."

He sat laxly in the chair, rubbing his hand over his head, his gaze brooding somewhere about his booted feet. Narcissa sat utterly quiet, shrunk back against the piano. She spoke at last:

"I am so sorry about your wife . . . John. I asked Miss Jenny to tell you when she. . . . . . . "

He sat rubbing his head slowly, in the brooding violence of his temporary repose.

"You aren't married yourself, are you?" he asked. She sat perfectly still. "Ought to try it," he added. "Everybody ought to get married once, like everybody ought to go to one war."

Miss Jenny returned with the keys, and he got his long abrupt body erect and left them.

"You can go on, now," she said. "He wont bother us again."

"No, I must go." Narcissa rose quickly and took her hat from the top of the piano.

"Why, you haven't been here any time, yet."

"I must go," Narcissa repeated. Miss Jenny rose.

"Well, if you must. I'll cut you some flowers. Wont take a minute."

"No, some other time; I—I have—I'll come out soon and get some. Goodbye." At the door she glanced swiftly down the hall; then she went on. Miss Jenny followed to the veranda. The other had descended the steps and she now went swiftly on toward her car.

"Come back again soon," Miss Jenny called.

"Yes. Soon," Narcissa answered. "Goodbye."

2

Young Bayard came back from Memphis in his car. Memphis was seventy-five miles away and the trip had taken an hour and forty minutes because some of the road was clay country road. The car was long and low and gray; the four cylinder engine had sixteen valves and eight spark-plugs, and the people had guaranteed that it would run eighty miles an hour, although there was a strip of paper pasted to the windshield, to which he payed no attention whatever, asking him in red letters not to do so for the first five hundred miles.

He came up the drive and stopped before the house, where his grandfather sat with his feet on the veranda railing and Miss Jenny stood trim in her black dress beside a post. She descended the steps and examined it, and opened the door and got in to try the seat. Simon came to the door and gave it a brief derogatory look and retired, and Isom appeared around the corner and circled the car quietly with an utter and yearning admiration. But old Bayard just looked down at the long, dusty thing, his cigar in his fingers, and grunted.

"Why, it's as comfortable as a rocking-chair," Miss Jenny said. "Come here and try it," she called to him. But he grunted again, and sat with his feet on the rail and watched young Bayard slide in under the wheel. The engine raced experimentally, ceased. Isom stood like a leashed hound beside it. Young Bayard glanced at him.

"You can go next time," he said.

"Why cant he go now?" Miss Jenny said. "Jump in, Isom."

Isom jumped in, and old Bayard watched them move soundlessly down the drive and watched the car pass from sight down the valley. Presently above the trees a cloud of dust rose into the azure afternoon and hung rosily fading in the sun, and a sound as of remote thunder died muttering behind it. Old Bayard puffed his cigar again. Simon appeared again in the door and stood there.

"Now whar you reckon dey gwine right here at supper-time?" he said. Bayard grunted, and Simon stood in the door, mumbling to himself.

Twenty minutes later the car slid up the drive and came to a halt almost in its former tracks. In the back seat Isom's face was like an open piano. Miss Jenny had worn no hat, and she held her hair with both hands, and when the car stopped she sat for a moment so. Then she drew a long breath.

"I wish I smoked cigarettes," she said, and then: "Is that as fast as it'll go?"

Isom got out and opened the door for her. She descended a little stiffly, but her eyes were shining and her dry old cheeks were flushed.

"How fer y'all been?" Simon asked from the door.

"We've been to town," she answered proudly, and her voice was clear as a girl's. Town was four miles away.

After that the significance grew slowly. He received intimations of it from various sources. But because of his deafness, these intimations came slowly since they must come directly to him and not through overheard talk. The actual evidence, the convincing evidence, came from old man Falls. Eight or ten times a year he walked in from the county farm, always stopping in at the bank.

One day a week later old man Falls came in to town and found old Bayard in his office. The office was also the directors' room. It was a large room containing a long table lined with chairs, and a tall cabinet where blank banking forms were kept, and old Bayard's roll-top desk and swivel chair and a sofa on which he napped for an hour each noon.

The desk, like the one at home, was cluttered with a variety of objects which bore no relation whatever to the banking business, and the mantel above the fireplace bore still more objects of an agricultural nature, as well as a dusty assortment of pipes and three or four jars of tobacco which furnished solace for the entire banking force from president to janitor and for a respectable portion of the bank's clientele. Weather permitting, old Bayard spent most of the day in a tilted chair in the street door, and when these patrons found him there, they went on back to the office and filled their pipes from the jars. It was a sort of unspoken convention not to take more than a pipeful at a time. Here old man Falls and old Bayard retired on the old man's monthly visits and shouted at one another (they were both deaf) for a half hour or so. You could hear them plainly from the street and in the adjoining store on either side.

Old man Falls' eyes were blue and innocent as a boy's and his first act was to open the parcel which old Bayard had for him and take out a plug of chewing tobacco, cut off a chew and put it in his mouth, replace the plug and tie the parcel neatly again. Twice a year the parcel contained an entire outfit of clothing, on the other occasions tobacco and a small sack of peppermint candy. He would never cut the string, but always untied it with his stiff, gnarled fingers and tied it back again. He would not accept money.

He sat now in his clean, faded overalls, with the parcel on his knees, telling Bayard about the automobile that had passed him on the road that morning. Everyone had seen or heard of young Bayard's low gray car, but old man Falls was the first to tell his grandfather how he drove it. Old Bayard sat quite still, watching him with his fierce old eyes until he had finished.

"Are you sure who it was?" he asked.

"Hit passed me too fast fer me to tell whether they was anybody in hit a-tall or not. I asked when I fetched town who 'twas. Seems like ever'body knows how fast he runs hit except you."

Old Bayard sat quietly for a time. Then he raised his voice: "Byron."

The door opened quietly and the book-keeper entered—a thin, youngish man with hairy hands and covert close eyes that looked always as though he were just blinking them, though you never saw them closed.

"Yes, sir, Colonel," he said in a slow, nasal voice without inflection.

"'Phone out to my house and tell my grandson not to touch that car until I come home."

"Yes, sir, Colonel." And he was gone as silently as he appeared.

Bayard slammed around in his swivel chair again and old man Falls leaned forward, peering at his face.

"What's that 'ere wen you got on yo' face, Bayard?" he asked.

"What?" Bayard demanded, then he raised his hand to a small spot which the suffusion of his face had brought into relief. "Here? I dont know what it is. It's been there about a week. Why?"

"Is it gittin' bigger?" the other asked. He rose and laid his parcel down and extended his hand. Old Bayard drew his head back.

"It's nothing," he said testily. "Let it alone." But old man Falls put the other's hand aside and touched the spot with his fingers.

"H'm," he said. "Hard's a rock. Hit'll git bigger, too. I'll watch hit, and when hit's right, I'll take hit off. 'Taint ripe, yit." The book-keeper appeared suddenly and without noise beside them.

"Yo' cook says him and Miss Jenny is off car-ridin' some-wheres. I left yo' message."

"Jenny's with him, you say?" old Bayard asked.

"That's what yo' cook says," the book-keeper repeated in his inflectionless voice.

"Well. All right."

The book-keeper withdrew and old man Falls picked up his parcel. "I'll be gittin' on too," he said. "I'll come in next week and take a look at hit. You better let hit alone till I git back." He followed the book-keeper from the room, and presently old Bayard rose and stalked through the lobby and tilted his chair in the door.

That afternoon when he arrived home, the car was not in sight, nor did his aunt answer his call. He mounted to his room and put on his riding-boots and lit a cigar, but when he looked down from his window into the back yard, neither Isom nor the saddled mare were visible. The old setter sat looking up at his window. When old Bayard's head appeared there the dog rose and went to the kitchen door and stood there; then it looked up at his window again. Old Bayard tramped down the stairs and on through the house and entered the kitchen, where Caspey sat at the table, eating and talking to Isom and Elnora.

"And one mo' time me and another boy——" Caspey was saying. Then Isom saw Bayard, and rose from his seat in the woodbox corner and his eyes rolled whitely in his bullet head. Elnora paused also with her broom, but Caspey turned his head without rising, and still chewing steadily he blinked his eyes at old Bayard in the door.

"I sent you word a week ago to come on out here at once, or not to come at all," Bayard said. "Did you get it?" Caspey mumbled something, still chewing, and old Bayard came into the room. "Get up from there and saddle my horse."

Caspey turned his back deliberately and raised his glass of buttermilk. "Git on, Caspey," Elnora hissed at him.

"I aint workin' here," he answered, just beneath Bayard's deafness. He turned to Isom. "Whyn't you go'n git his hoss fer him? Aint you workin' here?"

"Caspey, fer Lawd's sake!" Elnora implored. "Yes, suh, Cunnel; he's gwine," she said loudly.

"Who, me?" Caspey said. "Does I look like it?" He raised the glass steadily to his mouth, then Bayard moved again and Caspey lost his nerve and rose quickly before the other reached him, and crossed the kitchen toward the door, but with sullen insolence in the very shape of his back. As he fumbled with the door Bayard overtook him.

"Are you going to saddle that mare?" he demanded.

"Aint gwine skip it, big boy," Caspey answered, just below Bayard's deafness.

"What?"

"Oh, Lawd, Caspey!" Elnora moaned. Isom crouched into his corner. Caspey raised his eyes swiftly to Bayard's face and opened the screen door.

"I says, I aint gwine skip it," he repeated, raising his voice. Simon stood at the foot of the steps beside the setter, gaping his toothless mouth up at them, and old Bayard reached a stick of stove wood from the box at his hand and knocked Caspey through the opening door and down the steps at his father's feet.

"Now, you go saddle that mare," he said.

Simon helped his son to rise and led him away toward the

barn while the setter watched them, gravely interested. "I kep' tellin' you dem new-fangled war notions of yo'n wa'nt gwine ter work on dis place," he said angrily. "And you better thank de good Lawd fer makin' yo' haid hard ez hit is. You go'n git dat mare, en save dat nigger freedom talk fer townfolks: dey mought stomach it. Whut us niggers want ter be free fer, anyhow? Aint we got ez many white folks now ez we kin suppo't?"

That night at supper, old Bayard looked at his grandson across the roast of mutton. "Will Falls told me you passed him on the Poor House hill running forty miles an hour today."

"Forty fiddlesticks," Miss Jenny answered promptly, "it was fifty four. I was watching the—what do you call it, Bayard? speedometer."

Old Bayard sat with his head bent a little, watching his hands trembling on the carving knife and fork; hearing beneath the napkin tucked into his waistcoat, his heart a little too light and a little too fast; feeling Miss Jenny's eyes upon his face.

"Bayard," she said sharply, "what's that on your cheek?" He rose so suddenly that his chair tipped over backward with a crash, and he tramped blindly from the room.

3

"I know what you want me to do," Miss Jenny told old Bayard across her newspaper. "You want me to let my housekeeping go to the dogs and spend all my time in that car, that's what you want. Well, I'm not going to do it. I dont mind riding with him now and then, but I've got too much to do with my time to spend it keeping him from running that car fast. Neck, too," she added. She rattled the paper crisply.

She said: "Besides, you aint foolish enough to believe he'll drive slow just because there's somebody with him, are you? If you do think so, you'd better send Simon along. Lord knows Simon can spare the time. Since you quit using the carriage, if he does anything at all, I dont know it." She read the paper again.

Old Bayard's cigar smoked in his still hand.

"I might send Isom," he said.

Miss Jenny's paper rattled sharply and she stared at her nephew for a long moment. "God in heaven, man, why dont you put a block and chain on him and have done with it?"

"Well, didn't you suggest sending Simon with him, your-self? Simon has his work to do, but all Isom ever does is saddle my horse once a day, and I can do that myself."

"I was trying to be ironical," Miss Jenny said. "God knows, I should have learned better by this time. But if you've got to invent something new for the niggers to do, you let it be Simon. I need Isom to keep a roof over your head and some-thing to eat on the table." She rattled the paper. "Why dont you come right out and tell him not to drive fast? A man that has to spend eight hours a day sitting in a chair in that bank door ought not to have to spend the rest of the afternoon helling around the country in an automobile if he dont want to."

"Do you think it would do any good to ask him? There was never a damned one of 'em ever paid any attention to my wishes yet."

"Ask, the devil," Miss Jenny said. "Who said anything about ask? Tell him not to. Tell him that if you hear again of his going fast in it, that you'll frail the life out of him. I believe any-way that you like to ride in that car, only you wont admit it, and you just dont want him to ride in it when you cant go too." But old Bayard had slammed his feet to the floor and risen, and he tramped from the room.

Instead of mounting the stairs however Miss Jenny heard his footsteps die away down the hall, and presently she rose and followed to the back porch, where he stood in the darkness there. The night was dark, myriad with drifting odors of the spring and with insects. Dark upon lesser dark, the barn loomed against the sky.

"He hasn't come in yet," she said impatiently, touching his arm. "I could have told you. Go on up and go to bed, now; dont you know he'll let you know when he comes in? You're going to think him into a ditch somewhere, with these fool notions of yours." Then more gently: "You're too childish about that car. It's no more dangerous at night than it is in day-time. Come on, now."

He shook her hand off, but he turned obediently and entered the house. This time he mounted the stairs and she could hear him in his bedroom, thumping about. Presently he ceased slamming doors and drawers and lay beneath the read-ing lamp with his Dumas. After a time the door opened and young Bayard entered and came into the radius of the light with his bleak eyes.

His grandfather did not remark his presence and he touched his arm. Old Bayard looked up, and when he did so young Bayard turned and quitted the room.

After the shades on the windows were drawn at three oclock old Bayard retired to the office. Inside the grille the cashier and the book-keeper could hear him clattering and banging around beyond the door. The cashier paused, a stack of silver clipped neatly in his fingers.

"Hear 'im?" he said. "Something on his mind here, lately. Used to be he was quiet as a mouse back there until they come for him, but last few days he tromples and thumps around back there like he was fighting hornets."

The book-keeper said nothing. The cashier set the stack of silver aside, built up another one.

"Something on his mind, lately. That examiner must a put a bug in his ear, I reckon."

The book-keeper said nothing. He swung the adding machine to his desk and clicked the lever over. In the back room old Bayard moved audibly about. The cashier stacked the remaining silver neatly and rolled a cigarette. The book-keeper bent above the steady clicking of the machine, and the cashier sealed his cigarette and lit it and waddled to the window and lifted the curtain.

"Simon's brought the carriage, today," he said. "That boy finally wrecked that car, I reckon. Better call Colonel."

The book-keeper slid from his stool and went back to the door and opened it. Old Bayard glanced up from his desk with his hat on.

"All right, Byron," he said. The book-keeper returned to his desk.

Old Bayard stalked through the bank and opened the street door and stopped utterly, the doorknob in his hand.

"Where's Bayard?" he said.

"He aint comin'," Simon answered. Old Bayard crossed to the carriage.

"What? Where is he?"

"Him en Isom off somewhar in dat cyar," Simon said. "Lawd knows whar dey is by now. Takin' dat boy away fum his work in de middle of de day, cyar-ridin'." Old Bayard laid his hand on the stanchion, the spot on his face coming again into white relief. "Atter all de time I spent tryin' to git some sense inter Isom's haid," Simon continued. He held the horses' heads up, waiting for his employer to enter. "Cyar-ridin'," he said. "Cyar-ridin'."

Old Bayard got in and sank heavily into the seat.

"I'll be damned," he said, "if I haven't got the triflingest set of folks to make a living for God ever made. There's just one thing about it: when I finally have to go to the poorhouse, every damned one of you'll be there when I come."

"Now, here you quoilin' too," Simon said. "Miss Jenny yellin' at me twell I wuz plumb out de gate, and now you already started at dis en'. But ef Mist' Bayard dont leave dat boy alone, he aint gwine ter be no better'n a town nigger spite of all I kin do."

"Jenny's already ruined him," old Bayard said. "Even Bayard cant hurt him much."

"You sho' tole de troof den," Simon agreed. He shook the reins. "Come up, dar."

"Here, Simon," old Bayard said. "Hold up a minute."

Simon reined the horses back. "Whut you want now?"

The spot on old Bayard's cheek had resumed its normal appearance. "Go back to my office and get me a cigar out of that jar on the mantel," he said.

Two days later, as he and Simon tooled sedately homeward through the afternoon, simultaneously almost with the warning thunder of it the car burst upon him on a curve, slewed into the ditch and on to the road again and rushed on; and in the flashing instant he and Simon saw the whites of Isom's eyes and the ivory cropping of his teeth behind the steering wheel. When the car returned home that afternoon Simon conducted Isom to the barn and whipped him with a harness strap.

That night they sat in the office after supper. Old Bayard held his cigar unlighted in his fingers. Miss Jenny read the paper. Faint airs blew in, laden with spring.

Suddenly old Bayard said: "Maybe he'll get tired of it after a while."

Miss Jenny raised her head.

"And when he does," Miss Jenny said, "dont you know

what he'll get then? When he finds that car wont go fast enough?" she demanded, staring at him across the paper. He sat with his unlighted cigar, his head bent a little, not looking at her. "He'll buy an aeroplane." She rattled the paper and turned a page. "He ought to have a wife," she added, reading again. "Let him get a son, then he can break his neck as soon and as often as he pleases. Providence doesn't seem to have any judgment at all," she said, thinking of the two of them, of his dead brother. She said: "But Lord knows, I'd hate to see any girl I was fond of, married to him." She rattled the paper again, turned another page. "I dont know what else you expect of him. Of any Sartoris. You dont waste your afternoons riding with him just because you think it'll keep him from turning that car over: you go because when it does happen, you want to be in it, too. So do you think you've got any more considera- tion for folks than he has?" He held his cigar, his face still averted. Miss Jenny was watching him again across the paper.

"I'm coming down town in the morning, and we're going and have the doctor look at that bump on your face, you hear?"

In his room, as he removed his collar and tie before his chest of drawers, his eye fell upon the pipe which he had laid there four weeks ago, and he put the collar and tie down and picked up the pipe and held it in his hand, rubbing the charred bowl slowly with his thumb.

Then with sudden decision he quitted the room and tramped down the hall. At the end of the hall a stair mounted into the darkness. He fumbled the light switch beside it and mounted, following the cramped turnings cautiously in the dark, to a door set at a difficult angle, and opened it upon a broad, low room with a pitched ceiling, smelling of dust and silence and ancient disused things.

The room was cluttered with indiscriminate furniture— chairs and sofas like patient ghosts holding lightly in dry and rigid embrace yet other ghosts—a fitting place for dead Sartorises to gather and speak among themselves of glamorous and old disastrous days. The unshaded light swung on a single cord from the center of the ceiling. He unknotted it and drew it across to a nail in the wall above a cedar chest. He fastened it here and drew a chair across to the chest and sat down.

The chest had not been opened since 1901, when his son John had succumbed to yellow fever and an old Spanish bullet-wound. There had been two occasions since, in July and in October of last year, but the other grandson still possessed quickness and all the incalculable portent of his heritage. So he had forborne for the time being, expecting to be able to kill two birds with one stone, as it were.

Thus each opening was in a way ceremonial, commemorating the violent finis to some phase of his family's history, and while he struggled with the stiff lock it seemed to him that a legion of ghosts breathed quietly at his shoulder, and he pictured a double line of them with their arrogant identical faces waiting just beyond a portal and stretching away toward the invisible dais where Something sat waiting the latest arrival among them; thought of them chafing a little and a little bewildered, thought and desire being denied them, in a place where, immortal, there were no opportunities for vainglorious swashbuckling. Denied that Sartoris heaven in which they could spend eternity dying deaths of needless and magnificent violence while spectators doomed to immortality looked eternally on. The Valhalla which John Sartoris, turning the wine glass in his big, well-shaped hand that night at the supper table, had seen in its chaste and fragile bubble.

The lock was stiff, and he struggled patiently with it for some time. Rust shaled off, rubbed off onto his hands, and he desisted and rose and rummaged about and returned to the chest with a heavy, cast-iron candlestick and hammered the lock free and removed it and raised the lid. From the chest there rose a thin exhilarating odor of cedar, and something else: a scent drily and muskily nostalgic, as of old ashes. The first object was a garment. The brocade was richly hushed, and the fall of fine Mechlin was dustily yellow, pale and textureless as February sunlight. He lifted the garment carefully out. The lace cascaded mellow and pale as spilled wine upon his hands, and he laid it aside and lifted out next a rapier. It was a Toledo, a blade delicate and fine as the prolonged stroke of a violin bow, in a velvet sheath. The sheath was elegant and flamboyant and soiled, and the seams had cracked drily.

Old Bayard held the rapier upon his hands for a while, feeling the balance of it. It was just such an implement as a Sartoris would consider the proper equipment for raising tobacco in a virgin wilderness; it and the scarlet heels and the ruffled wristbands in which he broke the earth and fought his stealthy and simple neighbors. And old Bayard held it upon his two hands, seeing in its stained fine blade and shabby elegant sheath the symbol of his race; that too in the tradition: the thing itself fine and clear enough, only the instrument had become a little tarnished in its very aptitude for shaping circumstance to its arrogant ends.

He laid it aside. Next came a heavy cavalry sabre, and a rosewood case containing two duelling pistols with silver mountings and the lean, deceptive delicacy of race horses, and what old man Falls had called "that 'ere dang der'nger." It was a stubby, evil looking thing with its three barrels; viciously and coldly utilitarian, and between the other two weapons it lay like a cold and deadly insect between two flowers.

He removed next the blue army forage-cap of the 'forties and a small pottery vessel and a Mexican machete, and a long-necked oil can such as locomotive drivers use. It was of silver, and engraved upon it was the picture of a locomotive with a huge bell-shaped funnel and surrounded by an ornate wreath. Beneath it, the name, "Virginia" and the date, "August 9, 1873."

He put these aside and with sudden purposefulness he removed the other objects—a frogged and braided coat of Confederate gray and a gown of sprigged muslin scented faintly of lavender and evocative of old formal minuets and drifting honeysuckle among steady candle flames—and came upon a conglomeration of yellowed papers neatly bound in packets, and at last upon a huge, brass-bound bible. He lifted this to the edge of the chest and opened it. The paper was brown and mellow with years, and it had a texture like that of slightly-moist wood ashes, as though each page were held intact by its archaic and fading print. He turned the pages carefully back to the fly leaves. Beginning near the bottom of the final blank page, a column of names and dates rose in stark, fading simplicity, growing fainter and fainter where time had lain upon them. At the top they were still legible, as they were at the foot of the preceding page. But halfway up this page they ceased, and from there on the sheet was blank save for the faint soft mottlings of time and an occasional brownish penstroke significant but without meaning.

Bayard sat for a long time, regarding the stark dissolving apotheosis of his name. Sartorises had derided Time, but Time was not vindictive, being longer than Sartorises. And probably unaware of them. But it was a good gesture, anyway.

"In the nineteenth century," John Sartoris said, "genealogy is poppycock. Particularly in America, where only what a man takes and keeps has any significance, and where all of us have a common ancestry and the only house from which we can claim descent with any assurance, is the Old Bailey. Yet the man who professes to care nothing about his forbears is only a little less vain than he who bases all his actions on blood prece-

dent. And I reckon a Sartoris can have a little vanity and poppycock, if he wants it."

Yes, it was a good gesture, and Bayard sat and mused quietly on the tense he had unwittingly used. Was. Fatality: the
augury of a man's destiny peeping out at him from the roadside
hedge, if he but recognise it; and again he ran panting through
undergrowth while the fading thunder of the smoke-colored
stallion swept on in the dusk and the Yankee patrol crashed
behind him, crashed fainter and fainter until he crouched with
spent, laboring lungs in a brier thicket and heard the pursuit
rush on. Then he crawled forth and went to a spring he knew
that flowed from the roots of a beech; and as he leaned down to
it the final light of day was reflected onto his face, bringing into
sharp relief forehead and nose above the cavernous sockets of
his eyes and the panting snarl of his teeth, and from the still
water there stared back at him for a sudden moment, a skull.

The unturned corners of man's destiny. Well, heaven, that
crowded place, lay just beyond one of them, they claimed;
heaven, filled with every man's illusion of himself and with the
conflicting illusions of him that parade through the minds of
other illusions. . . . He stirred and sighed quietly, and took out
his fountain pen. At the foot of the column he wrote:

"John Sartoris. July 5, 1918."

and beneath that:

"Caroline White Sartoris and son. October 27, 1918."

When the ink was dry he closed the book and replaced it
and took the pipe from his pocket and put it in the rosewood
case with the duelling pistols and the derringer and replaced
the other things and closed the chest and locked it.

Miss Jenny found old Bayard in his tilted chair in the door, and he looked up at her with a fine assumption of surprise and his deafness seemed more pronounced than ordinary. But she got him up with cold implacability and led him still grumbling down the street, where merchants and others spoke to her as to a martial queen, old Bayard stalking along beside her with sullen reluctance.

They turned presently and mounted a narrow stairway debouching between two stores, beneath an array of dingy professional signs. At the top was a dark corridor with doors. The nearest door was of pine, its gray paint scarred at the bottom as though it had been kicked repeatedly at the same height and with the same force. In the door itself two holes an inch apart bore mute witness to the missing hasp, and from a staple in the jamb depended the hasp itself, fixed there by a huge rusty lock of an ancient pattern. Bayard offered to stop here, but Miss Jenny led him firmly on to a door across the hall.

This door was freshly painted and grained to represent walnut. Into the top half of it was let a pane of thick, opaque glass bearing a name in raised gilt letters, and two embracing office hours. Miss Jenny opened this door and Bayard followed her into a small cubbyhole of a room of spartan but suave asepsis. The walls were an immaculate new gray, with a reproduction of a Corot and two spidery dry-points in narrow frames, and it contained a new rug in warm buff tones and a bare table and four chairs in fumed oak—all impersonal and clean and inexpensive, but revealing at a glance the proprietor's soul; a soul hampered now by material strictures, but destined and determined to someday function amid Persian rugs and mahogany or teak, and a single irreproachable print on the chaste walls. A young woman in a starched white dress rose from a smaller table on which a telephone sat, and patted her hair.

"Good morning, Myrtle," Miss Jenny said. "Tell Dr Alford we'd like to see him, please."

"You have an appointment?" the girl said in a voice without any inflection at all.

"We'll make one now, then," Miss Jenny replied. "You dont mean to say Dr Alford dont come to work before ten oclock, do you?"

"Dr Alford dont—doesn't see anyone without an appointment," the girl parrotted, gazing at a point above Miss Jenny's head. "If you have no appointment, you'll have to have an ap—"

"Tut, tut," Miss Jenny interrupted briskly, "you run and tell Dr Alford Colonel Sartoris wants to see him, there's a good girl."

"Yessum, Miss Jenny," the girl said obediently and she crossed the room, but at the other door she paused again and again her voice became parrot-like. "Wont you sit down? I'll see if the doctor is engaged."

"You go and tell Dr Alford we're here," Miss Jenny repeated affably. "Tell him I've got some shopping to do this morning."

"Yessum, Miss Jenny," the girl agreed, and disappeared, and after a dignified interval she returned, once more clothed faultlessly in her professional manner. "The doctor will see you now. Come in, please." She held the door open and stood aside.

"Thank you, honey," Miss Jenny replied. "Is your mamma still in bed?"

"No'm, she's sitting up now, thank you."

"That's good," Miss Jenny agreed. "Come on, Bayard."

This room was smaller than the other, and brutally carbolized. There was a white enamelled cabinet filled with vicious nickel gleams, and a metal operating table and an array of electric furnaces and ovens and sterilizers. The doctor in a white linen jacket bent above a small desk, and for a while he proffered them his sleek oblivious profiles. Then he glanced up, and rose.

He was in the youthful indeterminate thirties; a newcomer to the town and nephew of an old resident. He had made a fine record in medical school and was of a personable exterior, but there was a sort of preoccupied dignity, a sort of erudite and cold unillusion regarding mankind, about him that precluded the easy intimacy of the small town and caused even those who remembered him as a visiting boy to address him as doctor or mister. He had a small moustache and a face like a mask—a comforting face, but cold; and while Bayard sat restively the doctor probed delicately with dry, scrubbed fingers at the wen on his face. Miss Jenny asked him a question, but he continued his exploration raptly, as though he had not heard, as though she had not even spoken; inserting a small electric bulb which he first sterilized, into Bayard's mouth and snapping its ruby glow on and off within his cheek. Then he removed it and sterilized it again and returned it to the cabinet.

"Well?" Miss Jenny said impatiently. The doctor shut the cabinet carefully and washed and dried his hands and came and stood over them, and with his thumbs hooked in his jacket pockets he became solemnly and unctuously technical, rolling the harsh words from his tongue with an epicurean deliberation.

"It should be removed at once," he concluded. "It should be removed while in its early stage; that is why I advise an immediate operation."

"You mean, it might develop into cancer?" Miss Jenny asked.

"No question about it at all, madam. Course of time. Neglect it, and I can promise you nothing; have it out now, and he need never worry about it again." He looked at Bayard again with lingering and chill contemplation. "It will be very simple. I'll remove it as easily as that." And he made a short gesture with his hand.

"What's that?" Bayard demanded.

"I say, I can take that growth off so easily you wont know it, Colonel Sartoris."

"I'll be damned if you do!" Bayard rose with one of his characteristic plunging movements.

"Sit down, Bayard," Miss Jenny ordered. "Nobody's going to cut on you without your knowing it. Should it be done right away?" she asked.

"Yes, ma'am. I wouldn't have that thing on my face overnight. Otherwise, it is only fair to warn you that no doctor can assume responsibility for what might ensue.... I could remove it in two minutes," he added, looking at Bayard's face again with cold speculation. Then he half turned his head and stopped in a listening attitude, and beyond the thin walls a voice in the other room boomed in rich rolling waves.

"Mawnin', sister," it said. "Didn't I hear Bayard Sartoris cussin' in here?" The doctor and Miss Jenny held their arrested attitudes, then the door surged open and the fattest man in Yocona county filled it. He wore a shiny alpaca coat over waist-coat and trousers of baggy black broadcloth; above a plaited shirt the fatty rolls of his dewlap practically hid his low collar and a black string tie. His Roman senator's head was thatched with a vigorous curling of silvery hair. "What the devil's the matter with you?" he boomed, then he sidled into the room, filling it completely, dwarfing its occupants and its furnishings.

This was Doctor Lucius Quintus Peabody, eighty-seven years old and weighing three hundred and ten pounds and possessing a digestive tract like a horse. He had practiced medicine in Yocona county when a doctor's equipment consisted of a saw and a gallon of whisky and a satchel of calomel; he had been John Sartoris' regimental surgeon, and up to the day of the automobile he would start out at any hour of the twenty-four in any weather and for any distance, over practically impassable roads in a lopsided buckboard to visit anyone, white or black, who sent for him; accepting for fee usually a meal of corn pone and coffee or perhaps a small measure of corn or fruit, or a few flower bulbs or graftings. When he was young and hasty he had kept a daybook, kept it meticulously until these hypothetical assets totalled $10,000.00. But that was forty years ago, and since then he hadn't bothered with a record at all; and now from time to time a countryman enters his shabby office and discharges an obligation, commemorating sometimes the payor's entry into the world, incurred by his father or grandfather and which Dr Peabody himself had long since forgotten about. Every one in the county knew him and sent him hams and wild game at Christmas, and it was said that he could spend the balance of his days driving about the county in the buckboard he still used, with never a thought for board and lodging and without the expenditure of a penny for either. He filled the room with his bluff and homely humanity, and as he crossed the floor and patted Miss Jenny's back with one flail-like hand the whole building trembled to his tread.

"Mawnin', Jenny," he said. "Havin' Bayard measured for insurance?"

"This damn butcher wants to cut on me," Bayard said querulously. "You come on and make 'em let me alone, Loosh."

"Ten A.M.'s might early in the day to start carvin' white folks," Dr Peabody boomed. "Nigger's different. Chop up a nigger any time after midnight. What's the matter with him, son?" he asked of Dr Alford.

"I dont believe it's anything but a wart," Miss Jenny said. "But I'm tired of looking at it."

"It's no wart," Dr Alford corrected stiffly. He recapitulated his diagnosis in technical terms while Dr Peabody enveloped them all in the rubicund benevolence of his presence.

"Sounds pretty bad, dont it?" he agreed, and he shook the floor again and pushed Bayard firmly into the chair with one huge hand, and with the other he dragged his face up to the light. Then he dug a pair of iron-bowed spectacles from the pocket of his coat and examined Bayard's wen through them. "Think it ought to come off, do you?"

"I do," Dr Alford answered coldly. "I think it is imperative that it be removed. Unnecessary there. Cancer."

"Folks got along with cancer a long time befo' they invented knives," Dr Peabody said drily. "Hold still, Bayard."

And people like you are one of the reasons, was on the tip of the younger man's tongue. But he forbore and said instead: "I can remove that growth in two minutes, Colonel Sartoris."

"Damned if you do," Bayard rejoined violently, trying to rise. "Get away, Loosh."

"Sit still," Dr Peabody said equably, holding him down while he probed at the wen. "Does it hurt any?"

"No. I never said it did. And I'll be damned—"

"You'll probably be damned anyway," Dr Peabody told him. "You'd be about as well off dead, anyhow. I dont know anybody that gets less fun out of living than you do."

"You told the truth for once," Miss Jenny agreed. "He's the oldest person I ever knew in my life."

"And so," Dr Peabody continued blandly, "I wouldn't worry about it. Let it stay there. Nobody cares what your face looks like. If you were a young fellow, now, out sparkin' the gals every night——"

"If Dr Peabody is permitted to interfere with impunity——" Dr Alford began.

"Will Falls says he can cure it," Bayard said.

"With that salve of his?" Dr Peabody asked quickly.

"Salve?" Dr Alford repeated. "Colonel Sartoris, if you permit any quack that comes along to treat that growth with homemade or patent remedies, you'll be dead in six months. Dr Peabody even will bear me out," he added with fine irony.

"I dont know," Dr Peabody replied slowly. "Will has done some curious things with that salve of his."

"I must protest against this," Dr Alford said. "Mrs Du Pre, I protest against a member of my profession sanctioning even negatively such a procedure."

"Pshaw, boy," Dr Peabody answered, "we aint goin' to let Will put his dope on Bayard's wart. It's all right for niggers and livestock, but Bayard dont need it. We'll just let this thing alone, long as it dont hurt him."

"If that growth is not removed immediately, I wash my hands of all responsibility," Dr Alford stated. "To neglect it will be as fatal as Mr Falls' salve. Mrs Du Pre, I ask you to witness that this consultation has taken this unethical turn through no fault of mine and over my protest."

"Pshaw, boy," Dr Peabody said again. "This aint hardly worth the trouble of cuttin' out. We'll save you an arm or a leg as soon as that fool grandson of his turns that automobile over with 'em. Come on with me, Bayard."

"Mrs Du Pre——" Dr Alford essayed.

"Bayard can come back, if he wants to." Dr Peabody patted the younger man's shoulder with his heavy hand. "I'm going to take him to my office and talk to him a while. Jenny can bring him back if she wants to. Come on, Bayard." And he led Bayard from the room. Miss Jenny rose also.

"That Loosh Peabody is as big a fogy as old Will Falls," she said. "Old people just fret me to death. You wait: I'll bring him right back here, and we'll finish this business." Dr Alford held the door open for her and she sailed in a stiff silk-clad rage

from the room and followed her nephew across the corridor
and through the scarred door with its rusty lock, and into a
room resembling a miniature cyclonic devastation mellowed
peacefully over with dust ancient and undisturbed.

"You, Loosh Peabody," Miss Jenny said.

"Sit down, Jenny," Dr Peabody told her, "and be quiet.
Unfasten your shirt, Bayard."

"What?" Bayard said belligerently. The other thrust him
into a chair.

"Want to see your chest," he explained. He crossed to an
ancient rolltop desk and rummaged through the dusty litter
upon it. There was litter and dust everywhere in the huge
room. Its four windows gave upon the square, but the elms and
sycamores ranged along the sides of the square shaded these
first floor offices, so that light entered them but tempered, like
light beneath water. In the corners of the ceiling were spider
webs thick and heavy as Spanish moss and dingy as old lace;
and the once-white walls were an even and unemphatic drab
save for a paler rectangle here and there where an outdated
calendar had hung and been removed. Besides the desk the
room contained three or four miscellaneous chairs in various
stages of decrepitude, a rusty stove in a sawdust filled box, and
a leather sofa holding mutely amid its broken springs the out-
line of Dr Peabody's recumbent shape; beside it and slowly
gathering successive layers of dust, was a stack of lurid paper
covered nickel novels. This was Dr Peabody's library, and on
this sofa he passed his office hours, reading them over and
over. Other books there were none.

But the waste basket beside the desk and the desk itself and
the mantel above the trash-filled fireplace, and the win-
dowledges too were cluttered with circular mail matter and
mail order catalogues and government bulletins of all kinds. In
one corner, on an upended packing-box, sat a water cooler of

stained oxidized glass; in another corner leaned a clump of cane fishing poles warping slowly of their own weight, and on every horizontal surface rested a collection of objects not to be found outside of a second-hand store—old garments, bottles, a kerosene lamp, a wooden box of tins of axle grease, lacking one, a clock in the shape of a bland china morning-glory supported by four garlanded maidens who had suffered sundry astonishing anatomical mishaps, and here and there among their dusty indiscrimination various instruments pertaining to the occupant's profession. It was one of these that Dr Peabody sought now, in the littered desk on which sat a single photograph in a wooden frame, and though Miss Jenny said again, "You, Loosh Peabody, you listen to me," he continued to seek it with bland and unhurried equanimity.

"You fasten your clothes and we'll go back to that doctor," Miss Jenny said to her nephew. "Neither you nor I can waste any more time with a doddering old fool."

"Sit down, Jenny," Dr Peabody repeated, and he drew out a drawer and removed from it a box of cigars and a handful of faded artificial trout flies and a soiled collar and lastly a stethescope, then he tumbled the other things back into the drawer and shut it with his knee.

Miss Jenny sat trim and outraged, fuming while he listened to Bayard's heart.

"Well," she snapped, "does it tell you how to take that wart off his face? Will Falls didn't need any telephone to find that out."

"It tells more than that," Dr Peabody answered. "It tells how Bayard'll get rid of all his troubles, if he keeps on riding in that hellion's automobile."

"Fiddlesticks," Miss Jenny said. "Bayard's a good driver. I never rode with a better one."

"It'll take more'n a good driver to keep this—" he tapped

Bayard's chest with his blunt finger—"goin', time that boy whirls that thing around another curve or two like I've seen him do."

"Did you ever hear of a Sartoris dying from a natural cause, like anybody else?" Miss Jenny demanded. "Dont you know that heart aint going to take Bayard off before his time? You get up from there, and come on with me," she added to her nephew. Bayard buttoned his shirt, and Dr Peabody sat on the sofa and watched him quietly.

"Bayard," he said suddenly, "why dont you stay out of that damn thing?"

"What?"

"If you dont keep out of that car, you aint goin' to need me nor Will Falls, nor that boy in yonder with all his hand-boiled razors, neither."

"What business is it of yours?" Bayard demanded. "By God, cant I break my neck in peace if I want to?" He rose. He was trembling, fumbling at his waistcoat buttons, and Miss Jenny rose also and made to help him, but he put her roughly aside. Dr Peabody sat quietly, thumping his fat fingers on one fat knee. "I have already outlived my time," Bayard continued more mildly. "I am the first of my name to see sixty years that I know of. I reckon Old Marster is keeping me for a reliable witness to the extinction of it."

"Now," Miss Jenny said icily, "you've made your speech, and Loosh Peabody has wasted the morning for you, so I reckon we can leave now and let Loosh go out and doctor mules for a while, and you can sit around the rest of the day, being a Sartoris and feeling sorry for yourself. Good morning, Loosh."

"Make him let that place alone, Jenny," Dr Peabody said.

"Aint you and Will Falls going to cure it for him?"

"You keep him from letting Will Falls put anything on it," Dr Peabody repeated equably. "It's all right. Just let it alone."

"We're going to a doctor, that's what we're going to do," Miss Jenny replied. "Come on here."

When the door had closed he sat motionless and heard them quarrelling beyond it. Then the sound of their voices moved on down the corridor toward the stairs, and still quarrelling loudly and on Bayard's part with profane emphasis, the voices died away. Then Dr Peabody lay back on the sofa shaped already to the bulk of him, and with random deliberation he reached a nickel thriller blindly from the stack at the head of the couch.

4

As they neared the bank Narcissa Benbow came along from the opposite direction, and they met at the door, where he made her a ponderous compliment on her appearance while she stood in her pale dress and shouted her grave voice into his deafness. Then he took his tilted chair, and Miss Jenny followed her into the bank and to the window. There was no one behind the grille at the moment save the book-keeper. He looked at them briefly and covertly across his shoulder, then slid from his stool and crossed to the window, but without raising his eyes again.

He took Narcissa's check, and while she listened to Miss Jenny's recapitulation of Bayard's and Loosh Peabody's stubborn masculine stupidity, she remarked the reddish hair which clothed his arms down to the second joints of his fingers; and remarked with a faint yet distinct distaste, and a little curiosity, since it was not particularly warm, the fact that his hands and arms were beaded with perspiration.

Then she made her eyes blank again and took the notes which he pushed under the grille to her and opened her bag.

From its blue satin maw the corner of an envelope and some of its superscription peeped suddenly, but she crumpled it quickly from sight and put the money in and closed the bag. They turned away, Miss Jenny still talking, and she paused at the door again, clothed in her still aura of quietness, while Bayard twitted her heavily on imaginary affairs of the heart which furnished the sole theme of conversation between them, shouting serenely at him in return. Then she went on, surrounded by tranquillity like a visible presence or an odor or a sound.

As long as she was in sight, the book-keeper stood at the window. His head was bent and his hand made a series of neat, meaningless figures on the pad beneath it. Then she went on and passed from sight. He moved, and in doing so he found that the pad had adhered to his damp wrist, so that when he removed his arm it came also, then its own weight freed it and it fell to the floor.

He finished the forenoon stooped on his high stool at his high desk beneath the green-shaded light, penning his neat figures into ledgers and writing words into them in the flowing spencerian hand he had been taught in a Memphis business college. At times he slid from the stool and crossed to the window with his covert evasive eyes and served a client, then returned to his stool and picked up his pen. The cashier, a rotund man with bristling hair and lapping jowls like a Berkshire hog, returned presently, accompanied by a director, who followed him inside the grille. They ordered coca-colas from a neighboring drug store by telephone and stood talking until the refreshment arrived by negro boy. Snopes had been included and he descended again and took his glass. The other two sipped theirs; he spooned the ice from his into a spittoon and emptied it at a draught and replaced the glass on the tray and spoke a general and ignored thanks in his sober country idiom and returned to his desk.

Noon came. Old Bayard rose crashing from his tilted chair and stalked back to his office, where he would eat his frugal cold lunch and then sleep for an hour, and banged the door behind him. The cashier took his hat and departed also: for an hour Snopes would have the bank to himself. Outside the square lay motionless beneath noon; the dinnerward exodus of lawyers and merchants and clerks did not disturb its atmosphere of abiding and timeless fixation; in the elms surrounding the courthouse no leaf stirred in the May sunlight. Across the bank windows an occasional shadow passed, but none turned into the door, and presently the square was motionless as a theatre drop.

Snopes drew a sheet of paper from a drawer and laid it beneath the light and wrote slowly upon it, pausing at intervals, drawing his pen through a sentence or a word, writing again. Someone entered; without looking up he slid the paper beneath a ledger, crossed to the window and served the customer, returned and wrote again. The clock on the wall ticked into the silence and into the slow, mouse-like scratching of the pen. The pen ceased at last, but the clock ticked on like a measured dropping of small shot.

He re-read the first draught, slowly. Then he drew out a second sheet and made a careful copy. When this was done he re-read it also, comparing the two; then he folded the copy again and again until it was a small square thickness, and stowed it away in the fob-pocket of his trousers. The original he carried across to the cuspidor, and holding it above the receptacle he struck a match to it and held it in his fingers until the final moment. Then he dropped it into the spittoon and when it was completely consumed, he crushed the charred thing to powder. Quarter to one. He returned to his stool and opened his ledgers again.

At one the cashier with a toothpick appeared at the door talking to someone, then he entered and went to old Bayard's office and opened the door. "One oclock, Colonel," he shouted into the room, and old Bayard's heels thumped heavily on the floor. As Snopes took his hat and emerged from the grille old Bayard stalked forth again and tramped on ahead and took the tilted chair in the doorway.

There is in Jefferson a boarding house known as the Beard hotel. It is a rectangular frame building with a double veranda, just off the square, and it is conducted theoretically by a countryman, but in reality by his wife. Beard is a mild, bleached man of indeterminate age and of less than medium size, dressed always in a collarless shirt and a black evil pipe. He also owns the grist mill near the square, and he may be found either at the mill, or on the outskirts of the checker-game in the courthouse yard, or sitting in his stocking feet on the veranda of his hostelry. He is supposed to suffer from some obscure ailment puzzling to physicians, which prevents him exerting himself physically. His wife is a woman in a soiled apron, with straggling, damp grayish hair and an air of spent but indomitable capability. They have one son, a pale, quiet boy of twelve or so, who is always on the monthly honor roll at school; he may be seen on spring mornings schoolward bound with a bouquet of flowers. His rating among his contemporaries is not high.

Men only patronize the Beard hotel. Itinerant horse- and cattle-traders; countrymen in town overnight during court or the holiday season or arrested perhaps by inclement weather, stop there; and juries during court week——twelve good men and true marching in or out in column of twos, or aligned in chairs and spitting across the veranda rail with solemn and awesome decorum; and two of the town young bloods keep a room there, in which it is rumored dice and cards progress Sundays and drinking is done. But no women. If a skirt (other than Mrs Beard's gray apron) so much as flashes in the vicinity of its celibate portals, the city fathers investigate immediately, and woe to the peripatetic Semiramis if she be run to earth. Here, in company with a number of other bachelors—clerks, mechanics and such—the book-keeper Snopes lives.

And here he repaired when the bank day was finished. The afternoon was a replica of the morning. Then at three oclock the green shades were drawn upon door and windows, and Snopes and the cashier went about striking a daily balance. At 3:30 young Bayard arrived in his car and old Bayard stalked forth and got in it and was driven away. Presently thereafter the janitor, an ancient, practically incapacitated negro called Doctor Jones, came in and doddered futilely with a broom. By 4:30 he was done, and the cashier locked the vault and switched on the light above it, and he and the book-keeper emerged and locked the front door, and the cashier shook it experimentally.

After the bank closed that afternoon Snopes crossed the square and entered a street and approached a square frame building with a double veranda, from which the mournful cacophony of a cheap talking-machine came upon the afternoon. He entered. The music came from the room to the right and as he passed the door he saw a man in a collarless shirt sitting in a chair with his sock feet on another chair, smoking a pipe, the evil reek of which followed him down the hall. The hall smelled of damp, harsh soap, and the linoleum carpet gleamed, still wet. He followed it and approached a sound of steady, savage activity, and came upon a woman in a shapeless gray garment, who ceased mopping and looked at him across her gray shoulder, sweeping her lank hair from her brow with a reddened forearm.

"Evenin', Miz Beard," Snopes said. "Virgil come home yet?"

"He was through here a minute ago," she answered. "If he aint out front, I reckon his paw sent him on a arr'nd. Mr Beard's taken one of his spells in the hip agin. He might a sent Virgil on a arr'nd." Her hair fell lankly across her face again. Again she brushed it aside with a harsh gesture. "You got some mo' work fer him?"

"Yessum. You dont know which-a-way he went?"

"Ef Mr Beard aint sont him nowheres he mought be in the back yard. He dont usually go fur away." Again she dragged her dank hair aside; shaped so long to labor, her muscles were restive under inaction. She grasped the mop again.

Snopes went on, and stood on the kitchen steps above an enclosed space barren of grass and containing a chicken pen also grassless, in which a few fowls huddled or moved about in forlorn distraction in the dust. On one hand was a small kitchen garden of orderly, tended rows. In the corner of the yard was an outhouse of some sort, of weathered boards.

"Virgil," he said. The yard was desolate with ghosts; ghosts of discouraged weeds, of food in the shape of empty tins, broken boxes and barrels, a pile of stove wood and a chopping block across which lay an axe whose helve had been mended with rusty wire amateurishly wound. He descended the steps, and the chickens raised a discordant clamor, anticipating food.

"Virgil."

Sparrows found sustenance of some sort in the dust among the fowls, but the fowls themselves, perhaps with a foreknowledge of frustration and of doom, huddled back and forth along the wire, discordant and distracted, watching him with predatory importunate eyes. He was about to turn and reenter the kitchen when the boy appeared silently and innocently from the outhouse, with his straw-colored hair and his bland eyes.

His mouth was pale and almost sweet, but secretive at the corners. His chin was negligible.

"Hi, Mr Snopes, you calling me?"

"Yes, if you aint doin' anything special," Snopes answered.

"I aint," the boy said. They entered the house and passed the room where the woman labored with drab fury. The reek of the pipe, the lugubrious reiteration of the phonograph, filled the hall, and they mounted stairs carpeted also with linoleum fastened to each step by a treacherous sheet-iron strip treated to resemble brass and scuffed and scarred by heavy feet. The upper hall was lined by two identical rows of doors. They entered one of these. The room contained a bed, a chair, a dressing-table and a washstand with a slop-jar beside it. The floor was covered with straw matting frayed in places. The single light hung unshaded from a greenish-brown cord; upon the wall above the paper-filled fireplace a framed lithograph of an Indian maiden in immaculate buckskin leaned her naked bosom above a formal moonlit pool of Italian marble. She held a guitar and a rose, and dusty sparrows sat on the window ledge and watched them brightly through the dusty screen.

The boy entered politely. His pale eyes took in the room and its contents at a comprehensive glance. He said: "That air gun aint come yet, has it, Mr Snopes?"

"No, it aint," Snopes answered. "It'll be here soon, though."

"You ordered off after it a long time, now."

"That's right. But it'll be here soon. Maybe they haven't got one in stock, right now." He crossed to the dresser and took from a drawer a few sheets of foolscap and laid them on the dresser top, and drew a chair up and dragged his suitcase from beneath the bed and set it on the chair. Then he took his fountain pen from his pocket and uncapped it and laid it beside the paper. "It ought to be here any day, now."

The boy seated himself on the suitcase and took up the pen. "They got 'em at Watts' hardware store," he suggested.

"If the one we ordered dont come soon, we'll git one there," Snopes said. "When did we order it, anyway?"

"Week ago Tuesday," the boy answered glibly. "I wrote it down."

"Well, it'll be here soon. You ready?"

The boy squared himself before the paper. "Yes, sir." Snopes took a folded paper from the top pocket of his trousers and spread it open.

"Code number forty eight. Mister Joe Butler, Saint Louis, Missouri," he read, then he leaned over the boy's shoulder, watching the pen. "That's right: up close to the top," he commended. "Now." The boy dropped down the page about two inches, and as Snopes read, he transcribed in his neat, copybook hand, pausing only occasionally to inquire as to the spelling of a word.

" 'I thought once I would try to forget you. But I cannot forget you because you cannot forget me. I saw my letter in your hand satchel today. Every day I can put my hand out and touch you you do not know it. Just to see you walk down the street To know what I know what you know. Some day we will both know to gether when you got use to it. You kept my letter but you do not anser. That is a good sign you do——' " The boy had reached the foot of the page. Snopes removed it, leaving the next sheet ready. He continued to read in his droning, inflectionless voice:

" '——not forget me you would not keep it. I think of you at night the way you walk down the street like I was dirt. You will get over this I can tell you something you will be surprised I know more than watch you walk down the street with cloths. I will some day you will not be surprised then. You pass me you do not know it I know it. You will know it some day. Be cause I will tell you.' Now," he said, and the boy dropped on to the foot of the page. " 'Yours truly Hal Wagner. Code number twenty one.' " Again he looked over the boy's shoulder. "That's right." He blotted the final sheet and gathered it up also. The boy recapped the pen and thrust the chair back, and Snopes produced a small paper bag from his coat.

The boy took it soberly. "Much obliged, Mr Snopes," he said. He opened it and squinted into it. "It's funny that air gun dont come on."

"It sure is," Snopes agreed. "I dont know why it dont come."

"Maybe it got lost in the postoffice," the boy suggested.

"It may have. I reckon that's about what happened to it. I'll write 'em again, tomorrow."

The boy rose, but he stood yet with his straw-colored hair and his bland, innocent face. He took a piece of candy from the sack and ate it without enthusiasm. "I reckon I better tell papa to go to the postoffice and ask 'em if it got lost."

"No, I wouldn't do that," Snopes said quickly. "You wait; I'll 'tend to it. We'll get it, all right."

"Papa wouldn't mind. He could go over there soon's he comes home and see about it. I could find him right now, and ask him to do it, I bet."

"He couldn't do no good," Snopes answered. "You leave it to me. I'll get that gun, all right."

"I could tell him I been working for you," the boy pursued. "I remember them letters."

"No, no, you wait and let me 'tend to it. I'll see about it first thing tomorrow."

"All right, Mr Snopes." He ate another piece of candy, without enthusiasm. He moved toward the door. "I remember ever' one of them letters. I bet I could sit down and write 'em all again. I bet I could. Say, Mr Snopes, who is Hal Wagner? Does he live in Jefferson?"

"No, no. You never seen him. He dont hardly never come to town. That's the reason I'm 'tending to his business for him. I'll see about that air gun, all right."

The boy opened the door, then he paused again. "They got 'em at Watts' hardware store. Good ones. I'd sure like to have one of 'em. Yes, sir, I sure would."

"Sure, sure," Snopes repeated. "Our'n'll be here tomorrow. You just wait: I'll see you git that gun."

The boy departed. Snopes locked the door, and for a while he stood beside it with his head bent, his hands slowly knotting and writhing together. Then he took up the folded sheet and burned it over the hearth and ground the carbonized ash to dust under his heel. With his knife he cut the address from the top of the first sheet, the signature from the bottom of the second, then he folded them and inserted them in a cheap envelope. He sealed this and stamped it, and took out his pen and with his left hand he addressed the envelope in labored printed characters. That night he took it to the station and mailed it on the train.

The next afternoon Virgil Beard killed a mockingbird. It was singing in the peach tree that grew in the corner of the chicken-yard.

5

At times, as Simon puttered about the place during the day, he could look out across the lot and into the pasture and see the carriage horses growing daily shabbier and less prideful with idleness and the lack of their daily grooming, or he would

pass the carriage motionless in its shed, its tongue propped at
an accusing angle on the wooden mechanism he had invented
for that purpose, and in the harness room the duster and tophat
gathered slow dust on the nail in the wall, holding too in their
mute waiting a patient and questioning uncomplaint. And at
times when he stood shabby and stooped a little with stubborn
bewilderment and age on the veranda with its ancient roses
and wistaria and all its spacious and steadfast serenity and
watched Sartorises come and go in a machine a gentleman of
his day would have scorned and which any pauper could own
and only a fool would ride in, it seemed to him that John Sartoris stood beside him with his bearded and hawklike face and
an expression of haughty and fine contempt.

And as he stood so, with afternoon slanting athwart the
southern end of the porch and the heady and myriad odors of
the waxing spring and the drowsy hum of insects and the
singing of birds steady upon it, Isom within the cool doorway
or at the corner of the house would hear his grandfather mumbling in a monotonous singsong in which were incomprehen-
sion and petulance and querulousness, and Isom would
withdraw to the kitchen where his mother labored steadily with
her placid yellow face and her endless crooning song.

"Pappy out dar talkin' to ole Marster agin," Isom told her.
"Gimme dem cole 'taters, mammy."

"Aint Miss Jenny got some work fer you dis evenin'?"
Elnora demanded, giving him the potatoes.

"No'm. She gone off in de cyar agin."

"Hit's de Lawd's blessin' you and her aint bofe gone in it,
like you is whenever Mist' Bayard'll let you. You git on outen
my kitchen, now. I got dis flo' mopped and I dont want it
tracked up."

Quite often these days Isom could hear his grandfather
talking to John Sartoris as he labored about the stable or the

flower beds or the lawn, mumbling away to that arrogant shade which dominated the house and the life that went on there and the whole scene itself across which the railroad he had built ran punily with distance but distinct with miniature verisimilitude, as though it were a stage set for the diversion of him whose stubborn dream, flouting him so deviously and cunningly while the dream was impure, had shaped itself fine and clear now that the dreamer was purged of the grossness of pride with that of flesh.

"Gent'mun equipage," Simon mumbled. He was busy again with his hoe in the salvia bed at the top of the drive. "Ridin' in dat thing, wid a gent'mun's proper equipage goin' ter rack en ruin in de barn." He wasn't thinking of Miss Jenny. It didn't make much difference what women rode in, their menfolks permitting. They only showed off a gentleman's equipage anyhow; they were but the barometers of his establishment, the glass of his gentility: horses themselves knew it. "Yo' own son, yo' own twin grandson ridin' right up in yo' face in a contraption like dat," he continued, "and you lettin' 'um do it. You bad ez dey is. You jes' got ter lay down de law ter 'um, Marse John; wid all dese foreign wars en sich de young folks is growed away fum de correck behavior; dey dont know how ter conduck deyselfs in de gent'mun way. Whut you reckon folks gwine think when dey sees yo' own folks ridin' in de same kine o' rig trash rides in? You jes' got ter resert yo'self, Marse John. Aint Sartorises sot de quality in dis country since befo' de War? And now jes' look at 'um."

He leaned on his hoe and watched the car swing up the drive and stop before the house. Miss Jenny and young Bayard got out and mounted to the veranda. The engine was still running, a faint shimmer of exhaust drifted upon the bright forenoon. Simon came up with his hoe and peered at the array of dials and knobs on the dash. Bayard turned in the door and spoke his name.

"Cut the switch off, Simon," he ordered.

"Cut de which whut off?" Simon said.

"That little bright lever by the steering wheel there. Turn it down."

"Naw, suh," Simon answered, backing away. "I aint gwine tech it. I aint gwine have it blowin' up in my face."

"It wont hurt you," Bayard said impatiently. "Just put your hand on it and pull it down. That little bright jigger there."

Simon peered doubtfully at the gadgets and things, but without coming any nearer, then he craned his neck further and stared over into the car. "I dont see nothin' but dis yere big lever stickin' up thoo de flo'. Dat aint de one you mentionin', is hit?" Bayard said "Hell." He descended in two strides and leaned across the door and cut the switch under Simon's curious blinking regard. The purr of the engine ceased.

"Well, now," Simon said. "Is dat de one you wuz talkin' erbout?" He stared at the switch for a time, then he straightened up and stared at the hood. "She's quit b'ilin' under dar, aint she? Is dat de way you stops her?" But Bayard had mounted the steps again and entered the house. Simon lingered a while longer, examining the gleaming long thing, dynamic as a motionless locomotive and little awesome, touching it lightly with his hand, then rubbing his hand on his thigh. He walked slowly around it and touched the tires, mumbling to himself and shaking his head, then he returned to his salvia bed, where Bayard emerged presently and found him.

"Want to take a ride, Simon?" he said.

Simon's hoe ceased and he straightened up. "Who, me?"

"Sure. Come on. We'll go up the road a piece." Simon stood with his static hoe rubbing his head slowly. "Come on," Bayard said, "we'll just go up the road a piece. It wont hurt you."

"Naw, suh," Simon agreed. "I dont reckon hit's gwine ter

hurt me." He allowed himself to be drawn gradually toward the
car, gazing at its various members with slow blinking speculation, now that it was about to become an actual quantity in his
life. At the door and with one foot raised to the running board
he made a final stand against the subtle powers of evil judgment. "You aint gwine run it thoo de bushes like you en Isom
done dat day, is you?"

Bayard reassured him, and he got in slowly, with mumbled
sounds of anticipatory concern, and he sat well forward on the
seat with his feet drawn under him, clutching the door with
one hand and a lump of shirt on his chest with the other as the
car moved down the drive. They passed through the gates and
onto the road and still he sat hunched forward on the seat, as
the car gained speed, and with a sudden convulsive motion he
caught his hat just as it blew off his head.

"I 'speck dis is fur ernough, aint it?" he suggested, raising
his voice. He pulled his hat down on his head, but when he
released it he had to clutch wildly at it again, and he removed
it and clasped it beneath his arm, and again his hand fumbled
at his breast and clutched something beneath his shirt. "I got to
weed dat bed dis mawnin'," he said, louder still. "Please, suh,
Mist' Bayard," he added and his wizened old body sat yet further forward on the seat and he cast quick covert glances at the
steadily increasing rush of the roadside growth.

Then Bayard leaned forward and Simon watched his forearm tauten, and then they shot forward on a roar of sound like
blurred thunder. Earth, the unbelievable ribbon of the road,
crashed beneath them and away behind into mad dust con-
volvulae: a dun moiling nausea of speed, and the roadside
greenery was a tunnel rigid and streaming and unbroken. But
he said no word, made no other sound, and when Bayard
glanced the lipless cruel derision of his teeth at him presently,
Simon knelt in the floor, his old disreputable hat under his

arm and his hand clutching a fold of his shirt on his breast. Later the white man glanced at him again, and Simon was watching him and the blurred irises of his eyes were no longer a melting pupilless brown: they were red, and in the blast of wind they were unwinking and in them was that mindless phosphorescence of an animal's. Bayard jammed the throttle down to the floor.

The wagon was moving drowsily and peacefully along the road. It was drawn by two mules and was filled with negro women asleep in chairs. Some of them wore drawers. The mules themselves didn't wake at all, but ambled sedately on with the empty wagon and the overturned chairs, even when the car crashed into the shallow ditch and surged back onto the road again and thundered on without slowing. The thunder ceased, but the car rushed on under its own momentum, and it began to sway from side to side as Bayard tried to drag Simon's hands from the switch. But Simon knelt in the floor with his eyes shut tightly and the air blast toying with the grizzled remnant of his hair, holding the switch off with both hands.

"Turn it loose!" Bayard shouted.

"Dat's de way you stops it, Lawd! Dat's de way you stops it, Lawd!" Simon chanted, keeping the switch covered with his hands while Bayard hammered them with his fist. And he clung to it until the car slowed and stopped. Then he fumbled the door open and climbed out. Bayard called to him, but he went on back down the road at a limping rapid shuffle.

"Simon!" Bayard called again. But Simon went on stiffly, like a man who has been deprived of the use of his legs for a long time. "Simon!" But he neither slowed nor looked back, and Bayard started the car again and drove on until he could turn it. Simon now stood in the ditch beside the road, his head bent above his hands when Bayard overtook him and stopped.

"Come on here and get in," he commanded.

"Naw, suh. I'll walk."

"Jump in, now," Bayard ordered sharply. He opened the door, but Simon stood in the ditch with his hand thrust inside his shirt, and Bayard could see that he was shaking as with an ague. "Come on, you old fool; I'm not going to hurt you."

"I'll walk home," Simon repeated stubbornly but without heat. "You git on wid dat thing."

"Ah, get in, Simon. I didn't know I'd scared you that bad. I'll drive slow. Come on."

"You git on home," Simon said again. "Dey'll be worried erbout you. You kin tell 'um whar I'm at."

Bayard watched him a moment, but Simon was not looking at him, and presently he slammed the door and drove on. Nor did Simon look up even then, even when the car burst once more into thunder and a soundless dun crash of fading dust. After a while the wagon emerged from the dust, the mules now at a high flop-eared trot, and jingled past him, leaving behind it upon the dusty insect-rasped air a woman's voice in a quavering wordless hysteria, passive and quavering and sustained. This faded slowly down the shimmering reaches of the valley and Simon removed from the breast of his shirt an object slung by a greasy cord about his neck. It was small and of no particular shape and it was covered with soiled napped fur: the first joint of the hind leg of a rabbit, caught supposedly in a graveyard in the dark of the moon, and Simon rubbed it through the sweat on his forehead and on the back of his neck, then he returned it to his bosom. His hands were still trembling, and he put his hat on and got back onto the road and turned toward home through the dusty noon.

Bayard drove on down the valley toward town, passing the iron gates and the serene white house among its old trees, and went on at speed. The sound of the unmuffled engine crashed into the dust and swirled it into lethargic bursting shapes, and faded across the planted land. Just outside of town he came upon another wagon and he held the car upon it until the mules reared, tilting the wagon; then he swerved and whipped past with not an inch to spare, so close that the yelling negro in the wagon could see the lipless and savage derision of his teeth.

He went on. In a mounting swoop like a niggard zoom the cemetery with his great-grandfather in pompous effigy gazing out across the valley and his railroad, flashed past, and he thought of old Simon trudging along the dusty road toward home, clutching his rabbit's foot, and again he felt savage and ashamed.

Town among its trees, its shady streets like green tunnels along which tight lives accomplished their peaceful tragedies, and he closed the muffler and at a sedate pace he approached the square. The clock on the courthouse lifted its four faces above the trees, in glimpses seen between arching vistas of trees. Ten minutes to twelve. At twelve exactly his grandfather would repair to the office in the rear of the bank and drink the pint of buttermilk which he brought in with him in a vacuum bottle every morning, and then sleep for an hour on the sofa there. When Bayard turned onto the square the tilted chair in the bank door was already vacant, and he slowed his car and eased it into the curb before a propped sandwich board. Fresh Catfish Today the board stated in letters of liquefied chalk, and through the screen doors beyond it came a smell of refrigerated food — cheese and pickle and such — with a faint overtone of fried grease.

He stood for a moment on the sidewalk while the noon throng parted and flowed about him. Negroes slow and aimless as figures of a dark placid dream, with an animal odor, murmuring and laughing among themselves. There was in their consonantless murmuring something ready with mirth, in their laughter something grave and sad; country people—men in overalls or corduroy or khaki and without neckties, women in shapeless calico and sunbonnets and snuff-sticks; groups of young girls in stiff mail-order finery, the young heritage of their bodies' grace dulled already by self-consciousness and labor and unaccustomed high heels and soon to be obscured forever by childbearing; youths and young men in cheap tasteless suits and shirts and caps, weather-tanned and clean-limbed as race horses and a little belligerently blatant. Against the wall squatting a blind negro beggar with a guitar and a wire frame holding a mouthorgan to his lips, patterned the background of smells and sounds with a plaintive reiteration of rich monotonous chords, rhythmic as a mathematical formula but without music. He was a man of at least forty and his was that patient resignation of many sightless years, yet he too wore filthy khaki with a corporal's stripes on one sleeve and a crookedly-sewn Boy Scout emblem on the other, and on his breast a button commemorating the fourth Liberty Loan and a small metal brooch bearing two gold stars, obviously intended for female adornment. His weathered derby was encircled by an officer's hat cord, and on the pavement between his feet sat a tin cup containing a dime and three pennies.

Bayard sought a coin in his pocket, and the beggar sensed his approach and his tune became a single repeated chord but without a break in the rhythm until the coin rang into the cup, and still without a break in the rhythm and the meaningless strains of the mouthorgan, his left hand dropped groping a little to the cup and read the coin in a single motion, then once more the guitar and mouthorgan resumed their monotonous pattern. As Bayard turned away someone spoke at his side—a broad squat man with a keen weathered face and gray temples. He wore corduroys and boots, and his body was the supple body of a horseman and his brown still hands were the hands that horses love. MacCallum his name, one of a family of six brothers who lived eighteen miles away in the hills, and with whom Bayard and John hunted foxes and 'coons during their vacations.

"Been hearing about that car of yourn," MacCallum said. "That's her, is it?" He stepped down from the curb and moved easily about the car, examining it, his hands on his hips. "Too much barrel," he said, "and she looks heavy in the withers. Clumsy. Have to use a curb on her, I reckon?"

"I dont," Bayard answered. "Jump in and I'll show you what she'll do."

"No, much obliged," the other answered. He stepped onto the pavement again, among the negroes gathered to stare at the car. The clock on the courthouse struck twelve, and already along the street there came in small groups children going home from school for the noon recess—little girls with colored boxes and skipping-ropes and talking sibilantly among themselves of intense feminine affairs, and boys in various stages of déshabillé shouting and scuffling and jostling the little girls, who shrank together and gave the little boys cold reverted glares. "Going to eat a snack," he explained. He crossed the pavement and opened the screen door. "You ate yet?" he asked, looking back. "Come on in a minute, anyway." And he patted his hip significantly.

The store was half grocery and confectionery and half restaurant. A number of customers stood about the cluttered but clean front section, with sandwiches and bottles of soda water, and the proprietor bobbed his head with flurried, slightly distrait affability above the counter to them. The rear half was filled with tables at which a number of men and a woman or so, mostly country people, sat eating with awkward and solemn decorum. Next to this was the kitchen, filled with frying odors and the brittle hissing of it, where two negroes moved like wraiths in a blue lethargy of smoke. They crossed this room and MacCallum opened a door set in an outthrust angle of the wall and they entered a smaller room, or rather a large closet. There was a small window high in the wall, and a bare table and three or four chairs, and presently the younger of the two negroes followed them.

"Yes, suh, Mr MacCallum and Mr Sartoris." He set two freshly rinsed glasses to which water yet adhered in sliding beads, on the table and stood drying his hands on his apron. He had a broad untroubled face, a reliable sort of face.

"Lemons and sugar and ice," MacCallum said. "You dont want none of that soda pop, do you?" The negro paused with his hand on the door.

"No," Bayard answered. "Rather have a toddy myself."

"Yes, suh," the negro agreed. "Y'all wants a toddy." And he bowed again with grave approval, and turned again and stepped aside as the proprietor in a fresh apron entered at his customary distracted trot and stood rubbing his hands on his thighs.

"Morning, morning," he said. "How're you, Rafe? Bayard, I saw Miss Jenny and the old Colonel going up to Doc Peabody's office the other day. Aint nothing wrong, is there?" His head was like an inverted egg; his hair curled meticulously away from the part in the center into two careful reddish-brown wings, like a toupée, and his eyes were a melting passionate brown.

"Come in here and shut that door," MacCallum ordered, drawing the other into the room. He produced from beneath his coat a bottle of astonishing proportions and set it on the table. It contained a delicate amber liquid and the proprietor rubbed his hands on his thighs and his hot mild gaze gloated upon it.

"Great Savior," he said, "where'd you have that demijohn hid? in your pants leg?" MacCallum uncorked the bottle and extended it and the proprietor leaned forward and sniffed it, his eyes closed. He sighed.

"Henry's," MacCallum said. "Best run he's made in six months. Reckon you'd take a drink if Bayard and me was to hold you?" The other cackled loudly, unctuously.

"Aint he a comical feller, now?" he asked Bayard. "Some joker, aint he?" He glanced at the table. "You aint got but two gl——" Someone tapped at the door: the proprietor leaned his conical head to it and waggled his hand at them. MacCallum concealed the bottle without haste as the other opened the door. It was the negro, with another glass, and lemons and sugar and a cracked bowl of ice. The proprietor admitted him.

"If they want me up front, tell 'em I've stepped out but I'll be back in a minute, Houston."

"Yes, suh," the negro replied, setting his burden on the table. MacCallum produced the bottle again.

"What do you keep on telling your customers that old lie, for?" he asked. "Everybody knows what you are doing."

The proprietor cackled again, gloating upon the bottle. "Yes, sir," he repeated, "he's sure some joker. Well, you boys have got plenty of time, but I got to get on back and keep things running."

"Go ahead," MacCallum told him, and the proprietor made himself a toddy. He raised the glass, stirring it and sniffing it alternately while the others followed suit. Then he removed his spoon and laid it on the table.

"Well, I hate to hurry a good thing mighty bad," he said, "but business dont wait on pleasure, you know."

"Work does interfere with a man's drinking," MacCallum agreed.

"Yes, sir, it sure does," the other replied. He raised his glass. "Your father's good health," he said. He drank. "I dont see the old gentleman in town much, now a days."

"No," MacCallum answered. "He aint never got over Buddy being in the Yankee army. Claims he aint coming to town again until the Democratic party denies Woodrow Wilson."

"It'll be the best thing they ever done, if they was to recall him and elect a man like Debs or Senator Vardaman president," the proprietor agreed sagely. "Well, that sure was fine. Henry's sure a wonder, aint he?" He set his glass down and turned to the door. "Well, you boys make yourselves at home. If you want anything, just call Houston." And he bustled out at his distracted trot.

"Sit down," MacCallum said. He drew up a chair, and Bayard drew another up opposite across the table. "Deacon sure ought to know good whisky. He's drunk enough of it to float his counters right on out the front door." He filled his glass and pushed the bottle across to Bayard, and they drank again, quietly.

"You look bad, son," MacCallum said suddenly, and Bayard raised his head and found the other examining him with his keen steady eyes. "Overtrained," he added, and Bayard made an abrupt gesture of negation and raised his glass again, but he could still feel the other watching him steadily. "Well, you haven't forgot how to drink good whisky, anyhow. . . . Why dont you come out and take a hunt with us? Got an old red we been saving for you. Been running him off and on for two years, now, with the young dogs. Aint put old General on him yet, because the old feller'll nose him out, and we wanted to save him for you boys. John would have enjoyed that fox. You remember that night Johnny cut across down to Samson's bridge ahead of the dogs, and when we got there, here come him and the fox floating down the river on that drift log, the fox on one end and Johnny on the other, singing that fool song as loud as he could yell? John would have enjoyed this here fox. He outsmarts them young dogs every time. But old General'll get him."

Bayard sat turning his glass in his hand. He reached a packet of cigarettes from his jacket and shook a few of them onto the table at his hand and flipped the packet across to the other. MacCallum drank his toddy steadily and refilled his glass. Bayard lit a cigarette and emptied his glass and reached for the bottle. "You look like hell, boy," MacCallum repeated.

"Dry, I reckon," Bayard answered in a voice as level as the other's. He made himself another toddy, his cigarette smoking on the table edge. He raised the glass, but instead of drinking he held it for a moment to his nose while the muscles at the base of his nostrils tautened whitely, then he swung the glass from him and with a steady hand he emptied it onto the floor. The other watched him quietly while he poured his glass half full of raw liquor and sloshed a little water into it and tilted it down his throat. "I've been good too damn long," he said aloud, and he fell to talking of the war. Not of combat, but rather of a life peopled by young men like fallen angels, and of a meteoric violence like that of fallen angels, beyond heaven or hell and partaking of both: doomed immortality and immortal doom.

MacCallum sat and listened quietly, drinking his whisky steadily and slowly and without appreciable effect, as though it were milk he drank; and Bayard talked on and presently found himself without surprise eating food. The bottle was now less than half full. The negro Houston had brought the food in and had his drink, taking it neat and without batting an eye. "Ef I had a cow dat give dat, de calf wouldn't git no milk a-tall," he said, "and I wouldn't never churn. Thanky, Mr MacCallum, suh."

Then he was out, and Bayard's voice went on, filling the

cubby-hole of a room, surmounting the odor of cheap food too quickly cooked and of sharp spilt whisky, with ghosts of a thing high-pitched as a hysteria, like a glare of fallen meteors on the dark retina of the world. Again a light tap at the door, and the proprietor's egg-shaped head and his hot diffident eyes.

"You gentlemen got everything you want?" he asked, rubbing his hands on his thighs.

"Come and get it," MacCallum said, jerking his head toward the bottle, and the other made himself a toddy in his stale glass and drank it while Bayard finished his tale of himself and an Australian major and two ladies in the Leicester lounge one evening (the Leicester lounge being out of bounds, and the Anzac lost two teeth and his girl, and Bayard himself got a black eye), watching the narrator with round melting astonishment.

"Great Savior," he said, "them av'aytors was sure some hellraisers, wadn't they? Well, I reckon they're wanting me up front again. You got to keep on the jump to make a living, these days." And he scuttled out again.

"I've been good too goddam long," Bayard repeated harshly, watching MacCallum fill the two glasses. "That's the only thing Johnny was ever good for. Kept me from getting in a rut. Bloody rut, with a couple of old women nagging at me, and nothing to do except scare niggers." He drank his whisky and set the glass down, still clutching it. "Damn ham-handed hun," he said. "He never could fly anyway. I kept trying to keep him from going up there on that goddam popgun," and he cursed his dead brother savagely. Then he raised his glass again, but halted it halfway to his mouth. "Where in hell did my drink go?"

MacCallum emptied the bottle into Bayard's glass, and he drank again and banged the thick tumbler on the table and rose and lurched back against the wall. His chair crashed over backward, and he braced himself, staring at the other. "I kept on trying to keep him from going up there, with that Camel. But he gave me a burst. Right across my nose."

MacCallum rose also. "Come on here," he said quietly, and he offered to take Bayard's arm, but Bayard evaded him and they passed through the kitchen and traversed the long tunnel of the store. Bayard walked steadily enough, and the proprietor bobbed his head at them across the counter.

"Call again, gentlemen," he said. "Call again."

"All right, Deacon," MacCallum answered. Bayard strode on. As they passed the soda-fountain a young lawyer standing beside a stranger, addressed him.

"Captain Sartoris, shake hands with Mr Gratton here. Gratton was up on the British front last spring." The stranger turned and extended his hand, but Bayard stared at him bleakly and strode so steadily on that the other involuntarily gave back in order not to be overborne.

"Why, God damn his soul," he said to Bayard's back. The lawyer grasped his arm.

"He's drunk," he whispered quickly, "he's drunk."

"I dont give a damn," the other exclaimed loudly. "Because he was a goddam shave-tail he thinks——"

"Shhhh, shhhh," the lawyer hissed. The proprietor came to the corner of his candy case, and peered out with hot round alarm.

"Gentlemen, gentlemen!" he exclaimed. The stranger made another violent movement, and Bayard stopped.

"Wait a minute while I bash his face in," he told MacCallum, turning. The stranger thrust the lawyer aside and stepped forward.

"You never saw the day——" he began. MacCallum took Bayard's arm firmly and easily.

"Come on here, boy."

"I'll bash his bloody face in," Bayard stated, looking bleakly at the angry stranger. The lawyer grasped his companion's arm again.

"Get away," the stranger said, flinging him off. "Just let him try it. Come on, you limey——"

"Gentlemen! Gentlemen!" the proprietor wailed.

"Come on here, boy," MacCallum said. "I've got to look at a horse."

"A horse?" Bayard repeated. He turned obediently, then he stopped and looked back. "Cant bash your face in now," he told the stranger. "Sorry. Got to look at a horse. Call for you later at the hotel." But the stranger's back was turned, and behind it the lawyer grimaced and waggled his hand at Mac-Callum.

"Get him away, MacCallum, for God's sake."

"Bash his face in later," Bayard repeated. "Cant bash yours, though, Eustace," he told the lawyer. "Taught us in ground-school never seduce a fool nor hit a cripple."

"Come on, here," MacCallum repeated, leading him on. At the door Bayard must stop again to light a cigarette; then they went on. It was three oclock and again they walked among school children in released surges. Bayard strode steadily enough, and a little belligerently, and soon MacCallum turned into a side street and they went on, passing negro stores, and between a busy grist mill and a silent cotton gin they turned into a lane filled with tethered horses and mules. From the end of the lane an anvil clanged. They passed the ruby glow of it and a patient horse standing on three legs in the blacksmith's doorway and the squatting overalled men along the shady wall, and came then to a high barred gate backing a long dun-colored brick tunnel smelling of ammonia. A few men sat on the top of the gate, others leaned their crossed arms upon it, and from the paddock itself came voices, then through

the slatted gate gleamed a haughty motionless shape of burnished flame.

The stallion stood against the yawning cavern of the livery
stable door like a motionless bronze flame, and along its burnished coat ran at intervals little tremors of paler flame, little
tongues of nervousness and pride. But its eye was quiet and
arrogant, and occasionally and with a kingly air its gaze swept
along the group at the gate with a fine disdain, without seeing
them as individuals at all, and again little tongues of paler
flame rippled flicking along its coat. About its head was a rope
hackamore; it was tethered to a door post, and in the background a white man moved about at a respectful distance with
a proprietorial air: beside him, a negro hostler with a tow sack
tied about his middle with a string. MacCallum and Bayard
halted at the gate, and the white man circled the stallion's
haughty immobility and crossed to them. The negro hostler
came forth also, with a soft dirty cloth and chanting in a mellow singsong. The stallion permitted him to approach and suffered him to erase with his rag the licking nervous little flames
that ran in renewed ripples under its skin.

"Aint he a picture, now?" the white man demanded of
MacCallum, leaning his elbow on the gate. A cheap nickel
watch was attached to his suspender loop by a length of raw
hide lace leather worn black and soft with age, and his shaven
beard was heaviest from the corners of his mouth to his chin;
he looked always as though he were chewing tobacco with his
mouth open. He was a horse trader by profession, and he was
constantly engaged in litigation with the railroad company
over the violent demise of his stock by its agency. "Look at that
nigger, now," he added. "He'll let Tobe handle him like a baby.
I wouldn't get within ten foot of him, myself. Dam'f I know
how Tobe does it. Must be some kin between a nigger and a
animal, I always claim."

"I reckon he's afraid you'll be crossing the railroad with him some day about the time 39 is due," MacCallum said drily.

"Yes, I reckon I have the hardest luck of any feller in this county," the other agreed. "But they got to settle this time: I got 'em dead to rights this time."

"Yes," MacCallum said. "The railroad company ought to furnish that stock of yourn with time tables." The other onlookers guffawed.

"Ah, the company's got plenty of money," the trader rejoined. Then he said: "You talk like I might have druv them mules in front of that train. Lemme tell you how it come about—"

"I reckon you wont never drive him in front of no train." MacCallum jerked his head toward the stallion. The negro burnished its shimmering coat, crooning to it in a monotonous singsong. The trader laughed.

"I reckon not," he admitted. "Not less'n Tobe goes, too. Just look at him, now. I wouldn't no more walk up to that animal than I'd fly."

"I'm going to ride that horse," Bayard said suddenly.

"What hoss?" the trader demanded, and the other onlookers watched Bayard climb the gate and vault over into the lot. "You let that hoss alone, young feller," the trader said. But Bayard paid him no heed. He went on; the stallion swept its regal regard upon him and away. "You let that hoss alone," the trader shouted, "or I'll have the law on you."

"Let him be," MacCallum said.

"And let him damage a fifteen hundred dollar stallion? That hoss'll kill him. You, Sartoris!"

From his hip pocket MacCallum drew a wad of bills enclosed by a rubber band. "Let him be," he repeated. "That's what he wants."

The trader glanced at the roll of money with quick calcu-
lation. "I take you gentlemen to witness——" he began loudly,
then he ceased and they watched tensely as Bayard approached
the stallion. The beast swept its haughty glowing eye upon him
again and lifted its head without alarm and snorted. The negro
glanced over his shoulder and crouched against the animal,
and his crooning chant rose to a swifter beat. "Go back, white
folks," he said. The beast snorted again and swept its head up,
snapping the rope like a gossamer thread, and the negro
grasped at the flying rope-end.

"Git away, white folks," he cried. "Git away, quick."

But the stallion eluded his hand. It cropped its teeth in a
vicious arc and the negro leaped sprawling as the animal
soared like a bronze explosion. Bayard had dodged beneath
the sabering hooves and as the horse swirled in a myriad flicking like fire, the spectators saw that the man had contrived to
take a turn with the rope-end about its jaws, then they saw the
animal rear again, dragging the man from the ground and
whipping his body like a rag upon its flashing arc. Then it
stopped trembling as Bayard closed its nostrils with the twisted
rope, and suddenly he was upon its back while it stood with
lowered head and rolling eyes, rippling its coat into quivering
tongues before exploding again.

The beast burst like bronze unfolding wings: a fluid desperation; the onlookers tumbled away from the gate and
hurled themselves to safety as the gate splintered to match-
wood beneath its soaring volcanic thunder. Bayard crouched
on its shoulders and dragged its mad head around and they
swept down the lane, spreading pandemonium among the
horses and mules tethered and patient about the blacksmith
shop and among the wagons there. Where the lane debouched
into the street a group of negroes scattered before them, and
without a break in its stride the stallion soared over a small

negro child clutching a stick of striped candy directly in its path. A wagon drawn by mules was just turning into the lane: these reared madly before the wild slack-jawed face of the white man in the wagon, and again Bayard sawed his thunderbolt around and headed it away from the square. Down the lane behind him the spectators ran, shouting through the dust, the trader among them, and Rafe MacCallum still clutching his roll of money.

The stallion moved beneath him like a tremendous mad music, uncontrolled, splendidly uncontrollable. The rope served only to curb its direction, not its speed, and among shouts from the pavement on either hand he swung the animal into another street. This was a quieter street; soon they would be in the country and the stallion could exhaust its rage without the added hazards of motors and pedestrians. Voices faded behind him in his own thunder: "Runaway! Runaway!" but the street was deserted save for a small automobile going in the same direction, and further along beneath the green tunnel, bright small spots of color scuttled out of the street. Children. Hope they stay there, he said to himself. His eyes were streaming a little; beneath him the surging lift and fall; in his nostrils a sharpness of rage and energy and violated pride like smoke from the animal's body, and he swept past the motor car, remarking in a flashing second a woman's face and a mouth partly open and two eyes round with tranquil astonishment. But the face flashed away without registering on his mind and he saw the children huddled on one side of the street, and on the opposite side a negro playing a hose on the sidewalk, and beside him a second negro with a pitchfork.

Someone screamed from a veranda, and the huddle of children broke, shrieking; a small figure in a white shirt and diminutive pale blue pants darted into the street, and Bayard leaned forward and wrapped the rope about his hand and

swerved the beast toward the opposite sidewalk, where the two
negroes stood gapemouthed. The small figure came on,
flashed safely behind, then a narrow band of rushing green; a
tree trunk like a wheel spoke in reverse, and the stallion struck
clashing fire from wet concrete. It slid, clashed, fighting for
balance, lunged and crashed down; and for Bayard, a red
shock, then blackness. The horse scrambled up and whirled
and poised and struck viciously at the prone man with its
hooves, but the negro with the pitchfork drove it away and it
trotted stiffly and with tossing head up the street and passed the
halted motor car. At the end of the street it stood trembling and
snorting and permitted the negro hostler to touch it. Rafe Mac-
Callum still clutched his roll of bills.

6

They gathered him up and brought him to town in a com-
mandeered motor car and roused Dr Peabody from slumber.
Dr Peabody profanely bandaged Bayard's head and gave him a
drink from the bottle which resided in the cluttered waste basket and threatened to telephone Miss Jenny if he didn't go
straight home. Rafe MacCallum promised to see that he did
so, and the owner of the impressed automobile offered to drive
him out. It was a ford body with, in place of a tonneau, a miniature one room cabin of sheet iron and larger than a dog kennel, in each painted window of which a painted housewife
simpered across a painted sewing machine, and in it an actual
sewing machine neatly fitted, borne thus about the countryside by the agent. The agent's name was V. K. Suratt and he
now sat with his shrewd plausible face behind the wheel.
Bayard with his humming head sat beside him, and to the
fender clung a youth with brown forearms and a slanted

extremely new straw hat, who let his limber body absorb the jolts with negligent ease as they rattled sedately out of town on the valley road.

The drink Dr Peabody had given him, instead of quieting his jangled nerves, rolled sluggishly and hotly in his stomach and served only to nauseate him a little, and against his closed eyelids red antic shapes coiled in throbbing and tedious cycles. He watched them dully and without astonishment as they emerged from blackness and swirled sluggishly and consumed themselves and reappeared, each time a little fainter as his mind cleared. And yet, somewhere blended with them, yet at the same time apart and beyond them with a tranquil aloofness and steadfast among their senseless convolutions, was a face. It seemed to have some relation to the instant itself as it culminated in crashing blackness; at the same time it seemed, for all its aloofness, to be a part of the whirling ensuing chaos; a part of it, yet bringing into the red vortex a sort of constant coolness like a faint, shady breeze. So it remained, aloof and not quite distinct, while the coiling shapes faded into a dull unease of physical pain from the jolting of the car, leaving about him like an echo that cool serenity and something else—a sense of shrinking yet fascinated distaste, of which he or something he had done, was the object.

Evening was coming. On either hand cotton and corn thrust green spears above the rich, dark soil, and in the patches of woodland where the sun slanted among violet shadows doves called moodily. After a time Suratt turned from the highway into a faint, rutted wagon road between a field and a patch of woods and they drove straight into the sun, and Bayard removed his hat and held it before his face.

"Sun hurt yo' haid?" Suratt asked. "'Taint long, now." The road wound presently into the woods where the sun was intermittent, and it rose to a gradual, sandy crest. Beyond this the

land fell away in ragged, ill-tended fields and beyond them in a
clump of sorry fruit trees and a stunted grove of silver poplar
shrubs pale as absinthe and twinkling ceaselessly with no wind,
a weathered small house squatted. Beyond it and much larger
loomed a barn gray and gaunt with age. The road forked here.
One faint arm curved sandily away toward the house; the other
went on between rank weeds toward the barn. The youth on
the fender leaned his head into the car. "Drive on to the barn,"
he directed.

Suratt obeyed. Beyond the bordering weeds a fence strag-
gled in limp dilapidation, and from the weeds beside it the
handles of a plow stood at a gaunt angle while its shard rusted
peacefully in the undergrowth, and other implements rusted
half concealed there—skeletons of labor healed over by the
earth they were to have violated, kinder than they. The fence
turned at an angle and Suratt stopped the car and the youth
stepped down and opened the warped wooden gate and Suratt
drove on into the barnyard where stood a wagon with drunken
wheels and a home-made bed, and the rusting skeleton of a
ford car. Low down upon its domed and bald radiator the two
lamps gave it an expression of beetling patient astonishment,
like a skull, and a lean cow ruminated and watched them with
moody eyes.

The barn doors sagged drunkenly from broken hinges,
held to the posts with twists of rusty wire; beyond, the cavern of
the hallway yawned in stale desolation—a travesty of earth's
garnered fullness and its rich inferences. Bayard sat on the
fender and leaned his bandaged head against the side of the
car and watched Suratt and the youth enter the barn and
mount slowly on invisible ladder rungs. The cow chewed in
slow dejection, and upon the yellow surface of a pond
enclosed by banks of trodden and sun-cracked clay, geese
drifted like small muddy clouds. The sun fell in a long slant

upon their rumps and upon their suave necks and upon the cow's gaunt rhythmically twitching flank, ridging her visible ribs with dingy gold. Presently Suratt's legs fumbled into view, followed by his cautious body, and after him the youth slid easily down the ladder in one-handed swoops.

He emerged carrying an earthen jug close against his leg. Suratt followed in his neat tieless blue shirt and jerked his head at Bayard, and they turned the corner of the barn among waist-high jimson weeds. Bayard overtook them as the youth with his jug slid with a single motion between two lax strands of barbed wire. Suratt stooped through more sedately and held the top strand taut and set his foot on the lower one until Bayard was through. Behind the barn the ground descended into shadow toward a junglish growth of willow and elder, against which a huge beech and a clump of saplings stood like mottled ghosts, and from which a cool dankness rose like a breath to meet them. The spring welled from the roots of the beech into a wooden frame sunk to its top in white sand that quivered ceaselessly and delicately beneath the water's limpid unrest, and went on into the willow and elder growth.

The earth about the spring was trampled smooth and packed as an earthen floor. Near the spring a blackened iron pot sat on four bricks, beneath it was a heap of pale wood-ashes and a litter of extinct brands and charred fagot-ends. Against the pot leaned a scrubbing board with a ridged metal face, and a rusty tin cup hung from a nail in the tree above the spring. The youth set the jug down and he and Suratt squatted beside it.

"I dont know if we aint a-goin' to git in trouble, givin' Mr Bayard whisky, Hub," Suratt said. "Still, Doc Peabody give him one dram hisself, so I reckon we kin give him one mo'. Aint that right, Mr Bayard?" Squatting he looked up at Bayard with his shrewd affable face. Hub twisted the corn cob stopper from the jug and passed it to Suratt, who tendered it to Bayard. "I

been knowin' Mr Bayard ever since he was a chap in knee
pants," Suratt confided to Hub, "but this is the first time me
and him ever taken a drink together. Aint that so, Mr
Bayard?. . . . I reckon you'll want a drinkin' cup, wont you?"
But Bayard was already drinking, with the jug tilted across his
horizontal forearm and the mouth held to his lips by the same
hand, as it should be done. "He knows how to drink outen a
jug, dont he?" Suratt added. "I knowed he was all right," he
said in a tone of confidential vindication. Bayard lowered the
jug and returned it to Suratt, who tendered it formally to Hub.

"Go ahead," Hub said. "Hit it." Suratt did so, with measured pistonings of his adam's apple. Above the stream gnats
whirled and spun in a levelling ray of sunlight like erratic
golden chaff. Suratt lowered the jug and passed it to Hub and
wiped his mouth on the back of his hand.

"How you feel now, Mr Bayard?" he asked. Then he said
heavily: "You'll have to excuse me. I reckon I ought to said
Cap'm Sartoris, oughtn't I?"

"What for?" Bayard asked. He squatted also on his heels,
against the bole of the beech tree. The rising slope of ground
behind them hid the barn and the house, and the three of them
squatted in a small bowl of peacefulness remote from the world
and time, and filled with the cool and limpid breathing of the
spring and a seeping of sunlight among the elders and willows
like a thinly diffused wine. On the surface of the spring the sky
lay reflected, stippled over with windless beech leaves. Hub
squatted leanly with his brown forearms clasped about his
knees, smoking a cigarette beneath the tilt of his hat. Suratt was
across the spring from him. He wore a faded blue shirt, and in
contrast to it his hands and his face were a rich even brown, like
mahogany. The jug sat rotundly, benignantly between them.

"Yes, sir," Suratt repeated, "I always find the best cure fer a
wound is plenty of whisky. Doctors, these here fancy young

doctors, 'll tell a feller different, but old Doc Peabody hisself cut off my granpappy's laig while granpappy laid back on the kitchen table with a demijohn in his hand and a mattress and a cheer acrost his laigs and fo' men a-holdin' him down, and him cussin' and singin' so scandalous the women-folks and the chillen went down to the pasture behind the barn and waited. Take some mo'," he said, and he reached the jug across the spring and Bayard drank again. "Reckon you're beginnin' to feel pretty fair, aint you?"

"Damned if I know," Bayard answered. "It's dynamite, boys."

Suratt poised the jug and guffawed, then he lipped it and his adam's apple pumped again in relief against the wall of elder and willow. The elder would soon flower, with pale clumps of tiny blooms. Miss Jenny made a little wine of it every year. Good wine, if you knew how and had the patience. Elder flower wine. Like a ritual for a children's game; a game played by little girls in small pale dresses, between supper and twilight. Above the bowl where sunlight yet came in a levelling beam, gnats whirled and spun like dust-motes in a still, disused room. Suratt's voice went on affably, ceaselessly recapitulant, in polite admiration of the hardness of Bayard's head and the fact that this was the first time he and Bayard had ever taken a drink together. They drank again, and Hub began to borrow cigarettes of Bayard and he too became a little profanely and robustly anecdotal in his country idiom, about whisky and girls and dice; and presently he and Suratt were arguing amicably about work. They appeared to be able to sit tirelessly and without discomfort on their heels, but Bayard's legs had soon grown numb and he straightened them, tingling with released blood, and he now sat with his back against the tree and his long legs straight before him, hearing Suratt's voice without listening to it.

His head was now no more than a sort of taut discomfort; at times it seemed to float away from his shoulders and hang against the green wall like a transparent balloon within which or beyond which that face that would neither emerge completely nor yet fade completely away, lingered with shadowy exasperation—two eyes round with a grave shocked astonishment, two lifted hands flashing behind little white shirt and blue pants swerving into a lifting rush plunging clatter crash blackness. . . . . . .

Suratt's slow plausible voice went on steadily, but without any irritant quality. It seemed to fit easily into the still scene, speaking of earthy things. "Way I learnt to chop cotton," he was saying, "my oldest brother taken and put me in the same row ahead of him. Started me off, and soon's I taken a lick or two, here he come behind me. And ever' time my hoe chopped once I could year his'n chop twice. I never had no shoes in them days, neither," he added drily. "So I had to learn to chop fast, with that 'ere hoe of his'n cuttin' at my bare heels. But I swo' then, come what mought, that I wouldn't never plant nothin' in the ground, soon's I could he'p myself. It's all right fer folks that owns the land, but folks like my folks was dont never own no land, and ever' time we made a furrow, we was scratchin' dirt fer somebody else." The gnats danced and whirled more madly yet in the sun above the secret places of the stream, and the sun's light was taking on a rich copper tinge. Suratt rose. "Well, boys, I got to git on back to'ds town, myself." He looked at Bayard again with his shrewd kind face. "I reckon Mr Bayard's clean fergot that knock he taken, aint he?"

"Dammit," Bayard said. "Quit calling me Mr Bayard."

Suratt picked up the jug. "I knowed he was all right, when you got to know him," he told Hub. "I been knowin' him since he was knee-high to a grasshopper, but me and him jest aint been throwed together like this. I was raised a pore boy, fellers, while Mr Bayard's folks has lived on that 'ere big place with plenty of money in the bank and niggers to wait on 'em. But he's all right," he repeated. "He aint goin' to say nothin' about who give him this here whisky."

"Let him tell, if he wants," Hub answered. "I dont give a damn."

They drank again. The sun was almost gone and from the secret marshy places of the stream came a fairy-like piping of young frogs. The gaunt invisible cow lowed barnward, and Hub replaced the corn cob in the jug and drove it home with a blow of his palm and they mounted the hill and crawled through the fence. The cow stood in the barn door and watched them approach and lowed again, moody and mournful, and the geese had left the pond and they now paraded sedately across the barnyard toward the house, in the door of which, framed by two crepe-myrtle bushes, a woman stood.

"Hub," she said in a flat country voice.

"Goin' to town," Hub answered shortly. "Sue'll have to milk."

The woman stood quietly in the door. Hub carried the jug into the barn and the cow followed him, and he heard her and turned and gave her a resounding kick in her gaunt ribs and cursed her without heat. Presently he reappeared and went on to the gate and opened it and Suratt drove through. Then he closed it and wired it to again and swung onto the fender. Bayard moved over and prevailed on Hub to get inside. The woman stood yet in the door, watching them quietly. About the doorstep the geese surged erratically with discordant cries, their necks undulant and suave as formal gestures in a pantomime.

The shadow of the fruit trees fell long across the untidy fields, and the car pushed its elongated shadow before it like the shadow of a huge humpshouldered bird. They mounted the sandy hill in the last of the sun and dropped downward out of sunlight and into violet dusk. The road was soundless with sand and the car lurched in the worn and shifting ruts and on to the highroad again.

The waxing moon stood overhead. As yet it gave off no light though, and they drove on toward town, passing an occasional country wagon homeward bound; these Suratt, who knew nearly every soul in the county, greeted with a grave gesture of his brown hand, and presently where the road crossed a wooden bridge among more willow and elder where dusk was yet denser and more palpable, Suratt stopped the car and climbed out over the door. "You fellers set still," he said. "I wont be but a minute. Got to fill that 'ere radiator." They heard him at the rear of the car, then he reappeared with a tin bucket and let himself gingerly down the roadside bank beside the bridge. Water chuckled and murmured beneath the bridge, invisible with twilight, its murmur burdened with the voice of cricket and frog. Above the willows that marked the course of the stream gnats still spun and whirled, for bullbats appeared from nowhere in long swoops, in midswoop vanished, then appeared again against the serene sky swooping, silent as drops of water on a window-pane; swift and noiseless and intent as though their wings were feathered with twilight and with silence.

Suratt scrambled up the bank, with his pail, and removed the cap and tilted the bucket above the radiator. The moon stood without emphasis overhead, yet a faint shadow of Suratt's head and shoulders fell upon the hood of the car and upon the pallid planking of the bridge the leaning willow fronds were faintly and delicately pencilled in shadow. The last of the water gurgled with faint rumblings into the engine's interior and Suratt replaced the pail and climbed over the blind door. The lights operated from a generator; he switched these on now. While the car was in low speed the lights glared to crescendo, but when he let the clutch in they dropped to a wavering glow no more than a luminous shadow.

Night was fully come when they reached town. Across the land the lights on the courthouse clock were like yellow beads above the trees, and upon the green afterglow a column of smoke stood like a balanced plume. Suratt put them out at the restaurant and drove on, and they entered and the proprietor raised his conical head and his round melting eyes from behind the soda fountain.

"Great Savior, boy," he exclaimed. "Aint you gone home yet? Doc Peabody's been huntin' you ever since four oclock, and Miss Jenny drove to town in the carriage, lookin' for you. You'll kill yourself."

"Get to hell on back yonder, Deacon," Bayard answered, "and bring me and Hub about two dollars' worth of ham and eggs."

Later they returned for the jug in Bayard's car, Bayard and Hub and a third young man, freight agent at the railway station, with three negroes and a bull fiddle in the rear seat. But they drove no further than the edge of the field above the house and stopped there while Hub went on afoot down the sandy road toward the barn. The moon stood pale and cold overhead, and on all sides insects shrilled in the dusty undergrowth. In the rear seat the negroes murmured among themselves.

"Fine night," Mitch, the freight agent, suggested. Bayard made no reply. He smoked moodily, his head closely helmeted in its white bandage. Moon and insects were one, audible and visible, dimensionless and unsourced.

After a while Hub materialized against the dissolving

vagueness of the road, crowned by the silver slant of his hat, and he came up and swung the jug onto the door and removed the stopper. Mitch passed it to Bayard.

"Drink," Bayard said, and Mitch did so, then the others drank.

"We aint got nothin' for the niggers to drink out of," Hub said.

"That's so," Mitch agreed. He turned in his seat. "Aint one of you boys got a cup or something?" The negroes murmured again, questioning one another in mellow consternation.

"Wait," Bayard said. He got out and lifted the hood and removed the cap from the breather-pipe. "It'll taste a little like oil for a drink or two, but you boys wont notice it after that."

"Naw, suh," the negroes agreed in chorus. One took the cup and wiped it out with the corner of his coat, and they too drank in turn, with smacking expulsions of breath. Bayard replaced the cap and got in the car.

"Anybody want another right now?" Hub asked, poising the corn cob.

"Give Mitch another," Bayard directed. "He'll have to catch up."

Mitch drank again. Then Bayard took the jug and tilted it. The others watched him respectfully.

"Dam'f he dont drink it," Mitch murmured. "I'd be afraid to hit it so often, if I was you."

"It's my damned head." Bayard lowered the jug and passed it to Hub. "I keep thinking another drink will ease it off some."

"Doc put that bandage on too tight," Hub said. "Want it loosened some?"

"I dont know." Bayard lit another cigarette and threw the match away. "I believe I'll take it off. It's been on there long enough." He raised his hands and fumbled at the bandage.

"You better let it alone," Mitch warned him. But he continued to fumble at the fastening, then he slid his fingers beneath a turn of the cloth and tugged at it savagely. One of the negroes leaned forward with a pocket knife and severed it, and they watched him as he stripped it off and flung it away.

"You ought not to done that," Mitch told him.

"Ah, let him take it off, if he wants," Hub said. "He's all right." He got in and stowed the jug away between his knees. Bayard backed the car around. The sandy road hissed beneath the broad tires of it and rose shaling into the woods again where the dappled moonlight was intermittent, treacherous with dissolving vistas. Invisible and sourceless among the shifting patterns of light and shade whip-poor-wills were like flutes tongued liquidly. The road passed out of the woods and descended, with sand in shifting and silent lurches, and they turned on to the valley road and away from town.

The car went on, on the dry hissing of the closed muffler. The negroes murmured among themselves with mellow snatches of laughter whipped like scraps of torn paper away behind. They passed the iron gates and Bayard's home serenely in the moonlight among its trees, and the silent box-like flag station and the metal-roofed cotton gin on the railroad siding. The road rose at last into hills. It was smooth and empty and winding, and the negroes fell silent as Bayard increased speed. But still it was not anything like what they had anticipated of him. Twice more they stopped and drank, and then from an ultimate hilltop they looked down upon another cluster of lights like a clotting of beads upon the pale gash where the railroad ran. Hub produced the breather cap and they drank again.

Through streets identical with those at home they moved slowly, toward an identical square. People on the square turned and looked after them curiously. They crossed the square and followed another street and went on between broad lawns and shaded windows, and presently beyond an iron fence and well back among black and silver trees, lighted windows hung in ordered tiers like rectangular lanterns strung among the branches.

They stopped here in shadow. The negroes descended and lifted the bass viol out, and a guitar. The third one held a slender tube frosted over with keys upon which the intermittent moon glinted in pale points, and they stood with their heads together, murmuring among themselves and touching plaintive muted chords from the strings. Then the one with the clarinet raised it to his lips.

The tunes were old tunes. Some of them were sophisticated tunes and formally intricate, but in the rendition this was lost and all of them were imbued instead with a plaintive similarity, a slurred and rhythmic simplicity, and they drifted in rich plaintive chords upon the silver air fading, dying in minor reiterations along the treacherous vistas of the moon. They played again, an old waltz. The college Cerberus came across the dappled lawn to the fence and leaned his arms upon it, a lumped listening shadow among other shadows. Across the street, in the shadows there, other listeners stood; a car approached and slowed into the curb and shut off engine and lights, and in the tiered windows heads leaned, aureoled against the lighted rooms behind, without individuality, feminine, distant, delicately and divinely young.

They played "Home, Sweet Home" and when the rich minor died away, across to them came a soft clapping of slender palms. Then Mitch sang "Goodnight, Ladies" in his true, oversweet tenor, and the young hands were more importunate; and as they drove away the slender heads leaned aureoled with bright hair in the lighted windows and the soft clapping drifted after them for a long while, fainter and fainter in the silver silence and the moon's infinitude.

At the top of the first hill out of town they stopped and Hub removed the breather cap. Behind them random lights among the trees, and it was as though there came yet to them across the hushed world that sound of young palms like flung delicate flowers before their masculinity and their youth, and they drank without speaking, lapped yet in the fading magic of the lost moment. Mitch sang to himself softly; the car slid purring on again. The road dropped curving smoothly, empty and blanched. Bayard spoke, his voice harsh, abrupt.

"Cut out, Hub," he said. Hub bent forward and reached under the dash and the car swept on with a steady leashed muttering like waking thunderous wings, then the road flattened in a long swoop toward another rise and the muttering leaped to crescendo and the car shot forward with neck-snapping violence. The negroes had stopped talking; one of them raised a wailing shout.

"Reno lost his hat," Hub said, looking back.

"He dont need it," Bayard replied. The car roared up this hill and rushed across the crest of it and flashed around a tight curve.

"Oh, Lawd," the negro wailed. "Mr Bayard!" The air-blast stripped his words away like leaves. "Lemme out, Mr Bayard!"

"Jump out, then," Bayard answered. The road fell from beneath them like a tilting floor and away across a valley, straight now as a string. The negroes clutched their instruments and held to one another. The speedometer showed 55 and 60 and turned gradually on. Sparse houses flashed slumbering away, and fields and patches of woodland like tunnels.

The road went on across the black and silver land. Whippoor-wills called on either side, one to another in quiring liquid reiterations; now and then as the headlights swept in the road's abrupt windings two spots of pale fire blinked in the dust before the bird blundered awkwardly somewhere beneath the radiator. The ridge rose steadily, with wooded slopes falling away on either hand. Sparse negro cabins squatted on the slopes or beside the road, dappled with shadow and lightless and profound with slumber; beneath trees before them wagons stood or warped farm implements leaned, shelterless, after the shiftless fashion of negroes.

The road dipped, then rose again in a long slant broken by another dip; then it stood directly before them like a wall. The car shot upward and over the dip, left the road completely, then swooped dreadfully on, and the negroes' concerted wail whipped forlornly away. Then the ridge attained its crest and the car's thunder ceased and it rolled to a stop. The negroes now sat in the bottom of the tonneau.

"Is dis heaven?" one murmured after a time.

"Dey wouldn't let you in heaven, wid licker on yo' breaf and no hat, feller," another said.

"Ef de Lawd dont take no better keer of me dan He done of dat hat, I dont wanter go dar, noways," the first rejoined.

"Mmmmmmmm," the second agreed. "When us come down dat 'ere las' hill, dis yere cla'inet almos' blowed clean outen my han', let 'lone my hat."

"And when us jumped over dat 'ere lawg er whutever it wuz back dar," the third one added, "I thought fer a minute dis whole auto'bile done blowed outen my han'."

They drank again. It was high here, and the air moved with grave coolness. On either hand lay a valley filled with silver mist and with whip-poor-wills; beyond these valleys the silver earth rolled on into the sky. Across it, mournful and far, a dog howled. Bayard's head was as cool and clear as a clapperless bell, within it that face emerged clearly at last: those two eyes round with grave astonishment, winged serenely by two dark wings of hair. It was that Benbow girl, he said to himself, and he sat for a while, gazing into the sky. The lights on the town

clock were steadfast and yellow and unwinking in the dissolving distance, but in all other directions the world rolled away
in slumberous ridges, milkily opaline.

All of her instincts were antipathetic toward him, toward
his violence and his brutally obtuse disregard of all the qualities which composed her being. His idea was like a trampling
of heavy feet in those cool corridors of hers, in that grave serenity in which her days accomplished themselves; at the very syllables of his name her instincts brought her upstanding and
under arms against him, thus increasing, doubling the sense of
violation by the act of repulsing him and by the necessity for it.
And yet, despite her armed sentinels, he still crashed with that
hot violence of his through the bastions and thundered at the
very inmost citadel of her being. Even chance seemed to abet
him, lending to his brutal course a sort of theatrical glamor, a
tawdry simulation of the virtues which the reasons (if he had
reasons) for his actions outwardly ridiculed. That mad flaming
beast he rode almost over her car and then swerved it with an
utter disregard of consequences to himself onto a wet sidewalk
in order to avoid a frightened child; the pallid, suddenly
dreaming calm of his bloody face from which violence had
been temporarily wiped as with a damp cloth, leaving it still
with that fine bold austerity of Roman statuary, beautiful as a
flame shaped in bronze and cooled: the outward form of its
energy but without its heat.

Her appetite was gone at supper, and Aunt Sally Wyatt
mouthed her prepared soft food and mumbled querulously at
her because she wouldn't eat.

"My mother saw to it that I drank a good cup of bark tea
when I come sulking to the table and wouldn't eat," Aunt Sally
stated, "but folks nowadays think the good Lord's going to keep
'em well and them lifting no finger."

"I'm all right," Narcissa insisted. "I just dont want any supper."

"That's what you say. Let yourself get down, and Lord knows, I aint strong enough to wait on you. In my day young folks had more consideration for their elders." She mouthed her food unprettily, querulously and monotonously retrospective, while Narcissa toyed restively with the food she could not eat.

Later Aunt Sally continued her monologue while she rocked with her interminable fancy-work on her lap. She would never divulge what it was to be when completed, nor for whom, and she had been working on it for fifteen years, carrying about with her a shapeless bag of dingy threadbare brocade containing odds and ends of colored fabric in all possible shapes. She could never bring herself to trim any of them to any pattern, so she shifted and fitted and mused and fitted and shifted them like pieces of a patient puzzle picture, trying to fit them to a pattern or to create a pattern about them without using her scissors, smoothing her colored scraps with flaccid, putty-colored fingers, shifting and shifting them. From the bosom of her dress the needle Narcissa had threaded for her dangled its spidery skein.

Across the room Narcissa sat, with a book. Aunt Sally's voice droned on with querulous interminability while Narcissa read. Suddenly she rose and laid the book down and crossed the room and entered the alcove where her piano sat. But she had not played four bars before her hands crashed in discord, and she shut the piano and went to the telephone.

Miss Jenny thanked her for her solicitude tartly, and dared to say that Bayard was all right, still an active member of the so-called human race, that is, since they had received no official word from the coroner. No, she had heard nothing of him since Loosh Peabody had phoned her at four oclock that

Bayard was on his way home with a broken head. The broken head she readily believed, but the other part of the message she had put no credence in whatever, having lived with those damn Sartorises eighty years and knowing that home would be the last place in the world a Sartoris with a broken head would ever consider going. No, she was not even interested in his present whereabouts, and she hoped he hadn't injured the horse? Horses were valuable animals.

Narcissa returned to the living room and explained to Aunt Sally whom she had been talking to and why, and drew a low chair to the lamp and took up her book.

"Well," Aunt Sally said after a time, "if you aint going to talk any. . . ." She fumbled her scraps together and crammed them into the bag. "I thank the Lord sometimes you and Horace aint any blood of mine, the way you all go on. But if you'd drink it, I dont know who's to get sassafras for you: I aint able to, and you wouldn't know it from dog fennel or mullein, yourself."

"I'm all right," Narcissa protested.

"Go ahead," Aunt Sally repeated, "get flat on your back, with me and that trifling nigger to take care of you. She aint wiped off a picture frame in six months, to my certain knowledge. And I've done everything but beg and pray."

She rose and said goodnight and hobbled from the room. Narcissa sat and turned the pages on, hearing the other mount the stairs with measured laborious tappings of her stick, and for a while longer she sat and turned the pages of her book. But presently she flung the book away and went to the piano again, but Aunt Sally thumped on the floor overhead with her stick, and she desisted and returned to her book. So it was with actual pleasure that she greeted Dr Alford a moment later.

"I was passing and heard your piano," he explained. "You haven't stopped?"

She explained that Aunt Sally had gone to bed, and he sat formally and talked to her in his stiff pedantic way on cold and erudite subjects for two hours. Then he departed and she stood in the door and watched him down the drive. The moon stood overhead; along the drive cedars in a rigid curve were pointed against the pale, faintly spangled sky.

She returned to the living room and got her book and turned out the lights and mounted the stairs. Across the hall Aunt Sally snored with genteel placidity, and Narcissa stood for a moment, listening to the homely noise. I will be glad when Horry gets home, she thought, going on.

She turned on her light and undressed and took her book to bed, where she again held her consciousness submerged deliberately as you hold a puppy under water until its struggles cease. And after a time her mind surrendered to the book and she read on, pausing from time to time to think warmly of sleep, reading again. And so when the negroes first blended their instruments beneath the window, she paid them only the most perfunctory notice. Why in the world are those jellybeans serenading me? she thought with faint amusement, visioning immediately Aunt Sally in her night-cap leaning from a window and shouting them away. And she lay with the book open, seeing upon the spread page the picture she had created while the plaintive rhythm of the strings and clarinet drifted into the open window.

Then she sat bolt upright, with a sharp and utter certainty, and clapped the book shut and slipped from bed. From the adjoining room she looked down.

The negroes were grouped on the lawn: the frosted clarinet, the guitar, the sober comic bulk of the viol. At the street entrance to the drive a motor car stood in shadow. The musicians played once, then a voice called from the car, and they retreated across the lawn and the car moved away, without lights. She was certain, then: no one else would play one tune beneath a lady's window, just enough to waken her from sleep, then go away.

She returned to her room. The book lay face down upon the bed, but she went to the window and stood there, between the parted curtains, looking out upon the black and silver world and the peaceful night. The air moved upon her face and amid the fallen dark wings of her hair with grave coolness. . . . "The beast, the beast," she whispered to herself. She let the curtains fall and on her silent feet she descended the stairs again and found the telephone in the darkness, muffling its bell when she rang.

Miss Jenny's voice came out of the night with its usual brisk and cold asperity, and without surprise or curiosity. No, he had not returned home, for he was by now safely locked up in jail, she believed, unless the city officers were too corrupt to obey a lady's request. Serenading? Fiddlesticks. What would he want to go serenading for? he couldn't injure himself serenading, unless someone killed him with a flat iron or an alarm clock. And why was she concerned about him?

Narcissa hung up, and for a moment she stood in the darkness, beating her fists on the telephone's unresponsive box. The beast, the beast.

She received three callers that night. One came formally, the second came informally, the third came anonymously. The garage which sheltered her car was a small brick building surrounded by evergreens. One side of it was a continuation of the garden wall. Beyond the wall a grass-grown lane led back to another street. The garage was about fifteen yards from the house and its roof rose to the level of the first-floor windows: Narcissa's bedroom windows looked out upon the slate roof of it.

This third caller entered by the lane and mounted onto

the wall and thence onto the garage roof, where he now lay in the shadow of a cedar, sheltered so from the moon. He had lain there for a long time. The room facing him was dark when he arrived, but he had lain in his fastness quiet as an animal and with an animal's patience, without movement save to occasionally raise his head and reconnoiter the immediate scene with covert dartings of his eyes.

But the room facing him remained dark while an hour passed. In the meantime a car entered the drive (he recognised it; he knew every car in town) and a man entered the house. The second hour passed and the room was still dark and the car stood yet in the drive. Then the man emerged and drove away, and a moment later the lights downstairs went out, and then the window facing him glowed and through the sheer curtains he saw her moving about the room, watched the shadowy motions of her disrobing. Then she passed out of his vision. But the light still burned and he lay with a still and infinite patience, lay so while another hour passed and another car stopped before the house and three men carrying an awkwardly shaped burden came up the drive and stood in the moonlight beneath the window; lay so until they played once and went away. When they had gone she came to the window and parted the curtains and stood for a while in the dark fallen wings of her hair, looking directly into his hidden eyes.

Then the curtains fell again, and once more she was a shadowy movement beyond them. Then the light went off, and he lay face down on the steep pitch of the roof, utterly motionless for a long time, darting from beneath his hidden face covert ceaseless glances, quick and darting and all-embracing as those of an animal.

To Narcissa's house they came finally. They had visited the dark homes of all the other unmarried girls one by one and sat in the car while the negroes stood on the lawn with their blended instruments. Heads had appeared at darkened windows, sometimes lights went up; once they were invited in, but Hub and Mitch hung diffidently back, once refreshment was sent out to them, once they were heartily cursed by a young man who happened to be sitting with the young lady on the dark veranda. In the meantime they had lost the breather cap, and as they moved from house to house all six of them drank fraternally from the jug, turn and turn about. At last they reached the Benbows' and played once beneath the cedars. There was a light yet in one window, but none came to it.

The moon stood well down the sky. Its light was now a cold silver upon things, spent and a little wearied, and the world was empty as they rolled without lights along a street lifeless and fixed in black and silver as any street in the moon itself. Beneath stippled intermittent shadows they went, passed quiet intersections dissolving away, occasionally a car motionless at the curb before a house. A dog crossed the street ahead of them trotting, and went on across a lawn and so from sight, but saving this there was no movement anywhere. The square opened spaciously about the absinthe-cloudy mass of elms that surrounded the courthouse. Among them the round spaced globes were more like huge pallid grapes than ever. Above the exposed vault in each bank burned a single bulb; inside the hotel lobby, before which a row of cars was aligned, another burned. Other lights there were none.

They circled the courthouse, and a shadow moved near the hotel door and detached itself from shadow and came to the curb, a white shirt glinting within a spread coat, and as the slow car swung away toward another street, the man hailed them. Bayard stopped and the man came through the blanched dust and laid his hand on the door.

"Hi, Buck," Mitch said. "You're up pretty late, aint you?"

The man had a sober, good-natured horse's face and he wore a metal star on his unbuttoned waistcoat. His coat humped slightly on his hip.

"What you boys doin'?" he asked. "Been to a dance?"

"Serenading," Bayard answered. "Want a drink, Buck?"

"No, much obliged." He stood with his hand on the door, gravely and goodnaturedly serious. "Aint you fellers out kind of late, yourselves?"

"It is gettin' on," Mitch agreed. The marshal lifted his foot to the running board. Beneath his hat his eyes were in shadow. "We're going in now," Mitch said. The other pondered quietly, and Bayard added:

"Sure; we're on our way home now."

The marshal moved his head slightly and spoke to the negroes.

"I reckon you boys are about ready to turn in, aint you?"

"Yes, suh," the negroes answered, and they got out and lifted the viol out. Bayard gave Reno a bill and they thanked him and said goodnight and picked up the viol and departed quietly down a side street. The marshal turned his head again.

"Aint that yo' car in front of Rogers' café, Mitch?" he asked.

"Reckon so. That's where I left it."

"Well, suppose you run Hub out home, lessen he's goin' to stay in town tonight. Bayard better come with me."

"Aw, hell, Buck," Mitch protested.

"What for?" Bayard demanded.

"His folks are worried about him," the other answered. "They aint seen hide nor hair of him since that stallion throwed him. Where's yo' bandage, Bayard?"

"Took it off," he answered shortly. "See here, Buck, we're going to put Mitch out and then Hub and me are going straight home."

"You been on yo' way home ever since fo' oclock, Bayard," the marshal replied soberly, "but you dont seem to git no nearer there. I reckon you better come with me tonight, like yo' aunt said."

"Did Aunt Jenny tell you to arrest me?"

"They was worried about you, son. Miss Jenny just 'phoned and asked me to kind of see if you was all right until mawnin'. So I reckon we better. You ought to went on home this evenin'."

"Aw, have a heart, Buck," Mitch protested.

"I ruther make Bayard mad than Miss Jenny," the other answered patiently. "You boys go on, and Bayard better come with me."

Mitch and Hub got out and Hub lifted out his jug and they said goodnight and went on to where Mitch's ford stood before the restaurant. The marshal got in beside Bayard. The jail was not far. It loomed presently above its walled court, square and implacable, its slitted upper windows brutal as sabre blows. They turned into an alley and the marshal descended and opened a gate. Bayard drove into the grassless littered compound and stopped while the other went on ahead to a small garage in which stood a ford. He backed this out and motioned Bayard forward. The garage was built to the ford's dimensions, and about a third of Bayard's car stuck out the door of it.

"Better'n nothin', though," the marshal said. "Come on." They entered through the kitchen, into the jailkeeper's living quarters, and Bayard waited in a dark passage until the other found a light. Then they entered a bleak neat room, containing spare conglomerate furnishings and a few scattered articles of masculine apparel.

"Say," Bayard objected. "Aren't you giving me your bed?"

"Wont need it befo' mawnin'," the other answered. "You'll be gone, then. Want me to he'p you off with yo' clothes?"

"No. I'm all right." Then, more graciously: "Goodnight, Buck, and much obliged."

"Goodnight," the marshal answered. He closed the door behind him and Bayard removed his coat and shoes and his tie and snapped the light off and lay on the bed. Moonlight seeped into the room impalpably, refracted and sourceless; the night was without any sound. Beyond the window a cornice rose in a succession of shallow steps against the opaline and dimensionless sky. His head was clear and cold. The whisky he had drunk was completely dead. Or rather, it was as though his head were one Bayard who watched curiously and impersonally that other Bayard who lay in a strange bed and whose alcohol-dulled nerves radiated like threads of ice through that body which he must drag forever about a bleak and barren world with him. "Hell," he said, lying on his back, staring out the window where nothing was to be seen, waiting for sleep, not knowing if it would come or not, not caring a particular damn either way. Nothing to be seen, and the long long span of a man's natural life. Three score and ten years, to drag a stubborn body about the world and cozen its insistent demands. Three score and ten, the bible said. Seventy years. And he was only twenty-six. Not much more than a third through it. Hell.

Three

1

Horace Benbow in his clean, wretchedly-fitting khaki which but served to accentuate his air of fine and delicate futility, and laden with an astonishing impedimenta of knapsacks and kitbags and paper-wrapped parcels, got off the two-thirty train. Across the tight clotting of descending and ascending passengers the sound of his spoken name reached him, and he roved his distraught gaze like a somnambulist rousing to avoid traffic, about the agglomerate faces. "Hello, hello," he said, then he thrust himself clear and laid his bags and parcels on the edge of the platform and moved with intent haste up the train toward the baggage car.

"Horace!" his sister called again, running after him. The station agent emerged from his office and stopped him and held him like a finely-bred restive horse and shook his hand, and thus his sister overtook him. He turned at her voice and came completely from out his distraction and swept her up in his arms until her feet were off the ground, and kissed her on the mouth.

"Dear old Narcy," he said, kissing her again. Then he set her down and stroked his hands on her face, as a child would. "Dear old Narcy," he repeated, touching her face with his fine spatulate hands, gazing at her as though he were drinking that constant serenity of hers through his eyes. He continued to say

Dear old Narcy, stroking his hands on her face, utterly oblivious of his surroundings until she recalled him.

"Where in the world are you going, up this way?"

Then he remembered, and released her and rushed on, she following, and stopped again at the door of the baggage car, from which the station porter and a trainhand were taking trunks and boxes as the baggage clerk tilted them out.

"Cant you send down for it?" she asked. But he stood peering into the car, oblivious of her again. The two negroes returned and he stepped aside, still looking into the car with peering, bird-like motions of his head. "Let's send back for it," his sister said again.

"What? Oh. I've seen it every time I changed cars," he told her, completely forgetting the sense of her words. "It'd be rotten luck to have it go astray right at my doorstep, wouldn't it?" Again the negroes moved away with a trunk, and he stepped forward again and peered into the car. "That's just about what happened to it; some clerk forgot to put it on the train at M—— There it is," he interrupted himself. "Easy now, cap," he called in the country idiom, in a fever of alarm as the clerk slammed into the door a box of foreign shape stencilled with a military address. "She's got glass in her."

"All right, colonel," the baggage clerk agreed. "We aint hurt her none, I reckon. If we have, all you got to do is sue us." The two negroes backed up to the door and Horace laid his hands on the box as the clerk tilted it outward. "Easy now, boys," he repeated nervously, and he trotted beside them as they crossed to the platform. "Set it down easy, now. Here, sis, lend a hand, will you?"

"We got it all right, cap'm," the station porter said. "We aint gwine drop it." But Horace continued to dab at it with his hands, and as they set it down he leaned his head to it. "She's all right, aint she?" the station porter asked.

"It's all right," the train porter assured him. He turned away. "Le's go," he called.

"I think it's all right," Horace agreed, his ear against the box. "I dont hear anything. It's packed pretty well." The engine whistled and Horace sprang erect, digging in his pocket, and ran to the moving cars. The porter was closing the vestibule, but he leaned down to Horace's hand and straightened up and touched his cap. Horace returned to his box and gave another coin to the second negro. "Put it in the house for me, careful, now," he directed. "I'll be back for it in a few minutes."

"Yes, suh, Mr Benbow. I'll look out fer it."

"I thought it was lost, once," he confided, slipping his arm inside his sister's, and they moved toward the car. "It was delayed at Brest and didn't come until the next boat. I had the first outfit I bought—a small one—with me, and I pretty near lost that one, too. I was blowing a small one in my cabin on the boat one day, when the whole thing, cabin and all, took fire. The captain decided that I'd better not try it again until we got ashore, what with all the men on board. The vase turned out pretty well, though," he babbled. "Lovely little thing. I'm catching on; I really am. Venice. A voluptuous dream, a little sinister. Must take you there, some day." Then he squeezed her arm and fell to repeating Dear old Narcy, as though the homely sound of the nickname on his tongue was a taste he loved and had not forgotten. A few people still lingered about the station. Some of them spoke to him and he stopped to shake their hands, and a marine private with the Second Division Indian head on his shoulder remarked the triangle on Horace's sleeve and made a vulgar sound of derogation through his pursed lips.

"Howdy, buddy," Horace said, turning upon him his shy startled gaze.

"Evenin', general," the marine answered. He spat, not

exactly at Horace's feet, and not exactly anywhere else. Narcissa clamped her brother's arm against her side.

"Do come on home and get into some decent clothes," she said in a lower tone, hurrying him along.

"Get out of uniform?" he said. "I rather fancied myself in khaki," he added, a little hurt. "You really think I am ridiculous in this?"

"Of course not," she answered immediately, squeezing his hand. "Of course not. I'm sorry I said that. You wear it just as long as you want to."

"It's a good uniform," he said soberly. "I dont mean this," he said, gesturing toward the symbol on his arm. They went on. "People will realize that in about ten years, when noncombatants' hysteria has worn itself out and the individual soldiers realize that the A.E.F. didn't invent disillusion."

"What did it invent?" she asked, holding his arm against her, surrounding him with the fond, inattentive serenity of her affection.

"God knows. . . . . . . Dear old Narcy," he said again, and they crossed the platform toward her car. "So you have dulled your palate for khaki."

"Of course not," she repeated, shaking his arm a little as she released it. "You wear it just as long as you want to." She opened the car door. Someone called after them and they looked back and saw the porter trotting after them with Horace's hand-luggage, which he had walked off and left lying on the platform.

"Oh, Lord," he exclaimed, "I worry with it for four thousand miles, then lose it on my own doorstep. Much obliged, Sol." The porter stowed the things in the car. "That's the first outfit I got," Horace added to his sister. "And the vase I blew on shipboard. I'll show it to you when we get home."

His sister got in under the wheel. "Where are your clothes? In the box?"

"Haven't any. Had to throw most of 'em away to make room for the other things. No room for anything else."

Narcissa sat and looked at him for a moment with fond exasperation. "What's the matter?" he asked innocently. "Forget something yourself?"

"No. Get in. Aunt Sally's waiting to see you."

They drove on and mounted the shady gradual hill toward the square, and Horace looked about happily upon familiar scenes. Sidings with freight cars; the platform which in the fall would be laden with cotton bales in serried rotund ranks; the town power plant, a brick building from which there came a steady, unbroken humming and about which in the spring gnarled heaven-trees swung ragged lilac bloom against the harsh ocher and Indian red of a clay cut-bank. Then a street of lesser residences, mostly new. Same tight little houses with a minimum of lawn—homes built by country-bred people and set close to the street after the country fashion; occasionally a house going up on a lot which had been vacant sixteen months ago when he went away. Then other streets opened away beneath arcades of green, shadier, with houses a little older and more imposing as they got away from the station's vicinity; and pedestrians, usually dawdling negro boys at this hour or old men bound townward after their naps, to spend the afternoon in sober futile absorptions.

The hill flattened away into the plateau on which the town proper had been built these hundred and more years ago, and the street became definitely urban presently with garages and small new shops with merchants in shirt-sleeves and customers; the picture show with its lobby plastered with life episodic in colored lithographic mutations. Then the square, with its unbroken low skyline of old weathered brick and fading dead names stubborn yet beneath scaling paint, and drifting negroes in casual and careless o.d. garments worn by both sexes and country people in occasional khaki too; and the brisker urbanites weaving among their placid chewing unhaste and among the men in tilted chairs before certain stores.

The courthouse was of brick too, with stone arches rising among elms, and among the trees the monument of the confederate soldier stood, his musket at order arms, shading his carven eyes with his stone hand. Beneath the porticoes of the courthouse and upon benches about the green, the city fathers sat and talked and drowsed, in uniform too, here and there. But it was the gray of Old Jack and Beauregard and Joe Johnston, and they sat in a grave sedateness of minor political sinecures, smoking and spitting about unhurried checkerboards. When the weather was bad they moved inside to the circuit clerk's office.

It was here that the young men loafed also, pitching dollars or tossing baseballs back and forth or lying on the grass until the young girls in their little colored dresses and cheap nostalgic perfume should come trooping down town through the late afternoon to the drug store. When the weather was bad the young men loafed in the drug stores or in the barber shop.

"Lots of uniforms yet," Horace remarked. "All be home by June. Have the Sartoris boys come home yet?"

"John is dead," his sister answered. "Didn't you know?"

"No," he answered quickly, with swift concern. "Poor old Bayard. Rotten luck they have. Funny family. Always going to wars, and always getting killed. And young Bayard's wife died, you wrote me."

"Yes. But he's here. He's got a racing automobile and he spends all his time tearing around the country. We are expecting every day to hear he's killed himself in it."

"Poor devil," Horace said, and again: "Poor old Colonel.

He used to hate an automobile like a snake. Wonder what he thinks about it."

"He goes with him."

"What? Old Bayard in a motor car?"

"Yes. Miss Jenny says it's to keep Bayard from turning it over. But she says Colonel Sartoris doesn't know it, but that Bayard would just as soon break both their necks. That he probably will before he's done." She drove on across the square, among tethered wagons and cars parked casually and without order. "I hate Bayard Sartoris," she said with sudden vehemence. "I hate all men." Horace looked at her quickly.

"What's the matter? What's Bayard done to you? No, that's backward. What have you done to Bayard?" But she didn't answer. She turned into another street bordered by negro stores of one story and shaded by metal awnings beneath which negroes lounged, skinning bananas or small florid cartons of sweet biscuits; and then a grist mill driven by a spasmodic gasoline engine. It oozed chaff and a sifting dust mote-like in the sun, and above the door a tediously hand-lettered sign: W. C. Beards Mill. Between it and a shuttered and silent gin draped with feathery soiled festoons of lint, an anvil clanged at the end of a short lane filled with wagons and horses and mules, and shaded by mulberry trees beneath which countrymen in overalls squatted. "He ought to have more consideration for the old fellow than that," Horace said fretfully. "Still, they've just gone through with an experience that pretty well shook the verities and the humanities, and whether they know it or not, they've got another one ahead of 'em that'll pretty well finish the business. Give him a little time. . . . . . . But I personally cant see why he shouldn't be allowed to kill himself, if that's what he thinks he wants. Sorry for Miss Jenny, though."

"Yes," his sister agreed, quietly again. "They're worried about Colonel Sartoris' heart, too. Everybody except him and

Bayard, that is. I'm glad I have you instead of one of those Sartorises, Horry." She laid her hand quickly and lightly on his thin knee.

"Dear old Narcy," he said, then his face clouded again. "Damn scoundrel," he said. "Well, it's their trouble. How's Aunt Sally been?"

"All right." And then: "I *am* glad you're home, Horry."

The shabby small shops were behind, and now the street opened away between old shady lawns, spacious and quiet. These homes were quite old, in appearance at least, and, set well back from the street and its dust, they emanated a gracious and benign peace, steadfast as a windless afternoon in a world without motion or sound. Horace looked about him and drew a long breath.

"Perhaps this is the reason for wars," he said. "The meaning of peace."

The meaning of peace. They turned into an intersecting street narrower but more shady and even quieter, with a golden Arcadian drowse, and turned through a gate in a honeysuckle-covered fence of iron pickets. From the gate the cinder-packed drive rose in a grave curve between cedars. The cedars had been set out by an English architect of the '40s, who had built the house (with the minor concession of a veranda) in the funereal light tudor which the young Victoria had sanctioned; and beneath and among them, even on the brightest days, lay a resinous exhilarating gloom. Mockingbirds loved them, and catbirds, and thrushes demurely mellifluous in the late afternoon; but the grass beneath them was sparse or nonexistent and there were no insects save fireflies in the dusk.

The drive ascended to the house and curved before it and descended again to the street in an unbroken arc of cedars. Within the arc rose a lone oak, broad and huge and low; around its trunk ran a wooden bench. About this halfmoon of lawn and without the arc of the drive, were bridal wreath and crepe-myrtle bushes old as time, and huge as age, would make them. Big as trees they were, and in one fence corner was an astonishing clump of stunted banana palms and in the other a lantana with its clotted wounds, which Francis Benbow had brought home from Barbados in a tophat-box in '71.

About the oak and from the funereal scimitar of the drive descending, lawn flowed streetward with good sward broken by random clumps of jonquil and narcissus and gladiolus. Originally the lawn was in terraces and the flowers a formal bed on the first terrace. Then Will Benbow, Horace's and Narcissa's father, had had the terraces obliterated. It was done with plows and scrapers and seeded anew with grass, and he had supposed the flower bed destroyed. But the next spring the scattered bulbs sprouted again, and now every year the lawn was stippled with bloom in yellow, white and pink without order. A certain few young girls asked and received permission to pick some of them each spring, and neighbors' children played quietly among them and beneath the cedars. At the top of the drive, where it curved away descending again, sat the brick doll's house in which Horace and Narcissa lived, surrounded always by that cool, faintly-stringent odor of cedar trees.

It was trimmed with white and it had mullioned casements brought out from England; along the veranda eaves and above the door grew a wistaria vine like heavy tarred rope and thicker than a man's wrist. The lower casements stood open upon gently billowing curtains; upon the sill you expected to see a scrubbed wooden bowl, or at least an immaculate and supercilious cat. But the window sill held only a wicker work-basket from which, like a drooping poinsettia, spilled an end of patchwork in crimson and white; and in the doorway Aunt Sally, a potty little woman in a lace cap, leaned upon a gold-headed ebony walking stick.

Just as it should be, and Horace turned and looked back at his sister crossing the drive with the parcels he had forgotten again. The meaning of peace.

He banged and splashed happily in his bathroom, shouting through the door to his sister where she sat on his bed. His discarded khaki lay upon a chair, holding yet through long association, in its harsh drab folds something of that taut and delicate futility of his. On the marble-topped dresser lay the crucible and tubes of his glass-blowing outfit, the first one he had bought, and beside it the vase he had blown on shipboard—a small chaste shape in clear glass not four inches tall, fragile as a silver lily and incomplete.

"They work in caves," he was shouting through the door, "down flights of stairs underground. You feel water seeping under your foot while you're reaching for the next step, and when you put your hand out to steady yourself against the wall, it's wet when you take it away. It feels just like blood."

"Horace!"

"Yes, magnificent. And way ahead you see the glow. All of a sudden the tunnel comes glimmering out of nothing, then you see the furnace, with things rising and falling before it, shutting the light off, and the walls go glimmering again. At first they're just shapeless things hunching about. Antic, with shadows on the bloody walls, red shadows; a glare, and black shapes like paper dolls weaving and rising and falling in front of it like a magic lantern shutter. And then a face comes out, blowing, and other faces sort of swell out of the red dark like painted balloons.

"And the things themselves! Sheerly and tragically beautiful. Like preserved flowers, you know. Macabre and inviolate; purged and purified as bronze, yet fragile as soap bubbles. Sound of pipes crystallized. Flutes and oboes, but mostly reeds. Oaten reeds. Damn it, they bloom like flowers right before your eyes. Midsummer night's dream to a salamander." His voice became unintelligible, soaring into measured phrases which she did not recognise, but which from the pitch of his voice she knew were Milton's archangels in their sonorous plunging ruin.

He emerged at last, in a white shirt and serge trousers but still borne aloft on his flaming verbal wings, and while his voice chanted in measured syllables she fetched a pair of shoes from the closet, and while she stood holding the shoes in her hands, he ceased chanting and touched her face again with his hands after that fashion of a child.

At supper Aunt Sally broke into his staccato babbling.

"Did you bring your Snopes back with you?" she asked. This Snopes was a young man, member of a seemingly inexhaustible family which for the last ten years had been moving to town in driblets from a small settlement known as Frenchman's Bend. Flem, the first Snopes, had appeared unheralded one day behind the counter of a small restaurant on a side street, patronized by country folk. With this foothold and like Abraham of old, he brought his blood and legal kin household by household, individual by individual, into town and established them where they could gain money. Flem himself was presently manager of the city light and water plant, and for the following few years he was a sort of handyman to the municipal government; and three years ago, to old Bayard's profane astonishment and unconcealed annoyance, he became vice-president of the Sartoris bank, where already a relation of his was a book-keeper.

He still retained the restaurant, and the canvas tent in the rear of it in which he and his wife and baby had passed the first few months of their residence in town, and it served as an alighting-place for incoming Snopeses, from which they spread to small third-rate businesses of various kinds—grocery stores, barber shops (there was one, an invalid of some sort, who operated a second-hand peanut parcher)—where they multiplied and flourished. The older residents, from their Jeffersonian houses and genteel stores and offices, looked on with amusement at first. But this was long since become something like consternation.

The Snopes to which Aunt Sally referred was named Montgomery Ward, and just before the draft law went into operation in '17 he applied to a recruiting officer in Memphis and was turned down because of his heart. Later, to everyone's surprise, particularly that of Horace Benbow's friends, he departed with Horace to a position in the Y.M.C.A. Later still it was told of him that he had travelled all the way to Memphis on that day when he had offered for service, with a plug of chewing tobacco beneath his left armpit. But he and his patron were already departed when that story got out.

"Did you bring your Snopes back with you?" Aunt Sally asked.

"No," he answered, and his thin, nerve-sick face clouded over with a fine cold distaste. "I was very much disappointed in him. I dont even care to talk about it."

"Anybody could have told you that when you left." Aunt Sally chewed slowly and steadily above her plate. Horace brooded for a moment, his thin hand tightened slowly about his fork.

"It's individuals like that, parasites——" he began, but his sister interrupted.

"Who cares about an old Snopes, anyway? Besides, it's too late at night to talk about the horrors of war." Aunt Sally made a moist sound through her food, a sound of vindicated superiority.

"It's the generals they have nowadays," she said. "General

Johnston or General Forrest wouldn't have took a Snopes in his army at all." Aunt Sally was no relation whatever. She lived next door but one with two maiden sisters, one younger and one older than she. She had been in and out of the house ever since Horace and Narcissa could remember, having arrogated to herself certain rights in their lives before they could walk; privileges which were never definitely expressed and which she never availed herself of, yet the mutual admission of whose existence she never permitted to fall into desuetude. She would walk into any room in the house unannounced, and she liked to talk tediously and a little tactlessly of Horace's and Narcissa's infantile ailments. It was said that she had once 'made eyes' at Will Benbow although she was a woman of thirty four or five when Will married; and she still spoke of him with a faintly disparaging possessiveness, and of his wife she always spoke pleasantly, too. "Julia was a right sweet-natured girl," she would say.

So when Horace went off to the war Aunt Sally moved over to keep Narcissa company: no other arrangement had ever occurred to any of the three of them; the fact that Narcissa must have Aunt Sally in the house for an indefinite year or two or three appeared as unavoidable as the fact that Horace must go to the war. Aunt Sally was a good old soul, but she lived much in the past, shutting her mind with a bland finality to anything which had occurred since 1901. For her, time had gone out drawn by horses, and into her stubborn and placid vacuum the squealing of automobile brakes had never penetrated. She had a lot of the crudities which old people are entitled to. She liked the sound of her own voice and she didn't like to be alone at any time, and as she had never got accustomed to the false teeth which she had bought twelve years ago and so never touched them other than to change weekly the water in which they reposed, she ate unprettily of unprepossessing but easily malleable foods. Narcissa reached her hand beneath the table and touched her brother's knee again.

"I *am* glad you're home, Horry."

He looked at her quickly, and the cloud faded from his face as suddenly as it had come, and his spirit slipped, like a swimmer into a tideless sea, into the serene constancy of her affection again.

He was a lawyer, principally through a sense of duty to the family tradition, and though he had no particular affinity to it other than a love for printed words, for the dwelling-places of books, he contemplated returning to his musty office with a glow of . . . not eagerness: no: of deep and abiding unreluctance, almost of pleasure. The meaning of peace. Old unchanging days; unwinged, perhaps, but undisastrous, too. You dont see it, feel it, save with perspective. Fireflies had not yet come, and the cedars flowed unbroken on either hand down to the street, like a curving ebony wave with rigid unbreaking crests pointed on the sky. Light fell outward from the window, across the porch and upon a bed of cannas, hardy, bronze-like—none of your flower-like fragility, theirs; and within the room Aunt Sally's quavering monotone. Narcissa was there too, beside the lamp with a book, filling the room with her still and constant presence like the odor of jasmine, watching the door through which he had passed; and Horace stood on the veranda with his cold pipe, surrounded by that cool astringency of cedars like another presence. The meaning of peace, he said to himself once more, releasing the grave words one by one within the cool bell of silence into which he had come at last again, hearing them linger with a dying fall pure as silver and crystal struck lightly together.

———————

"How's Belle?" he asked on the evening of his arrival.

"They're all right," his sister answered. "They have a new car."

"Dare say," Horace agreed with detachment. "The war should certainly have accomplished that much." Aunt Sally had left them at last and tapped her slow bedward way. Horace stretched his serge legs luxuriously and for a while he ceased striking matches to his stubborn pipe and sat watching his sister's dark head bent above the magazine upon her knees, lost from lesser and inconstant things. Her hair was smoother than any reposing wings, sweeping with burnished unrebellion to a simple knot low on her neck. "Belle's a rotten correspondent," he said. "Like all women."

She turned a page, without looking up. "Did you write to her often?"

"It's because they realize that letters are only good to bridge intervals between actions, like the interludes in Shakespeare's plays," he went on, oblivious. "And did you ever know a woman who read Shakespeare without skipping the interludes? Shakespeare himself knew that, so he didn't put any women in the interludes. Let the men bombast to one another's echoes while the ladies were backstage washing the dinner dishes or putting the children to bed."

"I never knew a woman that read Shakespeare at all," Narcissa corrected. "He talks too much."

Horace rose and stood above her and patted her dark head.

"O profundity," he said, "you have reduced all wisdom to a phrase, and measured your sex by the stature of a star."

"Well, they dont," she repeated, raising her face.

"No? why dont they?" He struck another match to his pipe, watching her across his cupped hands as gravely and with poised eagerness, like a striking bird. "Your Arlens and Sabatinis talk a lot, and nobody ever had more to say and more trouble saying it than old Dreiser."

"But they have secrets," she explained. "Shakespeare doesn't have any secrets. He tells everything."

"I see. Shakespeare had no sense of discrimination and no instinct for reticence. In other words, he wasn't a gentleman," he suggested.

"Yes. . . . . . . That's what I mean."

"And so, to be a gentleman, you must have secrets."

"Oh, you make me tired." She returned to her magazine and he sat beside her on the couch and took her hand in his and stroked it upon his cheek and upon the fine devastation of his hair.

"It's like walking through a twilit garden," he said. "The flowers you know are all there, in their shifts and with their hair combed out for the night, but you know all of them. So you dont bother 'em, you just walk on and sort of stop and turn over a leaf occasionally, a leaf you didn't notice before; perhaps you find a violet under it, or a bluebell or a lightning bug; perhaps only another leaf or a blade of grass. But there's always a drop of dew on it." He continued to stroke her hand upon his face. With her other hand she turned the magazine slowly on, listening to him with fond and serene detachment.

"Did you write to Belle often?" she repeated. "What did you say to her?"

"I wrote what she wanted to read. What all women want in letters. People are really entitled to half of what they think they should have."

"What did you tell her?" Narcissa persisted, turning the pages slowly, her passive hand in his, following the stroking movement of his.

"I told her I was unhappy. Perhaps I was," he added. His sister freed her hand quietly and laid it on the page. He said: "I

admire Belle. She's so cannily stupid. Once I feared her. Perhaps. . . . . . . No, I dont. I am immune to destruction: I have a
magic. Which is a good sign that I am due for it, say the sages,"
he added. "But then, acquired wisdom is a dry thing; it has a
way of crumbling to dust where a sheer and blind coursing of
stupid sap is impervious." He sat without touching her, in a
rapt and instantaneous repose. "Not like yours, O Serene," he
said, waking again. Then he fell to saying Dear old Narcy, and
again he took her hand. It did not withdraw; neither did it
wholly surrender.

"I dont think you ought to say I'm dull so often, Horry," she
said.

"Neither do I," he agreed. "But I must take some sort of
revenge on perfection."

Later she lay in her dark room. Across the corridor Aunt
Sally snored with placid regularity; in the adjoining room
Horace lay while that wild fantastic futility of his voyaged in
lonely regions of its own beyond the moon, about meadows
nailed with firmamented stars to the ultimate roof of things,
where unicorns filled the neighing air with galloping, or
grazed or lay supine in golden-hooved repose.

Horace was seven when she was born. In the background
of her sober babyhood were three beings whose lives and conduct she had adopted with rapt intensity—a lad with a wild
thin face and an unflagging aptitude for tribulation; a darkly
gallant shape romantic with smuggled edibles and with strong
hard hands that smelled always of a certain thrilling carbolic
soap—a being something like Omnipotence but without awe-
someness; and lastly, a gentle figure without legs or any infer-
ence of locomotion whatever, like a minor shrine, surrounded
always by an aura of gentle melancholy and an endless and delicate manipulation of colored silken thread. This last figure

was constant with a gentle and melancholy unassertion; the second revolved in an orbit which bore it at regular intervals into outer space, then returned it with its strong and jolly virility into her intense world again; but the first she had made her own by a sober and maternal perseverance. And so by the time she was five or six, people coerced Horace by threatening to tell Narcissa on him.

Julia Benbow died genteelly when Narcissa was seven, had been removed from their lives as a small sachet of lavender might be removed from a chest of linen, leaving a delicate lingering impalpability; and slept now amid pointed cedars and doves and serene marble shapes. Thus Narcissa acquired two masculine destinies to control and shape, and through the intense maturity of seven and eight and nine she cajoled and threatened and commanded and (very occasionally) stormed them into concurrence. And so through fourteen and fifteen and sixteen, while Horace was first at Sewanee and later at Oxford. Then Will Benbow's time came, and he joined his wife Julia among the marbles and the cedars and the doves, and the current of her maternalism had now but a single channel. For a time this current was dammed by a stupid mischancing of human affairs, but now Horace was home again and lay now beneath the same roof and the same recurrence of days, and the channel was undammed again.

"Why dont you marry, and let that baby look after himself for a while?" Miss Jenny Du Pre had demanded once, in her cold, abrupt way. Perhaps when she too was eighty, all men would be Sartorises to her, also. But that was a long time away. Sartorises. She thought of Bayard, but briefly, and without any tremor at all. He was now no more than the shadow of a hawk's flight mirrored fleetingly by the windless surface of a pool, and gone; where, the pool knew and cared not, leaving no stain.

2

He was settled soon and easily into the routine of days between his office and his home. The musty, solemn familiarity of calf-bound and never-violated volumes on whose dusty bindings prints of Will Benbow's dead fingers might probably yet be found; a little tennis in the afternoons, usually on Harry Mitchell's fine court; cards in the evenings, also with Belle and Harry as a general thing, or again and better still, with the ever accessible and never-failing magic of printed pages, while his sister sat across the table from him or played softly to herself in the darkened room across the hall. Occasionally men called on her; Horace received them with unfailing courtesy and a little exasperation, and departed soon to tramp about the streets or to read in bed. Dr Alford came stiffly once or twice a week, and Horace, being somewhat of an amateur casuist, amused himself by blunting delicately feathered metaphysical darts upon the doctor's bland scientific hide for an hour or so; it would not be until then that they realized that Narcissa had not spoken a word for sixty or seventy or eighty minutes. "That's why they come to see you," Horace told her—"for an emotional mud-bath."

Aunt Sally had returned home, with her bag of colored scraps and her false teeth, leaving behind her a fixed impalpability of a nebulous but definite obligation discharged at some personal sacrifice, and a faint odor of old female flesh which faded from the premises slowly, lingering yet in unexpected places, so that at times Narcissa, waking and lying for a while in the darkness, in the sensuous pleasure of having Horace home again, imagined that she could hear yet in the dark myriad silence of the house Aunt Sally's genteel and placid snores.

At times it would be so distinct that she would pause suddenly and speak Aunt Sally's name into an empty room. And sometimes Aunt Sally replied, having availed herself again of her prerogative of coming in at any hour the notion took her, unannounced, to see how they were getting along and to complain querulously of her own household. She was old, too old to react easily to change, and it was hard for her to readjust herself to her sisters' ways again after her long sojourn in a household where everyone gave in to her regarding all domestic affairs. At home her elder sister ran things in a capable shrewish fashion; she and the third sister persisted in treating Aunt Sally like the child she had been sixty five years ago, whose diet and clothing and hours must be rigorously and pettishly supervised.

"I cant even go to the bathroom in peace," she complained querulously. "I'm a good mind to pack up and move back over here, and let 'em get along the best they can." She rocked fretfully in the chair which by unspoken agreement was never disputed her, looking about the room with bleared protesting old eyes. "That nigger dont half clean up, since I left. That furniture, now. . . . . . . a damp cloth. . . . . . . "

"I wish you would take her back," Miss Sophia, the elder sister, told Narcissa. "She's got so crotchety since she's been with you that there's no living with her. What's this I hear Horace has taken up? making glassware?"

His proper crucibles and retorts had arrived intact. At first he had insisted on using the cellar, clearing out the lawn mower and the garden tools and all the accumulate impedimenta, and walling up the windows so as to make a dungeon of it. But Narcissa had finally persuaded him upon the upper floor of the garage and here he had set up his furnace and had set fire to the building once and had had four mishaps and produced one almost perfect vase of clear amber, larger, more richly and chastely serene and which he kept always on his night table and called by his sister's name in the intervals of apostrophising both of them impartially in his moments of rhapsody over the realization of the meaning of peace and the unblemished attainment of it, as Thou still unravished bride of quietude.

At times he found himself suddenly quiet, a little humble in the presence of the happiness of his winged and solitary cage. For a cage it was, barring him from freedom with trivial compulsions; but he desired a cage. A topless cage, of course, that his spirit might wing on short excursions into the blue, but far afield his spirit did not desire to go: its direction was always upward plummeting, for a plummeting fall.

Still unchanging days. They were doomed days; he knew it, yet for the time being his devious and uncontrollable impulses had become one with the rhythm of things as a swimmer's counter muscles become one with a current, and cage and all his life grew suave with motion, oblivious of destination. During this period not only did his immediate days become starkly inevitable, but the dead thwarted ones with all the spent and ludicrous disasters which his nature had incurred upon him, grew lustrous in retrospect and without regret, and those to come seemed as undeviating and logical as mathematical formulae beyond an incurious golden veil.

At Sewanee, where he had gone as his father before him, he had been an honor man in his class. As a Rhodes Scholar he had gone to Oxford, there to pursue the verities and humanities with that waiting law office in a Mississippi country town like a gate in the remote background through which he must someday pass, thinking of it not often and with no immediate perspective, accepting it with neither pleasure nor regret. Here, amid the mellow benignance of these walls, was a perfect life, a life accomplishing itself placidly in a region remote from time and into which the world's noises came only from afar and with only that glamorous remote significance of a parade passing along a street far away, with inferences of brass and tinsel fading beyond far walls, into the changeless sky. Here he developed a reasonably fine discrimination in alcohol and a brilliant tennis game, after his erratic electric fashion; but save for an occasional half sophomoric, half travelling-salesmanish sabbatical to the Continent in company with fellow-countrymen, his life was a golden and purposeless dream, without palpable intent or future with the exception of that law office to which he was reconciled by the sheer and youthful insuperability of distance and time.

There had come a day on which he stood in that mild pleasurable perplexity in which we regard our belongings and the seemingly inadequate volume of possible packing space, coatless among his chaotic possessions, slowly rubbing the fine unruly devastation of his head. About the bedroom bags and boxes gaped, and on the bed, on chairs, on the floor, were spread his clothes—jackets and trousers of all kinds and all individual as old friends. A servant moved about in the next room and he entered, but the man ignored him with silent and deft efficiency, and he went on to the window. The thin curtains stirred to a faint troubling exhalation of late spring. He put their gentle billowing aside and lit a cigarette and idly watched the match fall, its initial outward impulse fading into a wavering reluctance, as though space itself were languid in violation. Someone crossing the quad called up to him indistinguishably. He waved his hand vaguely in reply and sat on the window sill.

Outward, above and beyond buildings peaceful and gray and old, within and beyond trees in an untarnished and gracious resurgence of green, afternoon was like a blonde woman going slowly in a windless garden; afternoon and June were like blonde sisters in a windless garden-close, approaching without regret the fall of day. Walking a little slower, perhaps;

perhaps looking backward, but without sadness, untroubled as cows. Horace sat in the window while the servant methodically reduced the chaos of his possessions to the boxes and bags, gazing out across ancient gray roofs, and trees which he had seen in all their seasonal moods, in all moods matching his own. Had he been younger he would have said goodbye to them secretively or defiantly; older, he would have felt neither the desire to nor the impulse to suppress it. So he sat quietly in his window for the last time while the curtains stirred delicately against his hair, brooding upon their dreaming vistas where twilight was slowly finding itself and where, beyond dissolving spires, lingered grave evening shapes; and he knew a place where, had he felt like walking, he could hear a cuckoo, that symbol of sweet and timeless mischief, that augur of the fever renewed again.

All he wanted anyway was quiet and dull peace and a few women, preferably young and good looking and fair tennis players, with whom to indulge in harmless and lazy intrigue. So his mind was made up, and on the homeward boat he framed the words with which he should tell his father that he was going to be an Episcopal minister. But when he reached New York the wire waited him saying that Will Benbow was ill, and all thoughts of his future fled his mind during the journey home and during the two subsequent days that his father lived. Then Will Benbow was buried beside his wife, and Aunt Sally Wyatt was sombrely ubiquitous about the house and talked with steady macabre complacence of Will at meals and snored placidly by night in the guest room. The next day but one Horace opened his father's law office again.

His practice, what there was of it, consisted of polite interminable litigation that progressed decorously and pleasantly from conference to conference, the greater part of which were given to discussions of the world's mutations as exemplified by men or by printed words; conferences conducted as often as not across pleasant dinner tables or upon golf links or, if the conferee were active enough, upon tennis courts — conferences which wended their endless courses without threat of consummation or of advantage or detriment to anyone involved.

There reposed also in a fire-proof cabinet in his office — the one concession Will Benbow had ever made to progress — a number of wills which Horace had inherited and never read, the testators of which accomplished their lives in black silk and lace caps and an atmosphere of formal and timeless desuetude in stately, high ceiled rooms screened from the ceaseless world by flowering shrubs and old creeping vines; existences circumscribed by church affairs and so-called literary clubs and a conscientious, slightly contemptuous preoccupation with the welfare of remote and obtusely ungrateful heathen peoples. They did not interest themselves in civic affairs. To interfere in the lives or conduct of people whom you saw daily or who served you in various ways or to whose families you occasionally sent food and cast-off clothing, was not genteel. Besides, the heathen was far enough removed for his willy nilly elevation to annoy no one save his yet benighted brethren. Clients upon whom he called at rare intervals by formal and unnecessary request and who bade fair to outlive him as they had outlived his father and to be heired in turn by some yet uncorporeal successor to him. As if God, Circumstance, looking down upon the gracious if faintly niggard completeness of their lives, found not the heart to remove them from surroundings tempered so peacefully to their requirements, to any other of lesser decorum and charm.

The meaning of peace; one of those instants in a man's life, a neap tide in his affairs, when, as though with a premonition of disaster, the moment takes on a sort of fixed clarity in which his actions and desires stand boldly forth unshadowed and rhythmic one with another like two steeds drawing a single chariot along a smooth empty road, and during which the I in him stands like a tranquil deciduated tree above the sere and ludicrous disasters of his days.

3

Narcissa had failed to call at the office for him and he walked home and changed to flannels and the blue jacket with his Oxford club insignia embroidered upon the breast pocket, and removed his racket from its press. In trees and flower beds spring was accomplishing itself more and more with the accumulating days, and he walked on with the sunset slanting into his hair, toward Belle's. He strode on, chanting to himself, walking a little faster until the majestic monstrosity of the house came into view.

Someone piped thinly to him from beyond the adjoining fence; it was Belle's eight year old daughter, her dress of delicate yellow a single note of a chord of other small colored garments engaged in the intense and grave preoccupations of little girls. Horace waved his racket at her and went on, turning into the drive. The gravel slipped with short sibilance beneath his rubber soles. He did not approach the entrance to the house but continued instead along the drive toward the rear, where already against the further sunshot green of old trees and flowering shrubs he saw a figure in white tautly antic with motion in a single overarching sweep. They were playing already, someone. Belle would be there, already ensconced, Ahenobarbus' vestal, proprietorial and inattentive, preeningly dictatorial; removed from the dust and the heat and the blood; disdainful and the principal actor in the piece. O thou grave myrtle shapes amid which petulant Death.

But Belle was the sort of watcher he preferred, engaged as she would be in that outwardly faultless immersion, in the unflagging theatrics of her own part in the picture, surrounding him as she would with that atmosphere of surreptitious domesticity. Belle didn't play tennis herself: her legs were not good, and Belle knew it; but sat instead in a tea gown of delicate and irreproachable lines at a table advantageously placed and laden with books and magazines and the temporarily discarded impedimenta of her more Atalanta-esque sisters. There was usually a group around Belle's chair—other young women or a young man or so inactive between sets, with an occasional older woman come to see just exactly what was going on or what Belle wore at the time; watching Belle's pretty regal airs with the young men. "Like a moving picture," Aunt Sally Wyatt said once, with cold and curious interest.

And presently Meloney would bring tea out and lay it on the table at Belle's side. Between the two of them, Belle with her semblance of a peahen suave and preening and petulant upon clipped sward, before marble urns and formal balustrades, and Meloney in her starched cap and apron and her lean shining legs, they made a rite of the most casual gathering; lending a sort of stiffness to it which Meloney seemed to bring in on her tray and beneath which the calling ladies grew more and more reserved and coldly watchful and against which Belle flowered like a hot-house bloom, brilliant and petulant and perverse.

It had taken Belle some time to overcome Jefferson's prejudice against a formal meal between dinner and supper and to educate the group in which she moved to tea as a function in itself and not as something to give invalids or as an adjunct to a party of some sort. But Horace had assisted her, unwittingly and without self-consciousness; and there had been a youth, son of a carpenter, of whom Belle had made a poet and sent to

New Orleans and who, being a conscientious objector, had narrowly escaped prison during the war and who now served in a reportorial capacity on a Texas newspaper, holding the position relinquished by a besotted young man who had enlisted in the Marine Corps early in '17.

Bareheaded, in flannels and a blue jacket with his Oxford club insignia embroidered on the pocket and his racket under his arm, Horace passed on around the house and the court came into view with its two occupants in fluid violent action. Beneath an arcade of white pilasters and vine-hung beams Belle, surrounded by the fragile, harmonious impedimenta of the moment, was like a butterfly. Two sat with her, in bright relief against the dark foliage of a crepe-myrtle not yet in flower. The other woman (the third member of the group was a young girl in white and with a grave molasses bang and a tennis racket across her knees) spoke to him, and Belle greeted him with a sort of languid possessive desolation. Her hand was warm, prehensile, like mercury in his palm exploring softly with delicate bones and petulant scented flesh. Her eyes were like hothouse grapes and her mouth was redly mobile, rich with discontent; but waked now from its rouged repose, this was temporarily lost. She had lost Meloney, she told him.

"Meloney saw through your gentility," Horace said. "You grew careless, probably. Your elegance is much inferior to Meloney's. You surely didn't expect to always deceive anyone who can lend as much rigid discomfort to the function of eating and drinking as Meloney could, did you? Or has she got married some more?"

"She's gone in business," Belle answered fretfully. "A beauty shop. And why, I cant for the life of me see. Those things never do last, here. Can you imagine Jefferson women supporting a beauty shop, with the exception of us three? Mrs

Marders and I might; I'm sure we need it, but what use has Frankie for one?"

"What seems curious to me," the other woman said, "is where the money came from. People thought that perhaps you had given it to her, Belle."

"Since when have I been a public benefactor?" Belle said coldly. Horace grinned faintly. Mrs Marders said:

"Now, Belle, we all know how kindhearted you are; dont be modest."

"I said a public benefactor," Belle repeated. Horace said quickly:

"Well, Harry would swap a handmaiden for an ox, any day. At least, he can save a lot of wear and tear on his cellar, not having to counteract your tea in a lot of casual masculine tummies. I suppose there'll be no more tea out here, will there?" he added.

"Dont be silly," Belle said.

Horace said: "I realise now that it is not tennis that I come here for, but for the incalculable amount of uncomfortable superiority I always feel when Meloney . . . serves me tea. . . . I saw your daughter as I came along."

"She's somewhere around, I suppose," Belle agreed indifferently. "You haven't had your hair cut yet," she stated. "Why is it that men have no sense about barbers?" she said generally. The older woman watched Belle and Horace brightly, coldly across her two flaccid chins. The young girl sat quietly in her simple virginal white, her racket on her lap and one brown hand lying upon it like a sleeping tan puppy. She was watching Horace with sober interest but without rudeness, as children do. "They either wont go to the barber at all, or they insist on having their heads all gummed up with pomade and things," Belle added.

"Horace is a poet," the other woman said. Her flesh draped loosely from her cheek-bones like rich, slightly-soiled velvet; her eyes were like the eyes of an old turkey, predatory and unwinking; a little obscene. "Poets must be excused for what they do. You should remember that, Belle." Horace bowed toward her.

"Your race never fails in tact, Belle," he said. "Mrs Marders is one of the few people I know who give the law profession its true evaluation."

"It's like any other business, I suppose," Belle said. "You're late today. Why didn't Narcissa come?"

"I mean, dubbing me a poet," Horace explained. "The law, like poetry, is the final resort of the lame, the halt, the imbecile and the blind. I dare say Caesar invented the law business to protect himself against poets."

"You're so clever," Belle said. The young girl spoke suddenly:

"Why do you bother about what men put on their hair, Miss Belle? Mr Mitchell's bald."

The other woman laughed, unctuously, steadily, watching them with her lidless unlaughing eyes. She watched Belle and Horace and still laughed steadily, brightly and cold. " 'Out of the mouths of babes——' " she said. The young girl glanced from one to another with her clear sober eyes. She rose.

"I guess I'll see if I cant get a set now," she said.

Horace moved also. "Let's you and I——" he began. Without turning her head Belle touched him with her hand.

"Sit down, Frankie," she commanded. "They haven't finished the game yet. You shouldn't laugh so much on an empty stomach," she told Mrs Marders. "Do sit down, Horace."

The girl stood yet with slim and awkward grace, holding her racket. She looked at Belle a moment, then she turned her face to the court again. Horace took the chair beyond Belle;

her hand dropped hidden into his, with that secret movement, then it grew passive; it was as though she had turned a current off somewhere. Like one entering a dark room in search of something, finding it and pressing the light off again.

"Dont you like poets?" Horace spoke across Belle's body. The girl did not turn her head.

"They cant dance," she answered. "I guess they are all right, though. They went to the war, the good ones did. There was one was a good tennis player, that got killed. I've seen his picture, but I dont remember his name."

"Oh, dont start talking about the war, for heaven's sake," Belle said. Her hand stirred in Horace's. "I had to listen to Harry for two years. Explaining why he couldn't go. As if I cared whether he did or not."

"He had a family to support," Mrs Marders suggested brightly. Belle half reclined, her head against the chair-back, her hidden hand moving slowly in Horace's, exploring, turning, ceaselessly like a separate volition curious but without warmth.

"Some of them were aviators," the girl continued. She stood with one little unemphatic hip braced against the table, her racket clasped beneath her arm, turning the pages of a magazine. Then she closed the magazine and again she watched the two figures leanly antic upon the court. "I danced with one of those Sartoris boys once. I was too scared to know which one it was. I wasn't anything but a baby, then."

"Were they poets?" Horace asked. "I mean, the one that got back. I know the other one, the dead one, was."

"He sure can drive that car of his," she answered, still watching the players, her straight hair (hers was the first bobbed head in town) not brown not gold, her brief nose in profile, her brown still hands clasping her racket. Belle stirred and freed her hand.

"Do go on and play, you all," she said. "You make me nervous, both of you." Horace rose with alacrity.

"Come on, Frankie. Let's you and I take 'em on for a set."

The girl looked at him. "I'm not so hot," she said soberly. "I hope you wont get mad."

"Why? If we get beat?" They moved together toward the court where the two players were now exchanging sides. "Do you know what the finest sensation of all is?" Her straight brown head moved just at his shoulder. It's her dress that makes her arms and hands so brown, he thought. Little. He could not remember her at all sixteen months back, when he had gone away. They grow up so quickly, though, after a certain age. Go away again and return, and find her with a baby, probably.

"Good music?" she suggested tentatively, after a time.

"No. It's to finish a day and say to yourself: Here's one day during which I have accomplished nothing and hurt no one and had a whale of a good time. How does it go? 'Count that day lost whose low descending sun——'? Well, they've got it exactly backward."

"I dont know. I learned it in school, I guess," she answered indifferently. "But I dont remember it now. D'you reckon they'll let me play? I'm not so hot," she repeated.

"Of course they will," Horace assured her. And soon they were aligned: the two players, the book-keeper in the local department store and a youth who had been recently expelled from the state university for a practical joke (he had removed the red lantern from the barrier about a street excavation and hung it above the door of the girls' dormitory) against Horace and the girl. Horace was an exceptional player, electric and brilliant. One who knew tennis and who had patience and a cool head could have defeated him out of hand by letting him beat himself. But not these. The points see-sawed back and forth, but usually Horace managed to retrieve the advantage with stroking or strategy so audacious as to obscure the faultiness of his tactics.

Meanwhile he could watch her; her taut earnestness, her unflagging determination not to let him down, her awkward virginal grace. From the back line he outguessed their opponents with detached and impersonal skill, keeping the point in abeyance and playing the ball so as to bring her young intent body into motion as he might pull a puppet's strings. Hers was an awkward speed that cost them points, but from the base line Horace retrieved her errors when he could, pleasuring in the skimpy ballooning of her little dress moulded and dragged by her arms and legs, watching the taut revelations of her speeding body in a sort of ecstasy. Girlwhite and all thy little Oh. Not pink, no. For a moment I thought she'd no. Disgraceful, her mamma would call it. Or any other older woman. Belle's are pink O muchly "Oaten reed above the lyre," Horace chanted, catching the ball at his shoe-tops with a full swing, watching it duck viciously beyond the net. Oaten reed above the lyre. And Belle like a harped gesture, not sonorous. Piano, perhaps. Blended chords, anyway. Unchaste ? Knowledgeable better. Knowingly wearied. Weariedly knowing. Yes, piano. Fugue. Fugue of discontent. O moon rotting waxed overlong too long

Last point. Game and set. She made it with savage awkwardness; and turned at the net and stood with lowered racket as he approached. Beneath the simple molasses of her hair she was perspiring a little. "I kept on letting 'em get my alley," she explained. "You never bawled me out a single time. What ought I to do, to break myself of that?"

"You ought to run in a cheese-cloth shimmy on hills under a new moon," Horace told her. "With chained ankles, of course. But a slack chain. No, not the moon; but in a dawn like pipes. Green and gold, and maybe a little pink. Would you risk a little pink?" She watched him with grave curious eyes as he stood before her lean in his flannels and with his sick brilliant face and his wild hair. "No," he corrected himself again. "On sand. Blanched sand, with dead ripples. Ghosts of dead motion waved into the sand. Do you know how cold the sea can be just before dawn, with a falling tide? Like lying in a dead world, upon the dead respirations of the earth. She's too big to die all at once. Like elephants. . . . . . . How old are you?" Now all at once her eyes became secretive, and she looked away. "Now what?" he demanded. "What did you start to say then?"

"There's Mr Mitchell," she said. Harry Mitchell had come out, in tight flannels and a white silk shirt and new ornate sport shoes that cost twenty dollars per pair. With a new racket in a patent case and press, standing with his squat legs and his bald bullet head and his undershot jaw of rotting teeth beside the studied picture of his wife. Presently when he had been made to drink a cup of tea he would gather up all the men present and lead them through the house to his bathroom and give them whisky, pouring out a glass and fetching it down to Rachel. He would give you the shirt off his back. He was a cotton speculator and a good one; he was ugly as sin and kindhearted and dogmatic and talkative, and he called Belle "little mother" until she broke him of it. Belle lay yet in her chair; she was watching them as they turned together from the court.

"What was it?" Horace persisted.

"Sir?"

"What you started to say just then."

"Nothing," she answered. "I wasn't going to say anything."

"Oh, that's too feminine," Horace said. "I didn't expect that of you, after the way you play tennis." They moved on under the veiled contemplation of Belle's gaze.

"Feminine?" Then she added: "I hope I can get another set soon. I'm not a bit tired, are you?"

"Yes. Any woman might have said that. But maybe you're not old enough to be a woman."

"Horace," Belle said.

"I'm seventeen," the girl answered. "Miss Belle likes you, dont she?"

Belle spoke his name again, mellifluously, lazily peremptory. Mrs Marders sat now with her slack chins in a raised teacup. The girl turned to him with polite finality. "Thanks for playing with me," she said. "I'll be better some day, I hope. We beat 'em," she said generally.

"You and the little lady gave 'em the works, hey, big boy?" Harry Mitchell said, showing his discolored teeth. His heavy prognathous jaw narrowed delicately down, then nipped abruptly off into bewildered pugnacity.

"Mr Benbow did," the girl corrected in her clear voice, and she took the chair next Belle. "I kept on letting 'em get my alley."

"Horace," Belle said, "your tea is getting cold."

It had been fetched out by the combination gardener-stableman-chauffeur, temporarily impressed in a white jacket and smelling of vulcanized rubber and ammonia. Mrs Marders removed her chins from her cup. "Horace plays too well," she said, "really too well. The other men cant compare with him. You were lucky to have him for a partner, child."

"Yessum," the girl agreed. "I guess he wont risk me again."

"Nonsense," Mrs Marders rejoined. "Horace enjoyed playing with you, with a young, fresh girl. Didn't you notice it, Belle?"

Belle made no reply. She poured Horace's tea, and at this moment her daughter came across the lawn in her crocus-yellow dress. Her eyes were like stars, more soft and melting than any deer's, and she gave Horace a swift shining glance.

"Well, Titania?" he said.

Belle half turned her head, with the teapot poised above the cup, and Harry set his cup on the table and went and knelt on one knee in her path, as though he were cajoling a puppy. The child came up, still watching Horace with radiant and melting diffidence, and permitted her father to embrace her and fondle her with his short, heavy hands. "Daddy's gal," Harry said. She submitted to having her prim little dress mussed, pleasurably but a little restively; her eyes flew shining again.

"Dont muss your dress, sister," Belle said, and the child evaded her father's hands with a prim movement. "What is it now?" Belle asked. "Why aren't you playing?"

"Nothing. I just came home." She came and stood diffidently beside her mother's chair.

"Speak to the company," Belle said. "Dont you know better than to come where older people are, without speaking to them?" The little girl did so, shyly and faultlessly, greeting them in rotation, and her mother turned and pulled and patted at her straight soft hair. "Now, go on and play. Why do you always want to come around where grown people are? You're not interested in what we're doing."

"Ah, let her stay, mother," Harry said. "She wants to watch her daddy and Horace play tennis."

"Run along, now," Belle repeated with a final pat. "And do keep your dress clean."

"Yessum," the child agreed, and she turned obediently, giving Horace another quick shining look. He watched her and saw Rachel open the kitchen door and speak to her as she passed, saw her turn and mount the steps into the kitchen.

"What a beautifully mannered child," Mrs Marders said.

"They're so hard to do anything with," Belle said. "She has some of her father's traits. Drink your tea, Harry."

Harry took his cup from the table and sucked its lukewarm

contents into himself noisily and dutifully. "Well, big boy, how about a set? These squirrels think they can beat us."

"Frankie wants to play again," Belle interposed. "Let the child have the court for a little while, Harry." Harry was busy uncasing his racket. He paused and raised his savage undershot face and his dull kind eyes.

"No, no," the girl protested quickly. "I've had enough. I'd rather look on a while."

"Dont be silly," Belle said. "They can play any time. Make them let her play, Harry."

"Sure the little lady can play," Harry said. "Help yourself; play as long as you want to." He bent again and returned his racket to its intricate casing, twisting nuts here and there; his back was sullen, with a boy's sullenness.

"Please, Mr Mitchell," the girl said.

"Go ahead," Harry repeated. "Here, you jelly-beans, how about fixing up a set with the little lady?"

"Dont mind him," Belle told the girl. "He and Horace can play some other time. He'll have to make a fourth, anyway."

The two players stood now, politely waiting.

"Sure, Mr Harry, come on. Me and Frankie'll play you and Joe," one of them said.

"You folks go ahead and play a set," Harry repeated. "I've got a little business to talk over with Horace. You all go ahead." He overrode their polite protests and they took the court. Then he jerked his head significantly at Horace.

"Go on with him," Belle said. "The baby." Without looking at him, without touching him, she enveloped him with rich and smoldering promise. Mrs Marders sat across the table from them, curious and bright and cold with her teacup. "Unless you want to play with that silly child again."

"Silly?" Horace repeated. "She's too young to be unconsciously silly yet."

"Run along," Belle told him. "And hurry back. Mrs Marders and I are tired of one another."

Horace followed his host into the house, followed his short rolling gait and the bald indomitability of his head. From the kitchen, as they passed, little Belle's voice came steadily, recounting some astonishment of the day, with an occasional mellow ejaculation from Rachel for antistrophe. In the bathroom Harry got a bottle from a cabinet, and preceded by labored heavy footsteps mounting, Rachel entered without knocking, bearing a pitcher of ice water. "Whyn't y'all g'awn and play, ef you wants?" she demanded. "Whut you let that 'oman treat you and that baby like she do, anyhow?" she demanded of Harry. "You ought to take and lay her out wid a stick of wood. Messin' up my kitchen at fo' oclock in de evenin'. And you aint helpin' none, neither," she told Horace. "Gimme a dram, Mr Harry, please, suh."

She held her glass out and Harry filled it, and waddled heavily from the room; they heard her descend the stairs slowly and heavily on her fallen arches. "Belle couldn't get along without Rachel," Harry said. He rinsed two glasses with ice water and set them on the lavatory. "She talks too much, like all niggers." He poured into the two tumblers, set the bottle down. "To listen to her you'd think Belle was some kind of a wild animal. A dam tiger or something. But Belle and I understand each other. You've got to make allowances for women, anyhow. Different from men. Born contrary; complain when you dont please 'em and complain when you do." He added a little water to his glass; then he said, with astonishing irrelevance: "I'd kill the man that tried to wreck my home like I would a dam snake. Well, let's take one, big boy."

Presently he sloshed water into his empty glass and gulped that, too, and he reverted to his former grievance.

"Cant get to play on my own dam court," he said. "Belle

gets all these dam people here every day. What I want is a court
where I can come home from work and get in a couple of fast
sets every afternoon. Appetizer before supper. But every dam
day I get home from work and find a bunch of young girls and
jelly-beans, using it like it was a public court in a dam park."
Horace drank his more moderately, and Harry lit a cigarette
and threw the match onto the floor and hung his leg across the
lavatory. "I reckon I'll have to build another court for my own
use and put a hogwire fence around it with a yale lock, so Belle
cant give picnics on it. There's plenty of room down there by
the lot fence. No trees, too. Put it out in the dam sun, and I
reckon Belle'll let me use it now and then. Well, suppose we
get on back."

He led the way through his bedroom and stopped to show
Horace a new repeating rifle he had just bought, and to press
upon him a package of cigarettes which he imported from
South America, and they descended and emerged into afternoon become later. The sun was level now across the court
where three players leaped and sped with soft quick slapping of
rubber soles, following the fleeting impact of the ball. Mrs
Marders sat yet with her ceaseless chins, although she was
speaking of departure when they came up. Belle turned her
head against the chair-back, but Harry led Horace on.

"We're going to look over a location for a tennis court. I
think I'll take up tennis myself," he told Mrs Marders with
heavy irony. It was later still when they returned. Mrs Marders
was gone and Belle sat alone, with a magazine. A youth in a
battered ford had called for the girl Frankie, but another young
man had dropped in, and when Horace and Harry came up
the three youths clamored politely for Harry to join them.

Horace halted in his loose, worn flannels, with his thin
face brilliant and sick with nerves, smoking his host's cigarettes
and watching his hopeless indomitable head and his intent,

faintly comical body as he paced off dimensions and talked steadily in his harsh voice; paced back and forth and planned and calculated with something of a boy's fine ability for fabling, for shaping the incontrovertible present to a desire which he will presently lose in a recenter one and so forget.

"Take Horace here," Harry said, obviously pleased. "He'll give you a run for your money." But Horace demurred and the three continued to importune Harry. "Lemme get my racket, then," he said finally, and Horace followed the heavy scuttling of his backside across the court. Belle looked briefly up.

"Did you find a place?"

"Yes," Harry answered, uncasing his racket again. "Where I can play myself, sometimes. A place too far from the street for everybody that comes along to see it and stop." But Belle was reading again. Harry unscrewed his racket press and removed it. "I'll go in one set, then you and I can get in a fast one before dark," he told Horace.

"Yes," Horace agreed. He sat down and watched Harry stride heavily onto the court and take his position, watched the first serve. Then Belle's magazine rustled and slapped onto the table.

"Come," she said, rising. Horace rose, and Belle preceded him and they crossed the lawn and entered the house. Rachel moved about in the kitchen, and they went on through the house, where all noises were remote and the furniture gleamed peacefully indistinct in the dying evening light. Belle slid her hand into his, clutching his hand against her silken thigh, and led him on through a dusky passage and into her music room. This room was quiet too and empty and she stopped against him half turning, and they kissed. But she freed her mouth presently and moved again and he drew the piano bench out and they sat on opposite sides of it and kissed again. "You haven't told me you love me," Belle said, touching his face with her fingertips, and the fine devastation of his hair. "Not in a long time."

"Not since yesterday," Horace agreed, but he told her, she leaning her breast against him and listening with a sort of rapt voluptuous inattention, like a great still cat; and when he had done and sat touching her face and her hair with his delicate wild hands, she removed her breast and opened the piano and touched the keys. Saccharine melodies she played, from memory and in the current mode, that you might hear on any vaudeville stage, and with shallow skill, a feeling for their oversweet nuances. They sat thus for sometime while the light faded, Belle in another temporary vacuum of discontent, building for herself a world in which she moved romantically, finely and a little tragical; with Horace sitting beside her and watching both Belle in her self-imposed and tragic rôle, and himself performing his part like the old actor whose hair is thin and whose profile is escaping him via his chin, but who can play to any cue at a moment's notice while the younger men chew their bitter thumbs in the wings.

Presently the rapid heavy concussions of Harry's feet thumped again on the stairs mounting, and the harsh wordless uproar of his voice as he led someone else in the back way and up to his bathroom. Belle stopped her hands and leaned against him and kissed him again, clinging. "This is intolerable," she said, freeing her mouth with a movement of her head. For a moment she resisted against his arm, then her hands crashed discordantly upon the keys and slid through Horace's hair and down his cheeks tightening. She freed her mouth again. "Now, sit over there."

He obeyed; she on the piano bench was in half shadow. Twilight was almost accomplished; only the line of her bent head and her back, tragic and still, making him feel young again. We do turn corners upon ourselves, like suspicious old ladies spying on servants, Horace thought. No, like boys trying to head off a parade. "There's always divorce," he said.

"To marry again?" Her hands trailed off into chords; merged, faded again into a minor in one hand. Overhead Harry moved with his heavy staccato tread, shaking the house. "You'd make a rotten husband."

"I wont as long as I'm not married," Horace answered.

She said, "Come here," and he went to her, and in the dusk she was again tragic and young and familiar, with a haunting sense of loss, and he knew the sad fecundity of the world, and time's hopeful unillusion that fools itself. "I want to have your child, Horace," she said, and then her own child came up the hall and stood diffidently in the door.

For a moment Belle was an animal awkward and mad with fear. She surged away from him in a mad spurning movement; her hands crashed on the keys as she controlled her instinctive violent escape that left in the dusk a mindless protective antagonism, pervading, in steady cumulate waves, directed at Horace as well.

"Come in, Titania," Horace said.

The little girl stood diffidently in silhouette. Belle's voice was sharp with relief. "Well, what do you want? Sit over there," she hissed at Horace. "What do you want, Belle?" Horace drew away a little, but without rising.

"I've got a new story to tell you, soon," he said. But little Belle stood yet, as though she had not heard, and her mother said:

"Go on and play, Belle. Why did you come in the house? It isn't supper time, yet."

"Everybody's gone home," she answered. "I haven't got anybody to play with."

"Go to the kitchen and talk to Rachel then," Belle said. She struck the keys again, harshly. "You worry me to death, hanging around the house." The little girl stood for a moment longer; then she turned obediently and went away. "Sit over there," Belle repeated. Horace resumed his chair and Belle played again, loudly and swiftly, with cold hysterical skill. Overhead Harry thumped again across the floor; they descended the stairs. Harry was still talking; the voices passed on toward the rear, ceased. Belle continued to play; still about him in the darkening room that blind protective antagonism like a muscular contraction that remains after the impulse of fright has died. Without turning her head she said:

"Are you going to stay for supper?"

He was not, he answered, waking suddenly. She did not rise with him, did not turn her head, and he let himself out the front door and into the late spring twilight, where was already a faint star above the windless trees. On the drive just without the garage Harry's new car stood. At the moment he was doing something to the engine of it while the house-yard-stable boy held a patent trouble-lamp above the beetling crag of his head and his daughter and Rachel, holding tools or detached sections of the car's vitals, leaned their intent dissimilar faces across his bent back and into the soft bluish glare of the light. Horace went on homeward. Twilight, evening, came swiftly. Before he reached the corner where he turned, the street lamps sputtered and failed, then glared above the intersections, beneath the arching trees.

4

"General William Booth has gotten a leprechaun on Uriah's wife," Horace told himself, and gravely presented the flowers he had brought, and received in return the starry incense of her flying eyes. Mrs Marders was among the group of Belle's more intimate familiars in this room, affable and brightly cold, a little detached and volubly easy; she admired little Belle's gifts one by one with impeccable patience. Belle's voice came from the adjoining room where the piano was bowered for the occasion by potted palms and banked pots and jars of bloom, and where yet more ladies were sibilantly crescendic with an occasional soberly clad male on the outer fringe of their colorful chattering like rocks dumbly imponderable about the cauldron where seethed an hysterical tideflux. These men spoke to one another from the sides of their mouths and, when addressed by the ladies, with bleak and swift affability, from the teeth outward. Harry's bald bullet head moved among his guests, borne hither and yon upon the harsh uproar of his voice; presently, when the recital would have gotten underway and the ladies engaged, he would begin to lead the men one by one and on tiptoe from the room and up the back stairs to his apartments.

But now the guests stood and drifted and chattered, anticipatory and unceasing, and every minute or two Harry gravitated again to the dining room, on the table of which his daughter's gifts and flowers were arrayed and beside which little Belle in her pale lilac dress stood in a shining-eyed and breathless ecstasy.

"Daddy's gal," Harry, in his tight, silver-gray gabardine suit and his bright tie with the diamond stud, chortled, putting his short thick hands on her; then together they examined the latest addition to the array of gifts with utter if dissimilar sincerity—little Belle with quiet and shining diffidence, her father stridently, tactlessly overloud. Harry was smoking his cigarettes steadily, scattering ash; he had receptacles of them open on every available flat surface throughout the lighted rooms. "How's the boy?" he added, shaking Horace's hand.

"Will you look at that sumptuous bouquet Horace has

brought your daughter," Mrs Marders said. "Horace, it's really a shame. She'd have appreciated a toy or a doll much more, wouldn't you honey? Are you trying to make Belle jealous?"

Little Belle gave Horace her flying stars again. Harry squatted before her.

"Did Horace bring daddy's gal some flowers?" he brayed. "Just look at the flowers Horace brought her." He put his hands on her again. Mrs Marders said quickly:

"You'll burn her dress with that cigarette, Harry."

"Daddy's gal dont care," Harry answered. "Buy her a new dress tomorrow." But little Belle freed herself, craning her soft brown head in alarm, trying to see the back of her frock, and then Belle entered in pink beneath a dark blue frothing of tulle, and the rich bloody auburn of her hair. Little Belle showed her Horace's bouquet, and she knelt and fingered and patted little Belle's hair, and smoothed her dress.

"Did you thank him?" she asked. "I know you didn't."

"Of course she did," Horace interposed. "Just as you thank providence for breath every time you breathe." Little Belle looked up at him with her grave ecstatic shining. "We think girls should always have flowers when they play music and dance," he explained, gravely too. "Dont we?"

"Yes," little Belle agreed breathlessly.

"Yes, sir," Belle corrected fretfully. Patting and pulling at her daughter's delicate wisp of dress, with its tiny embroidered flowers at the yoke. Belle kneeling in a soft swishing of silk, with her rich and smoldering unrepose. Harry stood with his squat, tightly-clothed body, looking at Horace with the friendly, blood-shot bewilderment of his eyes.

"Yes, sir," little Belle piped obediently.

Belle rose, swishing again. "Come on, sister. It's time to begin. And dont forget and start pulling at your clothes."

―――――――

The indiscriminate furniture—dining-room chairs, rockers, sofas and all—were ranged in semicircular rows facing the corner where the piano was placed. Beside the piano and above little Belle's soft brown head and her little sheer frock and the tense, impotent dangling of her legs, the music teacher, a thin passionate spinster with cold thwarted eyes behind nose glasses, stood. The men clung stubbornly to the rear row of chairs, their sober decorum splotched sparsely among the cacophonous hues of the women's dresses. With the exception of Harry, that is, who now sat with the light full on his bald crag. Just beyond him and between him and Mrs Marders, Horace could see Narcissa's dark burnished head. Belle sat on the front row at the end, turned sideways in her chair. The other ladies were still now, temporarily, in a sort of sibilant vacuum of sound into which the tedious labored tinkling of little Belle's playing fell like a fairy fountain.

The music tinkled and faltered, hesitated, corrected itself to the intent nodding of little Belle's head and the strained meagre gestures of the teacher, tinkled monotonously and tunelessly on while the assembled guests sat in a sort of bland, waiting inattention; and Horace speculated on that persevering and senseless urge of parents (and of all adults) for making children a little ridiculous in their own eyes and in the eyes of other children. The clothes they make them wear, the stupid mature things they make them do. And he found himself wondering if to be cultured did not mean to be purged of all taste; civilized, to be robbed of all fineness of objective judgment regarding oneself. Then he remembered that little Belle also had been born a woman.

The music tinkled thinly, ceased; the teacher leaned forward with a passionate movement and removed the sheet from the rack, and the room swelled with a polite adulation of bored palms. Horace too; and little Belle turned on the bench, with her flying eyes, and Horace grinned faintly at his own masculine vanity. Sympathy here, when she was answering one of the oldest compulsions of her sex, a compulsion that taste nor culture nor anything else would ever cause to appear ridiculous to her. Then the teacher spoke to her and she turned on the bench again, with her rapt laborious fingers and the brown, intent nodding of her head.

Belle sat sideways in her chair. Her head was bent and her hands lay idle upon her lap and she sat brooding and remote. Horace watched her, the line of her neck, the lustrous stillness of her arm; trying to project himself into that region of rich and smoldering immobility into which she had withdrawn for the while. But he could not; she did not seem to be aware of him at all; the corridors where he sought her were empty, and he moved quietly in his seat beneath the thin tinkling of the music and looked about at the other politely attentive heads and beyond them, in the doorway, Harry making significant covert signs in his direction. Harry jerked his thumb toward his mouth and moved his head meaningly, but Horace flipped his hand briefly in reply, without moving. When he looked doorward again Harry was gone.

Little Belle ceased again. When the clapping died the heavy thump-thump-thump of Harry's heels sounded on the ceiling above. Ridiculous, like the innocent defenseless backside of a small boy caught delving into an apple barrel, and a few of the guests cast their eyes upward in polite astonishment. Belle raised her head sharply, with an indescribable gesture, then she looked at Horace with cold and blazing irritation, enveloping, savage, disdainful of who might see. The thumping ceased, became a cautious clumsy tipping, and Belle's anger faded, though her gaze was still full upon him. Little Belle played again and Horace looked away from the cold fixity of Belle's gaze, a little uncomfortably, and so saw Harry and one of the men guests enter surreptitiously and seat themselves; he turned his head again. Beneath the heavy shadow of her hair Belle still watched him, and he shaped three words with his lips. But Belle's mouth did not change its sullen repose, nor her eyes, and then he realized that she was not looking at him at all, perhaps had never been.

Later Belle herself went to the piano and played a trite saccharine waltz and little Belle danced to it with studied, meaningless gestures too thinly conceived and too airily executed to be quite laughable, and stood with her diffident shining among the smug palms. She would have danced again, but Belle rose from the piano, and the guests rose also with prompt unanimity and surrounded her in laudatory sibilance. Belle stood moodily beside her daughter in the center of it, and little Belle pleasurably. Horace rose also. Above the gabbling of the women he could hear Harry again overhead: thump-thump-thump, and he knew that Belle was also listening although she responded faultlessly to the shrill indistinguishable compliments of her guests. Beside little Belle the teacher stood, with her cold, sad eyes, proprietorial and deprecatory, touching little Belle's hair with a meagre passionate hand.

Then they drifted doorward, with their shrill polite uproar. Little Belle slid from among them and came, a little drunk with all the furore and her central figuring in it, and took Horace's hand. "What do you think was the best," she asked. "When I played, or when I danced?"

"I think they both were," he answered.

"I know. But what do you *think* was the best?"

"Well, I think the dancing was, because your mamma was playing for you."

"So do I," little Belle agreed. "They could see all of me when I was dancing, couldn't they? When you are playing, they cant see but your back."

"Yes," Horace agreed. He moved toward the door, little Belle still clinging to his hand.

"I wish they wouldn't go. Why do they have to go now? Cant you stay a while?"

"I must take Narcissa home. She cant go home by herself, you know."

"Yes," little Belle agreed. "Daddy could take her home in our car."

"I expect I'd better do it. But I'll be coming back soon."

"Well, all right, then." Little Belle sighed with weary contentment. "I certainly do like parties; I certainly do. I wish we had one every night." The guests clotted at the door, evacuating with politely trailing phrases into the darkness. Belle stood responding to their recapitulations with smoldering patience. Narcissa stood slightly aside, waiting for him, and Harry was among them again, strident and affable.

"Daddy's gal," he said. "Did Horace see her playing the piano and dancing? Want to go up and take one before you leave?" he asked Horace in a jarring undertone.

"No, thanks. Narcissa's waiting for me. Some other time."

"Sure, sure," Harry agreed, and Horace was aware of Belle beside him, speaking to little Belle, but when he turned his head she was moving away with her silken swishing and her heavy, faint scent. Harry was still talking. "How about a couple of sets tomorrow? Let's get over early, before Belle's gang comes, and get in a couple of fast ones, then let 'em have the court."

"All right," Horace agreed, as he always did to this arrangement, wondering as usual if that boy's optimism of Harry's really permitted him to believe that they could or would follow it out, or if he had just said the phrase so many times that the juxtaposition of the words no longer had any meaning in his liquor-fuddled brain. Then Narcissa was beside him, and they were saying Goodnight, and the door closed upon little Belle, and Harry's glazed squat dome and upon Belle's smoldering and sullen rage. She had said no word to him all evening.

It was the evening of little Belle's recital, the climacteric of her musical year. During the whole evening Belle had not looked at him, had said no word to him, even when, in the departing crush at the door and while Harry was trying to persuade him upstairs for a night-cap, he felt her beside him for an instant, smelled the heavy scent she used. But she said no word to him even then, and he put Harry aside at last and the door closed on little Belle and on Harry's glazed dome, and Horace turned into the darkness and found that Narcissa hadn't waited. She was halfway to the street. "If you're going my way, I'll walk along with you," he called to her. She made no reply, neither did she slacken her pace nor increase it when he joined her.

"Why is it," he began, "that grown people will go to so much trouble to make children do ridiculous things, do you suppose? Belle had a house full of people she doesn't care anything about and most of whom dont approve of her, and kept little Belle up three hours past her bedtime; and the result is Harry's about half tight, and Belle is in a bad humor, and little Belle is too excited to go to sleep, and you and I wish we were home and are sorry we didn't stay there."

"Why do you go there, then?" Narcissa asked. Horace was suddenly stilled. They walked on through the darkness, toward the next street light. Against it branches hung like black coral in a yellow sea.

"Oh," Horace said. Then: "I saw that old cat talking with you."

"Why do you call Mrs Marders an old cat? Because she told me something that concerns me and that everybody else seems to know already?"

"So that's who told you, is it? I wondered. . . . . . . " He slid his arm within her unresponsive one. "Dear old Narcy." They passed through the dappled shadows beneath the light, went on into darkness again.

"Is it true?" she asked.

"You forget that lying is a struggle for survival," he said. "Little puny man's way of dragging circumstance about to fit his preconception of himself as a figure in the world. Revenge on the sinister gods."

"Is it true?" she persisted. They walked on, arm in arm, she gravely insistent and waiting; he shaping and discarding phrases in his mind, finding time to be amused at his own fantastic impotence in the presence of her constancy.

"People dont usually lie about things that dont concern them," he answered wearily. "They are impervious to the world, even if they aren't to life. Not when the actuality is so much more diverting than their imaginings could be," he added. She freed her arm with grave finality.

"Narcy——"

"Dont," she said. "Dont call me that." The next corner, beneath the next light, was theirs; they would turn there. Above the arched canyon of the street the sinister gods stared down with pale, unwinking eyes. Horace thrust his hands into his jacket, and for a space he was stilled again while his fingers learned the unfamiliar object they had found in his pocket. Then he drew it forth: a sheet of heavy notepaper, folded twice and impregnated with a fading heavy scent. A familiar scent, yet baffling for the moment, like a face watching him from an arras. He knew the face would emerge in a moment, but as he held the note in his fingers and sought the face through the corridors of his present distraction, his sister spoke suddenly and hard at his side.

"You've got the smell of her all over you. Oh, Horry, she's dirty!"

"I know," he answered unhappily, and the face emerged clearly, and he was suddenly empty and cold and sad. "I know." It was like a road stretching on through darkness, into nothingness and so away; a road lined with black motionless trees O thou grave myrtle shapes amid which Death. A road along which he and Narcissa walked like two children drawn apart one from the other to opposite sides of it; strangers, yet not daring to separate and go in opposite ways, while the sinister gods watched them with cold unwinking eyes. And somewhere, everywhere, behind and before and about them pervading, the dark warm cave of Belle's rich discontent and the tiger-reek of it.

But the world was opening out before him fearsome and sad and richly moribund, as though he were again an adolescent, and filled with shadowy shapes of dread and of delight not to be denied: he must go on, though the other footsteps sounded fainter and fainter in the darkness behind him and then not at all. Perhaps they had ceased, or turned into a byway.

This byway led her back to Miss Jenny. It was now well into June, and the scent of Miss Jenny's transplanted jasmine drifted steadily into the house and filled it with constant cumulate waves like a fading resonance of viols. The earlier flowers were gone, and the birds had finished eating the strawberries and now sat about the fig bushes all day, waiting for them to ripen; zinnia and delphinium bloomed without any assistance from Isom who, since Caspey had more or less returned to normalcy and laying-by time was yet a while away, might be found on the shady side of the privet hedge along the garden fence, trimming the leaves one by one from a single twig with a pair of mule shears until Miss Jenny returned to the house; whereupon he retreated himself and lay on the creek-bank for the rest of the afternoon, his hat over his eyes and a cane fishing pole propped between his toes. Old Simon pottered querulously about the place. His linen duster and tophat gathered chaff and dust on the nail in the harness room and the horses waxed fat and lazy and insolent in the pasture. The duster and hat came down from the nail and the horses were harnessed to the carriage but once a week, now—on Sundays, to drive in to town to church. Miss Jenny said she was too far along to jeopardize salvation by driving to church at fifty miles an hour; that she had as many sins as her ordinary behavior could take care of, particularly as she had old Bayard's soul to get into heaven somehow, also, what with him and young Bayard tearing around the country every afternoon at the imminent risk of their necks. About young Bayard's soul Miss Jenny did not alarm herself at all: he had no soul.

Meanwhile he rode about the farm and harried the negro tenants in his cold fashion, and in two dollar khaki breeches and a pair of field boots that had cost fourteen guineas he tinkered with farming machinery and with the tractor he had persuaded old Bayard to buy: for the time being he had become almost civilized again. He went to town only occasionally now, and often on horseback, and all in all his days had become so usefully innocuous that both his aunt and his grandfather were growing a little nervously anticipatory.

"Mark my words," Miss Jenny told Narcissa on the day she drove out again. "He's storing up devilment that's going to burst loose all at once, someday, and then there'll be hell to pay. Lord knows what it'll be—maybe he and Isom will take his car and that tractor and hold a steeple chase with 'em. . . . What did you come out for? Got another letter?"

"I've got several more," Narcissa answered lightly. "I'm saving them until I get enough for a book, then I'll bring them all out for you to read." Miss Jenny sat opposite her, erect as a crack guardsman, with that cold briskness of hers that caused agents and strangers to stumble through their errands with premonitions of failure ere they began. The guest sat motionless, her limp straw hat on her knees. "I just came to see you," she added, and for a moment her face held such grave and still despair that Miss Jenny sat more erect yet and stared at her guest with her piercing gray eyes.

"Why, what is it, child? Did the man walk into your house?"

"No, no." The look was gone, but still Miss Jenny watched her with those keen old eyes that seemed to see so much more than you thought—or wished. "Shall I play a while? It's been a long time, hasn't it?"

"Well," Miss Jenny agreed, "if you want to."

There was dust on the piano; Narcissa opened it with a fine gesture. "If you'll let me get a cloth——"

"Here, lemme dust it," Miss Jenny said, and she caught up her skirt by the hem and mopped the keyboard violently. "There, that'll do." Then she drew her chair from behind the instrument and seated herself. She still watched the other's profile with speculation and a little curiosity, but presently the old tunes stirred her memory again, and in a while her eyes softened and the other and the trouble that had shown momentarily in her face, were lost in Miss Jenny's own vanquished and abiding dead days, and it was some time before she realized that Narcissa was weeping quietly while she played.

Miss Jenny leaned forward and touched her arm. "Now,

you tell me what it is," she commanded. And Narcissa told her in her grave contralto, still weeping quietly.

"Hmph," Miss Jenny said. "That's to be expected of a man that hasn't any more to do than Horace. I dont see why you are so upset over it."

"But that woman," Narcissa wailed suddenly, like a little girl, burying her face in her hands. "She's so dirty!"

Miss Jenny dug a man's handkerchief from the pocket of her skirt and gave it to the other:

"What do you mean?" she asked. "Dont she wash often enough?"

"Not that way. I m-mean she's—she's——" Narcissa turned suddenly and laid her head on the piano.

"Oh," Miss Jenny said. "All women are, if that's what you mean." She sat stiffly indomitable, contemplating the other's shrinking shoulders. "Hmph," she said again. "Horace has spent so much time being educated that he never has learned anything. . . . . . . Why didn't you break it up in time? Didn't you see it coming?"

The other wept more quietly now. She sat up and dried her eyes on Miss Jenny's handkerchief. "It started before he went away. Dont you remember?"

"That's so. I do sort of remember a lot of women's gabble. Who told you about it, anyway? Horace?"

"Mrs Marders did. And then Horace did. But I never thought that he'd—I never thought——" again her head dropped to the piano, hidden in her arms. "I wouldn't have treated Horace that way," she wailed.

"Sarah Marders, was it? I might have known. . . . . . . I admire strong character, even if it is bad," Miss Jenny stated. "Well, crying wont help any." She rose briskly. "We'll think what to do about it. Only I'd let him go ahead: it'll do him good if she'll just turn around and make a doormat of him. . . . . . .

Too bad Harry hasn't got spunk enough to. . . . But I reckon he'll be glad; I know I would—— There, there," she said, at the other's movement of alarm. "I dont reckon Harry'll hurt him. Dry your face, now. You better go to the bathroom and fix up. Bayard'll be coming in soon, and you dont want him to see you've been crying, you know." Narcissa glanced swiftly at the door and dabbed at her face with Miss Jenny's handkerchief.

At times the dark lifted, the black trees were no longer sinister, and then Horace and Narcissa walked the road in sunlight, as of old. Then he would seek her through the house and cross the drive and descend the lawn in the sunny afternoon to where she sat in the white dresses he loved beneath the oak into which a mockingbird came each afternoon and sang, bringing her the result of his latest venture in glass-blowing. He had five now, in different colors and all nearly perfect, and each of them had a name. And as he finished them and before they were scarce cooled, he must bring them across the lawn to where she sat with a book or with a startled caller perhaps, in his stained dishevelled clothes and his sooty hands in which the vase lay demure and fragile as a bubble, and with his face blackened too with smoke and a little mad, passionate and fine and austere.

But then the dark would descend once more, and beyond the black and motionless trees Belle's sultry imminence was like a presence, like the odor of death. And then he and Narcissa were strangers again, tugging and straining at the shackles of custom and old affection that bound them with slipping bonds.

And then they were no longer even side by side. At times he called back to her through the darkness, making no sound and receiving no reply; at times he hovered distractedly like a dark bird between the two of them. But at last he merged with himself, fused in the fatalism of his nature, and set his face steadily up the road, looking not back again. And then the footsteps behind him ceased.

5

For a time the earth held him in a hiatus that might have been called contentment. He was up at sunrise, planting things in the ground and watching them grow and tending them; he cursed and harried niggers and mules into motion and kept them there, and put the grist mill into running shape and taught Caspey to drive the tractor, and came in at mealtimes and at night smelling of machine oil and of stables and of the earth and went to bed with grateful muscles and with the sober rhythms of the earth in his body, and so to sleep. But he still waked at times in the peaceful darkness of his room and without previous warning, tense and sweating with old terror. Then, momentarily, the world was laid away and he was a trapped beast in the high blue, mad for life, trapped in the very cunning fabric that had betrayed him who had dared chance too much, and he thought again if, when the bullet found you, you could only crash upward, burst; anything but earth. Not death, no: it was the crash you had to live through so many times before you struck that filled your throat with vomit.

But his days were filled, at least, and he discovered pride again. Nowadays he drove the car into town to fetch his grandfather from habit alone, and though he still considered forty five miles an hour merely cruising speed, he no longer took cold and fiendish pleasure in turning curves on two wheels or in detaching mules from wagons by striking the whiffle-trees with his bumper in passing. Old Bayard still insisted on riding with him when he must ride, but with freer breath; and once he aired to Miss Jenny his growing belief that at last young Bayard had outworn his seeking for violent destruction.

Miss Jenny, being a true optimist—that is, expecting the worst at all times and so being daily agreeably surprised—promptly disillusioned him. Meanwhile she made young Bayard drink plenty of milk and otherwise superintended his diet and hours in her martinettish way, and at times she entered his room at night and sat for a while beside the bed where he slept.

Nevertheless, young Bayard improved in his ways. Without being aware of the progress of it, he had become submerged in a monotony of days, had been snared by a rhythm of activities repeated and repeated until his muscles grew so familiar with them as to get his body through the days without assistance from him at all. He had been so neatly tricked by earth, that ancient Delilah, that he was not aware that his locks were shorn, was not aware that Miss Jenny and old Bayard were wondering how long it would be before they grew out again. He needs a wife, was Miss Jenny's thought. Then maybe he'll stay sheared. "A young person to worry with him," she said to herself. "Bayard's too old, and I've got too much to do, to worry with the long devil."

He saw Narcissa about the house now and then, sometimes at the table these days, and he still felt her shrinking and her distaste, and at times Miss Jenny sat watching the two of them with a sort of speculation and an exasperation with their seeming obliviousness of one another. He treats her like a dog would treat a cut-glass pitcher, and she looks at him like a cut-glass pitcher would look at a dog, she told herself.

Then sowing time was over, and it was summer, and he found himself with nothing to do. It was like coming dazed out of sleep, out of the warm, sunny valleys where people lived into a region where cold peaks of savage despair stood bleakly above the lost valleys, among black and savage stars.

The road descended in a quiet red curve between pines through which the hot July winds swelled with a long sound like a far away passing of trains, descended to a mass of lighter green of willows, where a creek ran beneath a stone bridge. At the top of the grade the scrubby, rabbitlike mules stopped and the younger negro got down and lifted a gnawed white-oak sapling from the wagon and locked the off rear wheel by wedging the pole between the warped wire-bound spokes of it and across the axle-tree. Then he climbed back into the crazy wagon, where the other negro sat motionless with the rope-spliced reins in his hand and his head tilted creekward. "Whut 'us dat?" he said.

"Whut wuz whut?" the other asked. His father sat in his attitude of arrested attention, and the younger negro listened also. But there was no further sound save the long sough of the wind among the sober pines and the liquid whistling of a quail somewhere among the green fastnesses of them. "Whut you hear, pappy?" he repeated.

"Somethin' busted down dar. Tree fell, mebbe." He jerked the reins. "Hwup, mules." The mules flapped their jackrabbit ears and lurched the wagon into motion, and they descended among cool dappled shadows, on the jarring scrape of the locked wheel that left behind it a glazed bluish ribbon in the soft red dust. At the foot of the hill the road crossed the bridge and went on mounting again; beneath the bridge the creek rippled and flashed brownly among willows, and beside the bridge and bottom up in the water, a motor car lay. Its front wheels were still spinning and the engine ran at idling speed, trailing a faint shimmer of exhaust. The older negro drove onto the bridge and stopped, and the two of them sat and stared statically down upon the car's long belly. The younger negro spoke suddenly:

"Dar he is! He in de water under hit. I kin see his foots stickin' out."

"He liable ter drown, dar," the other said, with interest and disapproval, and they descended from the wagon. The younger negro slid down the creek bank; the other wrapped the reins deliberately about one of the stakes that held the bed on the frame and thrust his peeled hickory goad beneath the seat and went around and dragged the pole free of the locked wheel and put it in the wagon. Then he also slid gingerly down the bank to where his son squatted, peering at Bayard's submerged legs.

"Dont you git too clost ter dat thing, boy," he commanded. "Hit mought blow up. Dont you year hit still grindin' in dar?"

"We got to git dat man out," the younger one replied. "He gwine drown."

"Dont you tech 'im. White folks be sayin' we done it. We gwine wait right heer 'twell some white man comes erlong."

"He'll drown 'fo' dat," the other said. "Layin' in dat water." He was barefoot, and he stepped into the water and stood again with brown flashing wings of water stemming about his lean black calves.

"You, John Henry!" his father said. "You come 'way fum dat thing."

"We got to git 'im outen dar," the boy repeated, and the one in the water and the other on the bank, they wrangled amicably while the water rippled about Bayard's boot toes. Then the younger negro approached warily and caught Bayard's leg and tugged at it. The body responded, shifted, stopped again, and grunting querulously the older negro sat and removed his shoes and stepped into the water also. "He hung again," John Henry said, squatting in the water with his arm beneath the car. "He hung under de guidin' wheel. His haid aint quite under water, dough. Lemme git de pole."

He mounted the bank and got the sapling from the wagon and returned and joined his father where the other stood in sober, curious disapproval above Bayard's legs, and with the pole they lifted the car enough to drag Bayard out. They lifted him onto the bank and he sprawled there in the sun, with his calm wet face and his matted hair, while water drained out of his boots, and they stood above him on alternate legs and wrung out their overalls.

"Hit's Cunnel Sartorises boy, aint it?" the elder said at last, and he lowered himself stiffly to the sand, groaning and grunting, and donned his shoes.

"Yessuh," the other answered. "Is he daid, pappy?"

"Co'se he is," the other answered pettishly. "Atter dat otto'-bile jumped offen dat bridge wid 'im en den trompled 'im in de creek? Whut you reckon he is, ef he aint daid? And whut you gwine say when de law axes you how come you de onliest one dat foun' 'im daid? Tell me dat."

"Tell 'um you holp me."

"Hit aint none of my business. I never run dat thing offen dat bridge. Listen at it, dar, mumblin' and grindin' yit. You git on 'fo' hit blows up."

"We better git 'im into town," John Henry said. "Dey mought not nobody else be comin' 'long today." He stooped and lifted Bayard's shoulders and tugged him to a sitting position. "He'p me git 'im up de bank, pappy."

"Hit aint none o' my business," the other repeated, but he stooped and picked up Bayard's legs and they lifted him, and he groaned without waking.

"Dar, now," John Henry exclaimed. "Year dat? He aint daid." But he might well have been, with his long inert body and his head wrung excruciatingly against John Henry's shoulder. They shifted their grips and turned toward the road. "Hah," John Henry exclaimed. "Le's go!"

They struggled up the shaling bank with him and onto the road, where the elder let his end of the burden slip to the ground. "Whuf," he expelled his breath sharply. "He heavy ez a flou' bar'l."

"Come on, pappy," John Henry said. "Le's git 'im in de waggin." The other stooped again, and they raised Bayard with dust caked redly on his wet thighs, and heaved him by grunting stages into the wagon. "He look lak a daid man," John Henry added, "and he sho' do ack lak one. I'll ride back here wid 'im and keep his haid fum bumpin'."

"Git dat brakin' pole you lef' in de creek," his father ordered, and John Henry descended and retrieved the sapling and got in the wagon again and lifted Bayard's head onto his knees, and his father unwrapped the reins and mounted to the sagging seat and picked up his peeled wand.

"I dont lak dis kin' o' traffickin'," he repeated. "Hwup, mules." The mules lurched the wagon into motion once more, and they went on. Behind them the car lay on its back in the creek, its engine still muttering at idling speed.

Its owner lay in the springless wagon, lax and inert with the jolting of it. Thus for some miles, while John Henry held his battered straw hat between the white man's face and the sun. Then the jolting penetrated into that region where Bayard lay, and he groaned again. "Drive slower, pappy," John Henry said. "De joltin' wakin' 'im up."

"I caint he'p dat," the elder replied. "I never run dat otto'-bile offen dat bridge. I got to git on into town en git on back home. Git on dar, mules."

John Henry made to ease him to the jolting, and Bayard groaned again and raised his hand to his chest, and he moved and opened his eyes. But he closed them immediately against the sun and he lay with his head on John Henry's knees, cursing. Then he moved again, trying to sit up. John Henry held him down, and he opened his eyes again, struggling.

"Let go, God damn you!" he said. "I'm hurt."

"Yessuh, captain; ef you'll jes' lay still——"

Bayard heaved himself violently, clutching his side; his teeth glared between his drawn lips and he gripped John Henry's shoulder with a clutch like steel hooks. "Stop," he shouted, glaring wildly at the back of the older negro's head. "Stop him; make him stop! He's driving my damn ribs right through me." He cursed again, trying to get onto his knees, gripping John Henry's shoulder, clutching his side with his other hand. The older negro turned and looked back at him. "Hit him with something," Bayard shouted. "Make him stop. I'm hurt, God damn it!"

The wagon stopped. Bayard was now on all fours, his head hanging and swaying from side to side like a wounded beast. The two negroes watched him quietly, and still clutching his side he moved and essayed to climb out of the wagon. John Henry jumped down and helped him, and he got slowly out and leaned against the wheel, with his sweating, bloodless face and his clenched grin.

"Git back in de waggin, captain," John Henry said, "and le's git to town to de doctor."

The color seemed to have drained from his eyes too. He leaned against the wagon, moistening his lips with his tongue. He moved again and sat down at the roadside, fumbling at the buttons of his shirt. The two negroes watched him.

"Got a knife, son?" he said.

"Yessuh." John Henry produced it, and by Bayard's direction he slit the shirt off. Then with the negro's help Bayard bound it tightly about his body, and he got to his feet.

"Got a cigarette?"

John Henry had not. "Pappy got some chewin' terbacker," he suggested.

"Gimme a chew, then." They gave him a chew and helped him back into the wagon and onto the seat. The other negro took up the lines. They jingled and rattled interminably on in the red dust, from shadow to sunlight, up hill and down. Bayard clutched his chest with his arms and chewed and cursed steadily. On and on, and at every jolt, with every breath, his broken ribs stabbed and probed into his flesh; on and on from shadow to sunlight and into shadow again.

A final hill, and the road emerged from the shade and crossed the flat treeless valley and joined the highway, and here they stopped, the sun blazing downward on his naked shoulders and bare head while he and the old negro wrangled as to whether they should take Bayard home or not. Bayard raged and swore but the other was querulously adamant, whereupon Bayard took the reins from his hands and swung the mules up the valley and with the end of the reins lashed the astonished creatures into mad motion.

This last mile was the worst of all. On all sides of them cultivated fields spread away to the shimmering hills: earth was saturated with heat and broken and turned and saturated again and drunken with it; exuding heat like an alcoholic's breath. The trees along the road were sparse and but half grown, and the mules slowed to a maddening walk in their own dust. He surrendered the reins again, and in a red doze he clung to the seat, conscious only of dreadful thirst, knowing that he was becoming light headed. The negroes too realized that he was going out of his head, and the younger one removed his frayed hat and Bayard put it on.

The mules with their comical, over-large ears assumed fantastic shapes, merged into other shapes without significance;

shifted and merged again. At times it seemed to him that they were travelling backward, that they would crawl terrifically past the same tree or telephone pole time after time; and it seemed to him that the three of them and the rattling wagon and the two beasts were caught in a senseless treadmill: a motion without progress, forever and to no escape.

But at last and without his being aware of it, the wagon turned in between the iron gates, and shadow fell upon his naked shoulders, and he opened his eyes and his home swam and floated in a pale mirage. The jolting stopped and the two negroes helped him down and the younger one followed him to the steps, holding his arm. But he flung him off and mounted and crossed the veranda; in the hallway, after the outer glare, he could see nothing for a moment and he stood swaying and a little nauseated, blinking. Then Simon's eyeballs rolled out of the obscurity.

"Whut in de Lawd's name," Simon said, "is you been into now?"

"Simon?" he said. He swayed, staggered for balance, and blundered into something. "Simon?"

Simon moved quickly and touched him. "I kep' tellin' you dat car 'uz gwine kill you; I kep' tellin' you!" Simon slid his arm about Bayard and led him on toward the stairs. But he would not turn here, and they went on down the hall and Simon helped him into the office and he stopped, leaning on a chair.

"Keys," he said thickly. "Aunt Jenny. Get drink."

"Miss Jenny done gone to town wid Miss Benbow," Simon answered. "Dey aint nobody here, aint nobody here a-tall 'cep' de niggers. I kep' tellin' you!" he moaned again, pawing at Bayard. "Dey aint no blood, dough. Come to de sofa and lay down, Mist' Bayard."

Bayard moved again, and Simon supported him, and

Bayard lurched around the chair and slumped into it, clutching his chest. "Dey aint no blood," Simon babbled.

"Keys," Bayard repeated. "Get the keys."

"Yessuh, I'll git 'um." But he continued to flap his distracted hands about Bayard until Bayard swore at him and flung him violently off. Still moaning Dey aint no blood, Simon turned and scuttled from the room. Bayard sat forward, clutching his chest, and heard Simon mount the stairs, and cross the floor overhead. Then he was back, and Bayard watched him open the desk and extract the silver stoppered decanter. He set it down and scuttled out again and returned with a glass, to find Bayard beside the desk, drinking from the decanter. Simon helped him back to the chair and poured him a drink into the glass. Then he fetched him a cigarette and hovered futilely and distractedly about him. "Lemme git de doctuh, Mist' Bayard."

"No. Gimme another drink."

Simon obeyed. "Dat's three, already. Lemme go git Miss Jenny en de doctuh, Mist' Bayard, please, suh."

"No. Leave me alone. Get out of here."

He drank that one. The nausea, the mirage shapes, were gone, and he felt better. At every breath his side stabbed him with hot needles, so he was careful to breathe shallowly. If he could only remember that. . . . . . Yes, he felt much better, so he rose carefully and went to the desk and had another drink. Yes, that was the stuff for a wound, like Suratt had said. Like that time he got that tracer in his belly and nothing would stay on his stomach except gin-and-milk. And this, this wasn't anything: just a few caved slats. Patch up his fuselage with a little piano wire in ten minutes. Not like Johnny. They were all going right into his thighs. Damn butcher wouldn't even raise his sights a little. He must remember to breathe shallowly.

He crossed the room slowly. Simon flitted in the dim hall

before him, and he mounted the stairs slowly, holding to the rail while Simon flapped his hands and watched him. He entered his room, the room that had been his and John's, and he stood for a while against the wall until he could breathe shallowly again. Then he crossed to the closet and opened it, and kneeling carefully, with his hand against his side, he opened the chest which was there. There was not much in it: a garment; a small leather-bound book; a shotgun shell to which was attached by a bit of wire a withered bear's paw. It was John's first bear, and the shell with which he had killed it in the river bottom near MacCallum's when he was twelve years old. The book was a new testament; on the flyleaf in faded brown: 'To my son, John, on his seventh birthday, March 16, 1900, from his Mother.' He had one exactly like it; that was the year grandfather had arranged for the morning local freight to stop and pick them up and take them in to town to start to school. The garment was a canvas hunting coat, stained and splotched with what had once been blood and scuffed and torn by briers and smelling yet faintly of saltpeter.

Still kneeling, he lifted the objects out one by one and laid them on the floor. He picked up the coat again, and its fading stale acridity drifted in his nostrils with an intimation of life and warmth. "Johnny," he whispered, "Johnny." Suddenly he raised he garment toward his face but halted it as sharply, and with the coat half raised he looked swiftly over his shoulder. But immediately he recovered himself and turned his head and lifted the garment and laid his face against it, defiantly and deliberately, and knelt so for a time.

Then he rose and gathered up the book and the trophy and the coat and crossed to his chest of drawers and took from it a photograph. It was a picture of John's Princeton eating club group, and he gathered this also under his arm and descended the stairs and passed on out the back door. As he emerged

Simon was just crossing the yard with the carriage, and as he passed the kitchen Elnora was crooning one of her mellow endless songs.

Behind the smoke-house squatted the black pot and the wooden tubs where Elnora did her washing in fair weather. She had been washing today; the clothes line swung with its damp, limp burden, and beneath the pot smoke yet curled from the soft ashes. He thrust the pot over with his foot and rolled it aside, and from the woodshed he fetched an armful of rich pine and laid it on the ashes. Soon a blaze, pale in the sunny air; and when the wood was burning strongly he laid the coat and the bible and the trophy and the photograph on the flames and prodded them and turned them until they were consumed. In the kitchen Elnora crooned mellowly as she labored; her voice came rich and plaintful and sad along the sunny reaches of the air. He must remember to breathe shallowly.

Simon drove rapidly to town, but he had been forestalled. The two negroes had told a merchant about finding Bayard on the roadside and the news had reached the bank, and old Bayard sent for Dr Peabody. But Dr Peabody was gone fishing, so he took Dr Alford instead, and the two of them in Dr Alford's car passed Simon just on the edge of town. He turned about and followed them, but by the time he arrived home they had young Bayard anaesthetized and temporarily incapable of further harm; and when Miss Jenny and Narcissa drove unsuspectingly up the drive an hour later, he was bandaged and conscious again. They had not heard of it. Miss Jenny did not recognise Dr Alford's car standing in the drive, but she had one look at the strange motor. "That fool has killed himself at last," she said, and she got out of Narcissa's machine and sailed into the house and up the stairs.

Bayard lay white and still and a little sheepish in his bed. Old Bayard and the doctor were just leaving, and Miss Jenny waited until they were out of the room, then she raged and stormed at him and stroked his hair, while Simon bobbed and bowed in the corner between bed and wall. "Dasso, Miss Jenny, dasso! I kep' a-tellin' 'im!"

She left him then and descended to the veranda where Dr Alford stood in impeccable departure. Old Bayard sat in the car waiting for him, and on Miss Jenny's appearance he became his stiff self again and completed his departing, and he and old Bayard drove away.

Miss Jenny also looked up and down the veranda, then into the hall. "Where—" she said, then she called: "Narcissa." A reply; "Where are you?" she added. The reply came again and Miss Jenny reentered the house and saw Narcissa's white dress in the gloom where she sat on the piano bench. "He's awake," Miss Jenny said. "You can come up and see him." The other rose and turned her face to the light. "Why, what's the matter?" Miss Jenny demanded. "You look lots worse than he does. You're white as a sheet."

"Nothing," the other answered. "I——" She stared at Miss Jenny a moment, clenching her hands at her sides. "I must go," she said, and she emerged into the hall. "It's late, and Horace. . . . . . . "

"You can come up and speak to him, cant you?" Miss Jenny asked, curiously. "There's not any blood, if that's what you are afraid of."

"It isn't that," Narcissa answered. "I'm not afraid."

Miss Jenny approached her, piercing and curious. "Why, all right," she said kindly. "If you'd rather not. I just thought perhaps you'd like to see he's all right, as long as you are here. But dont, if you dont feel like it."

"Yes. Yes. I feel like it. I want to." She passed Miss Jenny

and went on. At the foot of the stairs she paused until Miss
Jenny came up behind her, then she went on, mounting
swiftly and with her face averted.

"What's the matter with you?" Miss Jenny demanded, trying to see the other's face. "What's happened to you? Have you
gone and fallen in love with him?"

"In love . . . him? Bayard?" She paused, then hurried on,
clutching the rail. She began to laugh thinly, and put her hand
to her mouth. Miss Jenny mounted beside her, piercing and
curious and cold; Narcissa hurried on. At the stair head she
stopped again, still with her face averted, and let Miss Jenny
pass her; and just without the door she stopped and leaned
against it, throttling her laughter and her trembling. Then she
entered the room, where Miss Jenny stood beside the bed
watching her.

There was a sickish-sweet lingering of ether in the room,
and she approached the bed blindly and stood beside it with
her hidden clenched hands. Bayard's head was pallid and
calm, like a chiseled mask brushed lightly over with his spent
violence, and he was watching her, and for a while she gazed at
him; and Miss Jenny and the room and all, swam away.

"You beast, you beast," she cried thinly. "Why must you
always do these things where I've got to see you?"

"I didn't know you were there," Bayard answered mildly,
with weak astonishment.

Every few days, by Miss Jenny's request, she came out and
sat beside his bed and read to him. He cared nothing at all
about books; it is doubtful if he had ever read a book on his
own initiative; but he would lie motionless in his cast while her
grave contralto voice went on and on in the quiet room. Sometimes he tried to talk to her, but she ignored his attempts and
read on; if he persisted, she went away and left him. So he soon

learned to lie, usually with his eyes closed, voyaging alone in the bleak and barren regions of his despair, while her voice flowed on and on above the remoter sounds that came up to them—Miss Jenny scolding Simon or Isom downstairs or in the garden; the twittering of birds in the tree just beyond the window; the ceaseless groaning of the water pump below the barn. At times she would cease and look at him and find that he was peacefully sleeping.

6

Old man Falls came through the lush green of early June, came into town through the yet horizontal sunlight of morning, and in his dusty neat overalls he now sat opposite old Bayard in immaculate linen and a geranium like a merry wound. The room was cool and still, with the clear morning light and the casual dust of a negro janitor's casual and infrequent disturbing. Now that old Bayard was aging, and what with the deaf tenor of his stiffening ways, he was showing more and more a preference for surrounding himself with things of a like nature; showing an incredible aptitude for choosing servants who shaped their days to his in a sort of pottering and hopeless futility. The janitor, who dubbed old Bayard General and whom old Bayard and the other clients for whom he performed seemingly interminable duties of a slovenly and minor nature, addressed as Dr Jones, was one of these. He was black and stooped with querulousness and age, and he took advantage of everyone who would permit him, and old Bayard swore at him all the time he was around and allowed him to steal his tobacco and the bank's winter supply of coal by the scuttleful and peddle it to other negroes.

The windows behind which old Bayard and his caller sat

gave upon a vacant lot of rubbish and dusty weeds. It was bounded by the weathered rears of sundry one storey board buildings within which small businesses—repair- and junk-shops and such—had their lowly and ofttimes anonymous being. The lot itself was used by day by country people as a depot for their teams; already some of these were tethered som-nolent and ruminant there, and about the stale ammoniac droppings of their patient generations sparrows swirled in gar-rulous clouds, or pigeons slanted with sounds like rusty shut-ters, or strode and preened in burnished and predatory pomposity, crooning among themselves with guttural unem-phasis.

Old man Falls sat on the opposite side of the trash-filled fireplace, mopping his face with a clean blue bandanna.

"It's my damned old legs," he roared, faintly apologetic. "Used to be I'd walk twelve-fifteen mile to a picnic or a singin' with less study than what that 'ere little old three mile into town gives me now." He mopped the handkerchief about that face of his browned and cheerful these many years with the simple and abounding earth. "Looks like they're fixin' to give out on me, and I aint but ninety-three, neither." He held his parcel in his other hand, but he continued to mop his face, making no motion to open it.

"Why didn't you wait on the road until a wagon came along?" old Bayard shouted. "Always some damn feller with a field full of weeds coming to town."

"I reckon I mought," the other agreed. "But gittin' here so quick would spile my holiday. I aint like you townfolks. I aint got so much time I kin hurry it." He stowed the handkerchief away and rose and laid his parcel carefully on the mantel, and from his shirt he produced a small object wrapped in a clean frayed rag. Beneath his tedious and unhurried fingers there emerged a tin snuff-box polished long since to the dull soft sheen of silver by handling and age. Old Bayard sat and watched, watched quietly as the other removed the cap of the box and put this, too, carefully aside.

"Now, turn yo' face up to the light," old man Falls directed.

"Loosh Peabody says that stuff will give me blood-poisoning, Will."

The other continued his slow preparations, his blue innocent eyes raptly preoccupied. "Loosh Peabody never said that," he corrected quietly. "One of them young doctors told you that, Bayard. Lean yo' face to the light." Old Bayard sat tautly back in his chair, his hands on the arms of it, watching the other with his piercing old eyes soberly, a little wistful; eyes filled with unnameable things like the eyes of old lions, and intent.

Old man Falls poised a dark gob of his ointment on one finger and set the box carefully on his vacated chair, and put his hand on old Bayard's face. But old Bayard still resisted, though passively, watching him with unutterable things in his eyes. Old man Falls drew his face firmly and gently into the light from the window.

"Come on, here. I aint young enough to waste time hurtin' folks. Hold still, now, so I wont spot yo' face up. My hand aint steady enough to lift a rifle ball offen a hot stove-led no mo'."

Bayard submitted then, and old man Falls patted the salve onto the wen with small deft touches. Then he took the bit of cloth and removed the surplus from Bayard's face and wiped his fingers and dropped the rag onto the hearth and knelt stiffly and touched a match to it. "We allus do that," he explained. "My granny got that 'ere from a Choctaw woman nigh a hundred and thutty year ago. Aint none of us never told what hit air nor left no after trace." He rose stiffly and dusted his knees. He recapped the box with the same unhurried care and put it away and picked up his parcel from the mantel and resumed his chair.

"Hit'll turn black tomorrer, and long's hit's black, hit's workin'. Dont put no water on yo' face befo' mawnin', and I'll come in again in ten days and dose hit again, and on the——" he mused a moment, computing slowly on his gnarled fingers; his lips moved, but with no sound. "——the ninth day of July, hit'll drap off. And dont you let Miss Jenny nor none of them doctors worry you about hit."

He sat with his knees together. The parcel lay on his knees and he now opened it after the ancient laborious ritual, picking patiently at the pink knot until a younger person would have screamed at him. Old Bayard merely lit a cigar and propped his feet against the fireplace, and in good time old man Falls solved the knot and removed the string and laid it across his chair-arm. It fell to the floor and he bent and fumbled it into his blunt fingers and laid it again across the chair-arm and watched it a moment lest it fall again, then he opened the parcel. First was his carton of tobacco, and he removed a plug and sniffed it, turned it about in his hand and sniffed it again. But without biting into it he laid it and its fellows aside and delved further yet. He spread open the throat of the resulting paper bag, and his innocent boy's eyes gloated soberly into it.

"I'll declare," he said. "Sometimes I'm right ashamed for havin' sech a consarned sweet-tooth. Hit dont give me no rest a-tall." Still carefully guarding the other objects on his knees he tilted the sack and shook two or three of the striped, shrimp-like things into his palm, returned all but one, which he put into his mouth. "I'm afeard now I'll be loosin' my teeth some-day and I'll have to start gummin' 'em or eatin' soft ones. I never did relish soft candy." His leathery cheek bulged slightly, with slow regularity like a respiration. He peered into the sack again, and he sat weighing it in his hand.

"They was times back in sixty three and fo' when a feller could a bought a section of land and a couple of niggers with this yere bag of candy. Lots of times I mind, with ever'thing goin' agin us like, and sugar and cawfee gone and food scace, eatin' stole cawn when they was any to steal and ditch weeds ef they wa'nt; bivouackin' at night in the rain, more'n like. . . . . . ." His voice trailed away among ancient phantoms of the soul's and body's tribulations, into those regions of glamorous and useless strivings where such ghosts abide. He chuckled and mouthed his peppermint again.

"I mind that day we was a-dodgin' around Grant's army, headin' nawth. Grant was at Grenada then, and Cunnel had rousted us boys out and we taken hoss and jined Van Dorn down that-a-way. That was when Cunnel had that 'ere silver stallion. Grant was still at Grenada, but Van Dorn lit out one day, headin' nawth; why, us boys didn't know. Cunnel mought have knowed, but he never told us. Not that we keered much, long's we was headin' to'ds home.

"So our boys was ridin' along to ourselves, goin' to jine up with the balance of 'em later. Leastways the rest of 'em thought we was goin' to jine 'em. But Cunnel never had no idea of doin' that; his cawn hadn't been laid by yit, and he was goin' home fer a spell. We wasn't runnin' away," he explained. "We knowed Van Dorn could handle 'em all right fer a week or two. He usually done it. He was a putty good man," old man Falls said. "A putty good man."

"They were all pretty good men in those days," old Bayard agreed. "But you damn fellers quit fighting and went home too often."

"Well," old man Falls rejoined defensively, "even ef the hull country's overrun with bears, a feller cant hunt bears all the time. He's got to quit once in a while, ef hit's only to rest up the dawgs and hosses. But I reckon them dogs and hosses could stay on the trail long as any," he added with sober pride. "'Course ever'body couldn't keep up with that 'ere mist-colored stallion. They wasn't but one animal in the Confedrit army could tech him—that last hoss Zeb Fothergill fotch back outen one of Sherman's cavalry pickets on his last trip into Tennessee.

"Nobody never did know what Zeb done on them trips of his'n; Cunnel claimed hit was jest to steal hosses. But he never got back with lessen one. One time he come back with seven of the orneriest critters that ever walked, I reckon. He tried to swap 'em fer meat and cawn-meal, but wouldn't nobody have 'em; then he tried to give 'em to the army, but even the army wouldn't have 'em. So he finally turned 'em loose and requisitioned to Joe Johnston's haidquarters fer ten hosses sold to Forrest's cavalry. I dont know ef he ever got air answer. Nate Forrest wouldn't a had them hosses. I doubt ef they'd even a et 'em in Vicksburg. . . . . . . I never did put no big reliability in Zeb Fothergill, him comin' and goin' by hisself like he done. But he knowed hosses, and he usually fotch a good 'un home ever' time he went away to'ds the war. But he never got anoth- er'n like this befo'."

The bulge was gone from his cheek and he produced his pocket knife and cut a neat segment from his plug of tobacco and lipped it from the knife-blade. Then he rewrapped his par- cel and tied the string about it. The ash of old Bayard's cigar trembled delicately about its glowing heart, but did not yet fall.

Old man Falls spat neatly and brownly into the cold fire- place. "That day we was in Calhoun county," he continued. "Hit was as putty a summer mawnin' as you ever see; men and hosses rested and fed and feelin' peart, trottin' along the road through the woods and fields whar birds was a-singin' and young rabbits lopin' acrost the road. Cunnel and Zeb was ridin' along side by side on them two hosses, Cunnel on Jupiter and Zeb on that sorrel two-year-old, and they was a-braggin' as usual. We all knowed Cunnel's Jupiter, but Zeb kep' a-contendin' he wouldn't take no man's dust. The road was putty straight across the bottom to'ds the river and Zeb kep' on a-aggin' the Cunnel fer a race, until Cunnel says All right. He told us boys to come on and him and Zeb would wait fer us at the river bridge 'bout fo' mile ahead, and him and Zeb lined up and lit out.

"Them hosses was the puttiest livin' things I ever seen. They went off together like two hawks, neck and neck. They was outen sight in no time, with dust swirlin' behind, but we could foller 'em fer a ways by the dust they left, watchin' it kind of suckin' on down the road like one of these here ottomobiles was in the middle of it. When they come to whar the road drapped down to the river Cunnel had Zeb beat by about three hundred yards. Thar was a spring-branch jest under the ridge, and when Cunnel sailed over the rise, thar was a comp'ny of Yankee cavalry with their hosses picketed and their muskets stacked, eatin' dinner by the spring. Cunnel says they was a-settin' thar gapin' at the rise when he come over hit, holdin' cups of cawfee and hunks of bread in their hands and their muskets stacked about fo'ty foot away, buggin' their eyes at him.

"It was too late fer him to turn back, anyhow, but I dont reckon he would ef they'd been time. He jest spurred down the ridge and rid in amongst 'em, scatterin' cook-fires and guns and men, shoutin' 'Surround 'em, boys! Ef you move, you air dead men.' One or two of 'em made to break away, but Cunnel drawed his pistols and let 'em off, and they come back and scrouged in amongst the others, and thar they set, still a-holdin' their dinner, when Zeb come up. And that was the way we found 'em when we got thar ten minutes later." Old man Falls spat again, neatly and brownly, and he chuckled. His eyes shone like periwinkles. "That cawfee was sho' mighty fine," he added.

"And thar we was, with a passel of prisoners we didn't have

no use fer. We held 'em all that day and et their grub; and when night come we taken and throwed their muskets into the crick and taken their ammunition and the rest of the grub and put a gyard on their hosses, then the rest of us laid down. And all that night we laid thar in them fine Yankee blankets, listenin' to them prisoners sneakin' away one at a time, slippin' down the bank into the crick and wadin' off. Time to time one would slip er make a splash er somethin', then they'd all git right still fer a spell. But putty soon we'd hear 'em at it again, crawlin' through the bushes to'ds the crick, and us layin' thar with blanket aidges held agin our faces. Hit was nigh dawn 'fore the last one had snuck off in a way that suited 'im.

"Then Cunnel from whar he was a-layin' let out a yell them pore critters could hear fer a mile.

" 'Go it, Yank,' he says, 'and look out fer moccasins!'

"Next mawnin' we saddled up and loaded our plunder and ever' man taken him a hoss, and lit out fer home. We'd been home two weeks and Cunnel had his cawn laid by, when we heard 'bout Van Dorn ridin' into Holly Springs and burnin' Grant's sto's. Seems like he never needed no help from us, noways." He chewed his tobacco for a time, quietly retrospective, reliving in the company of men now dust with the dust for which they had, unwittingly perhaps, fought, those gallant, pinch-bellied days into which few who now trod that earth could enter with him.

Old Bayard shook the ash from his cigar. "Will," he said, "what the devil were you folks fighting about, anyhow?"

"Bayard," old man Falls answered. "Be damned ef I ever did know."

After old man Falls had departed with his small parcel and his innocently bulging cheek, old Bayard sat and smoked his cigar. Presently he raised his hand and touched the wen on his face, but lightly, remembering old man Falls' parting stricture; and recalling this, the thought that it might not yet be too late, that he might yet remove the paste with water, followed.

He rose and crossed to the lavatory in the corner of the room. Above it was fixed a small cabinet with a mirror in the door, and in it he examined the black spot on his cheek, touching it again with his fingers, then examining his hand. Yes, it might still come off. . . . . . . But be damned if he would; be damned to a man who didn't know his own mind. And Will Falls, too; Will Falls, hale and sane and sound as a dollar; Will Falls who, as he himself had said, was too old to have any reason for injuring anyone. He flung his cigar away and quitted the room and tramped through the lobby toward the door where his chair sat. But before he reached the door he turned about and came up to the cashier's window, behind which the cashier sat in a green eyeshade.

"Res," he said.

The cashier looked up. "Yes, Colonel?"

"Who is that damn boy that hangs around here, looking through that window all day?" Old Bayard lowered his voice within a pitch or so of an ordinary conversational tone.

"What boy, Colonel?" Old Bayard pointed, and the cashier raised himself on his stool and peered over the partition and saw beyond the indicated window a boy of ten or twelve watching him with an innocently casual air. "Oh. That's Will Beard's boy, from up at the boarding house," he shouted. "Friend of Byron's, I think."

"What's he doing around here? Every time I walk through here, there he is looking in that window. What does he want?"

"Maybe he's a bank robber," the cashier suggested.

"What?" Old Bayard cupped his ear fiercely in his palm.

"Maybe he's a bank robber," the other shouted, leaning forward on his stool. Old Bayard snorted and tramped violently on and slammed his chair back against the door. The cashier sat lumped and shapeless on his stool, rumbling deep within his gross body. He said, without turning his head: "Colonel's let Will Falls treat him with that salve." Snopes at his desk made no reply; did not raise his head. After a time the boy moved, and drifted casually and innocently away.

Virgil Beard now possessed a pistol that projected a stream of ammoniac water excruciatingly painful to the eyes, a small magic lantern, and an ex-candy showcase in which he kept birds' eggs and an assortment of insects that had died slowly on pins, and a modest hoard of nickels and dimes. With a child's innocent pleasure he divulged to his parents the source of this beneficence, and his mother took Snopes to her gray heart, fixing him special dishes and performing trifling acts to increase his creature comfort with bleak and awkward gratitude.

At times the boy, already dressed and with his bland shining face, would enter his room and waken him from his troubled sleep and sit on a chair while Snopes donned his clothing, talking politely and vaguely of certain things he aimed to do, and of what he would require to do them successfully with. Or if not this, he was on hand at breakfast while his harried gray mother and the slatternly negress bore dishes back and forth from the kitchen, quiet but proprietorial; blandly and innocently portentous. And all during the banking day (it was summer now, and school was out) Snopes never knew when he would look over his shoulder and find the boy lounging without the plate glass window of the bank, watching him with profound and static patience. Presently he would take himself away, and for a short time Snopes would be able to forget him until, wrapped in his mad unsleeping dream, he mounted the boarding house veranda at supper time and found the boy sitting there and waiting patiently his return; innocent and bland, steadfast and unassertive as a minor but chronic disease. "Got another business letter to write tonight, Mr Snopes?"

And sometimes after he had gone to bed and his light was out, he lay in the mad darkness against which his sleepless desire moiled in obscene images and shapes, and heard presently outside his door secret, ratlike sounds; and lay so tense in the dark, expecting the door to open and, preceded by breathing above him sourceless and invisible: "Going to write another letter, Mr Snopes?" And he waked sweating from dreams in which her image lived and moved and thwarted and mocked him, with the pillow crushed against his mean, half insane face, while the words produced themselves in his ears: "Got air other letter to write yet, Mr Snopes?"

So he changed his boarding house. He gave Mrs Beard an awkward, stumbling explanation; vague, composed of sentences with frayed ends. She was sorry to see him go, but she permitted him to pack his meagre belongings and depart without either anger or complaint, as is the way of country people.

He went to live with a relation, that I. O. Snopes who ran the restaurant—a nimble, wiry little man with a talkative face like a nutcracker, and false merry eyes—in a small frame house painted a sultry prodigious yellow, near the railway station. Snopeses did not trust one another enough to develop any intimate relations, and he was permitted to go and come when he pleased. So he found this better than the boarding house, the single deterrent to complete satisfaction being the hulking but catlike presence of I.O.'s son Clarence. But, what with his secretive nature, it had even been his custom to keep all his possessions under lock and key, so this was but a minor matter. Mrs Snopes was a placid mountain of a woman who swung all day in a faded wrapper, in the porch swing. Not reading, not doing anything: just swinging.

He liked it here. It was more private; no transients appearing at the supper table and tramping up and down the hallways all night; no one to try to engage him in conversation on the veranda after supper. Now, after supper he could sit undisturbed on the tight barren little porch in the growing twilight and watch the motor cars congregating at the station across the way to meet the 7:30 train; could watch the train draw into the station with its rows of lighted windows and the hissing plume from the locomotive, and go on again with bells, trailing its diminishing sound into the distant evening, while he sat on the dark porch with his desperate sleepless lust and his fear. Thus, until one evening after supper he stepped through the front door and found Virgil Beard sitting patiently and blandly on the front steps in the twilight.

So he had been run to earth again, and drawn, and hounded again into flight. Yet outwardly he pursued the even tenor of his days, unchanged, performing his duties with his slow meticulous care. But within him smoldered something of which he himself grew afraid, and at times he found himself gazing at his idle hands on the desk before him as though they were not his hands, wondering dully at them and at what they were capable, nay importunate, to do. And day by day that lust and fear and despair that moiled within him merged, becoming desperation—a thing blind and vicious and hopeless, like that of a cornered rat. And always, if he but raised his head and looked toward the window, there was the boy watching him with bland and innocent eyes beneath the pale straw of his hair. Sometimes he blinked; then the boy was gone; sometimes not. So he could never tell whether the face had been there at all, or whether it was merely another face swum momentarily from out the seething of his mind. In the meanwhile he wrote another letter.

7

Miss Jenny's exasperation and rage when old Bayard arrived home that afternoon was unbounded. "You stubborn old fool," she stormed. "Cant Bayard kill you fast enough, that you've got to let that old quack of a Will Falls give you blood poisoning? After what Dr Alford told you, when even Loosh Peabody, who thinks a course of quinine or calomel will cure anything from a broken neck to chilblains, agreed with him? I'll declare, sometimes I just lose all patience with you folks; wonder what crime I seem to be expiating by having to live with you. Soon as Bayard sort of quiets down and I can quit jumping every time the 'phone rings, you have to go and let that old pauper daub your face up with axle grease and lamp black. I'm a good mind to pack up and get out, and start life over in some place where they never heard of a Sartoris." She raged and stormed on; old Bayard raged in reply, with violent words and profane, and their voices swelled and surged through the house until Elnora and Simon in the kitchen moved furtively, with cocked ears. Finally old Bayard tramped from the house and mounted his horse and rode away, leaving Miss Jenny to wear her rage out upon the empty air, and then there was peace for a time.

But at supper the storm brewed and burst again. Behind the swing door of the butler's pantry Simon could hear them and young Bayard too, trying to shout them down. "Let up, let up," he howled, "for God's sake. I can't hear myself chew, even."

"And you're another one," Miss Jenny turned promptly on him. "You're just as trying as he is. You and your stiff-necked, sullen ways. Helling around the country in that car just because you think there may be somebody who cares a whoop whether or not you break your worthless neck, and then coming into the supper table smelling like a stable-hand! Just because you went to a war. Do you think you're the only person in the world that ever went to a war? Do you reckon that when my Bayard came back from The War, he made a nuisance of himself to everybody that had to live with him? But he was a gentleman: he raised the devil like a gentleman, not like you Mississippi country people. Clod-hoppers. Look what he did with just a horse," she added. "He didn't need any flying machine."

"Look at the little two-bit war he went to," young Bayard rejoined, "a war that was so sorry that grandfather wouldn't even stay up there in Virginia where it was."

"And nobody wanted him at it," Miss Jenny retorted. "A man that would get mad just because his men deposed him and elected a better colonel in his place. Got mad and came back to the country to lead a bunch of red-neck brigands."

"Little two-bit war," young Bayard repeated. "And on a horse. Anybody can go to a war on a horse. No chance for him to do anything much."

"At least he got himself decently killed," Miss Jenny snapped. "He did more with a horse than you could do with that aeroplane."

"Sho," Simon breathed against the pantry door. "Aint dey gwine it? Takes white folks to sho' 'nough quoil." And so it surged and ebbed through the succeeding days; wore itself out, then surged again when old Bayard returned home with another application of salve. But by this time Simon was having troubles of his own, troubles which he finally consulted old Bayard about one afternoon. Young Bayard was laid up in bed with his crushed ribs, with Miss Jenny mothering him with savage and cherishing affection, and Miss Benbow to visit with him and read aloud to him; and Simon came into his own again. The tophat and the duster came down from the nail, and old Bayard's cigars depleted daily by one, and the fat matched horses spent their accumulated laziness between home and the bank, before which Simon swung them to a halt each afternoon as of old, with his clamped cigar and smartly-furled whip and all the theatrics of the fine moment. "De otto-mobile," Simon philosophised, "is all right fer pleasure en excitement, but fer de genu-wine gen'lemun tone, dey aint but one thing: dat's hosses."

Thus Simon's opportunity came ready to his hand, and once they were clear of town and the team had settled into its gait, he took advantage of it.

"Well, Cunnel," he began, "looks lak me en you's got to make some financial 'rangements."

"What?" Old Bayard brought his attention back from where it wandered about the familiar planted fields and blue shining hills beyond.

"I says, it looks lak me en you's got to arrange erbout a little cash money."

"Much obliged, Simon," old Bayard answered, "but I dont need any money right now. Much obliged, though."

Simon laughed heartily. "I declare, Cunnel, you sho' is comical. Rich man lak you needin' money!" Again he laughed, with unctuous and abortive heartiness. "Yes, suh, you sho' is comical." Then he ceased laughing and became engrossed with the horses for a moment. Twins they were: Roosevelt and Taft, with sleek hides and broad, comfortable buttocks. "You, Taf', lean on dat collar! Laziness gwine go in on you someday, en kill you, sho'." Old Bayard sat watching his apelike head and the swaggering tilt of the tophat. Simon turned his wizened, plausible face over his shoulder again. "But sho' 'nough, now, we is got to quiet dem niggers somehow."

"What have they done? Cant they find anybody to take their money?"

"Well, suh, hit's lak dis," Simon explained. "Hit's kind of all 'round cu'i's. You see, dey been collectin' buildin' money fer dat church whut burnt down, en ez dey got de money up, dey turnt hit over ter me, whut wid my 'ficial position on de church boa'd en bein' I wuz a member of de bes' fambly 'round here. Dat 'uz erbout las' Chris'mus time, en now dey wants de money back."

"That's strange," old Bayard said.

"Yessuh," Simon agreed readily. "Hit struck me jes' 'zackly dat way."

"Well, if they insist, I reckon you'd better give it back to 'em."

"Now you's gittin' to it." Simon turned his head again; his manner was confidential, and he exploded his bomb in a hushed melodramatic tone: "De money's gone."

"Dammit, I know that," old Bayard answered, his levity suddenly gone. "Where is it?"

"I went and put it out," Simon told him, and his tone was still confidential, with a little pained astonishment at the world's obtuseness. "And now dem niggers 'cusin' me of stealin' it."

"Do you mean to tell me that you took charge of money belonging to other people, and then went and loaned it to somebody else?"

"You does de same thing ev'y day," Simon answered. "Aint lendin' out money yo' main business?"

Old Bayard snorted violently. "You get that money back and give it to those niggers, or you'll be in jail, you hear?"

"You talks jes' lak dem uppity town niggers," Simon told him in a pained tone. "Dat money done been put out, now," he reminded his patron.

"Get it back. Haven't you got collateral for it?"

"Is I got which?"

"Something worth the money, to keep until the money is paid back."

"Yessuh, I got dat." Simon chuckled again, unctuously, a satyrish chuckle rich with complacent innuendo. "Yessuh, I got dat, all right. Only I never heard hit called collateral befo'. Naw, suh, not dat."

"Did you give that money to some nigger wench?" old Bayard demanded.

"Well, suh, hit's lak dis——" Simon began, but the other interrupted him.

"Ah, the devil. And now you expect me to pay it back, do you? How much is it?"

"I dont rightly ricollick. Dem niggers claims hit wuz sevumty er ninety dollars er somethin'. But dont you pay 'um no mind; you jes' give 'um whut ever you think is right: dey'll take it."

"I'm damned if I will. They can take it out of your worthless hide, or send you to jail—whichever they want to, but I'm damned if I'll pay one cent of it."

"Now, Cunnel," Simon said, "you aint gwine let dem town niggers 'cuse a member of yo' fambly of stealin', is you?"

"Drive on!" old Bayard shouted. Simon turned on the seat and clucked to the horses and drove on, his cigar tilted toward his hatbrim, his elbows out and the whip caught smartly back in his hand, glancing now and then at the field niggers laboring among the cotton rows with tolerant and easy scorn.

Old man Falls replaced the cap on his tin of salve, wiped the tin carefully with the bit of rag, then knelt on the cold hearth and held a match to the rag.

"I reckon them doctors air still a-tellin' you hit's gwine to kill you, aint they?" he said.

Old Bayard propped his feet against the hearth, cupping a

match to his cigar, cupping two tiny matchflames in his eyes. He flung the match away and grunted.

Old man Falls watched the rag take fire sluggishly, with a pungent pencil of yellowish smoke that broke curling in the still air. "Ever' now and then a feller has to walk up and spit in deestruction's face, sort of, fer his own good. He has to kind of put a aidge on hisself, like he'd hold his axe to the grindstone," he said, squatting before the pungent curling of the smoke as though in a pagan ritual in miniature. "Ef a feller'll show his face to deestruction ever' now and then, deestruction'll leave 'im be 'twell his time comes. Deestruction likes to take a feller in the back."

"What?" old Bayard said.

Old man Falls rose and dusted his knees carefully.

"Deestruction's like ary other coward," he roared. "Hit wont strike a feller that's a-lookin' hit in the eye lessen he pushes hit too clost. Your paw knowed that. Stood in the do' of that sto' the day them two cyarpet-baggers brung them niggers in to vote 'em that day in '72. Stood thar in his prince albert coat and beaver hat, with his arms folded, when ever'body else had left, and watched them two Missouri fellers herdin' them niggers up the road to'ds the sto'; stood right in the middle of the do' while them two cyarpet-baggers begun backin' off with their hands in their pockets until they was clar of the niggers, and cussed him. And him standin' thar jest like this." He crossed his arms on his breast, his hands in sight, and for a moment old Bayard saw, as through a cloudy glass, that arrogant and familiar shape which the old man in shabby overalls had contrived in some way to immolate and preserve in the vacuum of his own abnegated self.

"Then, when they was gone on back down the road, Cunnel reached around inside the do' and taken out the ballot box and sot hit between his feet.

" 'You niggers come hyer to vote, did you?' he says. 'All right, come up hyer and vote.'

"When they had broke and scattered he let off that 'ere dang der'nger over their haids a couple of times, then he loaded hit agin and marched down the road to Miz Winterbottom's, whar them two fellers boa'ded.

" 'Madam,' he says, liftin' his beaver, 'I have a small matter of business to discuss with yo' lodgers. Permit me,' he says, and he put his hat back on and marched up the stairs steady as a parade, with Miz Winterbottom gapin' after him with her mouth open. He walked right into the room whar they was a-settin' behind a table facin' the do', with their pistols layin' on the table.

"When us boys outside heard the three shots we run in. Thar wuz Miz Winterbottom standin' thar, a-gapin' up the stairs, and in a minute hyer comes Cunnel with his hat cocked over his eye, marchin' down steady as a co't jury, breshin' the front of his coat with his hank'cher. And us standin' thar, a-watchin' him. He stopped in front of Miz Winterbottom and lifted his hat agin.

" 'Madam,' he says, 'I was fo'ced to muss up yo' guest-room right considerable. Pray accept my apologies, and have yo' nigger clean it up and send the bill to me. My apologies agin, madam, fer havin' been put to the necessity of exterminatin' vermin on yo' premises. Gentlemen,' he says to us, 'good mawnin'. And he cocked that 'ere beaver on his head and walked out.

"And, Bayard," old man Falls said, "I sort of envied them two nawthuners, be damned ef I didn't. A feller kin take a wife and live with her fer a long time, but after all they aint no kin. But the feller that brings you into the world or sends you outen hit. . . . . . . "

———————

Lurking behind the pantry door Simon could hear the steady storming of Miss Jenny's and old Bayard's voices; later when they had removed to the office and Elnora and Caspey and Isom sat about the table in the kitchen waiting for him, the concussion of Miss Jenny's raging and old Bayard's rocklike stubbornness came in muffled surges, as of far away surf.

"Whut dey quoilin' erbout now?" Caspey asked. "Is you been and done somethin'?" he demanded of his nephew.

Isom rolled his eyes quietly above his steady jaws. "Naw, suh," he mumbled. "I aint done nothin'."

"Seems like dey'd git wo' out, after a while. Whut's pappy doin', Elnora?"

"Up dar in de hall, listenin'. Go tell 'im to come on and git his supper, so I kin git done, Isom."

Isom slid from his chair, still chewing, and left the kitchen. The steady raging of the two voices increased; where the shapeless figure of his grandfather stood like a disreputable and ancient bird in the dark hallway Isom could distinguish words:. . . . . . . poison. . . . . . . blood. . . . . . . think you can cut your head off and cure it?. . . . . . . fool put it on your foot, but. . . . . . face, head. . . . . . dead and good riddance. . . . . . fool of you dying because of your own bullheaded folly. . . . . . . you first lying on your back, though. . . . . . .

"You and that damn doctor are going to worry me to death." Old Bayard's voice drowned the other temporarily. "Will Falls wont have a chance to kill me. I cant sit in my chair in town without that damn squirt sidling around me and look-ing disappointed because I'm still alive on my feet. And when I come home to get away from him, you cant even let me eat supper in peace. Have to show me a lot of damn colored pic-tures of what some fool thinks a man's insides look like."

"Who gwine die, pappy?" Isom whispered.

Simon turned his head. "Whut you hangin' eround here fer, boy? Go'n back to dat kitchen, whar you belongs."

"Supper waitin'," Isom said. "Who dyin', pappy?"

"Aint nobody dyin'. Does anybody soun' dead? You git on outen de house, now."

Together they returned down the hall and entered the kitchen. Behind them the voices raged and stormed, blurred a little by walls, but dominant and unequivocal.

"Whut dey fightin' erbout, now?" Caspey, chewing, asked.

"Dat's white folks' bizness," Simon told him. "You tend to yo'n, and dey'll git erlong all right." He sat down and Elnora rose and filled a cup from the coffee pot on the stove, and brought it to him. "White folks got dey troubles same as niggers is. Gimme dat dish o' meat, boy."

In the house the storm ran its nightly course, ceased as though by mutual consent, both parties still firmly entrenched; resumed at the supper table the next evening. And so on, day after day, until the second week in July and six days after young Bayard had been fetched home with his chest crushed, Miss Jenny and old Bayard and Dr Alford went to Memphis to consult a well known authority on blood and glandular diseases with whom Dr Alford, with some difficulty, had made a formal engagement. Young Bayard lay upstairs in his cast, but Narcissa Benbow had promised to come out and keep him company during the day.

Between the two of them they got old Bayard on the early train, still protesting profanely like a stubborn and bewildered ox. There were others who knew them in the car and who remarked Dr Alford's juxtaposition and became curious and solicitous. Old Bayard took these opportunities to assert himself again, with violent rumblings which Miss Jenny ignored.

They took him, like a sullen small boy, to the clinic where

the specialist was to meet them, and in a room resembling an easy and informal summer hotel lobby they sat among quiet, waiting people talking in whispers, and an untidy clutter of papers and magazines, waiting for the specialist to arrive. They waited a long time. Meanwhile Dr Alford from time to time assaulted the impregnable affability of the woman at the switchboard, was repulsed and returned and sat stiffly beside his patient, aware that with every minute he was losing ground in Miss Jenny's opinion of him. Old Bayard was cowed too, by now, though occasionally he rumbled hopefully at Miss Jenny. "Oh, stop swearing at me," she interrupted him at last. "You cant walk out now. Here, here's the morning paper—take it and be quiet."

Then the specialist entered briskly and went to the switchboard woman, where Dr Alford saw him and rose and went to him. The specialist turned—a brisk, dapper man, who moved with arrogant jerky motions, as though he were exercising with a small sword, and who in turning, almost stepped on Dr Alford. He gave Dr Alford a glassy, impatient stare; then he shook his hand and broke into a high, desiccated burst of words. "On the dot, I see. Promptness. Promptness. That's good. Patient here? Stood the trip all right, did she?"

"Yes, Doctor, he's——"

"Good; good. Undressed and all ready, eh?"

"The patient is a m——"

"Just a moment." The specialist turned. "Oh, Mrs Smith."

"Yes, Doctor." The woman at the switchboard did not raise her head, and at that moment another specialist of some kind, a large one, with a majestic, surreptitious air like a royal undertaker, entered and addressed him, and for a while the two of them rumbled and rattled at one another while Dr Alford stood ignored nearby, fuming stiffly and politely, feeling himself sinking lower and lower in Miss Jenny's opinion of his professional status. Then the two specialists had done, and Dr Alford led his man toward his patient.

"Got the patient all ready, you say? Good; good; save time. Lunching down town today. Had lunch yourself?"

"No, Doctor. But the patient is a —— "

"Daresay not," the specialist agreed. "Plenty of time, though." He turned briskly toward a curtained exit, but Dr Alford took his arm firmly but courteously and halted him. Old Bayard was reading the paper. Miss Jenny was watching them frigidly, her bonnet on the exact top of her head.

"Mrs Du Pre; Colonel Sartoris," Dr Alford said. "This is Dr Brandt. Colonel Sartoris is your p—— "

"How d'ye do? How d'ye do? Come along with the patient, eh? Daughter? Grand-daughter?" Old Bayard looked up.

"What?" he said, cupping his ear, and found the specialist staring at his face.

"What's that on your face?" he demanded, jerking his hand forth and touching the blackened excrescence. When he did so, the thing came off in his fingers, leaving on old Bayard's withered but unblemished cheek a round spot of skin rosy and fair as any baby's.

On the train that evening old Bayard, who had sat for a long time in deep thought, spoke suddenly.

"Jenny, what day of the month is this?"

"The ninth," Miss Jenny answered. "Why?"

Old Bayard sat for a while longer. Then he rose. "Think I'll go up and smoke a cigar," he said. "I reckon a little tobacco wont hurt me, will it, Doctor?"

Three weeks later they got a bill from the specialist for fifty dollars. "Now I know why he's so well known," Miss Jenny said acidly. Then to her nephew: "You better thank your stars it wasn't your hat he lifted off."

Toward Dr Alford her manner is fiercely and belligerently

protective; to old man Falls she gives the briefest and coldest nod and sails on with her nose in air; but to Loosh Peabody she does not speak at all.

8

She passed from the fresh, hot morning into the cool hall, where Simon uselessly and importantly proprietorial with a duster, bobbed his head to her. "Dey done gone to Memphis today," he told her. "But Mist' Bayard waitin' fer you. Walk right up, missy."

"Thank you," she answered, and she went on and mounted the stairs and left him busily wafting dust from one surface to another and then back again. She mounted into a steady drift of air that blew through the open doors at the end of the hall; through these doors she could see a segment of blue hills and salt-colored sky. At Bayard's door she stopped and stood there for a time, clasping the book to her breast.

The house, despite Simon's activity in the hall below, was a little portentously quiet, without the reassurance of Miss Jenny's bustling presence. Faint sounds reached her from far away—out-of-doors sounds whose final drowsy reverberations drifted into the house on the vivid July air; sounds too somnolent and remote to die away.

But from the room before her no sound came at all. Perhaps he was asleep; and the initial impulse—her given word, and the fortitude of her desperate heart which had enabled her to come out despite Miss Jenny's absence—having served its purpose and deserted her, she stood just without the door, hoping that he was asleep, that he would sleep all day.

But she would have to enter the room in order to find out

if he slept, so she touched her hands to her face, as though by that she would restore to it its wonted serene repose for him to see, and entered.

"Simon?" Bayard said, having felt her presence through that sharpened sixth sense of the sick. He lay on his back, his hands beneath his head, gazing out the window across the room, and she paused again just within the door. At last, roused by her silence, he turned his head and his bleak gaze. "Well, I'm damned. I didn't believe you'd come out today."

"Yes," she answered. "How do you feel?"

"Not after the way you sit with one foot in the hall all the time Aunt Jenny's out of the room," he continued. "Did she make you come anyway?"

"She asked me to come out. She doesn't want you to be alone all day, with just Simon in the house. Do you feel better today?"

"So?" he drawled. "Wont you sit down, then?" She crossed to where her customary chair had been moved into a corner and drew it across the floor. He was watching her as she turned the chair about and seated herself. "What do you think about it?"

"About what?"

"About coming out to keep me company?"

"I've brought a new book," she said. "One H——one I just got. I hope you'll like this one."

"I hope so," he agreed, but without conviction. "Seems like I'd like one after a while, dont it? But what do you think about coming out here today?"

"I dont think a sick person should be left alone with just negroes around," she said, her face lowered over the book. "The name of this one is——"

"Why not send a nurse out, then? No use your coming way

out here." She met his gaze at last, with her grave desperate eyes. "Why do you come, when you dont want to?" he persisted.

"I dont mind," she answered. She opened the book. "The name of this one is——"

"Dont," he interrupted. "I'll have to listen to that damn thing all day. Let's talk a while." But her head was bent and her hands were still on the open book. "What makes you afraid to talk to me?"

"Afraid?" she repeated. "Had you rather I'd go?"

"What? No, damn it. I want you to be human for one time and talk to me. Come over here." She would not look at him, and she raised her hands between them as though he did not lie helpless on his back two yards away. "Come over here closer," he commanded. She rose, clutching the book.

"I'm going," she said. "I'll tell Simon to stay where he can hear you call. Goodbye."

"Here," he exclaimed. She went swiftly to the door.

"Goodbye."

"After what you just said, about leaving me alone with just niggers on the place?" She paused at the door, and he added with cold cunning: "After what Aunt Jenny told you? What'll I tell her, tonight? Why are you afraid of a man flat on his back, in a damn cast-iron strait-jacket, anyway?" But she only looked at him with her sober, hopeless eyes. "All right, dammit," he said violently. "Go, then." And he jerked his head on the pillow and stared again out the window while she returned to her chair. He said, mildly: "What's the name of this one?" She told him. "Let her go, then. I reckon I'll be asleep soon, anyway."

She opened the book and began to read, swiftly, as though she were crouching behind the screen of words her voice raised between them. She read steadily on for some time, while he on the bed made no movement, her head bent over the book, aware of time passing, as though she were in a contest with time. She finished a sentence and ceased, without raising her head, but almost immediately he spoke. "Go on; I'm still here. Better luck next time."

The forenoon passed on. Somewhere a clock rang the quarter hours, but saving this there was no other sound in the house. Simon's activity below stairs had ceased long since, but a murmur of voices reached her at intervals from somewhere, murmurously indistinguishable. The leaves on the branch beyond the window did not stir in the hot air, and upon it a myriad noises blended in a drowsy monotone—the negroes' voices, sounds of animals in the barnyard, the rhythmic groaning of the water pump; a sudden cacophony of fowls in the garden beneath the window, interspersed with Isom's meaningless cries as he drove them out.

Bayard was asleep now, and as she realized this she realized also that she did not know just when she had stopped reading. And she sat with the page open upon her knees, a page whose words left no echoes whatever in her mind, looking at his calm face. It was again like a bronze mask, purged by illness of the heat of its violence, yet with the violence still slumbering there and only refined a little. . . . She looked away and sat with the book open, her hands lying motionless upon the page, gazing out the window. The curtains hung without motion. On the branch athwart the window the leaves hung motionless beneath the intermittent fingers of the sun, and she sat also without life, the fabric of her dress unstirred by her imperceptible breathing, thinking that there would be peace for her only in a world where there were no men at all.

The clock rang twelve times. Immediately after, a stertorous breathing and surreptitious sounds as of a huge rat, and yet other furtive ratlike sounds in the hall, Simon thrust his head around the door, like the grandfather of all apes. "Is you 'sleep Mist' Bayard?" he said in a rasping whisper.

"Shhhhhhhh," Narcissa said, lifting her hand. Simon entered on tiptoe, breathing heavily, scraping his feet on the floor. "Hush," Narcissa said quickly, "you'll wake him."

"Dinner ready," Simon said, still in that rasping whisper.

"You can keep his warm until he wakes up, cant you?" Narcissa whispered. "Simon!" she whispered. She rose, but he had already crossed to the table, where he fumbled clumsily at the stack of books and contrived at last to topple it to the floor in a random crash. Bayard opened his eyes.

"Good God," he said, "are you here again?"

"Well, now," Simon exclaimed with ready dismay, "ef me en Miss Benbow aint waked him up."

"Why you cant bear to see anybody lying on their back with their eyes closed, I cant see," Bayard said. "Thank God you were not born in a drove, like mosquitoes."

"Des lissen at 'im!" Simon said. "Go to sleep quoilin' en wake up quoilin'. Elnora got dinner ready fer y'all."

"Why didn't you bring it up, then?" Bayard said. "Miss Benbow's too. Unless you'd rather go down?" he added.

In all his movements Simon was a caricature of himself. He now assumed an attitude of shocked reproof. "Dinin' room de place fer comp'ny," he said.

"No," Narcissa said, "I'll go down. I wont put Simon to that trouble."

"'Taint no trouble," Simon disclaimed. "Only hit aint no—"

"I'll come down," Narcissa said. "You go on and see to Mr Bayard's tray."

"Yes'm," Simon said. He moved toward the door. "You kin

walk right down. Elnora have hit on de table time you git dar."
He went out.

"I try to keep—" Narcissa began.

"I know," Bayard interrupted. "He wont let anybody sleep
through meal time. And you'd better go and have yours, or
he'll carry everything back to the kitchen. And you dont have
to hurry back just on my account," he added.

"Dont have to hurry back?" She paused at the door and
looked back at him. "What do you mean?"

"I thought you might be tired of reading."

"Oh," she said, and looked away and stood for a moment
clothed in her grave despair.

"Look here," he said suddenly. "Are you sick or anything?
Had you rather go home?"

"No," she answered. She moved again. "I'll be back soon."

She had her meal in lonely state in the sombre dining
room while Simon, having dispatched Bayard's tray by Isom,
moved about the table and pressed dishes upon her with bland
insistence or leaned against the sideboard and conducted a
rambling monologue that seemed to have had no beginning
and held no prospect of any end. It still flowed easily behind
her as she went up the hall; when she stood in the front door it
was still going on, volitionless, as though entranced with its
own existence and feeding on its own momentum. Beyond the
porch the salvia bed lay in an unbearable glare of white light,
in clamorous splashes. Beyond it the drive shimmered with
heat until, arched over with locust and oak, it descended in a
cool green tunnel to the gates and the sultry ribbon of the highroad. Beyond the road fields spread away shimmering, broken
here and there by motionless clumps of wood, on to the hills
dissolving bluely in the July haze.

She leaned for a while against the door, in her white dress, her cheek against the cool, smooth plane of the jamb, in a faint draft that came steadily from somewhere, though no leaf stirred. Simon had finished in the dining room and a drowsy murmur of voices came up the hall from the kitchen, borne upon that thin stirring of air too warm to be called a breeze.

At last she heard a movement from above stairs and she remembered Isom with Bayard's tray, and she turned and slid the parlor doors ajar and entered. The shades were drawn closely, and the crack of light that followed her but deepened the gloom. She found the piano and stood beside it for a while, touching its dusty surface and thinking of Miss Jenny erect and indomitable in her chair beside it. She heard Isom descend the stairs; soon his footsteps died away down the hall, and she drew out the bench and sat down and laid her arms along the closed lid.

Simon entered the dining room again, mumbling to himself and followed presently by Elnora, and they clashed dishes and talked with a mellow rise and fall of consonantless and indistinguishable words. Then they went away, but still she sat with her arms along the cool wood, in the dark quiet room where even time stagnated a little.

The clock rang again, and she moved. I've been crying, she thought. "I've been crying," she said in a sad whisper that savored its own loneliness and its sorrow. At the tall mirror beside the parlor door she stood and peered at her dim reflection, touching her eyes with her fingertips. Then she went on, but paused again at the stairs, listening, then she mounted briskly and entered Miss Jenny's room and went on to her bathroom and bathed her face.

Bayard lay as she had left him. He was smoking a cigarette now, between puffs he dabbed it casually at a saucer on the bed beside him. "Well?" he said.

"You're going to set the house on fire that way," she told

him, removing the saucer. "You know Miss Jenny wouldn't let you do that."

"I know it," he agreed, a little sheepishly, and she dragged the table up and set the saucer on it.

"Can you reach it now?"

"Yes, thanks. Did they give you enough to eat?"

"Oh, yes. Simon's very insistent, you know. Shall I read some more, or had you rather sleep?"

"Read, if you dont mind. I think I'll stay awake, this time."

"Is that a threat?" He looked at her quickly as she seated herself and picked up the book.

"Say, what happened to you?" he demanded. "You acted like you were all in before dinner. Simon give you a drink, or what?"

"No, not that bad." And she laughed, a little wildly, and opened the book. "I forgot to mark the place," she said, turning the leaves swiftly. "Do you remember——No, you were asleep, weren't you? Shall I go back to where you stopped listening?"

"No, just read anywhere. It's all about alike, I guess. If you'll move a little nearer, I believe I can stay awake."

"Sleep, if you want to. I dont mind."

"Meaning you wont come any nearer?" he asked, watching her with his bleak gaze. She moved her chair nearer and opened the book again and turned the pages on.

"I think it was about here," she said, with indecision. "Yes." She read to herself for a line or two, then she began aloud, read to the end of the page, where her voice trailed off in grave consternation. She turned the next page then flipped it back. "I read this once; I remember it now." She turned the leaves on, her serene brow puckered a little. "I must have been asleep too," she said, and she glanced at him with friendly bewilderment. "I seem to have read pages and pages. . . . . . ."

"Oh, begin anywhere," he repeated.

"No: wait; here it is." She read again and picked up the thread of the story. Once or twice she raised her eyes swiftly and found him watching her, bleakly but quietly. After a while he was no longer watching her, and at last, finding that his eyes were closed, she thought he slept. She finished the chapter and stopped.

"No," he said drowsily. "Not yet." Then, when she failed to resume, he opened his eyes and asked for a cigarette. She laid the book aside and struck the match for him, and picked up the book again.

The afternoon wore away. The negroes had gone, and there was no sound about the house save her voice, and the clock at quarter hour intervals; outside the shadows slanted more and more, peaceful harbingers of evening. He was asleep now, despite his contrary conviction, and after a while she stopped and laid the book away. The long shape of him lay stiffly in its cast beneath the sheet, and she sat and looked at his bold still face and the broken travesty of him and her tranquil sorrow overflowed in pity for him. He was so utterly without any affection for any thing at all; so—so...... hard (no, that's not the word—but cold eluded her; she could comprehend hardness, but not coldness. ...)

Afternoon drew on; evening was finding itself. She sat musing and still and quiet, gazing out of the window where no wind yet stirred the leaves, as though she were waiting for someone to tell her what to do next, and she had lost all account of time other than as a dark unhurrying stream into which she gazed until the mesmerism of water conjured the water itself away.

He made an indescribable sound, and she turned her head quickly and saw his body straining terrifically in its cast, and his clenched hands and his teeth beneath his lifted lip, and as she sat blanched and incapable of further movement he made the sound again. His breath hissed between his teeth and he screamed, a wordless sound that merged into a rush of profanity; and when she rose at last and stood over him with her hands against her mouth, his body relaxed and from beneath his sweating brow he watched her with wide intent eyes in which terror lurked, and mad, cold fury, and despair.

"He damn near got me, then," he said in a dry, light voice, still watching her from beyond the fading agony in his wide eyes. "There was a sort of loop of 'em around my chest, and every time he fired, he twisted the loop a little tighter. . . . . . . " He fumbled at the sheet and tried to draw it up to his face. "Can you get me a handkerchief? Some in that top drawer there."

"Yes," she said. "Yes," and she went to the chest of drawers and held her shaking body upright by clinging to it, and found a handkerchief and brought it to him. She tried to dry his brow and face, but at last he took the handkerchief from her and did it himself. "You scared me," she moaned. "You scared me so bad. I thought. . . . . . . "

"Sorry," he answered shortly. "I dont do that on purpose. I want a cigarette."

She gave it to him and struck the match, and again he had to grasp her hand to hold the flame steady, and still holding her wrist he drew deeply several times. She tried to free her wrist, but his fingers were like steel, and her trembling body betrayed her and she sank into her chair again, staring at him with terror and dread. He consumed the cigarette in deep, swift draughts, and still holding her wrist, he began talking of his dead brother, without preamble, brutally. It was a brutal tale, without beginning, and crassly and uselessly violent and at times profane and gross, though its very wildness robbed it of offensiveness just as its grossness kept it from obscenity. And beneath it all, the bitter struggling of his false and stubborn pride; and she sitting with her arm taut in his grasp and her other hand pressed against her mouth, watching him with ter- rified fascination.

"He was zigzagging: that was why I couldn't get on the hun. Every time I got my sights on him, John'd barge in between us again, and then I'd have to hoick away before one of the others got on me. Then he quit zigzagging. Soon as I saw him sideslip I knew it was all over. Then I saw the fire streaking out along his wing, and he was looking back. He wasn't looking at the hun at all; he was looking at me. The hun stopped shoot- ing then, and all of us sort of just sat there for a while. I couldn't tell what John was up to until I saw him swing his feet out. Then he thumbed his nose at me like he was always doing and flipped his hand at the hun and kicked his machine out of the way and jumped. He jumped feet first. You cant fall far feet first, you know, and pretty soon he sprawled out flat. There was a bunch of cloud right under us and he smacked on it right on his belly, like what we used to call gut-busters in swimming. But I never could pick him up below the cloud. I know I got down before he could have come out, because after I was down there his machine came diving out right at me, burning good. I pulled away from it, but the damn thing zoomed past and did a split-turn and came at me again, and I had to dodge. And so I never could pick him up when he came out of the cloud. I went down fast, until I knew I was below him, and looked again. But I couldn't find him and then I thought that maybe I hadn't gone far enough, so I dived again. I saw the machine crash about three miles away, but I never could pick John up again. And then they started shooting at me from the ground——"

He talked on and her hand came away from her mouth and slid down her other arm and tugged at his fingers. "Please," she whispered. "Please!" He ceased and looked at her and his fingers shifted, and just as she thought she was free they clamped again, and now both of her wrists were prisoners. She struggled, staring at him dreadfully, but he grinned his white cruel teeth at her and pressed her crossed arms down upon the bed beside him. "Please, please," she implored, struggling; she could feel the flesh of her wrists, feel the bones turn in it like a loose garment; could see his bleak eyes and the fixed derision of his teeth, and suddenly she swayed forward in her chair and her head dropped between her prisoned arms and she wept with hopeless and dreadful hysteria.

After a while there was no sound in the room again, and he moved his head and looked at the dark crown of her head. He lifted his hand and saw the bruised discolorations where he had gripped her wrists. But she did not stir even then, and he dropped his hand upon her wrists again and lay quietly, and after a while even her shuddering and trembling had ceased. "I'm sorry," he said. "I wont do it again." He could see only the top of her dark head, and her hands lay passive beneath his. "I'm sorry," he repeated. "I wont do it anymore."

"You wont drive that car fast anymore?" she asked, without moving; her voice was muffled.

"What?"

She made no answer, and with infinite small pains and slowly he turned himself, cast and all, by degrees onto his side, chewing his lip and swearing under his breath, and laid his other hand on her hair.

"What are you doing?" she asked, still without raising her head. "You'll break your ribs again."

"Yes," he agreed, stroking her hair awkwardly.

"That's the trouble, right there," she said. "That's the way you act: doing things that—that—You do things to hurt yourself just to worry people. You dont get any fun out of doing them."

"No," he agreed, and he lay with his chest full of hot needles, stroking her dark head with his hard, awkward hand. Far above him now the peak among the black and savage stars, and about him the valleys of tranquillity and of peace. It was later still; already shadows were growing in the room and losing themselves in shadow, and beyond the window sunlight was a diffused radiance, sourceless yet palpable; from somewhere cows lowed one to another, moody and mournful. At last she sat up, touching her face and her hair.

"You're all twisted. You'll never get well, if you dont behave yourself. Turn on your back, now." He obeyed, slowly and painfully, his lip between his teeth and faint beads on his forehead, while she watched him with grave anxiety. "Does it hurt?"

"No," he answered, and his hand shut again on her wrists that made no effort to withdraw. The sun was gone, and twilight, foster-dam of quietude and peace, filled the fading room and evening had found itself.

"And you wont drive that car fast anymore?" she persisted from the dusk.

"No," he answered.

9

Meanwhile she had received another letter from her anonymous correspondent. Horace when he came in one night, had brought it in to her as she lay in bed with a book; tapped at her door and opened it and stood for a moment diffidently, and for a while they looked at one another across the barrier of their estrangement and their stubborn pride.

"Excuse me for disturbing you," he said stiffly. She lay beneath the shaded light, with the dark splash of her hair upon the pillow, and only her eyes moved as he crossed the room and stood above her where she lay with her lowered book, watching him with sober interrogation.

"What are you reading?" he asked. For reply she shut the book on her finger, with the jacket and its colored legend upward. But he did not look at it. His shirt was open beneath his silk dressing gown and his thin hand moved among the objects on the table beside the bed; picked up another book. "I never knew you to read so much."

"I have more time for reading, now," she answered.

"Yes." His hand still moved about the table, touching things here and there. She lay waiting for him to speak. But he did not, and she said:

"What is it, Horace?"

He came and sat on the edge of the bed. But still her eyes were antagonistic and interrogatory and the shadow of her mouth was stubbornly cold. "Narcy?" he said. She lowered her eyes to the book, and he added: "First, I want to apologise for leaving you alone so often at night."

"Yes?"

He laid his hand on her knee. "Look at me." She raised her face, and the antagonism of her eyes. "I want to apologise for leaving you alone at night," he repeated.

"Does that mean you aren't going to do it anymore, or that you're not coming in at all?"

For a time he sat, brooding upon the wild repose of his hand lying on her covered knee. Then he rose and stood beside the table again, touching the objects there, then he returned and sat on the bed. She was reading again, and he tried to take the book from her hand. She resisted.

"What do you want, Horace?" she asked impatiently.

He mused again while she watched his face. He looked up. "Belle and I are going to be married," he blurted.

"Why tell me? Harry is the one to tell. Unless you and Belle are going to dispense with the formality of divorce."

"Yes," he said. "He knows it." He laid his hand on her knee again, stroking it through the covers. "You aren't even surprised, are you?"

"I'm surprised at you, but not at Belle. Belle has a backstairs nature."

"Yes," he agreed; then: "Who said that to you? You didn't think of that yourself." She lay with her book half raised, watching him. He took her hand roughly; she tried to free it, but vainly. "Who was it?" he demanded.

"Nobody told me. Dont, Horace."

He released her hand. "I know who it was. It was Mrs Du Pre."

"It wasn't anybody," she repeated. "Go away and leave me alone, Horace." And behind the antagonism her eyes were hopeless and desperate. "Don't you see that talking doesn't help any?"

"Yes," he said wearily, but he sat for a while yet, stroking her knee. Then he rose and thrust his hands into his gown, but turning, he paused again and drew forth an envelope from his pocket. "Here's a letter for you. I forgot it this afternoon. Sorry."

She was reading again. "Put it on the table," she said, without raising her eyes. He laid the letter on the table and quitted the room. At the door he looked back, but her head was bent over her book.

As he removed his clothes it did seem that that heavy fading odor of Belle's body clung to them, and to his hands even after he was in bed; and clinging, shaped in the darkness beside him Belle's rich voluption, until within that warm, not-yet-sleeping region where dwells the mother of dreams, Belle grew palpable in ratio as his own body slipped away from him. And Harry too, with his dogged inarticulateness and his hurt groping which was partly damaged vanity and shock, yet mostly a boy's sincere bewilderment, that freed itself terrifically in the form of movie subtitles. Just before he slept his mind, with the mind's uncanny attribute of irrelevant recapitulation, reproduced with the startling ghostliness of a dictaphone, an incident which at the time he had considered trivial. Belle had freed her mouth, and for a moment, her body still against his, she held his face in her two hands and stared at him with intent questioning eyes. "Have you plenty of money, Horace?" And "Yes," he had answered immediately. "Of course I have." And then Belle again, enveloping him like a rich and fatal drug, like a motionless and cloying sea in which he watched himself drown.

The letter lay on the table that night, forgotten; it was not until the next morning that she discovered it and opened it.

"I am trying to forget you I cannot forget you Your big eyes your black hair how white your black hair make you look. And how you walk I am watching you a smell you give off like a flowr. Your eyes shine with mistry and how you walk makes me sick like a fevver all night thinking how you walk. I could touch you you would not know it Every day. But I can not I must pore out on paper must talk You do not know who. Your lips like cupids bow when the day comes when I will press them to mine like I dreamed like a fevver from heaven to hell. I know what you do I know more than you think I see men visting you with bitter twangs. Be care full I am a desprate man Nothing any more to me now If you unholy love a man I will kill him.

"You do not anser. I know you got it I saw one in your hand bag. You better anser soon I am desprate man eat up with fevver I can not sleep for. I will not hurt you but I am desprate. Do not forget I will not hurt you but I am a desprate man."

Meanwhile the days accumulated. Not sad days nor

lonely: they were too feverish to be sorrowful, what with her nature torn in two directions, and the walls of her serene garden cast down, and she herself like a night animal or bird caught in a beam of light and trying vainly to escape. Horace had definitely gone his way; and like two strangers they followed the routine of their physical days, in an unbending estrangement of long affection and similar pride beneath a shallow veneer of trivialities. She sat with Bayard almost every day now, but at a discreet distance of two yards. At first he tried to override her with bluster, then with cajolery. But she was firm and at last he desisted and lay gazing quietly out the window or sleeping while she read. From time to time Miss Jenny would come to the door and look in at them and go away. Her shrinking, her sense of anticipation and dread while with him, was gone now, and at times instead of reading they talked, quietly and impersonally, with the ghost of that other afternoon between them, though neither ever referred to it. Miss Jenny had been a little curious about that day, but Narcissa was gravely and demurely noncommittal about it; nor had Bayard ever talked of it, and so there was another bond between them, but unirksome. Miss Jenny had heard gossip about Horace and Belle, but on this subject also Narcissa had nothing to say.

"Have it your own way," Miss Jenny said tartly. "I can draw my own conclusions. I imagine Belle and Horace can produce quite a mess together. And I'm glad of it. That man is making an old maid out of you. It isn't too late now, but if he'd waited five years later to play the fool, there wouldn't be anything left for you except to give music lessons. But you can get married, now."

"Would you advise me to marry?" Narcissa asked.

"I wouldn't advise anybody to marry. You wont be happy, but then, women haven't got civilized enough yet to be happy unmarried, so you might as well try it. We can stand anything, anyhow. And change is good for folks. They say it is, at least."

But Narcissa didn't believe that. I shall never marry, she told herself. Men. . . . . . . that was where unhappiness lay, getting men into your life. And if I couldn't keep Horace, loving him as I did. . . . . . . Bayard slept. She picked up the book and read on to herself, about antic people in an antic world where things happened as they should. The shadows lengthened eastward. She read on, lost from mutable things.

After a while Bayard waked, and she fetched him a cigarette and a match. "You wont have to do this any more," he said. "I reckon you're sorry."

His cast would come off tomorrow, he meant, and he lay smoking his cigarette and talking of what he would do when he was about again. He would see about getting his car repaired first thing; have to take it to Memphis, probably. And he planned a trip for the three of them—Miss Jenny, Narcissa, and himself—while the car was in the shop. "It'll take about a week," he added. "She must be in pretty bad shape. Hope I didn't hurt her guts any."

"But you aren't going to drive it fast anymore," she reminded him. He lay still, his cigarette burning in his fingers. "You promised," she insisted.

"When did I promise?"

"Don't you remember? That. . . . . . . afternoon, when they were. . . . . . . "

"When I scared you?" She sat watching him with her grave troubled eyes. "Come here," he said. She rose and went to the bed and he took her hand.

"You wont drive it fast again?" she persisted.

"No," he answered. "I promise." And they were still so, her hand in his. The curtains stirred in the breeze, and the leaves on the branch beyond the window twinkled and turned and lisped against one another. Sunset was not far away; it would cease then. He moved.

"Narcissa," he said, and she looked at him. "Lean your face down here."

She looked away, and for a while there was no movement, no sound between them.

"I must go," she said at last, quietly, and he released her hand.

His cast was gone, and he was up and about again, moving a little gingerly, to be sure, but already Miss Jenny was beginning to contemplate him a little anxiously. "If we could just arrange to have one of his minor bones broken every month or so, just enough to keep him in the house. . . ."

"That wont be necessary," Narcissa told her. "He's going to behave from now on."

"How do you know?" Miss Jenny demanded. "What in the world makes you think that?"

"He promised he would."

"He'll promise anything when he's flat on his back," Miss Jenny retorted. "They all will; always have. But what makes you think he'll keep it?"

"He promised me he would," Narcissa replied serenely.

His first act was to see about his car. It had been pulled into town and patched up after a fashion until it would run under its own power, but it would be necessary to take it to Memphis to have the frame straightened and the body repaired. Bayard was all for doing this himself, fresh-knit ribs and all, but Miss Jenny put her foot down and after a furious half hour, he was vanquished. And so the car was driven in to Memphis by a youth who hung around one of the garages in town. "Narcissa'll take you driving in her car, if you must ride," Miss Jenny told him.

"In that little peanut parcher?" Bayard said derisively. "It wont do more than twenty one miles an hour."

"No, thank God," Miss Jenny answered. "And I've written to Memphis and asked 'em to fix yours so it'll run just like that, too."

Bayard stared at her with humorless bleakness. "Did you do any such damn thing as that?"

"Oh, take him away, Narcissa," Miss Jenny exclaimed. "Get him out of my sight. I'm so tired of looking at you."

But he wouldn't ride in Narcissa's car at first. He missed no opportunity to speak of it with heavy, facetious disparagement, but he wouldn't ride in it. Dr Alford had evolved a tight elastic bandage for his chest so that he could ride his horse, but he had developed an astonishing propensity for lounging about the house when Narcissa was there. And Narcissa came quite often. Miss Jenny thought it was on Bayard's account and pinned the guest down in her forthright way; whereupon Narcissa told her about Horace and Belle while Miss Jenny sat indomitably erect on her straight chair beside the piano.

"Poor child," she said, and "Lord, aint they fools?" and then: "Well, you're right; I wouldn't marry one of 'em either."

"I'm not," Narcissa answered. "I wish there weren't any of them in the world."

Miss Jenny said, "Hmph."

And then one afternoon they were in Narcissa's car and Bayard was driving, over her protest at first. But he was behaving himself quite sensibly, and at last she relaxed. They drove down the valley road and turned into the hills and she asked where they were going, but his answer was vague. So she sat quietly beside him and the road mounted presently in long curves among dark pines in the slanting afternoon. The road wound on, with changing sunshot vistas of the valley and the opposite hills at every turn, and always the sombre pines and their faint exhilarating odor. After a time they topped a hill and Bayard slowed the car. Beneath them the road sank, then flattened away toward a line of willows, crossed a stone bridge and rose again curving redly from sight among the dark trees.

"There's the place," he said.

"The place?" she repeated dreamily; then as the car rolled forward again, gaining speed, she roused herself and understood what he meant. "You promised," she cried, but he jerked the throttle down its ratchet and she clutched him and tried to scream. But she could make no sound, nor could she close her eyes as the narrow bridge hurtled dancing toward them. And then her breath stopped and her heart as they flashed with a sharp reverberation like hail on a tin roof, between willows and a crashing glint of water and shot on up the next hill. The small car swayed on the curve, lost its footing and went into the ditch, bounded out and hurled across the road. Then Bayard straightened it out and with diminishing speed it rocked on up the hill, and stopped. She sat beside him, her bloodless mouth open, beseeching him with her wide hopeless eyes. Then she caught her breath, wailing.

"I didn't mean—" he began awkwardly. "I just wanted to see if I could do it," and he put his arms around her and she clung to him, moving her hands crazily about his shoulders. "I didn't mean——" he essayed again, and then her crazed hands were on his face and she was sobbing wildly against his mouth.

10

Through the morning hours and following his sleepless night, he bent over his desk beneath the green-shaded light, penning his neat, meticulous figures into the ledgers. The routine of the bank went on; old Bayard sat in his tilted chair in the fresh August morning while passers went to and fro, greeting him with florid cheerful gestures and receiving in return his half military salute—people cheerful and happy with their orderly affairs; the cashier served the morning line of depositors and swapped jovial anecdote with them. For this was the summer cool spell and there was a vividness in the air, a presage of the golden days of frost and yellowing persimmons in the wornout fields, and of sweet small grapes in the matted vines along the sandy branches, and the scent of cooking sorghum upon the smoky air. But Snopes crouched over his desk after his sleepless night, with jealousy and thwarted desire and furious impotent rage in his vitals.

His head felt hot and dull, and heavy, and to the cashier's surprise, he offered to buy the coca-colas, ordering two for himself, drank them one after the other and returned to his ledgers. So the morning wore away. His neat figures accumulated slowly in the ruled columns, steadily and with a maddening aloofness from his own turmoil and without a mistake although his mind coiled and coiled upon itself, tormenting him with fleeing obscene images in which she moved with another. He had thought it dreadful when he was not certain that there was another; but now to know it, to find knowledge of it on every tongue. . . . . . . and young Sartoris, at that: a man whom he had hated instinctively with all his sense of inferiority and all the venom of his worm-like nature. Married, married. Adultery, concealed if suspected, he could have borne; but this, boldly, in the world's face, flouting him with his own impotence. . . . . . . He dug a cheap, soiled handkerchief from his hip pocket and wiped the saliva from his jaws.

By changing his position a little he could see old Bayard, could catch a glint of his white suit where he sat oblivious in the door. There was a sort of fascination in the old fellow now, serving as he did as an object upon which Snopes could vent the secret, vicarious rage of his half-insane mind. And all during the morning he watched the other covertly; once old Bayard entered the cage and passed within arms' length of him, and when he moved his hand to wipe his drooling mouth, he found that the page had adhered to his wrist, blotting the last entry he had made. With his knife blade he erased the smear and rewrote it.

All the forenoon he bent over his ledgers, watching his hand pen the neat figures into the ruled columns with a sort of astonishment. After his sleepless night he labored in a kind of stupor, his mind too spent even to contemplate the coiling images of his lust, thwarted now for all time, save with a dull astonishment that the images no longer filled his blood with fury and despair, so that it was some time before his dulled nerves reacted to a fresh threat and caused him to raise his head. Virgil Beard was just entering the door.

He slid hurriedly from his stool and slipped around the corner and darted through the door of old Bayard's office. He crouched within the door, heard the boy ask politely for him, heard the cashier say that he was there a minute ago but that he reckoned he had stepped out; heard the boy say well, he reckoned he'd wait for him. And he crouched within the door, wiping his drooling mouth with his handkerchief.

After a while he opened the door cautiously. The boy squatted patiently and blandly on his heels against the wall, and Snopes stood again with his clenched trembling hands. He did not curse: his desperate fury was beyond words; but his breath came and went with a swift ah-ah-ah sound in his throat and it seemed to him that his eyeballs were being drawn back and back into his skull, turning further and further until the cords that drew them reached the snapping point. He opened the door.

"Hi, Mr Snopes," the boy said genially, rising; but Snopes strode on and entered the grille and approached the cashier.

"Res," he said, in a voice scarcely articulate, "gimme five dollars."

"What?"

"Gimme five dollars," he repeated hoarsely. The cashier did so, scribbled a notation and speared it on the file at his elbow. The boy had come up to the second window, but Snopes went on and he followed the man back to the office, his bare feet hissing on the linoleum floor.

"I tried to find you last night," he explained. "But you wasn't to home." Then he looked up and saw Snopes' face, and after a moment he screamed and broke his trance and turned to flee. But the man caught him by his overalls, and he writhed and twisted, screaming with utter terror as the man dragged him across the office and opened the door that gave onto the vacant lot. Snopes was trying to say something in his mad, shaking voice, but the boy screamed steadily, hanging limp from the other's hand as he tried to thrust the bill into his pocket. At last he succeeded and the boy, who staggered away, found his legs, and fled.

"What were you whuppin' that boy, for?" the cashier asked curiously, when Snopes returned to his desk.

"For not minding his own business," he snapped, opening his ledger again.

During the hour the cashier was out to lunch Snopes was his outward usual self—uncommunicative but efficient, a little covertly sullen, with his mean, close-set eyes and his stubby

features; patrons remarked nothing unusual in his bearing.
Nor did the cashier when he returned, sucking a toothpick and
belching at intervals. But instead of going home to dinner,
Snopes repaired to a street occupied by negro stores and barber
shops and inquired from door to door. After a half hour search
he found the negro he sought, held a few minutes' conversation with him, then returned across town to his cousin's restaurant and had a platter of hamburger steak and a cup of coffee.
At two oclock he was back at his desk.

The afternoon passed. Three oclock came; he went
around and touched old Bayard's shoulder and he rose and
dragged his chair inside and Snopes closed the doors and drew
the green shades upon the windows. Then he totaled his
ledgers while the cashier counted the cash. In the meantime
Simon drove up to the door and presently old Bayard stalked
forth and got in the carriage and was driven off. Snopes and the
cashier compared notes and struck a balance, and while the
other stacked the money away in receptacles he carried his
ledgers one by one into the vault. The cashier followed with
the cash and put it away and they emerged as the cashier was
about to close the vault, when Snopes stopped him. "Forgot
that cash-book," he explained. The cashier returned to his window and Snopes carried the book into the vault and put it away
and emerged and clashed the door to, and hiding the dial with
his body, he rattled the knob briskly. The cashier had his back
turned, rolling a cigarette.

"See it's throwed good," he said. Snopes rattled the knob
again, then shook the door.

"That's got it." They took their hats and emerged from the
cage and locked it behind them, and passed through the front
door, which the cashier closed and shook also. He struck a
match to his cigarette.

"See you tomorrow," he said.

"All right," Snopes agreed, and he stood looking after the other's shapeless back in its shabby alpaca coat. He produced his soiled handkerchief and wiped his mouth again.

That evening about eight oclock he was back downtown. He stood for a time with the group that sat nightly in front of the drug store on the corner; stood quietly among them, listening but saying nothing, as was his way. Then he moved on, without being missed, and walked slowly up the street and stopped at the bank door. One or two passers spoke to him while he was finding his key and opening the door; he responded in his flat country idiom and entered and closed the door behind him. A single bulb burned above the vault. He raised the shade on the window beside it and entered the grilled cage and turned on the light above his desk. Here passers could see him, could have watched him for several minutes as he bent over his desk, writing slowly. It was his final letter, in which he poured out his lust and his hatred and his jealousy, and the language was the obscenity which his jealousy and desire had hoarded away in his temporarily half-crazed mind and which the past night and day had liberated. When it was finished he blotted it carefully and folded it and put it in his pocket, and snapped his light off. He entered the directors' room and in the darkness he unlocked the door which gave onto the vacant lot, closed it and left it unlocked.

He returned to the front and drew the shade on the window, and drew the other shades to their full extent, until no crack of light showed at their edges, emerged and locked the door behind him. On the street he looked casually back at the windows. The shades were drawn close; the interior of the bank was invisible from the street.

The group still talked in front of the drug store and he stopped again on the outskirts of it. People passed back and forth along the street and in or out of the drug store; one or two of the group drifted away, and newcomers took their places. An automobile drew up to the curb, was served by a negro lad; drove away. The clock on the courthouse struck nine measured strokes.

Soon, with a noise of starting engines, motor cars began to stream out of a side street and onto the square, and presently a flux of pedestrians appeared. It was the exodus from the picture show, and cars one after another drew up to the curb with young men and girls in them, and other youths and girls in pairs turned into the drug store with talk and shrill laughter and cries one to another, with slender bodies in delicate colored dresses, shrill as apes and awkward, divinely young. Then the more sedate groups—a man with a child or so gazing longingly into the scented and gleaming interior of the store, followed by three or four women—his wife and a neighbor or so—talking sedately among themselves; more children—little girls in prim and sibilant clots, and boys scuffling and darting with changing adolescent shouts. A few of the sitters rose and joined passing groups.

More belated couples came up the street and entered the drug store, and other cars; other couples emerged and strolled on. The night watchman came along presently, with his star on his open vest and a pistol and a flash light in his hip pockets; he too stopped and joined in the slow, unhurried talk. The last couple emerged from the drug store, and the last car drove away. And presently the lights behind them flashed off and the proprietor jingled his keys in the door and rattled it, and stood for a moment among them, then went on. Ten oclock. Snopes rose to his feet.

"Well, I reckon I'll turn in," he said generally.

"Time we all did," another said, and they rose also. "Good night, Buck."

"Good night, gentlemen," the night watchman replied.

As he crossed the now empty square he looked up at the lighted face of the clock. It was ten minutes past eleven. There was no sign of life save the lonely figure of the night marshal in the door of the lighted postoffice lobby.

He left the square and entered a street and went steadily beneath the arc lights, having the street to himself and the regular recapitulation of his striding shadow dogging him out of the darkness, through the pool of the light and into darkness again. He turned a corner and followed a yet quieter street and turned presently from it into a lane between massed banks of honeysuckle higher than his head and sweet on the night air. The lane was dark and he increased his pace. On either hand the upper stories of houses rose above the honeysuckle, with now and then a lighted window among the dark trees. He kept close to the wall and went swiftly on, passing now between back premises. After a while another house loomed, and a serried row of cedars against the paler sky, and he stole beside a stone wall and so came opposite the garage. He stopped here and sought in the lush grass beneath the wall and stooped and picked up a pole, which he leaned against the wall. With the aid of the pole he mounted on to the wall and thence to the garage roof.

But the house was dark, and presently he slid to the ground and stole across the lawn and stopped beneath a window. There was a light somewhere toward the front, but no sound, no movement, and he stood for a time listening, darting his eyes this way and that, covert and ceaseless as a cornered animal.

The screen responded easily to his knife and he raised it and listened again. Then with a single scrambling motion he was in the room, crouching. Still no sound save the thudding of his heart, and the whole house gave off that unmistakable

emanation of temporary desertion. He drew out his handkerchief and wiped his mouth.

The light was in the next room, and he went on. The stairs
rose from the end of this room and he scuttled silently across it
and mounted swiftly into the upper darkness and groped forward until he touched a wall, then a door. The knob turned
under his fingers.

It was the right room; he knew that at once: her presence
was all about him, and for a time his heart thudded and thudded in his throat and fury and lust and despair shook him. He
pulled himself together; he must get out quickly, and he
groped his way across to the bed and lay face down upon it, his
head buried in the pillows, writhing and making smothered,
animal-like moanings. But he must get out, and he got up and
groped across the room again. What little light there was was
behind him now, and instead of finding the door he blundered
into a chest of drawers, and stood there a moment, learning its
shape with his hands. Then he opened one of the drawers and
fumbled in it. It was filled with a faintly scented fragility of garments, but he could not distinguish one from another with his
hands.

He found a match in his pocket and struck it beneath the
shelter of his palm, and by its light he chose one of the soft garments, discovering as the match died a packet of letters in the
corner of the drawer. He recognised them at once, dropped the
dead match to the floor and took the packet from the drawer
and put it in his pocket, and placed the letter he had just written in the drawer, and he stood for a time with the garment
crushed against his face; remained so for some time, until a
sound caused him to jerk his head up, listening. A car was
coming up the drive, and as he sprang to the window, its lights
swept beneath him and fell full upon the open garage, and he
crouched at the window in a panic. Then he sped to the door

and stopped again crouching, panting and snarling with indecision.

He ran back to the window. The garage was dark, and two dark figures were approaching the house and he crouched beside the window until they had passed from sight. Then, still clutching the garment, he climbed out the window and swung from the sill a moment by his hands, and closed his eyes and dropped.

A crash of glass and he sprawled numbed by shock amid lesser crashes and a burst of stale, dry dust. He had fallen into a shallow flower pit and he scrambled out and tried to stand and fell again, while nausea swirled in him. It was his knee, and he lay sick and with drawn, gasping lips while his trouser leg sopped slowly and warmly, clutching the garment and staring at the dark sky with wide, mad eyes. He heard voices in the house, and a light came on behind the window above him and he turned crawling, and at a scrambling hobble he crossed the lawn and plunged into the shadow of the cedars beside the garage, where he lay watching the window in which a man leaned, peering out; and he moaned a little while his blood ran between his clasped fingers. He drove himself onward again and dragged his bleeding leg on up to the wall and dropped into the lane and cast the pole down. A hundred yards further he stopped and drew his torn trousers aside and tried to bandage the gash in his leg. But the handkerchief stained over almost at once, and still blood ran and ran down his leg and into his shoe.

Once in the back room of the bank, he rolled his trouser leg up and removed the handkerchief and bathed the gash at the lavatory. It still bled, and the sight of his own blood sickened him, and he swayed against the wall, watching his blood. Then he removed his shirt and bound it as tightly as he could about his leg. He still felt nausea, and he drank long of the tepid water from the tap. Immediately it welled salinely within him and he clung to the lavatory, sweating, trying not to vomit, until the spell passed. His leg felt numb and dead, and he was weak and he wished to lie down but he dared not.

He entered the grille, his left heel showing yet a red print at each step. The vault door opened soundlessly; without a light he found the key to the cash box and opened it. He took only banknotes, but he took all he could find. Then he closed the vault and locked it, returned to the lavatory and wetted a towel and removed his heel prints from the linoleum floor. Then he passed out the back door, threw the latch so it would lock behind him. The clock on the courthouse rang midnight.

In an alley between two negro stores a man sat in a battered ford, waiting. He gave the negro a bill and the negro cranked the engine and came and stared curiously at the bloody cloth beneath his torn trousers. "Whut happened, boss? Y'aint hurt, is you?"

"Run into some wire," he answered shortly. "She's got plenty gas, aint she?" The negro said yes, and he drove on. As he crossed the square the night marshal, Buck, stood beneath the light before the postoffice, and Snopes cursed him with silent and bitter derision. He drove on and entered another street and passed from view, and presently the sound of his going had died away.

He drove through Frenchman's Bend at two oclock, without stopping. The village was dark; Varner's store, the blacksmith shop (now a garage too, with a gasoline pump), Mrs Littlejohn's huge, unpainted boarding house—all the remembered scenes of his boyhood—were without life; he went on. He drove now along a rutted wagon road, between swampy jungle, at a snail's pace. After a half hour the road mounted a small knoll wooded with scrub oak and indiscriminate saplings, and faded into a barren, sun-baked surface in the middle of which squatted a low, broken backed log house. His lights swept across its gaping front, and a huge gaunt hound descended from the porch and bellowed at him. He stopped and switched the lights off.

His leg was stiff and dead, and when he descended he was forced to cling to the car for a time, moving it back and forth until it would bear his weight. The hound stood ten feet away and thundered at him in a sober conscientious fury until he spoke to it, whereupon it ceased its clamor but stood yet in an attitude of watchful belligerence. He limped toward it, and it recognised him, and together they crossed the barren plot in the soundless dust and mounted the veranda. "Turpin," he called in a guarded voice.

The dog had followed him onto the porch, and it flopped noisily and scratched itself. The house consisted of two wings joined by an open hall; through the hall he could see sky, and another warped roof tree on the slope behind the house. His leg tingled and throbbed as with pins of fire. I got that 'ere bandage too tight, he thought. "Turpin."

A movement from the wing at his left, and into the lesser obscurity of the hall a shape emerged and stood in vague relief against the sky, in a knee-length night-shirt and a shot gun. "Who's thar?" the shape demanded.

"Byron Snopes."

The man leaned the gun against the wall and came onto the porch, and they shook hands limply. "What you doin', this time of night? Thought you was in town."

"On a trip for the bank," Snopes explained. "Just drove in, and I got to git right on. Might be gone some time, and I wanted to see Minnie Sue."

The other rubbed the wild shock of his head, then he scratched his leg. "She's a-sleepin'. Caint you wait till daylight?"

"I got to git on," he repeated. "Got to be pretty nigh Alabama by daybreak."

The man brooded heavily, rubbing his flank. "Well," he said finally. "Ef you caint wait till mawnin'." He padded back into the house and vanished. The hound flopped again at Snopes' feet and sniffed noisily. From the river bottom a mile away an owl hooted with its mournful rising inflection. Snopes thrust his hand into his coat and touched the wadded delicate garment. In his breast pocket the money bulked against his arm.

Another figure stepped soundlessly into the hall, against the lighter sky; a smaller figure and even more shapeless, that stood for a moment, then came out to him. He put his arms around her, feeling her free body beneath the rough garment she had hastily donned. "Byron?" she said. "What is it, Byron?" He was trying to kiss her, and she suffered him readily, but withdrew her face immediately, peering at him. He drew her away from the door.

"Come on," he whispered. His voice was shaking and hoarse, and his body was trembling also. He led her to the steps and tried to draw her on, but she held back a little, peering at him.

"Let's set on the steps," she said. "What's the matter, Byron? You got a chill?"

"I'm all right. Let's git away where we can talk."

She let him draw her forward and down the steps, but as they moved further and further away from the house she began to resist, with curiosity and growing alarm. "Byron," she said again and stopped. His hands were trembling upon her, moving about her body, and his voice was shaking so that she could not understand him.

"You aint got on nothing under here but your nightgown, have you?" he whispered.

"What?" He drew her a little farther, but she stopped firmly and he could not move her; she was as strong as he. "You tell me what it is, now," she commanded. "You aint ready fer our marryin' yet, are you?"

But he made no answer. He was trembling more than ever, pawing at her. They struggled, and at last he succeeded in dragging her to the ground and he sprawled beside her, pawing at her clothing; whereupon she struggled in earnest, and soon she held him helpless while he sprawled with his face against her throat, babbling a name not hers. When he was still she turned and thrust him away, and rose to her feet.

"You come back tomorrer, when you git over this," she said, and she ran silently toward the house, and was gone.

He sat where she had left him for a long time, with his half-insane face between his knees and madness and helpless rage and thwarted desire coiling within him. The owl hooted again from the black river bottom; its cry faded mournfully across the land, beneath the chill stars, and the hound came silently through the dust and sniffed at him, and went away. After a time he rose and limped to the car and started the engine.

Four

1

It was a sunny Sunday afternoon in October. Narcissa and Bayard had driven off soon after dinner, and Miss Jenny and old Bayard were sitting on the sunny end of the veranda when, preceded by Simon, the deputation came solemnly around the corner of the house from the rear. It consisted of six negroes in a catholic variety of Sunday raiment and it was headed by a huge, bull-necked negro in a hind-side-before collar and a prince albert coat, with an orotund air and a wild, compelling eye.

"Yere dey is, Cunnel," Simon said, and without pausing he mounted the steps and turned about, leaving no doubt in any one's mind as to which side he considered himself aligned with. The deputation halted and milled a little, solemnly decorous.

"What's this?" Miss Jenny asked. "That you, uncle Bird?"

"Yessum, Miss Jenny." One of the committee uncovered his grizzled wool and bowed. "How you gittin' on?" The others shuffled their feet, and one by one they removed their hats. The leader clasped his across his chest like a congressman being photographed.

"Here, Simon," old Bayard demanded. "What's this? What did you bring these niggers around here for?"

"Dey come fer dey money," Simon explained.

"What?"

"Money?" Miss Jenny repeated with interest. "What money, Simon?"

"Dey come fer de money you promised 'um," Simon shouted.

"I told you I wasn't going to pay that money," old Bayard said. "Did Simon tell you I was going to pay it?" he demanded of the deputation.

"What money?" Miss Jenny repeated. "What are you talking about, Simon?" The leader of the committee was shaping his face for words, but Simon forestalled him.

"Why, Cunnel, you tole me yo'self to tell dem niggers you wuz gwine pay 'um."

"I didn't do any such thing," old Bayard answered violently. "I told you that if they wanted to put you in jail, to go ahead and do it. That's what I told you."

"Why, Cunnel, you said it des' ez plain. You jes' fergot erbout it. I kin prove it by Miss Jenny you tole me——"

"Not by me," Miss Jenny interrupted. "This is the first I heard about it. Whose money is it, Simon?"

Simon gave her a pained, reproachful look. "He tole me to tell 'um he wuz gwine pay it."

"I'm damned if I did," old Bayard shouted. "I told you I wouldn't pay a damn cent of it. And I told you that if you let 'em worry me about it, I'd skin you alive, sir."

"I aint gwine let 'um worry you," Simon answered soothingly. "Dat's whut I'm fixin' now. You jes' give 'um dey money, en me en you kin fix it up later."

"I'll be eternally damned, if I will; if I let a lazy nigger that aint worth his keep——"

"But somebody got to pay 'um," Simon pointed out patiently. "Aint dat right, Miss Jenny?"

"That's right," Miss Jenny agreed. "But I aint the one."

"Yessuh, dey aint no argument dat somebody got to pay 'um. Ef somebody dont quiet 'um down, dey'll put me in de jail. And den whut'll y'all do, widout nobody to keep dem hosses fed en clean, en to clean de house en wait on de table? Co'se I dont mine gwine to jail, even ef dem stone flo's aint gwine do my mis'ry no good." And he drew a long and affecting picture, of high and grail-like principles, and of patient abnegation. Old Bayard slammed his feet to the floor.

"How much is it?"

The leader swelled within his prince albert. "Brudder Mo'," he said, "will you read out de total emoluments owed to de pupposed Secon' Baptis' church by de late Deacon Strother in his capacity ez treasurer of de church boa'd?"

Brother Moore created a mild disturbance in the rear of the group, emerging presently by the agency of sundry willing hands—a small, reluctant ebon negro in sombre, overlarge black—where the parson majestically made room for him, contriving by some means to focus attention on him. He laid his hat on the ground at his feet and from the right hand pocket of his coat he produced in order, a red bandanna handkerchief; a shoe horn; a plug of chewing tobacco, and holding these in his free hand he delved again, with an expression of mildly conscientious alarm. Then he replaced the objects, and from his left pocket he produced a pocket knife; a stick on which was wound a length of soiled twine; a short piece of leather strap attached to a rusty and apparently idle buckle, and lastly a greasy, dogeared notebook. He crammed the other things back into his pocket, dropping the strap, which he stooped and recovered, then he and the parson held a brief whispered conversation. He opened the notebook and fumbled at the leaves, fumbled at them until the parson leaned over his shoulder and found the proper page and laid his finger upon it.

"How much is it, reverend?" old Bayard asked impatiently.

"Brudder Mo' will now read out de amount," the parson intoned. Brother Moore looked at the page with his tranced gaze and mumbled something in a practically indistinguishable voice.

"What?" old Bayard demanded, cupping his ear.

"Make 'im talk up," Simon said. "Cant nobody tell whut he sayin'."

"Louder," the parson rumbled, with just a trace of impatience.

"Sixty sevum dollars en fawty cents," Brother Moore enunciated at last. Old Bayard slammed back in his chair and swore for a long minute while Simon watched him with covert anxiety. Then he rose and tramped up the veranda and into the house, still swearing. Simon sighed and relaxed. The deputation milled again, and Brother Moore faded briskly into the rear rank of it. The parson however still retained his former attitude of fateful and impressive profundity.

"What became of that money, Simon?" Miss Jenny asked curiously. "You had it, didn't you?"

"Dat's whut dey claims," Simon answered.

"What did you do with it?"

"Hit's all right," Simon assured her. "I jes' put it out, sort of."

"I bet you did," she agreed drily. "I bet it never even got cool while you had it. They deserve to lose it for ever giving it to you in the first place. Who did you put it out to?"

"Oh, me en Cunnel done fix dat up," Simon said easily. "Long time ago." Old Bayard tramped in the hall again, and emerged flapping a check in his hand.

"Here," he commanded, and the parson approached the railing and took it and folded it away in his pocket. "And if you folks are fools enough to turn any more money over to him, dont come to me for it, you hear?" He glared at the deputation a moment; then he glared at Simon. "And the next time you steal money and come to me to pay it back, I'm going to have you arrested and prosecute you myself. Get those niggers out of here."

The deputation had already stirred, with a concerted movement, but the parson halted them with a commanding hand. He faced Simon again. "Deacon Strother," he said, "ez awdained minister of de late Fust Baptis' church, en recalled minister of de pupposed Secon' Baptis' church, en chairman of dis committee, I hereby reinfestes you wid yo' fawmer capacity of deacon in de said pupposed Secon' Baptis' church. Amen. Cunnel Sartoris en ma'am, good day." Then he turned and herded his committee from the scene.

"Thank de Lawd, we got dat offen our mind," Simon said, and he came and lowered himself to the top step, groaning pleasurably.

"And you remember what I said," old Bayard warned him. "One more time, now——"

But Simon was craning his head in the direction the church board had taken. "Dar now," he said. "Whut you reckon dey wants now?" For the committee had returned and it now peered diffidently around the corner of the house.

"Well," old Bayard demanded. "What is it now?"

They were trying to thrust Brother Moore forward again, but he won this time. At last the parson spoke.

"You fergot de fawty cents, white folks."

"What?"

"He says you lef' out de extry fawty cents," Simon shouted. Old Bayard exploded; Miss Jenny clapped her hands to her ears and the committee rolled its eyes in fearsome admiration while he soared to magnificent heights, alighting finally upon Simon.

"You give him that forty cents, and get 'em out of here," old Bayard stormed. "And if you ever let 'em come back here again, I'll take a horsewhip to the whole passel of you."

"Lawd, Cunnel, I aint got no fawty cents, en you knows it. Cant dey do widout dat, after gittin' de balance of it?"

"Yes you have, Simon," Miss Jenny said. "You had a half a dollar left after I ordered those shoes for you last night." Again Simon looked at her with pained astonishment.

"Give it to 'em," old Bayard commanded. Slowly Simon reached into his pocket and produced a half dollar and turned it slowly in his palm.

"I mought need dis money, Cunnel," he protested. "Seems like dey mought leave me dis."

"Give 'em that money!" old Bayard thundered. "I reckon you can pay forty cents of it, at least." Simon rose reluctantly, and the parson approached.

"Whar's my dime change?" Simon demanded, nor would he surrender the coin until two nickels were in his hand. Then the committee departed.

"Now," old Bayard said, "I want to know what you did with that money."

"Well, suh," Simon began readily, "it wuz like dis. I put dat money out." Miss Jenny rose.

"My Lord, are you all going over that again?" And she left them. In her room, where she sat in a sunny window, she could still hear them—old Bayard's stormy rage, and Simon's bland and plausible evasion rising and falling on the drowsy Sabbath air.

There was a rose, a single remaining rose. Through the sad, dead days of late summer it had continued to bloom, and now though persimmons had long swung their miniature suns among the caterpillar-festooned branches, and gum and maple and hickory had flaunted two gold-and-scarlet weeks, and the grass, where grandfathers of grasshoppers squatted sluggishly like sullen octogenarians, had been pencilled twice delicately with frost, and the sunny noons were scented with sassafras, it still bloomed. Overripe now, and a little gallantly blowsy, like a fading burlesque star. Miss Jenny worked in a sweater, nowadays, and her trowel glinted in her earthy glove.

"It's like some women I've known," she said. "It just dont know how to give up gracefully and be a grandmamma."

"Let it have the summer out," Narcissa in her dark woolen dress, protested. She had a trowel too, and she pottered serenely after Miss Jenny's scolding brisk impatience, accomplishing nothing. Worse than nothing, worse than Isom even, because she demoralized Isom, who had immediately given his unspoken allegiance to the Left, or passive, Wing. "It's entitled to its summer."

"Some folks dont know when summer's over," Miss Jenny rejoined. "Indian summer's no excuse for senile adolescence."

"It isn't senility, either."

"All right. You'll see, some day."

"Oh, someday. I'm not quite prepared to be a grand-mother, yet."

"You're doing pretty well." Miss Jenny trowelled a tulip bulb carefully and expertly up and removed the clotted earth from its roots. "We seem to have pretty well worn out Bayard, for the time being," she continued. "I reckon we'd better name him John this time."

"Yes?"

"Yes," Miss Jenny repeated. "We'll name him John. You, Isom!"

The gin had been running steadily for a month, now, what with the Sartoris cotton and that of other planters further up the valley, and of smaller croppers with their tilted fields among the hills. The Sartoris place was farmed on shares. Most of the tenants had picked their cotton, and gathered the late corn; and of late afternoons, with Indian summer upon the land and an ancient sadness sharp as woodsmoke on the windless air, Bayard and Narcissa would drive out to where, beside a spring on the edge of the woods, the negroes brought their cane and made their communal winter sorghum molasses. One of the negroes, a sort of patriarch among the tenants, owned the mill and the mule that furnished the motive power. He did the grinding and superintended the cooking of the sap for a tithe, and when Bayard and Narcissa arrived the mule would be plodding in a monotonous and patient circle, its feet rustling in the dried cane-pith, while one of the patriarch's grandsons fed the cane into the crusher.

Round and round the mule went, setting its narrow, deer-like feet delicately down in the hissing cane-pith, its neck bobbing limber as a section of rubber hose in the collar, with its trace-galled flanks and flopping, lifeless ears, and its half-closed eyes drowsing venomously behind pale lids, apparently asleep with the monotony of its own motion. Some Homer of the cotton fields should sing the saga of the mule and of his place in the South. He it was, more than any other one creature or thing, who, steadfast to the land when all else faltered before the hopeless juggernaut of circumstance, impervious to conditions that broke men's hearts because of his venomous and patient preoccupation with the immediate present, won the prone South from beneath the iron heel of Reconstruction and taught it pride again through humility and courage through adversity overcome; who accomplished the well-nigh impossible despite hopeless odds, by sheer and vindictive patience. Father and mother he does not resemble, sons and daughters he will never have; vindictive and patient (it is a known fact that he will labor ten years willingly and patiently for you, for the privilege of kicking you once); solitary but without pride, self-sufficient but without vanity; his voice is his own derision. Outcast and pariah, he has neither friend, wife, mistress nor sweetheart; celibate, he is unscarred, possesses neither pillar nor desert cave, he is not assaulted by temptations nor flagellated by dreams nor assuaged by visions; faith, hope and charity are not his. Misanthropic, he labors six days without reward for one creature whom he hates, bound with chains to another whom he despises, and spends the seventh day kicking or being kicked by his fellows. Misunderstood even by that creature (the nigger who drives him) whose impulses and mental processes most closely resemble his, he performs alien actions among alien surroundings; he finds bread not only for a race, but for an entire form of behavior; meek, his inheritance is cooked away from him along with his soul in a glue factory. Ugly, untiring and perverse, he can be moved neither by reason, flattery, nor promise of reward; he performs his humble monotonous duties without complaint, and his meed is blows. Alive, he is haled through the world, an object of general derision; unwept, unhonored and unsung, he bleaches his awkward, accusing bones among rusting cans and broken crockery and worn-out automobile tires on lonely hillsides, while his flesh soars unawares against the blue in the craws of buzzards.

As they approached, the groaning and creaking of the mill would be the first intimation, unless the wind happened to blow toward them. Then it would be the sharp, subtly exciting odor of fermentation and of boiling molasses. Bayard liked the smell of it, and they would drive up and stop for a time while the boy rolled his eyes covertly at them as he fed cane into the mill, while they watched the patient mule and the old man stooped above the simmering pot. Sometimes Bayard got out and went over and talked to him, leaving Narcissa in the car, lapped in the ripe odors of the failing year and all its rich, vague sadness, her gaze brooding upon Bayard and the old negro—the one lean and tall and fatally young and the other stooped with time, and her spirit went out in serene and steady waves, surrounding him unawares.

Then he would return and get in beside her, and she would touch his rough clothing but so lightly that he was not conscious of it, and they would drive back along the faint uneven road, beside the flaunting woods, and soon, above turning locusts and oaks, the white house simple and huge and steadfast, and the orange disc of the harvest moon getting above the ultimate hills, ripe as cheese.

Sometimes they went back after dark. The mill was still then, its long arm motionless across the firelit scene. The mule was munching in stable, or stamping and nuzzling its empty manger, or asleep standing, boding not of tomorrow; and against the firelight many shadows moved. The negroes had gathered now: old men and women sitting on crackling cushions of cane about the blaze which one of their number fed with pressed stalks until its incense-laden fury swirled licking at the boughs overhead, making more golden still the twinkling golden leaves; and young men and girls, and children squatting and still as animals, staring into the fire. Sometimes they sang—quavering, wordless chords in which plaintive minors blent with mellow bass in immemorial and sad suspense, their grave dark faces bent to the flames and with no motion of lips. But when the white folks arrived the singing ceased, and they sat or lay about the fire on which the blackened pot simmered, talking in broken murmurous overtones ready with sorrowful mirth, while in shadowy beds among the dry whispering canestalks youths and girls murmured and giggled.

Always one of them, and sometimes both, stopped in the office where old Bayard and Miss Jenny were. There was a fire of logs on the hearth now, and they would sit in the glow of it— Miss Jenny beneath the light with her lurid daily paper; old Bayard with his slippered feet propped against the fireplace, his head wreathed in smoke and the old setter dreaming fitfully beside his chair, reliving proud and ancient stands perhaps, or further back still, the lean, gawky days of his young doghood, when the world was full of scents that maddened the blood in him and pride had not taught him self-restraint; Narcissa and Bayard between them—Narcissa dreaming too in the firelight, grave and tranquil, and young Bayard smoking his cigarettes in his leashed and moody repose.

At last old Bayard would throw his cigar into the fire and drop his feet to the floor, and the dog would wake and raise its head and blink and yawn with such gaping deliberation that Narcissa, watching him, invariably yawned also. "Well, Jenny?"

Miss Jenny would lay her paper aside and rise. "Let me," Narcissa would say. "Let me go." But Miss Jenny never would, and presently she would return with a tray and three glasses, and old Bayard would unlock his desk and fetch the silver-stoppered decanter and compound three toddies with ritualistic care.

Once Bayard persuaded her into khaki and boots and carried her 'possum hunting. Caspey with a streaked lantern and a cow's horn slung over his shoulder, and Isom with a gunny sack and an axe, and four shadowy, restless hounds waited for them at the lot gate and they set off among ghostly shocks of corn, where every day Bayard kicked up a covey of quail, toward the woods.

"Where we going to start tonight, Caspey?" Bayard asked.

"Back of Unc' Henry's. Dey's one in dat grape vine behine de cotton house. Blue treed 'im down dar las' night."

"How do you know he's there tonight, Caspey?" Narcissa asked.

"He be back," Caspey answered confidently. "He right dar now, watchin' dis lantern wid his eyes scrooched up, listenin' to hear ef de dawgs wid us."

They climbed through a fence and Caspey stooped and set the lantern down. The dogs moiled and tugged about his legs with sniffings and throaty growls at one another as he unleashed them. "You, Ruby! Stan' still, dar. Hole up here, you potlickin' fool." They whimpered and surged, their eyes melting in fluid brief gleams, then they faded soundlessly and swiftly into the darkness. "Give 'um a little time," Caspey said. "Let 'um see ef he dar yit." From the darkness ahead a dog yapped three times on a high note. "Dat's dat young dog," Caspey said. "Jes' showin' off. He aint smelt nothin'." Overhead the stars swam vaguely in the hazy sky; the air was not yet chill, the earth still warm to the touch. They stood in a steady oasis of lantern light in a world of but one dimension, a vague cistern of darkness filled with meagre light and topped with an edgeless canopy of ragged stars. The lantern was smoking and emanating a faint odor of heat. Caspey raised it and turned the wick down and set it at his feet again. Then from the darkness there came a single note, resonant and low and grave.

"Dar he," Isom said.

"Hit's Ruby," Caspey agreed, picking up the lantern. "She got 'im." The young dog yapped again, with fierce hysteria, then the single low cry chimed. Narcissa slid her arm through Bayard's. "'Taint no rush," Caspey told her. "Dey aint treed yit. Whooy. H'mawn, dawg." The young dog had ceased its yapping, but still at intervals the other one bayed her single timbrous note, and they followed it. "H'mawn, dawg."

They stumbled a little over fading plow-scars, after Caspey's bobbing lantern, and the darkness went suddenly crescendic with short steady cries in four keys. "Dey got 'im," Isom said.

"Dat's right," Caspey replied. "Le's go. Hold 'im, dawg!" They trotted now, Narcissa clinging to Bayard's arm, and plunged through rank grass and over another fence and so among trees. Eyes gleamed fleetingly from the darkness ahead, and another gust of barking interspersed with tense and eager whimperings, and among stumbling half-lit shadows dogs surged about them. "He up dar," Caspey said. "Ole Blue sees 'im."

"Dar Unc' Henry's dawg, too," Isom said.

Caspey grunted. "I knowed he'd be here. He cant keep up wid a 'possum no mo', but jes' let a dog tree whar he kin hear 'im. . . ." He set the lantern upon his head and peered up into the vine-matted sapling, and Bayard drew a flashlight from his pocket and turned its beam into the tree. The three older hounds and Uncle Henry's ancient, moth-eaten beast sat in a tense circle about the tree, whimpering or barking in short spaced gusts, but the young one yapped steadily in mad, hysterical rushes. "Kick dat puppy still," Caspey commanded.

"You, Ginger, hush yo' mouf," Isom shouted; he laid his axe and sack down and caught the puppy and held it between his knees. Caspey and Bayard moved slowly about the tree, among the eager dogs; Narcissa followed them. "Dem vines is so thick up dar. . . . . . . " Caspey said.

"Here he is," Bayard said suddenly. "I've got 'im." He steadied his light and Caspey moved behind him and looked over his shoulder.

"Where?" Narcissa asked. "Can you see it?"

"Dat's right," Caspey agreed. "Dar he is. Ruby dont lie. When she say he dar, he dar."

"Where is he, Bayard?" Narcissa repeated. He drew her before him and trained the light over her head, into the tree,

and presently from the massed vines two reddish points of fire
not a match-breadth apart, gleamed at her, winked out, then
shone again.

"He movin'," Caspey said. "Young 'possum. Git up dar and
shake 'im out, Isom." Bayard held his light on the creature's
eyes and Caspey set his lantern down and herded the dogs
together at his knees. Isom scrambled up into the tree and vanished in the mass of vine, but they could follow his progress by
the shaking branches and his panting ejaculations as he threatened the animal with a mixture of cajolery and adjuration.

"Hah," he grunted. "Aint gwine hurt you. Aint gwine do
nothin' ter you but th'ow you in de cook-pot. Look out, mister;
I'se comin' up dar." More commotion; it ceased, they could
hear him moving the branches cautiously. "Here he," he
called suddenly. "Hole dem dawgs, now."

"Little 'un, aint he?" Caspey asked.

"Cant tell. Can't see nothin' but his face. Watch dem
dawgs." The upper part of the sapling burst into violent and
sustained fury; Isom whooped louder and louder as he shook
the branches. "Whooy, here he comes," he shouted, and something dropped sluggishly and reluctantly from branch to invisible branch, stopped, and the dogs set up a straining clamor.
The thing fell again, and Bayard's light followed a lumpy
object that plumped with a resounding thud to the ground and
vanished immediately beneath a swirl of hounds. Caspey and
Bayard leaped among them with shouts, and at last succeeded
in dragging them clear, and Narcissa saw the creature in the
pool of the flashlight, lying on its side in a grinning curve, its
eyes closed and its pink, baby-like hands doubled against its
breast. She looked at the motionless thing with pity and distinct loathing—such a paradox, its vulpine, skull-like grin and
those tiny, human-looking hands, and the long, rat-like tail of
it. Isom dropped from the tree, and Caspey turned the three

straining clamorous dogs he held over to his nephew and picked up the axe, and while Narcissa watched in shrinking curiosity, he laid the axe across the thing's neck and put his foot on either end of the helve, and grasped the animal's tail. . . . . . . She turned and fled, her hand to her mouth.

But the wall of darkness stopped her and she stood trembling and a little sick, watching them as they moved about the lantern. Then Caspey drove the dogs away, giving Uncle Henry's octogenarian a hearty and resounding kick that sent him homeward with bloodcurdling and astonished wails, and Isom swung the lumpy sack to his shoulder, and Bayard turned and looked for her. "Narcissa?"

"Here," she answered. He came to her.

"That's one. We ought to get a dozen, tonight."

"Oh, no," she shuddered. "No." He peered at her; then he snapped his flashlight full on her face. She lifted her hand and put it aside.

"What's the matter? Not tired already, are you?"

"No." She went on, "I just. . . . Come on; they're leaving us."

Caspey led them on into the woods. They walked now in a dry sibilance of leaves and crackling undergrowth. Trees loomed in to the lantern light; above them, among the thinning branches, stars swam in the hushed, vague sky. The dogs were on ahead, and they went on among the looming tree trunks, sliding down into ditches where sand gleamed in the lantern's pool and where the scissoring shadow of Caspey's legs was enormous, struggled through snatching briers and up the other bank.

"We better head away fum de creek bottom," Caspey suggested. "Dey mought strike a 'coon, and den dey wont git home 'fo' day." He bore away toward the open again; they emerged from the woods and crossed a field of sedge, odorous of sun and dust, in which the lantern was lightly nimbused. "H'mawn, dawg." They entered the woods again. Narcissa was beginning to tire, but Bayard strode on with a fine obliviousness of that possibility, and she followed without complaint. At last, from some distance away, came that single ringing cry. Caspey stopped. "Le's see which way he gwine." They stood in the darkness, in the sad, faintly chill decline of the year, among the dying trees, listening. "Whooy," Caspey shouted mellowly. "Go git 'im."

The dog replied, and they moved again, slowly, pausing at intervals to listen. The hound bayed; there were two voices now, and they seemed to be moving in a circle across their path. "Whooy," Caspey called, his voice ebbing in falling echoes among the trees. They went on. Again the dogs gave tongue, half the circle away from where the first cry had come. "He ca'yin' 'um right back whar he come fum," Caspey said. "We better wait 'twell dey gits 'im straightened out." He set the lantern down and squatted beside it, and Isom sloughed his burden and squatted also, and Bayard sat against a tree trunk and drew Narcissa down beside him. The dogs bayed again, nearer. Caspey stared off into the darkness toward the sound.

"I believe hit's a 'coon dey got," Isom said.

"Mought be. Hill 'coon."

"Headin' fer dat holler tree, aint he?"

"Soun' like it." They listened, motionless. "We have a job, den. Whooy." there was a faint chill in the air now, as the day's sunlight cooled from the ground, and Narcissa moved closer to Bayard. He took a packet of cigarettes from his jacket and gave Caspey one and lit one for himself. Isom squatted on his heels, his eyes rolling whitely in the lantern light.

"Gimme one, please, suh," he said.

"You aint got no business smokin', boy," Caspey told him. But Bayard gave him one, and he squatted leanly on his haunches, holding the white tube in his black diffident hand. There was a scurrying noise in the leaves behind them and a tense whimpering, and the young dog came into the light and slid with squeaking whimpers, and the diffident, fleeting phosphorous of its eyes against Caspey's leg. "Whut you want?" Caspey said, dropping his hand on its head. "Somethin' skeer you out dar?" The puppy genuflected its gawky young body and nuzzled whimpering at Caspey's hand. "He mus' a foun' a bear down yonder," Caspey said. "Wouldn't dem other dawgs he'p you ketch 'im?"

"Poor little fellow," Narcissa said. "Did he really get scared, Caspey? Come here, puppy."

"De other dawgs jes' went off and lef' 'im," Caspey answered. The puppy moiled diffidently about Caspey's knees; then it scrambled up and licked his face.

"Git down fum here!" Caspey exclaimed, and he flung the puppy away. It flopped awkwardly in the dry leaves and scrambled to its feet, and at that moment the hounds bayed again, mellow and chiming and timbrous in the darkness, and the puppy whirled and sped yapping shrilly toward the sound. The dogs bayed again; Isom and Caspey listened. "Yes, suh," Caspey repeated. "He headin' fer dat down tree."

"You know this country like you do the back yard, dont you, Caspey?" Narcissa said.

"Yessum, I ought to. I been over it a hund'ed times since I wuz bawn. Mist' Bayard do too. He been huntin' it long ez I is, pretty near. Him and Mist' Johnny bofe. Miss Jenny send me wid 'um when dey had dey fust gun; me and dat 'ere single bar'l gun I use ter have ter tie together wid a string. You 'member dat ole single bar'l, Mist' Bayard? But hit would shoot. Many's de fox squir'l we shot in dese woods. Rabbits, too." Bayard was leaning back against the tree. He was gazing off into the treetops and the soft sky beyond, his cigarette burning slowly in his hand. She looked at his bleak profile against the lantern glow, then she moved closer against him. But he did not respond, and she slid her hand into his. But it too was cold, and again he had left her for the lonely heights of his despair. Caspey was speaking again, in his slow, consonantless voice with its overtones of mellow sadness. "Mist' Johnny, now, he sho' could shoot. You 'member dat time me and you and him wuz——"

Bayard rose. He dropped his cigarette and crushed it carefully with his heel. "Let's go," he said. "They aint going to tree." He drew Narcissa to her feet and turned and went on. Caspey got up and unslung his horn and put it to his lips. The sound swelled about them, grave and clear and prolonged, then it died into echoes and so into silence again, leaving no ripple in the still darkness.

It was near midnight when they left Caspey and Isom at their cabin and followed the lane toward the house. The barn loomed presently beside them, and the house among its thinning trees, against the hazy sky. He opened the gate and she passed through and he followed and closed it, and turning he found her beside him, and stopped. "Bayard?" she whispered, leaning against him, and he put his arms around her and stood so, gazing above her head into the sky. She took his face between her palms and drew it down, but his lips were cold and upon them she tasted fatality and doom, and she clung to him for a time, her head bowed against his chest.

After that she would not go with him again. So he went alone, returning anywhere between midnight and dawn, ripping his clothing off quietly in the darkness and sliding cautiously into bed. But when he was still, she would touch him and speak his name in the dark beside him, and turn to him warm and soft with sleep. And they would lie so, holding to one another in the darkness and the temporary abeyance of his despair and the isolation of that doom he could not escape.

2

"Well," Miss Jenny said briskly, above the soup. "Your girl's gone and left you, and now you can find time to come out and see your kin folks, cant you?"

Horace grinned a little. "To tell the truth, I came out to get something to eat. I dont think that one woman in ten has any aptitude for keeping house, but my place is certainly not in the home."

"You mean," Miss Jenny corrected, "that not one man in ten has sense enough to marry a decent cook."

"Maybe they have more sense and consideration for others than to spoil decent cooks," he suggested.

"Yes," young Bayard said. "Even a cook'll quit work when she gets married."

"Dat's de troof," Simon, propped in a slightly florid attitude against the sideboard, in a collarless boiled shirt and his Sunday pants (it is Thanksgiving day) and reeking a little of whisky in addition to his normal odors, agreed. "I had to fin' Euphrony fo' new cookin' places de fust two mont' we wuz ma'ied."

Dr Peabody said: "Simon must have married somebody else's cook."

"I'd rather marry somebody else's cook than somebody else's wife," Miss Jenny snapped.

"Miss Jenny!" Narcissa reproved. "You hush."

"I'm sorry," Miss Jenny said immediately. "I wasn't saying

that at you, Horace: it just popped into my head. I was talking to you, Loosh Peabody. You think, just because you've eaten off of us Thanksgiving and Christmas for sixty years, that you can come into my own house and laugh at me, dont you?"

"Hush, Miss Jenny!" Narcissa repeated. Horace put down his spoon, and Narcissa's hand found his beneath the table.

"What's that?" Old Bayard, his napkin tucked into his waistcoat, lowered his spoon and cupped his hand to his ear.

"Nothing," young Bayard told him. "Aunt Jenny and Doc fighting again. Come alive, Simon." Simon stirred and removed the soup plates, but laggardly, still giving his interested attention to the altercation.

"Yes," Miss Jenny rushed on. "Just because that old fool of a Will Falls put axle grease on a little bump on his face without killing him dead, you have to go around swelled up like a poisoned dog. What did you have to do with it? You certainly didn't take it off. Maybe you conjured it on his face to begin with?"

"Haven't you got a piece of bread or something Miss Jenny can put in her mouth, Simon?" Dr Peabody asked mildly. Miss Jenny glared at him a moment, then flopped back in her chair.

"You, Simon! Are you dead?" Simon removed the plates and bore them out, and the guests sat avoiding one another's eyes a little, while Miss Jenny behind her barricade of cups and urns and jugs and things, continued to breathe fire and brimstone.

"Will Falls," old Bayard repeated. "Jenny, tell Simon, when he fixes that basket, to come to my office: I've got something to go in it." This something was the pint flask of whisky which he included in old man Falls' Thanksgiving and Christmas basket and which the old fellow divided out in spoonsful as far as it would go among his ancient and homeless cronies on those days; and invariably old Bayard reminded her to tell Simon of something which neither of them had overlooked.

"All right," she returned. Simon reappeared, with a huge silver coffee-urn, set it beside Miss Jenny, and retreated to the kitchen.

"How many of you want coffee now?" she asked generally. "Bayard will no more sit down to a meal without his coffee than he'd fly. Will you, Horace?" He declined, and without looking at Dr Peabody she said: "I reckon you'll have to have some, wont you?"

"If it's no trouble," he answered mildly. He winked at Narcissa and assumed an expression of lugubrious diffidence. Miss Jenny drew two cups, and Simon appeared with a huge platter borne gallantly and precariously aloft and set it before old Bayard with a magnificent flourish.

"My God, Simon," young Bayard said, "where did you get a whale this time of year?"

"Dat's a fish in dis worl', mon," Simon agreed. And it was a fish. It was a yard long and broad as a saddle blanket; it was a jolly red color and it lay gaping on the platter with an air of dashing and rollicking joviality.

"Dammit, Jenny," old Bayard said pettishly, "what did you want to have this thing, for? Who wants to clutter his stomach up with fish, in November, with a kitchen full of 'possum and turkey and squirrel?"

"There are other people to eat here besides you," she retorted. "If you dont want any, dont eat it. We always had a fish course at home," she added. "But you cant wean these Mississippi country folks away from bread and meat to save your life. Here, Simon." Simon set a stack of plates before old Bayard and he now came with his tray and Miss Jenny put two coffee cups on it, and he served them to old Bayard and Dr Peabody. Miss Jenny drew a cup for herself, and Simon passed sugar and cream. Old Bayard carved the fish, still rumbling heavily.

"I aint ever found anything wrong with fish at any time of year," Dr Peabody said.

"You wouldn't," Miss Jenny snapped. Again he winked heavily at Narcissa.

"Only," he continued, "I like to catch my own, out of my own pond. Mine have mo' food value."

"Still got your pond, Doc?" young Bayard asked.

"Yes. But the fishin' aint been so good, this year. Abe had the flu last winter, and ever since he's been goin' to sleep on me, and I have to sit there and wait until he wakes up and takes the fish off and baits my hook again. But finally I thought about tyin' one end of a cord to his leg and the other end to the bench, and now when I get a bite, I just reach around and give the string a yank and wake 'im up. You'll have to bring yo' wife out, someday, Bayard. She aint never seen my pond."

"You haven't?" Bayard asked Narcissa. She had not. "He's got benches all around it, with footrests, and a railing just high enough to prop your pole on, and a nigger to every fisherman to bait his hook and take the fish off. I dont see why you feed all those niggers, Doc."

"Well, I've had 'em around so long I dont know how to get shut of 'em, 'less I drown 'em. Feedin' 'em is the main trouble, though. Takes every thing I can make. If it wasn't for them, I'd a quit practicin' long ago. That's the reason I dine out whenever I can: every time I get a free meal, it's the same as a half holiday to a workin' man."

"How many have you got, Doctor?" Narcissa asked.

"I dont rightly know," he answered. "I got six or seven registered ones, but I dont know how many scrubs I have. I see a new yearlin' every day or so." Simon was watching him with rapt interest.

"You aint got no extry room out dar, is you, Doctuh?" he asked. "Here I slaves all de livelong day, keepin' 'um in vittles en sech."

"Can you eat cold fish and greens every day?" Dr Peabody asked him solemnly.

"Well, suh," Simon answered doubtfully, "I aint so sho' erbout dat. I burnt out on fish once, when I wuz a young man, en I aint had no right stomach fer it since."

"Well, that's about all we eat, out home."

"All right, Simon," Miss Jenny said. Simon was propped statically against the sideboard, watching Dr Peabody with musing astonishment.

"En you keeps yo' size on cole fish en greens? Gentlemun, I'd be a bone-rack on dem kine o' vittles in two weeks, I sholy would."

"Simon!" Miss Jenny raised her voice sharply. "Why wont you let him alone, Loosh, so he can 'tend to his business?" Simon came abruptly untranced and removed the fish. Beneath the table Narcissa slipped her hand in Horace's again.

"Lay off of Doc, Aunt Jenny," young Bayard said. He touched his grandfather's arm. "Cant you make her let Doc alone?"

"What's he doing, Jenny?" old Bayard asked. "Wont he eat his dinner?"

"None of us'll get to eat anything, if he sits there and talks to Simon about cold fish and greens," Miss Jenny replied.

"I think you're mean, to treat him like you do, Miss Jenny," Narcissa said.

"Well, it gives me something to be thankful for," Dr Peabody answered, "that you never took me when you had the chance. I went and proposed to Jenny once," he told them.

"You old gray-headed liar," Miss Jenny said, "you never did any such a thing!"

"Oh, yes, I did. Only I did it on John Sartoris' account. He said he was havin' mo' trouble than he could stand with politics outside his home. And, do you know——"

"Loosh Peabody, you're the biggest liar in the world!"

"——I pretty near had her persuaded for a while? It was that first spring them weeds she brought out here from Ca'lina bloomed, and there was a moon and we were in the garden and there was a mockin'bird——"

"No such thing!" Miss Jenny shouted. "There never was——"

"Look at her face, if you believe I'm lyin'," Dr Peabody said.

"Look at her face," young Bayard echoed rudely. "She's blushing!"

And she was blushing, but her cheeks were like banners, and her head was still high amid the gibing laughter. Narcissa rose and came to her and laid her arm about her trim erect shoulders. "You all hush this minute," she said. "You'd better consider yourselves lucky that any of us ever marry you, and flattered even when we refuse."

"I am flattered," Dr Peabody rejoined, "or I wouldn't be a widower now."

"Who wouldn't be a widower, the size of a hogshead and living on cold fish and turnip greens?" Miss Jenny said. "Sit down, honey. I aint scared of any man alive."

Narcissa resumed her seat, and Simon appeared again, with Isom in procession now, and for the next few minutes they moved steadily between kitchen and dining room with a roast turkey and a smoked ham and a dish of quail and another of squirrel, and a baked 'possum in a bed of sweet potatoes; and squash and pickled beets, and sweet potatoes and Irish potatoes, and rice and hominy, and hot biscuit and beaten biscuit and delicate long sticks of cornbread, and strawberry and pear preserves, and quince and apple jelly, and stewed cranberries and pickled peaches.

Then they ceased talking for a while and really ate, glancing now and then across the table at one another in a rosy glow of amicability and steamy odors. From time to time Isom entered with hot bread, while Simon stood overlooking the field somewhat as Caesar must have stood looking down into Gaul, once it was well in hand, or the Lord God Himself when He contemplated His latest chemical experiment and saw that it was good.

"After this, Simon," Dr Peabody said, and he sighed a little, "I reckon I can take you on and find you a little side meat now and then."

"I 'speck you kin," Simon agreed, watching them like an eagle-eyed general who rushes reserves to the threatened points, pressing more food upon them as they faltered. But even Dr Peabody allowed himself vanquished after a time, and then Simon brought in pies of three kinds, and a small, deadly plum pudding, and cake baked cunningly with whisky and nuts and fruit as ravishing as odors of heaven and treacherous and fatal as sin; and at last, with an air sibylline and solemnly profound, a bottle of port. The sun lay hazily in the glowing west, falling levelly through the windows and upon the silver arrayed upon the sideboard, dreaming in mellow gleams among its placid rotundities and upon the colored panes in the fanlight high in the western wall.

But that was November, the season of hazy, languorous days, when the first flush of autumn was over and winter beneath the sere horizon breathed yet a spell. November, when like a shawled matron among her children the earth died peacefully, without pain and of no disease. Early in December the rains set in and the year turned gray beneath the season of dissolution and of death. All night and all day it whispered upon the roof and along the eaves; the trees shed their final stubborn leaves in it and gestured their black and sorrowful branches against ceaseless vistas; only a lone hickory at the foot of the park kept its leaves yet, gleaming like a sodden flame on the eternal azure; beyond the valley the hills were hidden by a swaddling of rain.

Almost daily, despite Miss Jenny's strictures and commands and the grave protest in Narcissa's eyes, Bayard went forth with a shotgun and the two dogs, to return just before dark wet to the skin. And cold; his lips would be chill on hers, and his eyes bleak and haunted, and in the yellow firelight of their room she would cling to him, or lie crying quietly in the darkness beside his rigid body with a ghost between them.

"Look here," Miss Jenny said, coming upon her as she sat brooding before the fire in old Bayard's den. "You spend too much time this way; you're getting moony. Stop worrying about him: he's spent half his life soaking wet, yet neither one of 'em ever had a cold, even, that I can remember."

"Hasn't he?" she answered listlessly. Miss Jenny stood beside her chair, watching her keenly. Then she laid her hand on Narcissa's head, quite gently, for a Sartoris.

"Are you worrying because maybe he dont love you like you think he ought to?"

"It isn't that," she answered. "He doesn't love anybody. He wont even love the baby. He doesn't seem to be glad, or sorry, or anything."

"No," Miss Jenny agreed. The fire crackled and leaped among the resinous logs. Beyond the gray window the day dissolved endlessly. "Listen," Miss Jenny said abruptly. "Dont you ride in that car with him any more. You hear?"

"No. It wont make him drive slowly. Nothing will."

"Of course not. Nobody believes it will, not even Bayard.

He goes along for the same reason that boy himself does. Sartoris. It's in the blood. Savages, everyone of 'em. No earthly use to anybody." Together they gazed into the leaping flames, Miss Jenny's hand still lying on Narcissa's head. "I'm sorry I got you into this."

"You didn't do it. Nobody got me into it. I did it myself."

"H'm," Miss Jenny said. And then: "Would you do it over again?" The other did not reply, and she repeated the question. "Would you?"

"Yes," Narcissa answered. "Dont you know I would?" Again there was silence between them, in which without words they sealed their hopeless pact with that fine and passive courage of women. Narcissa rose. "I believe I'll go in and spend the day with Horace, if you dont mind," she said.

"All right," Miss Jenny agreed. "I believe I would, too. Horace probably needs a little looking after, by now. He looked sort of gaunt when he was out here last week. Like he wasn't getting proper food."

When she entered the kitchen door Eunice, the cook, turned from the bread board and lifted her daubed hands in a soft dark gesture. "Well, Miss Narcy," she said. "We aint seed you in a mont'. Is you come all de way in de rain?"

"I came in the carriage. It was too wet for the car." She came into the room. Eunice watched her with grave pleasure. "How are you all getting along?"

"He gits enough to eat, all right," Eunice answered. "I sees to dat. But I has to make 'im eat it. He needs you back here."

"I'm here, for the day, anyhow. What have you got for dinner?" Together they lifted lids and peered into the simmering vessels on the stove and in the oven. "Oh, chocolate pie!"

"I has to toll 'im wid dat," Eunice explained. "He'll eat

anything, ef I jes' makes 'im a chocolate pie," she added proudly.

"I bet he does," Narcissa agreed. "Nobody can make chocolate pies like yours."

"Dis one aint turnt out so well," Eunice said, deprecatory. "I aint so pleased wid it."

"Why, Eunice! It's perfect."

"No'm, it aint up to de mark," Eunice insisted. But she beamed, gravely diffident, and for a few minutes the two of them talked amicably while Narcissa pried into cupboards and boxes.

Then she returned to the house and mounted to her room. The dressing table was bare of its intimate silver and crystal, and the drawers were empty, and the entire room with its air of still and fading desolation, reproached her. Chill, too; there had been no fire in the grate since last spring, and on the table beside the bed, in a blue vase, was a small faded bunch of flowers, forgotten and withered and dead. Touching them, they crumbled in her fingers, leaving a stain, and the water in the vase smelled of rank decay. She opened the window and threw them out.

The room was too chill to stop in long, and she decided to ask Eunice to build a fire on the hearth, for the comfort of that part of her which still lingered here, soberly and a little sorrowful in the chill and reproachful desolation. At her chest of drawers she paused again and remembered those letters, fretfully and with a little musing alarm, deprecating anew her carelessness in not destroying them. But maybe she had, and so she entered again into the closed circle of her bewilderment and first fear, trying to remember what she had done with them. But she was certain she had left them in the drawer with her underthings, positive that she had put them there. Yet she had never been able to find them, nor had Eunice nor Horace seen them. The day she had missed them was the day before her wedding, when she packed her things. That day she had missed them, finding in their stead one in a different handwriting, which she did not remember having received. The gist of it was plain enough, although she had not understood some of it literally. But on that day, she read it with tranquil detachment: it and all it brought to mind was definitely behind her now. And lacking even this, she would not have been shocked if she had comprehended it. Curious a little, perhaps, at some of the words, but that is all.

But what she had done with those other letters she could not remember, and not being able to gave her moments of definite fear when she considered the possibility that people might learn that someone had thought such things about her and put them into words. Well, they were gone; there was nothing to do save hope that she had destroyed them as she had the last one, or if she had not, to trust that they would never be found. Yet that brought back the original distaste and dread: the possibility that the intactness of her deep and heretofore inviolate serenity might be the sport of circumstance; that she must trust to chance against the eventuality of a stranger casually picking a stray bit of paper from the ground. . . . . . .

But she would put this firmly aside, for the time being, at least. This should be Horace's day, and her own too; a surcease from that ghost-ridden dream to which she clung, waking. She descended the stairs. There was a fire in the living room. It had burned down to embers however, and she put coal on it and punched it to a blaze. That would be the first thing he'd see when he entered; perhaps he'd wonder; perhaps he'd know before he entered, having sensed her presence. She considered telephoning him, and she mused indecisively for a moment

before the fire; then decided to let it be a surprise. But suppos-
ing he didn't come home to dinner because of the rain. She
considered this, and pictured him walking along a street in the
rain, and immediately and with instinctive foreknowledge, she
went to the closet beneath the stairs and opened the door. It
was as she had known: his overcoat and raincoat both hung
there; the chances were he didn't even have an umbrella, and
again irritation and exasperation and untroubled affection
welled within her, and it was as it had been of old again, and all
that had since come between them, rolled away like clouds.

Heretofore her piano had always been rolled into the living room when cold weather came. But now it stood yet in the
smaller alcove. There was a fireplace here, but no fire had
been lighted yet, and the room was chilly. Beneath her hands
the cold keys gave forth a sluggish chord, accusing, reproving
too; and she returned to the fire and stood where she could see
through the window the drive beneath its sombre, dripping
cedars. The small clock on the mantel behind her chimed
twelve, and she went to the window and stood with her nose
touching the chill glass and her breath frosting it over. Soon,
now: he was erratic in his hours, but never tardy, and everytime
an umbrella came into sight, her heart leaped a little. But it
was not he, and she followed the bearer's plodding passage
until he shifted the umbrella enough for her to recognise him,
and so she did not see Horace until he was half way up the
drive. His hat was turned down about his face and his coat collar was hunched to his ears, and as she had known, he didn't
even have an umbrella.

"Oh, you idiot," she said and ran to the door and through
the curtained glass she saw his shadowy shape come leaping up
the steps. He flung the door open and entered, whipping his
sodden hat against his leg, and so did not see her until she
stepped forth. "You idiot," she said. "Where's your raincoat?"

For a moment he stared at her with his wild and diffident unrepose, then he said "Narcy!" and his face lighted and he swept her into his wet arms.

"Dont," she cried. "You're wet!" But he swung her from the floor, against his sopping chest, repeating Narcy, Narcy; then his cold nose was against her face and she tasted rain.

"Narcy," he said again, hugging her, and she ceased resisting and clung to him. Then abruptly he released her and jerked his head up and stared at her with sober intensity.

"Narcy," he said, still staring at her, "has that surly blackguard   ?"

"No, of course not," she answered sharply. "Have you gone crazy?" Then she clung to him again, wet clothes and all, as though she would never let him go. "Oh, Horry," she said, "I've been a beast to you!"

"I was hoping," he said—they had eaten the chocolate pie and Horace now stood before the living room fire, his coffee cup on the mantel, striking matches to his pipe—"That you might have come home for good. That they had sent you back."

"No," she answered. "I wish. . . . . . ."

"What?"

But she only said: "You'll be having somebody, soon." And then: "When is it to be, Horry?"

He sucked intently at his pipe; in his eyes little twin matchflames rose and fell. "I dont know. Next spring, I suppose. Whenever she will."

"You dont want to," she stated quietly. "Not after what it's all got to be now."

"She's in Reno now," he added, puffing at his pipe, his face averted a little. "Little Belle wrote me a letter about mountains."

She said: "Poor Harry." She sat with her chin in her palms, gazing into the fire.

"He'll have little Belle," he reminded her. "He cares more for her than he does for Belle, anyway."

"You dont know," she told him soberly. "You just say that because you want to believe it."

"Dont you think he's well off, rid of a woman who doesn't want him, who doesn't even love his child very much?"

"You dont know," she repeated. "People cant—cant—You cant play fast and loose with the way things ought to go on, after they've started off."

"Oh, people." He raised the cup and drained it, and sat down. "Barging around through a lifetime, clotting for no reason, breaking apart again for no reason still. Chemicals. No need to pity a chemical."

"Chemicals," she mused, her serene face rosy in the firelight. "Chemicals. Maybe that's the reason so many of the things people do smell bad."

"Well, I dont know that I ever thought of it in exactly that way," he answered gravely. "But I daresay you're right, having femininity on your side." He brooded himself, restlessly. "But I suppose it's all sort of messy: living and seething corruption glossed over for a while by smoothly colored flesh; all foul, until the clean and naked bone." He mused again, she quietly beside him. "But it's something there, something you go after; must; driven. Not always swine. A plan somewhere, I suppose, known to Whoever first set the fermentation going. Perhaps it's just too big to be seen, like a locomotive is a porous mongrel substance without edges to the grains of sand that give it traction on wet rails. Or perhaps He has forgotten Himself what the plan was."

"But do you like to think of a woman who'll willingly give up her child in order to marry another man a little sooner?"

"Of course I dont. But neither do I like to remember that I have exchanged you for Belle, or that she has red hair and is going to be fat someday, or that she has lain in another man's arms and has a child that isn't mine, even though she did voluntarily give it up. Yet there are any number of virgins who love children walking the world today, some of whom look a little like you, probably, and a modest number of which I allow myself to believe, without conceit, that I could marry. And yet. . . . . . . " He struck another match to his pipe, but he let it go out again and sat forward in his chair, the pipe held loosely in his joined hands. "That may be the secret, after all. Not any subconscious striving after what we believe will be happiness, contentment; but a sort of gadfly urge after the petty, ignoble impulses which man has tried so vainly to conjure with words out of himself. Nature, perhaps, watching him as he tries to wean himself away from the rank and richly foul old mire that spawned him, biding her time and flouting that illusion of purifaction which he has foisted upon himself and calls his soul. But it's something there, something you—you—" He brooded upon the fire, holding his cold pipe. She put her hand out and touched his, and he clasped it and looked at her with his groping and wide intensity. But she was gazing into the fire, her cheek in her palm, and she drew his hand to her and stroked it on her face.

"Poor Horry," she said.

"Not happiness," he repeated. "I'm happier now than I'll ever be again. You dont find that, when you suddenly swap the part of yourself which you want least, for the half of someone else that he or she doesn't want. Do you? Did you find it?"

But she only said "Poor Horry" again. She stroked his hand slowly against her cheek as she stared into the shaling ruby of the coals. The clock chimed again, with blent small silver bells. She spoke without moving.

"Aren't you going back to the office this afternoon?"

"No." His tone was again the grave, lightly casual one which he employed with her. "I'm taking a holiday. Next time you come, I may have a case and cant."

"You never have cases: you have functions," she answered. "But I dont think you ought to neglect your business," she added with grave reproof.

"Neither do I," he agreed. "But whatever else is business for, then?"

"Dont be silly. . . . . . . Put on some coal, Horry."

But later he reverted again to his groping and tragic premonitions. They had spent the afternoon sitting before the replenished fire; later she had gone to the kitchen and made tea. The day still dissolved ceaselessly and monotonously without, and they sat and talked in a sober and happy isolation from their acquired ghosts, and again their feet chimed together upon the dark road and, their faces turned inward to one another's, the sinister and watchful trees were no longer there. But the road was in reality two roads become parallel for a brief mile and soon to part again, and now and then their feet stumbled.

"It's having been younger once," he said. "Being dragged by time out of a certain day like a kitten from a tow sack, being thrust into another sack with shreds of the first one sticking to your claws. Like the burro that the prospector keeps on loading down with a rock here and a rock there until it drops, leaving him in the middle of his desert, surrounded by waiting buzzards," he added, musing in metaphors. "Plunder. That's all it is. If you could just be translated every so often, given a blank, fresh start, with nothing to remember. Dipped in Lethe every decade or so. . . . . . . "

"Or every year," she added. "Or day."

"Yes." The rain dripped and dripped, thickening the twilight; the room grew shadowy. The fire had burned down again; its steady fading glow fell upon their musing faces and brought the tea things on the low table beside them, out of the obscurity in quiet rotund gleams; and they sat hand in hand in the fitful shadows and the silence, waiting for something. And at last it came: a thundering knock at the door, and they knew then what it was they waited for, and through the window they saw the carriage curtains gleaming in the dusk and the horses stamping and steaming on the drive, in the ceaseless rain.

3

Horace had seen her on the street twice, his attention caught by the bronze splendor of her hair and by an indefinable something in her air, her carriage. It was not boldness and not arrogance exactly, but a sort of calm, lazy contemptuousness that left him seeking in his mind after an experience lost somewhere within the veils of years that swaddled his dead childhood; an experience so sharply felt at the time that the recollection of it lingered yet somewhere just beneath his consciousness although the motivation of its virginal clarity was lost beyond recall. The wakened ghost of it was so strong that during the rest of the day he roused from periods of abstraction to find that he had been searching for it a little fearfully among the crumbled and long unvisited corridors of his mind, and later as he sat before his fire at home, with a book. Then, as he lay in bed thinking of Belle and waiting for sleep, he remembered it.

He was five years old and his father had taken him to his first circus, and clinging to the man's hard, reassuring hand in a daze of blaring sounds and sharp cries and scents that tight-

ened his small entrails with a sense of fabulous and unimagin-
able imminence and left him a little sick, he raised his head
and found a tiger watching him with yellow and lazy contemplation; and while his whole small body was a tranced and
soundless scream, the animal gaped and flicked its lips with an
unbelievably pink tongue. It was an old tiger and toothless, and
it had doubtless gazed through these same bars at decades and
decades of Horaces, yet in him a thing these many generations
politely dormant waked shrieking, and again for a red moment
he dangled madly by his hands from the lowermost limb of a
tree.

That was it, and though that youthful reaction was dulled
now by the years, he found himself watching her on the street
somewhat as a timorous person is drawn with delicious revul-
sions to gaze into a window filled with knives. He found himself thinking of her often, wondering who she was. A stranger,
he had never seen her in company with anyone who might
identify her. She was always alone and always definitely going
somewhere; not at all as a transient, a visitor idling about the
streets. And always that air of hers, lazy, predatory and coldly
contemptuous. The sort of woman men stare after on the street
and who does not even do them the honor of ignoring them.

The third time he saw her he was passing a store, a newly-
opened department store, just as she emerged at that free, purposeful gait he had come to know. In the center of the door sill
was a small iron ridge onto which the double doors locked,
and she caught the heel of her slipper on this ridge and
emerged stumbling in a cascade of small parcels, and swearing. It was a man's bold swearing, and she caught her balance
and stamped her foot and kicked one of her dropped parcels
savagely into the gutter. Horace retrieved it and turning saw
her stooping for the others, and together they gathered them

up and rose, and she glanced at him briefly with level eyes of a thick, dark brown and shot with golden lights somehow paradoxically cold.

"Thanks," she said, without emphasis, taking the packages from him. "They ought to be jailed for having a mantrap like that in the door." Then she looked at him again, a level stare without boldness or rudeness. "You're Horace Benbow, aren't you?" she asked.

"Yes, that is my name. But I dont believe——"

She was counting her packages. "One more yet," she said, glancing about her feet. "Must be in the street." He followed her to the curb, where she had already picked up the other parcel, and she regarded its muddy side and swore again. "Now I'll have to have it rewrapped."

"Yes, too bad, isn't it?" he agreed. "If you'll allow me——"

"I'll have it done at the drug store. Come along, if you're not too busy. I want to talk to you."

She seemed to take it for granted that he would follow, and he did so, with curiosity and that feeling stronger than ever of a timorous person before a window of sharp knives. When he drew abreast of her she looked at him again (she was almost as tall as he) from beneath her level brows. Her face was rather thin, with broad nostrils. Her mouth was flat though full, and there was in the ugly distinction of her face an indescribable something; a something boding and leashed, yet untamed. Carnivorous, he thought. A lady tiger in a tea gown and remarking something of his thoughts in his face, she said: "I forgot: of course you dont know who I am. I'm Belle's sister."

"Oh, of course. You're Joan. I should have known."

"How? Nobody yet ever said we look alike. And you never saw me before."

"No," he agreed. "But I've been expecting for the last three months that some of Belle's kinfolks would be coming here to see what sort of animal I am."

"They wouldn't have sent me, though," she replied. "You can be easy on that." They went on along the street. Horace responded to greetings, but she strode on with that feline poise of hers; he was aware that men turned to look after her but in her air there was neither awareness nor disregard of it conscious or otherwise. And again he remembered that tiger yawning with bored and lazy contempt while round and static eyes stared down its cavernous pink gullet. "I want to stop here," she said, as they reached the drug store. "Do you have to go back to the store, or whatever it is?"

"Office," he corrected. "Not right away."

"That's right," she agreed, and he swung the door open for her. "You're a dentist, aren't you? Belle told me."

"Then I'm afraid she's deceiving us both," he answered drily. She glanced at him with her level, speculative gaze, and he added: "She's got the names confused and sent you to the wrong man."

"You seem to be clever," she said over her shoulder. "And I despise clever men. Dont you know any better than to waste cleverness on women? Save it for your friends." A youthful clerk in a white jacket approached, staring at her boldly; she asked him with contemptuous politeness to rewrap her parcel. Horace stopped beside her.

"Women friends?" he asked.

"Women what?" She stooped down, peering into a show-case of cosmetics. "Well, maybe so," she said indifferently. "But I never believe 'em, though. Cheap sports." She straightened up. "Belle's all right, if that's what you want to ask. It's done her good. She doesn't look so bad-humored and settled down, now. Sort of fat and sullen."

"I'm glad you think that. But what I am wondering is, how you happened to come here. Harry's living at the hotel, isn't he?"

"He's opened the house again, now. He just wanted somebody to talk to. I came to see what you look like," she told him.

"What I look like?"

"Yes, to see the man that could make old Belle kick over the traces." Her eyes were coldly contemplative, a little curious. "What did you do to her? I'll bet you haven't even got any money to speak of."

Horace grinned a little. "I must seem rather thoroughly impossible to you, then," he suggested.

"Oh, there's no accounting for the men women pick out. I sometimes wonder at myself. Only I've never chosen one I had to nurse, yet." The clerk returned with her package, and she made a trifling purchase and gathered up her effects. "I suppose you have to stick around your office all day, dont you?"

"Yes. It's the toothache season now, you know."

"You sound like a college boy now," she said coldly. "I suppose Belle's ghost will let you out at night, though?"

"It goes along too," he answered.

"Well, I'm not afraid of ghosts. I carry a few around, myself."

"You mean dripping flesh and bloody bones, dont you?" She looked at him again, with her flecked eyes that should have been warm but were not.

"I imagine you could be quite a nuisance," she told him. He opened the door and she passed through it. And gave him a brief nod, and while he stood on the street with his hat lifted she strode on, without even a conventional Thank you or Goodbye.

That evening while he sat at his lonely supper, she telephoned him, and thirty minutes later she came in Harry's car for him. And for the next three hours she drove him about while he sat hunched into his overcoat against the raw air. She wore no coat herself and appeared impervious to the chill, and she carried him on short excursions into the muddy winter countryside, the car sliding and skidding while he sat with tensed anticipatory muscles. But mostly they drove monotonously around town while he felt more and more like a fatted and succulent eating-creature in a suave parading cage. Sometimes she talked, but usually she drove in a lazy preoccupation, seemingly utterly oblivious of him.

Later, when she had begun coming to his house, coming without secrecy and with an unhurried contempt for possible eyes and ears and tongues—a contempt that also disregarded Horace's acute unease on that score, she still fell frequently into those periods of aloof and purring repose. Then, sitting before the fire in his living room, with the bronze and electric disorder of her hair and the firelight glowing in little red points in her unwinking eyes, she was like a sheathed poniard, like Chablis in a tall-stemmed glass. At these times she would utterly ignore him, cold and inaccessible. Then she would rouse and talk brutally of her lovers. Never of herself, other than to give him the salient points in her history that Belle had hinted at with a sort of belligerent prudery. The surface history was brief and simple enough. Married at eighteen to a man three times her age, she had deserted him in Honolulu and fled to Australia with an Englishman, assuming his name; was divorced by her husband, discovered by first hand experience that no Englishman out of his native island has any honor about women; was deserted by him in Bombay, and in Calcutta, she married again. An American, a young man, an employee of the Standard oil company. A year later she divorced him, and since then her career had been devious and a little obscure, due to her restlessness. Her family would know

next to nothing of her whereabouts, receiving her brief, infrequent letters from random points half the world apart. Her first
husband had made a settlement on her, and from time to time
and without warning she returned home and spent a day or a
week or a month in the company of her father's bitter reserve
and her mother's ready tearful uncomplaint, while neighbors,
older people who had known her all her life, girls with whom
she had played in pinafores and boys with whom she had
sweethearted during the spring and summer of adolescence
and newcomers to the town, looked after her on the street.

Forthright and inscrutable and unpredictable: sometimes
she stayed an hour motionless before the fire while he sat
nearby and did not dare touch her; sometimes she lay beside
him while the firelight, fallen to a steady glow of coals, filled
his bedroom with looming and motionless shadows until midnight or later, talking about her former lovers with a brutality
that caused him hopeless and despairing anger and something
of a child's hurt disillusion; speaking of them with that same
utter lack of vanity and conventional modesty with which she
discussed her body, asking him to tell her again that he thought
her body beautiful, asking him if he had ever seen a match for
her legs, then taking him with a savage and carnivorous sud-
denness that left him spent. Yet all the while remote beyond
that barrier of cold inscrutability which he was never able to
break down, and rising at last, again that other feline and inaccessible self and departing without even the formality of a final
kiss or a Goodbye and leaving him to wonder, despite the evi-
dences of her presence, whether he had not dreamed it, after
all.

She made but one request of him: that he refrain from
talking to her of love. "I'm tired of having to listen to it and talk
and act a lot of childish stupidity," she explained. "I dont know
anything about it, and I dont care to."

"You dont think there is any such thing?" he asked.

"I've never found it. And if we can get anything from each other worth having, what's the use in talking about it? And it'll take a race of better people than we are to bear it, if there's any such thing. Save that for Belle: you'll probably need it."

One night she did not depart at all. That was the night she revealed another feline trait: that of a prowling curiosity about dark rooms. She had paused at Narcissa's door, and although he tried to draw her onward, she opened the door and found the light switch and pressed it on. "Whose room is this?"

"Narcissa's," he answered shortly. "Come away."

"Oh, your sister's. The one that married that Sartoris." She examined the room quietly. "I'd like to have known that man," she said in a musing tone. "I think I'd be good for him. Marrying women, then leaving them after a month or two. Only one man ever left me," she stated calmly. "I was practically a child, or that wouldn't have. . . . . . . Yes, I'd have been just the thing for him." She entered the room; he followed and took her arm again.

"Come away, Joan."

"But I dont know," she added. "Maybe it's a good thing he's gone, after all. For both of us."

"Yes. Come away."

She turned her head and stared at him with her level inscrutable eyes, beneath the bronze disorder of her hair. "Men are funny animals," she said. "You carry so much junk around with you." There was in her eyes a cold derisive curiosity. "What do you call it? sacrilege? desecration?"

"Come away," he repeated.

Next day, in the gray December forenoon among the musty books in his office, the reaction found him. It was more than reaction: it was revulsion, and he held a spiritual stock-taking with a sort of bleak derision: for a moment, in company with the sinister gods themselves, he looked down upon Horace Benbow as upon an antic and irresponsible worm. It was worse; it was conduct not even becoming a college sophomore—he, who had thought to have put all such these ten years behind him; and he thought of his sister and he felt unclean. On the way home at noon he saw Harry Mitchell approaching, and he ducked into a store and hid—a thing Belle had never caused him to do.

He would not go to his room, where the impact of her presence must yet linger, and Eunice served his meal with her face averted, emanating disapproval and reproach; and he angered slowly and asked her the direct question. "Has Mrs Heppleton gone yet, Eunice?"

"I dont know, suh," Eunice answered, still without looking at him. She turned doorward.

"You dont know when she left?"

"I dont know, suh," Eunice repeated doggedly, and the swing door slapped behind her in dying oscillations.

But he would not mount to his room, and soon he was back down town again. It was a gray, raw day, following the two recent weeks of bright frosty weather. Christmas was not a week away, and already the shop windows bloomed in toy fairylands, with life in its mutations in miniature among cedar branches and cotton batting and dusted over with powdered tinsel, amid which Santa Claus in his myriad avatars simpered in fixed and rosy benignance; and with fruit and cocoanuts and giant sticks of peppermint; and fireworks of all kinds—roman candles and crackers and pinwheels; and about the muddy square fetlock-deep horses stood hitched to wagons laden with berried holly and mistletoe.

He was too restless to remain in one place, and through the short afternoon, on trivial pretexts or on no pretext at all, he descended the stairs and walked along the streets among the

slow throngs of black and white in the first throes of the long
winter vacation; and at last he realized that he was hoping to
see her, realized it with longing and with dread, looking along
the street before him for a glimpse of her shapeless marten coat
and the curbed wild blaze of her hair, and the lithe and purposeful arrogance of her carriage, ready to flee when he did so.

But by the time he reached home in the early dusk the
dread was still there, but it was only the savor of the longing,
and without even pausing to remove his hat and coat he went
to the telephone in its chill and darkling alcove beneath the
stairs. And he stood with the chill receiver to his ear and watching the cloudy irregularity of his breath upon the nickel
mouthpiece, waiting until out of the twilight and the chill the
lazy purring of her voice should come. After a time he asked
central to ring again, with polite impatience. He could hear
the other instrument shrill again and he thought of her long
body rising from its warm nest in her chair before a fire somewhere in the quiet house, imagined he could hear her feet on
stairs nearer and nearer "Now. Now she is lifting her hand to
the receiver now Now." But it was Rachel, the cook. Naw, suh,
Miz Heppleton aint here. Yes, suh, she gone away. Suh? Naw,
suh, she aint comin' back. She went off on de evenin' train.
Naw, suh, Rachel didn't know where she was going.

It used to be that he'd fling his coat and hat down and Narcissa would come along presently and hang them up. But
already bachelordom was getting him house-broke—
accomplishing what affection never had and never would—
and he hung his coat, in the pocket of which an unopened
letter from Belle lay forgotten, carefully in the closet beneath
the stairs, fumbling patiently with his chilled hands until he
found a vacant hook. Then he mounted the stairs and opened
his door and entered the cold room where between the secret
walls she lingered yet in a hundred palpable ways—in the mir-

ror above his chest of drawers, in the bed, the chairs; on the deep rug before the hearth where she had crouched naked and drowsing like a cat. The fire had burned out; the ashes were cold and the room was icy chill: outside, the graying twilight. He built up the fire and drew his chair close to the hearth and sat before it, his thin delicate hands spread to the crackling blaze.

4

. . . . this time it was a ford car, and Bayard saw its wild skid as the driver tried to jerk it across the treacherous thawing road, and in the flashing moment and with swift amusement, he saw, between the driver's cravatless collar and the woman's stocking bound around his head beneath his hat and tied under his chin, his adam's apple like a scared puppy in a tow sack. This flashed on and behind, and Bayard wrenched the wheel, and the stalled ford swam sickeningly into view again as the big car slewed greasily upon the clay surface, its declutched engine roaring. Then the other car swam from sight again as he wrenched the wheel over and slammed the clutch in for more stability; and once more that sickening, unhurried rush as the car refused to regain its feet and the frosty December world swept laterally across his vision. Old Bayard lurched against him: from the corner of his eye he could see the old fellow's hand clutching at the top of the door. Now they were facing the bluff on which the cemetery lay; directly over them John Sartoris' effigy lifted its florid stone gesture, and from among motionless cedars gazed out upon the valley where for two miles the railroad he had built ran beneath his carven eyes. Bayard wrenched the wheel once more.

On the other side of the road a precipice dropped sheer

away, among scrub cedars and corroded ridges skeletoned brittly with frost and muddy ice where the sun had not yet reached; the rear end of the car hung timelessly over this before it swung again, with the power full on, swung on until its nose pointed down hill again, with never a slackening of its speed. But still it would not come into the ruts again and it had lost the crown of the road, and though they had almost reached the foot of the hill, Bayard saw they would not make it. Just before they slipped off he wrenched the steering wheel over and swung the nose straight over the bank, and the car poised lazily for a moment, as though taking breath. "Hang on," he shouted to his grandfather. Then they plunged.

An interval utterly without sound and in which all sensation of motion was lost. Then scrub cedar burst crackling about them and whipping branches of it exploded upon the radiator and slapped viciously at them as they leaned with braced feet, and the car slewed in a long bounce. Another vacuum-like interval, then a shock that banged the wheel into Bayard's chest and jerked it in his tight hands, wrenching his arm-sockets. Beside him his grandfather lurched forward and he threw out his arm just in time to keep the other from crashing through the windshield. "Hang on," he shouted again. The car had never faltered and he dragged the leaping wheel over and swung it down the ravine and opened the engine again, and with the engine and the momentum of the plunge, they rocked and crashed on down the ditch and turned and heaved up the now shallow bank and onto the road again. Bayard brought it to a stop.

He sat motionless for a moment. "Whew," he said. And then: "Great God in the mountain." His grandfather sat motionless beside him, his hand still clutching the door and his head bent a little. "Think I'll have a cigarette, after that," Bayard added. He dug one from his pocket, and a match; his hands were shaking. "I thought of that damn concrete bridge again, just as she went over," he explained, apologetically. He took a deep draught at his cigarette and glanced at his grandfather. "Y'all right?" Old Bayard made no reply, and with the cigarette poised, Bayard looked at him. He sat as before, his head bent a little and his hand on the door. "Grandfather?" Bayard said sharply. Still old Bayard didn't move, even when his grandson flung the cigarette away and shook him roughly.

5

Up the last hill the tireless pony bore him, and in the low December sun their shadow fell longly across the ridge and into the valley beyond, from which the high, shrill yapping of the dogs came again upon the frosty windless air. Young dogs, Bayard told himself, and he sat his horse in the faint scar of the road, listening as the high-pitched hysteria of them swept echoing across his aural field. Motionless, he could feel frost in the air. Above him the pines, though there was no wind in them, made a continuous dry, wild sound, as though the frost in the air had found voice; above them against the high evening blue, a shallow V of geese slid. There'll be ice tonight, he thought, watching them and thinking of black backwaters where they would come to rest, of rank bayonets of dead grasses about which water would shrink soon in fixed glassy ripples in the brittle darkness. Behind him the earth rolled away ridge on ridge blue as woodsmoke, on into a sky like thin congealed blood. He turned in his saddle and stared unwinking into the sun that spread like a crimson egg broken upon the ultimate hills. That meant weather: he snuffed the still tingling air, hoping he smelled snow.

The pony snorted and tossed his head experimentally, and

found the reins slack and lowered his nose and snorted again into the dead leaves and the delicate sere needles of pine beneath his feet. "Come up, Perry," Bayard said, jerking the reins. Perry raised his head and broke into a stiff, jolting trot, but Bayard lifted him smartly out of it and into his steady fox-trot again. He had not gone far when the dogs broke again into clamorous uproar to his left, and suddenly near, and as he reined Perry back and peered ahead along the fading scar of the road, he saw the fox trotting sedately toward him in the middle of it. Perry saw it at the same time and laid his fine ears back and rolled his young eyes. But the animal came on unawares at its steady, unhurried trot, glancing back over its shoulder from time to time. "Well, I'll be damned," Bayard whispered, holding Perry rigid between his knees. The fox was not forty yards away, yet still it came on, seemingly utterly unaware of the horseman. Then Bayard shouted.

The animal glanced at him; the level sun swam redly and fleetingly in its eyes, then with a single modest flash of brown it was gone. Bayard expelled his breath: his heart was thumping against his ribs. "Whooy," he yelled. "Come on, dogs!" The din of them swelled to a shrill pandemonium and the pack boiled into the road in a chaos of spotted hides and flapping tongues and ears. None of them was more than half grown, and ignoring the horse and rider they surged still clamoring into the undergrowth where the fox had vanished and shrieked frantically on; and as Bayard stood in his stirrups and gazed after them, preceded by yapping in a still higher and more frantic key, two even smaller puppies swarmed out of the woods and galloped past him on their short legs, with whimpering cries and expressions of ludicrous and mad concern. Then the clamor died into hysterical echoes, and so away.

He rode on. On either hand was a ridge: the one darkling like a bronze bastion, upon the other the final rays of the sun lying redly. The air crackled and tingled in his nostrils and seared his lungs with exhilarating needles. The road followed the valley; but half the sun now showed above the western wall, and among intermittent trees, he rode stirrup-deep in shadow like cold water. He would just about reach the house before dark, and he shook Perry up a little. The clamor of the dogs swelled again ahead of him, approaching the road again, and he lifted Perry into a canter.

Presently before him lay a glade—an old field, sedge-grown, its plow-scars long healed over. The sun filled it with dying gold, and he pulled Perry short upstanding: there, at the corner of the field beside the road, sat the fox. It sat there on its haunches like a dog, watching the trees across the glade, and Bayard shook Perry forward again. The fox turned its head and looked at him with a covert, fleeting glance, but without alarm, and Bayard halted Perry in intense astonishment. The clamor of the dogs swept nearer through the woods, yet still the fox sat on its haunches, watching the man with covert stolen glances, paying the dogs no heed. It revealed no alarm whatever, not even when the puppies burst yapping madly into the glade. They moiled at the wood's edge for a time while the fox divided its attention between them and the man. At last the largest puppy, evidently the leader, saw the quarry. Immediately they stopped their noise and trotted across the glade and squatted in a circle facing the fox, their tongues lolling. Then with one accord they turned about and faced the darkening woods, from which and nearer and nearer, came that spent, frantic yapping in a higher key. The largest dog barked once; the yapping among the trees swelled with frantic relief and the two smaller puppies appeared and burrowed like moles through the sedge and came up. Then the fox rose and cast another quick, furtive glance at the horseman, and surrounded by the amicable weary calico of the puppies, trotted up the road and vanished among the trees. "Well, I'll be damned," Bayard said, gazing after them. "Come up, Perry."

At last a pale and windless plume of smoke stood above the trees ahead, and he emerged from the woods, and in the rambling wall of the house a window glowed with ruddy invitation across the twilight. Dogs had already set up a resonant bell-like uproar; above it Bayard could distinguish the clear tenor of puppies and a voice shouting at them, and as he halted Perry in the yard, the fox was vanishing diffidently but without haste beneath the house. A lean figure faced him in the dusk, with an axe in one hand and an armful of wood, and Bayard said:

"What the devil's that thing, Buddy? That fox?"

"That's Ethel," Buddy answered. He put the wood down deliberately, and the axe, and he came and shook Bayard's hand once, limply, in the country fashion, but his hand was hard and firm. "How you?"

"All right," Bayard answered. "I came out to get that old fox Rafe was telling me about."

"Sure," Buddy agreed in his slow, infrequent voice. "We been expectin' you. Git down and lemme take yo' pony."

"No, I'll do it. You take the wood on in; I'll put Perry up." But Buddy was firm, without insistence or rudeness, and Bayard surrendered the horse to him.

"Henry," Buddy shouted at the house. "Henry." A door opened upon jolly leaping flames; a figure stood squatly in it. "Here's Bayard," he said. "Go on in and warm," he added leading Perry away. Dogs surrounded Bayard; he picked up the wood and the axe and went on toward the house in a ghostly spotted surge of dogs, and the figure stood in the lighted door while he mounted the veranda and leaned the axe against the wall.

"How you?" Henry said, and again the handshake was limp; again the hand was firm and kind, flabbier though than

Buddy's hard young flesh. He relieved Bayard of the wood and they entered the house. The walls were of chinked logs; upon them hung two or three outdated calendars and a patent medicine lithograph in colors. The floor was bare, of hand-trimmed boards scuffed with heavy boots and polished by the pads of generations of dogs; two men could lie side by side in the fireplace. In it now four foot logs blazed against the clay fireback, swirling in wild plumes into the chimney's dark maw, and in silhouette against it, his head haloed by the shaggy silver disorder of his hair, Virginius MacCallum sat. "Hyer's Bayard Sartoris, pappy," Henry said.

The old man turned in his chair with grave, leonine deliberation and extended his hand without rising. In 1861 he was sixteen and he had walked to Lexington, Virginia, and enlisted, served four years in the Stonewall brigade and walked back to Mississippi and built himself a house and got married. His wife's *dot* was a clock and a dressed hog; his own father gave them a mule. His wife was dead these many years, and her successor was dead, but he sat now before the fireplace at which that hog had been cooked, beneath the roof he had built in '66, and on the mantel above him the clock sat, deriding that time whose servant it once had been. "Well, boy?" he said. "You took yo' time about comin'. How's yo' folks?"

"Pretty well, sir," Bayard answered. He looked at the old man's hale ruddy face intently and sharply. No, they hadn't heard yet.

"We been expectin' you ever since Rafe seen you in town last spring. Henry, tell Mandy to put another plate on."

Four dogs had followed him into the room. Three of them watched him gravely with glowing eyes; the other one, a blue-ticked hound with an expression of majestic gravity, came up and touched its cold nose to his hand. "Hi, Gen'ral," he said, rubbing its ears; whereupon the other dogs approached and thrust their noses against his hands.

"Pull up a cheer," Mr MacCallum said. He squared his own chair around and Bayard obeyed, and the dogs followed him, surging with blundering decorum about his knees. "I keep sendin' word in to git yo' granpappy out hyer," the old man continued, "but he's too 'tarnal proud, or too damn lazy to come. Hyer, Gen'ral! Git away from thar. Kick 'em away, Bayard. Henry!" he shouted. Henry appeared. "Take these hyer damn dawgs out till after supper."

Henry drove the dogs from the room. Mr MacCallum picked up a long pine sliver from the hearth and fired it and lit his pipe, and smothered the sliver in the ashes and laid it on the hearth again. "Rafe and Lee air in town today," he said. "You could have come out in the waggin with them. But I reckon you'd ruther have yo' own hoss."

"Yes, sir," he answered quietly. Then they would know. He stared into the fire for a time, rubbing his hands slowly on his knees, and for an instant he saw the recent months of his life coldly in all their headlong and heedless wastefulness; saw its entirety like the swift unrolling of a film, culminating in that which he had been warned against and that any fool might have foreseen. Well, damn it, suppose it had: was he to blame? had he insisted that his grandfather ride with him? had he given the old fellow a bum heart? And then, coldly: *You were afraid to go home. You made a nigger sneak your horse out to you. You, who deliberately do things your judgment tells you may not be successful, even possible, are afraid to face the consequences of your own acts.* Then again something bitter and deep and sleepless in him blazed out in vindication and justification and accusation; what, he knew not, blazing out at what, Whom, he did not know: *You did it! You caused it all: you killed Johnny.*

Henry had drawn a chair up to the fire, and after a while the old man tapped his clay pipe carefully out against his palm and drew a huge, turnip-shaped silver watch from his corduroy vest. "Half after five," he said. "Aint them boys got in yet?"

"They're here," Henry answered briefly. "Heard 'em takin' out when I put out the dawgs."

"Git the jug, then," his father ordered. Henry rose and departed again, and presently feet clumped heavily on the porch and Bayard turned in his chair and stared bleakly at the door. It opened and Rafe and Lee entered.

"Well, well," Rafe said, and his lean dark face lighted a little. "Got here at last, did you?" He shook Bayard's hand, and Lee followed him. Lee's face, like all of them, was a dark, saturnine mask. He was not so stocky as Rafe, and least talkative of them all. His eyes were black and restless; behind them lurked something wild and sad: he shook Bayard's hand without a word.

But Bayard was watching Rafe. There was nothing in Rafe's face; no coldness, no questioning—Was it possible that he could have been to town, and not heard? Or had Bayard himself dreamed it? But he remembered that unmistakable feel of his grandfather when he had touched him, remembered how he had suddenly slumped as though the very fibre of him, knit so erect and firm for so long by pride and the perverse necessity of his family doom, had given way all at once, letting his skeleton rest at last. Mr MacCallum spoke.

"Did you git to the express office?"

"We never got to town," Rafe answered. "Axle tree broke just this side of Vernon. Had to uncouple the wagon and drive to Vernon and get it patched up. Too late to go in, then. We got our supplies there and come on home."

"Well, hit dont matter. You'll be goin' in next week, for Christmas," the old man said. Bayard drew a long breath and lit a cigarette, and on a draft of vivid darkness Buddy entered and came and squatted leanly in the shadowy chimney corner.

"Got that fox you were telling me about hid out yet?" Bayard asked Rafe.

"Sure. And we'll get 'im, this time. Maybe tomorrow. Weather's changin'."

"Snow?"

"Might be. What's it goin' to do tonight, pappy?"

"Rain," the old man answered. "Tomorrow, too. Scent wont lay good till Wen'sday. Henry!" After a moment he shouted Henry again, and Henry entered, with a blackened kettle trailing a faint plume of vapor and a stoneware jug and a thick tumbler with a metal spoon in it. There was something domestic, womanish, about Henry, with his squat, slightly tubby figure and his mild brown eyes and his capable, unhurried hands. He it was who superintended the kitchen (he was a better cook now than Mandy) and the house, where he could be found most of the time, pottering soberly at some endless task. He visited town almost as infrequently as his father; he cared little for hunting, and his sole relaxation was making whisky, good whisky and for family consumption alone, in a secret fastness known only to his father and to the negro who assisted him, after a recipe handed down from lost generations of his usquebaugh-bred forbears. He set the kettle and the jug and the tumbler on the hearth, and took the clay pipe from his father's hand and put it on the mantel, and reached down a cracked cup of sugar and seven tumblers, each with a spoon in it. The old man leaned forward into the firelight and made the toddies one by one, with tedious and solemn deliberation. When he had made one around, there were two glasses left. "Aint them other boys come in yet?" he asked. Nobody answered, and he corked the jug. Henry set the two extra glasses back on the mantel.

Mandy came to the door presently, filling it with her homely calico expanse. "Y'all kin come on in now," she said, and as she turned waddling Bayard spoke to her and she stopped as the men rose. The old man was straight as an Indian, and with the exception of Buddy's lean and fluid length, he towered above his sons by a head. Mandy waited beside the door and gave Bayard her hand. "You aint been out in a long while, now," she said. "And I bet you aint fergot Mandy, neither."

"Sure I haven't," Bayard answered. But he had. Money, to Mandy, did not compensate for some trinket of no value which John never forgot to bring her when he came. He followed the others into the frosty darkness again. Beneath his feet the ground was already stiffening; overhead the sky was brilliant with stars. He stumbled a little behind the crowding backs until Rafe opened a door into a separate building, and stood aside until they had entered. This room was filled with warmth and a thin blue haze pungent with cooking odors, in which a kerosene lamp burned steadily on a long table. At one end of the table was a single chair; the other three sides were paralleled by backless wooden benches. Against the further wall was the stove, and a huge cupboard of split planks, and a woodbox. Behind the stove two negro men and a half grown boy sat, their faces shining with heat and their eyeballs rolling whitely; about their feet five puppies snarled with mock savageness at one another or chewed damply at the negroes' static ankles or prowled about beneath the stove and the adjacent floor with blundering, aimless inquisitiveness.

"Howdy, boys," Bayard said, calling them by name, and they bobbed their heads at him with diffident flashes of teeth and polite murmurs.

"Put dem puppies up, Richud," Mandy ordered. The negroes gathered the puppies up one by one and tumbled them into a smaller box behind the stove, where they continued to move about with sundry scratchings and bumpings and an occasional smothered protest. From time to time during the meal a head would appear, staring above the rim of the box with blinking and solemn curiosity, then vanish with an abrupt scuffling thump and more protests, and moiling, infant-like noises rose again. "Hush up dawgs! G'awn to sleep, now," Richard would say, rapping the box with his knuckles. After a while the noise ceased.

The old man took the lone chair, his sons around him, and the guest; some coatless, all collarless, with their dark, saturnine faces stamped all clearly from the same die. They ate. Sausage, and spare ribs, and a dish of hominy and one of fried sweet potatoes, and corn bread and a molasses jug of sorghum, and Mandy poured coffee from a huge enamelware pot. In the middle of the meal the two missing ones came in—Jackson, the eldest, a man of fifty-two, with a broad, high forehead and thick brows and an expression at once dreamy and intense—a sort of shy and impractical Cincinnatus; and Stuart, forty-four and Rafe's twin. Yet although they were twins, there was no closer resemblance between them than between any two of them. As though the die was too firm and made too clean an imprint to be either hurried or altered, even by nature. Stuart had none of Rafe's easy manner (Rafe was the only one of them that, by any stretch of the imagination, could have been called loquacious); on the other hand, he had much of Henry's placidity. He was a good farmer and a canny trader, and he had a respectable bank account of his own. Henry, fifty, was the second son.

They ate with silent and steady decorum, with only the barest essential words, but amicably. Mandy moved back and forth between table and stove.

Before they had finished a sudden bell-like uproar of dogs

floated up from the night and seeped through the tight walls, into the room. "Dar, now." The negro Richard cocked his head. Buddy poised his coffee.

"Wher are they, Dick?"

"Right back of de spring-house. Dey got 'im, too." Buddy rose and slid leanly from his corner.

"I'll go with you," Bayard said, rising also. The others ate steadily. Richard got a lantern down from the cupboard top and lit it, and the three of them passed out into the chill darkness across which the baying of the dogs came in musical gusts, ringing as frosty glass. It was chill and dark. The house loomed, its rambling low wall broken only by the ruddy glow of the window. "Ground's about hard already," Bayard remarked.

"'Twont freeze tonight," Buddy answered. "Will it, Dick?"

"Naw, suh. Gwine rain."

"Go on," Bayard said. "I dont believe it."

"Pappy said so," Buddy replied. "Warmer'n 'twas at sundown."

"Dont feel like it, to me," Bayard insisted. They passed the wagon motionless in the starlight, its tires glinting like satin ribbons, and the long, rambling stable, from which placid munchings came, and an occasional snuffing snort as the lantern passed. Then the lantern twinkled among tree trunks as the path descended; the clamor of the dogs swelled just beneath them and the ghostly shapes of them shifted in the faint glow, and in a sapling just behind the spring house they found the 'possum, curled motionless and with its eyes tightly shut, in a fork not six feet from the ground. Buddy lifted it down by the tail, unresisting. "Hell," Bayard said.

Buddy called the dogs away, and they mounted the path again. In a disused shed behind the kitchen what seemed like at least fifty eyes gleamed in matched red points as Buddy swung the lantern in and flashed it onto a cage screened with chicken wire, from which rose a rank, warm odor and in which grizzled furry bodies moved sluggishly or swung sharp, skull-like faces into the light. He opened the door and dumped his latest capture in among its fellows and gave the lantern to Richard. They emerged. Already the sky was hazed over a little, losing some of its brittle scintillation.

The others sat in a semicircle before the blazing fire; at the old man's feet the blue-ticked hound dozed. They made room for Bayard, and Buddy squatted again in the chimney corner.

"Git 'im?" Mr MacCallum asked.

"Yes, sir," Bayard answered. "Like lifting your hat off a nail in the wall."

The old man puffed again. "We'll give you a sho' 'nough hunt befo' you leave."

Rafe said: "How many you got now, Buddy?"

"Aint got but fo'teen," Buddy answered.

"Fo'teen?" Henry repeated. "We wont never eat fo'teen 'possums."

"Turn 'em 'loose and run 'em again, then," Buddy answered. The old man puffed slowly at his pipe. The others smoked or chewed also, and Bayard produced his cigarettes and offered them to Buddy. Buddy shook his head.

"Buddy aint never started yet," Rafe said.

"You haven't?" Bayard asked. "What's the matter, Buddy?"

"Dont know," Buddy answered, from his shadow. "Just aint had time to learn, I reckon."

The fire crackled and swirled; from time to time Stuart, nearest the box, put another log on. The dog at the old man's feet dreamed, snuffed; soft ashes swirled on the hearth at its nose and it sneezed, waking itself, and raised its head and blinked up at the old man's face, then dozed again. They sat without word and with very little movement, their grave, aquiline faces as though carved by the firelight out of the shadowy darkness, shaped by a single thought and smoothed and colored by the same hand. The old man tapped his pipe carefully out upon his palm and consulted his fat silver watch. Eight oclock.

"We'uns git up at fo' oclock, Bayard," he said. "But you dont have to git up till daylight. Henry, git the jug."

"Four oclock," Bayard repeated, as he and Buddy undressed in the lamplit chill of the lean-to room in which, in a huge wooden bed with a faded patchwork quilt, Buddy slept. "I dont see why you bother to go to bed at all." As he spoke his breath vaporized in the chill air.

"Yes," Buddy agreed, ripping his shirt over his head and kicking his lean, racehorse shanks out of his shabby khaki pants. "Dont take long to spend the night at our house. You're comp'ny, though," he added, and in his voice was just a trace of envy and of longing. Never again after twenty-five will sleep in the morning be so golden. His preparations for sleeping were simple: he removed his boots and pants and shirt and went to bed in his woolen underwear, and he now lay with only his round head in view, watching Bayard who stood in a sleeveless jersey and short thin trunks. "You aint goin' to sleep warm that a way," Buddy said. "You want one o' my heavy 'uns?"

"I'll sleep warm, I guess," Bayard answered. He blew the lamp out and groped his way to the bed, his toes curling away from the icy floor, and got in. The mattress was filled with corn shucks: it rattled beneath him, drily sibilant, and whenever he or Buddy moved at all or took a deep breath even, the shucks shifted with small ticking sounds.

"Git that 'ere quilt tucked in good over thar," Buddy advised from the darkness, expelling his breath in a short explosive sound of relaxation. He yawned, audible but invisible. "Aint seen you in a long while," he suggested.

"That's right. Let's see, when was it? Two—three years, wasn't it?"

"Nineteen fifteen," Buddy answered. "Last time you and him. . . . . . " Then he added quietly: "I seen in a paper, when it happened. The name. Kind of knowed right off 'twas him. It was a limey paper."

"You did? Where were you?"

"Up there," Buddy answered. "Where them limeys was. Where they sent us. Flat country. Dont see how they ever git it drained enough to make a crop, with all that rain."

"Yes." Bayard's nose was like a lump of ice. He could feel his breath warming his nose a little, could almost see the pale smoke of it as he breathed; could feel the inhalation chilling his nostrils again. It seemed to him that he could feel the planks of the ceiling as they sloped down to the low wall on Buddy's side, could feel the atmosphere packed into the low corner, bitter and chill and thick, too thick for breathing, like invisible slush; and he lay beneath it. . . . He was aware of the dry ticking of shucks beneath him and discovered so that he was breathing in deep troubled draughts and he wished dreadfully to be up, moving, before a fire, light; anywhere, anywhere. Buddy lay beside him in the oppressive, half-congealed solidity of the chill, talking in his slow, inarticulate idiom of the war. It was a vague, dreamy sort of tale, without beginning or end and filled with stumbling references to places wretchedly pronounced—you got an impression of people, creatures without initiation or background or future, caught timelessly in a maze of solitary conflicting preoccupations, like bumping tops, against an imminent but incomprehensible nightmare.

"How'd you like the army, Buddy?" Bayard asked.

"Not much," Buddy answered. "Aint enough to do. Good

life for a lazy man." He mused a moment. "They gimme a charm," he added, in a burst of shy, diffident confidence and sober pleasure.

"A charm?" Bayard repeated.

"Uhuh. One of them brass gimcracks on to a colored ribbon. I aimed to show it to you, but I fergot. Do it tomorrow. That 'ere flo's too dang cold to tech till I have to. I'll watch a chance tomorrow when pappy's outen the house."

"Why? Dont he know you got it?"

"He knows," Buddy answered. "Only he dont like it because he claims it's a Yankee charm. Rafe says pappy and Stonewall Jackson aint never surrendered."

"Yes," Bayard repeated. Buddy ceased talking and presently he sighed again, emptying his body for sleep. But Bayard lay rigidly on his back, his eyes wide open. It was like being drunk and whenever you close your eyes, the room starts going round and round, and so you lie rigid in the dark with your eyes wide open, not to get sick. Buddy had ceased talking; presently his breathing became longer, steady and regular, and the shucks shifted with sibilant complaint as Bayard turned slowly onto his side.

Buddy breathed on in the darkness, steadily and peacefully. Bayard could hear his own breathing also, but above it, all around it, enclosing him, that other breathing. As though he were one thing breathing with restrained laboring pants, within himself breathing with Buddy's breathing; using up all the air so that the lesser thing must pant for it. Meanwhile the greater thing breathed deeply and steadily and unawares, asleep, remote; ay, perhaps dead. Perhaps he was dead, and he recalled that morning, relived it again with strained attention from the time he had seen the first tracer smoke, until from his steep sideslip he watched the flame burst like the gay flapping of an orange pennon from the nose of John's Camel and saw his brother's familiar gesture and the sudden awkward sprawl of his plunging body as it lost equilibrium in midair; relived it again as you might run over a printed oft-read tale, trying to remember, feel, a bullet going into his body or head that might have slain him at the same instant. That would account for it, would explain so much: that he too was dead and this was hell, through which he moved forever and ever with an illusion of quickness, seeking his brother who in turn was somewhere seeking him, never the two to meet. He turned onto his back again; the shucks whispered beneath him with dry derision.

The house was full of noises; to his sharpened senses the silence was myriad: the dry agony of wood in the black frost; the ticking of shucks as he breathed; the very atmosphere itself like slush ice in the vise of the cold, oppressing his lungs. His feet were cold, his limbs sweated with it, and about his hot heart his body was rigid and shivering and he raised his naked arms above the covers and lay for a time with the cold like a lead cast about them. And all the while Buddy's steady breathing and his own restrained and panting breath, both sourceless yet involved one with the other.

Beneath the covers again his arms were cold across his chest and his hands were like ice upon his ribs, and he moved with infinite caution while the chill croached from his shoulders downward and the hidden shucks chattered at him, and swung his legs to the floor. He knew where the door was and he groped his way to it on curling toes. It was fastened by a wooden bar, smooth as ice, and fumbling at it he touched something else beside it, something chill and tubular and upright, and his hand slid down it and he stood for a moment in the icy pitch darkness with the shotgun in his hands, and as he stood so, his numb fingers fumbling at the breach, he remembered the box of shells on the wooden box on which the lamp sat. A moment longer he stood so, his head bent a little and the gun in his numb hands; then he leaned it again in the corner and lifted the wooden bar from its slots carefully and without noise. The door sagged from the hinges and after the first jarring scrape, he grasped the edge of it and lifted it back, and stood in the door.

In the sky no star showed, and the sky was the sagging corpse of itself. It lay upon the earth like a deflated balloon; into it the dark shape of the kitchen rose without depth, and the trees beyond, and homely shapes like sad ghosts in the chill corpse-light—the woodpile; a farming tool; a barrel beside the broken stoop at the kitchen door, where he had stumbled, supperward. The gray chill seeped into him like water into sand, with short trickling runs; halting, groping about an obstruction, then on again, trickling at last along his unimpeded bones. He was shaking slowly and steadily with cold; beneath his hands his flesh was rough and without sensation, yet still it jerked and jerked as though something within the dead envelope of him strove to free itself. Above his head, upon the plank roof, there sounded a single light tap, and as though at a signal, the gray silence began to dissolve. He shut the door silently and returned to bed.

In the bed he lay shaking more than ever, to the cold derision of the shucks under him, and he lay quietly on his back, hearing the winter rain whispering on the roof. There was no drumming, as when summer rain falls through the buoyant air, but a whisper of unemphatic sound, as though the atmosphere lying heavily upon the roof dissolved there and dripped sluggishly and steadily from the eaves. His blood ran again, and the covers felt like iron or like ice; but while he lay motionless beneath the rain his blood warmed yet more, until at last his body ceased trembling and he lay presently in something like a tortured and fitful doze, surrounded by coiling images and shapes of stubborn despair and the ceaseless striving for . . . not vindication so much as comprehension, a hand, no matter whose, to touch him out of his black chaos. He would spurn it, of course, but it would restore his cold sufficiency again.

The rain dripped on, dripped and dripped; beside him Buddy breathed placidly and steadily: he had not even changed his position. At times Bayard dozed fitfully: dozing, he was wide awake; waking, he lay in a hazy state filled with improbable moiling and in which there was neither relief nor rest: drop by drop the rain wore the night away, wore time away. But it was so long, so damn long. His spent blood, wearied with struggling, moved through his body in slow beats, like the rain, wearing his flesh away. *It comes to all . . . bible . . . some preacher, anyway. Maybe he knew. Peace. It comes to all*

At last, from beyond walls, he heard movement. It was indistinguishable, yet he knew it was of human origin, made by people whose names and faces he knew waking again into the world he had not been able even temporarily to lose, people to whom he was . . . and he was comforted. The sounds continued; unmistakably he heard a door, and a voice which with a slight effort of concentration he knew he could name; and best of all, knew that now he could rise and go where they were gathered about a crackling fire where light was, and warmth. And he lay, at ease at last, intending to rise the next moment and go to them, putting it off a little longer while his blood beat slowly through his body and his heart was quieted. Buddy breathed steadily beside him, and his own breath was untroubled now as Buddy's while the human sounds came murmurously into the cold room with grave and homely reassurance. *It comes to all, it comes to all* his tired heart comforted him, and at last he slept.

He waked in the gray morning, his body weary and heavy and dull: his sleep had not rested him. Buddy was gone, and it still rained, though now it was a definite purposeful sound on the roof and the air was warmer, with a rawness that probed to the very bones of him; and in his stockings and carrying his boots in his hands, he crossed the cold room where Lee and Rafe and Stuart slept, and found Rafe and Jackson before the living room fire.

"We let you sleep," Rafe said, then he said: "Good Lord, boy, you look like a hant. Didn't you sleep last night?"

"Yes, I slept all right," Bayard answered. He sat down and stamped into his boots and buckled the thongs below his knees. Jackson sat at one side of the hearth; in the shadowy corner near his feet a number of small, living creatures moiled silently, and still bent over his boots Bayard said:

"What you got there, Jackson? What sort of puppies are them?"

"New breed I'm tryin'," Jackson answered, and Rafe returned with a half a tumbler of Henry's pale amber whisky.

"Them's Ethel's pups," he said. "Git Jackson to tell you about 'em after you eat. Here, drink this. You look all wore out. Buddy must a kept you awake, talkin'," he added, with dry irony.

Bayard drank the whisky and lit a cigarette. "Mandy's got yo' breakfast on the stove," Rafe said.

"Ethel?" Bayard repeated. "Oh, that fox. I aimed to ask about her, last night. Y'all raise her?"

"Yes. She growed up with last year's batch of puppies. Buddy caught her. And now Jackson aims to revolutionize the huntin' business, with her. Aims to raise a breed of animals with a hound's wind and bottom, and a fox's smartness and speed."

Bayard approached the corner and examined the small creatures with interest and curiosity. "I never saw many fox pups," he said at last, "but I never saw any that looked like them."

"That's what Gen'ral seems to think," Rafe answered.

Jackson spat into the fire and stooped over the creatures. They knew his hands, and the moiling of them became more intense, and Bayard then noticed that they made no sound at all, not even puppy whimperings. "Hit's a experiment," Jackson explained. "The boys makes fun of 'em, but they haint no more'n weaned, yit. You wait and see."

"Dont know what you'll do with 'em," Rafe said brutally. "They wont be big enough fer work stock. Better git yo' breakfast, Bayard."

"You wait and see," Jackson repeated. He touched the scramble of small bodies with his hands, in a gentle, protective gesture. "You cant tell nothin' 'bout a dawg 'twell hit's at least two month old, can you?" he appealed to Bayard, looking up at him with his vague, intense gaze from beneath his shaggy brows.

"Go git yo' breakfast, Bayard," Rafe insisted. "Buddy's done gone and left you."

He bathed his face with icy water in a tin pan on the porch, and ate his breakfast—ham and eggs and flapjacks and sorghum—while Mandy talked to him about his brother. When he returned to the house old Mr MacCallum was there. The puppies moiled inextricably in their corner, and the old man sat with his hands on his knees, watching them with bluff and ribald enjoyment, while Jackson sat nearby in a sort of hovering concern, like a hen.

"Come hyer, boy," the old man ordered when Bayard appeared. "Hyer, Rafe, git me that 'ere bait line." Rafe went out, returning presently with a bit of pork rind on the end of a string. The old man took it and hauled the puppies ungently into the light, where they crouched abjectly—as strange a litter as Bayard had ever seen. No two of them looked alike, and none of them looked like any other living creature—Neither fox nor hound; partaking of both, yet neither; and despite their soft infancy, there was about them something monstrous and contradictory and obscene. Here a fox's keen, cruel muzzle between the melting, sad eyes of a hound and its mild ears; there limp ears tried valiantly to stand erect and failed ignobly in flapping points; and limp brief tails brushed over with a faint, golden fuzz like the inside of a chestnut burr. As regards color, they ranged from reddish brown through an indiscriminate brindle to pure ticked beneath a faint dun cast; and one of them had, feature for feature, old General's face in comical miniature, even to his expression of sad and dignified disillusion. "Watch 'em, now," the old man directed.

He got them all facing forward, then he dangled the meat directly behind them. Not one became aware of its presence; he swept it back and forth just above their heads; not one looked up. Then he swung it directly before their eyes; still they crouched diffidently on their young, unsteady legs and gazed at the meat with curiosity but without any personal interest whatever and fell again to moiling soundlessly among themselves.

"You cant tell nothin' about a dawg——" Jackson began. His father interrupted him.

"Now, watch." He held the puppies with one hand and with the other he forced the meat into their mouths. Immediately they surged clumsily and eagerly over his hand, but he moved the meat away and at the length of the string he dragged it along the floor just ahead of them until they had attained a sort of scrambling lope. Then in midfloor he flicked the meat slightly aside, but without swerving the puppies blundered on and into a shadowy corner, where the wall stopped them and from which there rose presently the patient, voiceless confusion of them. Jackson crossed the floor and picked them up and brought them back to the fire.

"Now, what do you think of them, fer a pack of huntin' dawgs?" the old man demanded. "Cant smell, cant bark, and damn ef I believe they kin see."

"You cant tell nothin' about a dawg——" Jackson essayed patiently.

"Gen'ral kin," his father interrupted. "Hyer, Rafe, call Gen'ral in hyer."

Rafe went to the door and called, and presently General entered, his claws hissing a little on the bare floor and his ticked coat beaded with rain, and he stood and looked into the old man's face with grave inquiry. "Come hyer," Mr MacCallum said, and the dog moved again, with slow dignity. At that moment he saw the puppies beneath Jackson's chair. He paused in midstride and for a moment he stood looking at them with fascination and bafflement and a sort of grave horror, then he gave his master one hurt, reproachful look and turned and departed, his tail between his legs. Mr MacCallum sat down and rumbled heavily within himself.

"You cant tell about dawgs——" Jackson repeated. He stooped and gathered up his charges, and rose.

Mr MacCallum continued to rumble and shake. "Well, I dont blame the old feller," he said. "Ef I had to look around on a passel of chaps like them and say to myself Them's my boys——" But Jackson was gone. The old man sat and rumbled again, with heavy enjoyment. "Yes, suh, I reckon I'd feel 'bout as proud as he does. Rafe, han' me down my pipe."

All that day it rained, and the following day and the one after that. The dogs lurked about the house all morning, underfoot, or made brief excursions into the weather, returning to sprawl before the fire, drowsing and malodorous and steaming, until Henry came along and drove them out; twice from the door Bayard saw the fox, Ethel, fading with brisk diffidence across the yard. With the exception of Henry and Jackson, who had a touch of rheumatism, the others were somewhere out in the rain most of the day. But at mealtimes they gathered again, shucking their wet outer garments on the porch and stamping in to thrust their muddy, smoking boots to the fire while Henry fetched the kettle and the jug. And last of all, Buddy, soaking wet.

Buddy had a way of getting his lean length up from his niche beside the chimney at any hour of the day and departing without a word, to return in two hours or six or twelve or forty eight, during which periods and despite the presence of Jackson and Henry and usually Lee, the place had a vague air of desertion, until Bayard realized that the majority of the dogs were absent, also. Hunting, they told him when Buddy had been missing since breakfast.

"Why didn't he let me know?" he demanded.

"Maybe he thought you wouldn't keer to be out in the weather," Jackson suggested.

"Buddy dont mind weather," Henry explained. "One day's like another to him."

"Nothin' aint anything to Buddy," Lee said, in his bitter, passionate voice. He sat brooding in the fire, his womanish hands moving restlessly on his knees. "He'd spend his whole life in that 'ere river bottom, with a hunk of cold cawn bread to eat and a passel of dawgs fer comp'ny." He rose abruptly and quitted the room. Lee was in the late thirties. As a child he had been sickly. He had a good tenor voice and he was much in demand at Sunday singings. He was supposed to be keeping company with a young woman living in the hamlet of Mount

Vernon, six miles away. He spent much of his time tramping moodily and alone about the countryside.

Henry spat into the fire and jerked his head after the departing brother. "He been to Vernon lately?"

"Him and Rafe was there two days ago," Jackson answered.

Bayard said: "Well, I wont melt. I wonder if I could catch up with him now?"

They pondered for a while, spitting gravely into the fire. "I misdoubt it," Jackson said at last. "Buddy's liable to be ten mile away by now. You ketch 'im next time 'fo' he starts out."

After that Bayard did so, and he and Buddy tried for birds in the skeletoned fields in the rain, in which the guns made a flat, mournful sound that lingered in the streaming air like a spreading stain, or tried the stagnant backwaters along the river channel for duck and geese; or, accompanied now and then by Rafe, hunted 'coon and wildcat in the bottom. At times and far away, they would hear the shrill yapping of the young dogs in mad career. "'Ther goes Ethel," Buddy would remark. Then toward the end of the week the weather cleared, and in a twilight imminent with frost and while the scent lay well upon the wet earth, old General started the red fox that had baffled him so many times.

All through the night the ringing, bell-like tones quavered and swelled and echoed among the hills, and all of them save Henry followed on horseback, guided by the cries of the hounds but mostly by the old man's and Buddy's uncanny and seemingly clairvoyant skill in anticipating the course of the race. Occasionally they stopped while Buddy and his father wrangled about where the quarry would head next, but usually they agreed, apparently anticipating the animal's movements before it knew them itself; and once and again they halted their mounts upon a hill and sat so in the frosty starlight until the dogs' voices welled out of the darkness mournful and chiming, swelled louder and nearer and swept invisibly past not half a mile away; faded diminishing and with a falling suspense, as of bells, into the silence again.

"Thar, now!" the old man exclaimed, shapeless in his overcoat, upon his white horse. "Aint that music fer a man, now?"

"I hope they git 'im this time," Jackson said. "Hit hurts Gen'ral's conceit so much ever' time he fools 'im."

"They wont git 'im," Buddy said. "Soon's he gits tired, he'll hole up in them rocks."

"I reckon we'll have to wait till them pups of Jackson's gits big enough," the old man agreed, "unless they'll refuse to run they own granddaddy. They done refused ever' thing else excep' vittles."

"You jest wait," Jackson repeated, indefatigable. "When them puppies gits old enough to——"

"Listen."

The talking ceased, and again across the silence the dogs' voices rang among the hills. Long, ringing cries fading, falling with a quavering suspense, like touched bells or strings, repeated and sustained by bell-like echoes repeated and dying among the dark hills beneath the stars, lingering yet in the ears crystal-clear, mournful and valiant and a little sad.

"Too bad Johnny aint here," Stuart said quietly. "He'd enjoy this race."

"He was a feller fer huntin', now," Jackson agreed. "He'd keep up with Buddy, even."

"John was a fine boy," the old man said.

"Yes, suh," Jackson repeated, "a right warm-hearted boy. Henry says he never come out hyer withouten he brung Mandy and the boys a little sto'-bought somethin'."

"He never sulled on a hunt," Stuart said. "No matter how

cold and wet it was, even when he was a little chap, with that 'ere single bar'l he bought with his own money, that kicked 'im so hard ever' time he shot it. And yit he'd tote it around, instead of that 'ere sixteen old Colonel give 'im, jest because he saved up his own money and bought hit hisself."

"Yes," Jackson agreed. "Ef a feller gits into somethin' on his own accord, he ought to go through with hit cheerful."

"He was sho' a feller fer singin' and shoutin'," Mr MacCallum said. "Skeer all the game in ten mile. I mind that night he up and headed off a race down at Samson's bridge, and next we knowed, here him and the fox come a-floatin' down river on that 'ere drift lawg, and him singin' away loud as he could yell."

"That 'uz Johnny, all over," Jackson agreed. "Gittin' a whoppin' big time outen ever' thing that come up."

"He was a fine boy," Mr MacCallum said again.

"Listen."

Again the hounds gave tongue in the darkness below them. The sound floated up upon the chill air, died into echoes that repeated the sound again until its source was lost and the very earth itself might have found voice, grave and sad and wild with all regret.

Christmas was two days away, and they sat again about the fire after supper; again old General dozed at his master's feet. Tomorrow was Christmas eve and the wagon was going into town, and although, with that grave and unfailing hospitality of theirs, no word had been said to Bayard about his departure, he believed that in all their minds it was taken for granted that he would return home the following day for Christmas; and, since he had not mentioned it himself, a little curiosity and quiet speculation also.

It was cold again, with a vivid chill that caused the blazing logs to pop and crackle with vicious sparks and small embers that leaped out upon the floor, to be crushed out by a lazy boot, and Bayard sat drowsily, his tired muscles relaxed in cumulate waves of heat as in a warm bath, and his stubborn wakeful heart glozed over too, for the time being. Time enough tomorrow to decide whether to go or not. Perhaps he'd just stay on, without even offering that explanation which would never be demanded of him. Then he realized that Rafe, Lee, whoever went, would talk to people, would learn about that which he had not the courage to tell them.

Buddy had come out of his shadowy niche and he now squatted in the center of the semicircle, his back to the fire and his arms around his knees, with his motionless and seemingly tireless ability for sitting timelessly on his heels. He was the baby, twenty years old. His mother had been the old man's second wife, and his hazel eyes and the reddish thatch cropped close to his round head was a noticeable contrast to his brothers' brown eyes and black hair. But the old man had stamped Buddy's face as clearly as ever a one of the other boys', and despite its youth, it too was like the others—aquiline and spare, reserved and grave though a trifle ruddy with his fresh coloring and finer skin.

The others were of medium height or under, ranging from Jackson's faded, vaguely ineffectual lankness, through Henry's placid rotundity and Rafe's (Raphael Semmes he was) and Stuart's poised and stocky muscularity, to Lee's thin and fiery unrepose; but Buddy with his sapling-like leanness stood eye to eye with that father who wore his seventy-seven years as though they were a thin coat. "Long, spindlin' scoundrel," the old man would say, with bluff derogation. "Keeps hisself wore to a shadder totin' around all that 'ere grub he eats." And they would sit in silence, looking at Buddy's jack-knifed length with the same identical thought, a thought which each believed peculiar to himself and which none ever divulged—that someday Buddy would marry and perpetuate the name.

Buddy also bore his father's name, though it is doubtful if anyone outside the family and the War Department knew it. He had run away at seventeen and enlisted; at the infantry concentration camp in Arkansas to which he had been sent, a fellow recruit called him Virge and Buddy had fought him steadily and without anger for seven minutes; at the New Jersey embarkation depot another man had done the same thing, and Buddy had fought him, again steadily and thoroughly and without anger. In Europe, still following the deep but uncomplex compulsions of his nature, he had contrived, unwittingly perhaps, to perpetrate something which was later ascertained by authority to have severely annoyed the enemy, for which Buddy had received his charm, as he called it. What it was he did, he could never be brought to say, and the gaud not only failing to placate his father's rage over the fact that a son of his had joined the Federal army, but on the contrary adding fuel to it, the bauble languished among Buddy's sparse effects and his military career was never mentioned in the family circle; and now as usual Buddy squatted among them, his back to the fire and his arms around his knees, while they sat about the hearth with their bed-time toddies, talking of Christmas.

"Turkey," the old man was saying, with fine and rumbling disgust. "With a pen full of 'possums, and a river bottom full of squir'ls and ducks, and a smoke-house full of hawg meat, you damn boys have got to go clean to town and buy a turkey fer Christmas dinner."

"Christmas aint Christmas lessen a feller has a little somethin' different from ever' day," Jackson pointed out mildly.

"You boys jest wants a excuse to git to town and loaf around all day and spend money," the old man retorted. "I've seen a sight mo' Christmases than you have, boy, and ef hit's got to be sto'-bought, hit aint Christmas."

"How 'bout town folks?" Rafe asked. "You aint allowin' them no Christmas a-tall."

"Dont deserve none," the old man snapped. "Livin' on a little two-by-fo' lot, jam right up in the next feller's back do', eatin' outen tin cans."

"'Sposin' they all broke up in town," Stuart said, "and moved out here and took up land; you'd hear pappy cussin' town then. You couldn't git along without town to keep folks bottled up in, pappy, and you knows it."

"Buyin' turkeys," Mr MacCallum repeated with savage disgust. "Buyin' 'em. I mind the time when I could take a gun and step out that 'ere do' and git a gobbler in thutty minutes. And a ven'son ham in a hour mo'. Why, you fellers dont know nothin' about Christmas. All you knows is a sto' winder full of cocoanuts and Yankee-made popguns and sich."

"Yes, suh," Rafe said, and he winked at Bayard. "That was the biggest mistake the world ever made, when Lee surrendered. The country aint never got over it."

The old man snorted. "I be damned ef I aint raised the damdest smartest set of boys in the world. Cant tell 'em nothin', cant learn 'em nothin'; cant even set in front of my own fire fer the whole passel of 'em tellin' me how to run the whole damn country. Hyer, you boys, git on to bed."

Next morning Jackson and Rafe and Stuart and Lee left for town at sunup in the wagon. Still none of them had made any sign, expressed any curiosity as to whether they would find him there when they returned that night, or whether it would be another three years before they saw him again. And Bayard stood on the frost-whitened porch, smoking a cigarette in the chill, vivid sunrise, and looked after the wagon with its four muffled figures and wondered if it would be three years again, or ever. The hounds came and nuzzled about him and he dropped his hand among their icy noses and the warm flicking of their tongues, gazing at the trees from beyond which the dry rattling of the wagon came unimpeded upon the clear and soundless morning.

"Ready to go?" Buddy said behind him, and he turned and picked up his shotgun where it leaned against the wall. The hounds surged about them with eager whimperings and frosty breaths and Buddy led them across to their pen and huddled them inside and fastened the door upon their astonished protests. From another kennel he unleashed the young pointer, Dan. Behind them the hounds continued to lift their baffled and mellow expostulations.

Until noon they hunted the ragged, fallow fields and woods-edges in the warming air. The frost was soon gone, and the air warmed to a windless languor; and twice in brier thickets they saw redbirds darting like arrows of scarlet flame. At last Bayard lifted his eyes unwinking into the sun.

"I've got to go back, Buddy," he said. "I'm going home this afternoon."

"All right," Buddy agreed without protest, and he called the dog in. "You come back next month."

Mandy got them some cold food and they ate, and while Buddy was saddling Perry, Bayard went into the house where he found Henry laboriously soling a pair of boots and the old man reading a week-old newspaper through steel-bowed spectacles.

"I reckon yo' folks will be lookin' fer you," Mr MacCallum agreed, removing his spectacles. "We'll be expectin' you back next month, though, to git that 'ere fox. Ef we dont git 'im soon, Gen'ral wont be able to hold up his haid befo' them puppies."

"Yes, sir," Bayard answered. "I will."

"And try to git yo' gran'pappy to come out with you. He kin lay around hyer and eat his haid off well as he kin in town thar."

"Yes, sir, I will."

Buddy led the pony up, and the old man extended his hand without rising, and Henry put aside his cobbling and followed him onto the porch. "Come out again," he said diffidently, giving Bayard's hand a single pump-handle shake; and from a slobbering inquisitive surging of half grown hounds Buddy reached up his hand.

"Be lookin' fer you," he said briefly, and Bayard wheeled away, and when he looked back they lifted their hands gravely. Then Buddy shouted after him and he reined Perry about and returned. Henry had vanished, and he reappeared with a weighted towsack.

"I nigh fergot it," he said. "Jug of cawn pappy's sendin' in to yo' granddaddy. You wont git no better 'n this in Looeyvul ner nowhar else, neither," he added with quiet pride. Bayard thanked him, and Buddy fastened the sack to the pommel, where it lay solidly against his leg.

"There. That'll ride."

"Yes, that'll ride. Much obliged."

"So long."

"So long."

Perry moved on, and he looked back. They still stood there, quiet and grave and steadfast. Beside the kitchen door the fox, Ethel, sat, watching him covertly; near her the half-grown puppies rolled and played in the sunlight. The sun was an hour high above the western hills; the road wound on into the trees. He looked back again. The house sprawled its rambling length in the wintry afternoon, its smoke like a balanced plume on the windless sky. The door was empty and he shook

Perry into his easy, tireless foxtrot, the jug of whisky jouncing a little against his knee.

6

Where the dim, infrequent road to MacCallum's left the main road, rising, he halted Perry and sat for a while in the sunset. Jefferson, 14 miles. Rafe and the other boys would not be along for some time, yet, what with Christmas eve in town and the slow festive gathering of the county. Still, they may have left town early, so as to get home by dark; might not be an hour away. The sun's rays, slanting, released the chill they had held prisoned in the ground during the perpendicular hours, and it rose slowly about him as he sat Perry in the middle of the road, and slowly his blood cooled with the cessation of Perry's motion. He turned the pony's head away from town and shook him into his foxtrot again.

Darkness overtook him soon, but he rode on beneath the leafless trees, along the pale road in the gathering starlight. Already Perry was thinking of stable and supper and he went on with tentative, inquiring tossings of his head, but obediently and without slackening his gait, knowing not where they were going nor why, save that it was away from home, and a little dubious, though trustfully. The chill grew in the silence and the loneliness and the monotony. Bayard reined Perry to a halt and untied the jug and drank, and fastened it to the saddle again.

The hills rose wild and black about him; no sign of any habitation, no trace of man's hand did they encounter. On all sides the hills rolled blackly away in the starlight, or when the road dipped into valleys where the ruts were already stiffening into iron-like shards that clattered beneath Perry's hooves, they stood darkly towering and sinister overhead, lifting their leaf-less trees against the spangled sky. Where a stream of winter seepage trickled across the road Perry's feet crackled brittlely in thin ice, and Bayard slacked the reins while the pony snuffed at the water, and drank again from the jug.

He fumbled a match clumsily in his numb fingers and lit a cigarette, and pushed his sleeve back from his wrist. Eleven-thirty. "Well, Perry," his voice sounded loud and sudden in the stillness and the darkness and the cold. "I reckon we better look for a place to hole up till morning." Perry raised his head and snorted, as though he understood the words, as though he would enter the bleak loneliness in which his rider moved, if he could. They went on, mounting again.

The darkness spread away, lessening a little presently where occasional fields lay in the vague starlight, breaking the monotony of trees; and after a time during which he rode with the reins slack on Perry's neck and his hands in his pockets seeking warmth between leather and groin, a cotton house squatted beside the road, its roof dusted over with a frosty sheen as of hushed silver. Not long, he told himself, leaning forward and laying his hand on Perry's neck, feeling the warm, tireless blood there. "House soon, Perry, if we look sharp."

Again Perry whinnied a little, as though he understood, and presently he swerved from the road, and as Bayard reined him up he too saw the faint wagon trail leading away toward a low vague clump of trees. "Good boy, Perry," he said, slacken-ing the reins again.

The house was a cabin. It was dark, but a hound came gauntly from beneath it and bayed at him and continued its uproar while he reined Perry to the door and knocked upon it with his numb hand. From within the house at last a voice, and he shouted "Hello" again. Then he added: "I'm lost. Open the door." The hound bellowed at him indefatigably. After a moment the door cracked upon a dying glow of embers, emitting a rank odor of negroes, and against the crack of warmth, a head.

"You, Jule," the head commanded, "hush yo' mouf." The hound ceased obediently and retired beneath the house, though still growling. "Who dar?"

"I'm lost," Bayard repeated. "Can I stay in your barn tonight?"

"Aint got no barn," the negro answered. "Dey's anudder house down de road a piece."

"I'll pay you." Bayard fumbled in his pocket with his numb hand. "My horse is tired out." The negro's head peered around the door, against the crack of firelight. "Come on, uncle," Bayard added impatiently. "Dont keep a man standing in the cold."

"Who is you, whitefolks?"

"Bayard Sartoris, from Jefferson. Here," and he extended his hand. The negro made no effort to take it.

"Banker Sartorises folks?"

"Yes. Here."

"Wait a minute." The door closed. But Bayard tightened the reins and Perry moved readily and circled the house confidently and went on among frost-stiffened cotton stalks that clattered drily about his knees. As Bayard dismounted onto frozen rutted earth beneath a gaping doorway, a lantern appeared from the cabin, swung low among the bitten stalks and the shadowy scissoring of the man's legs, and the negro came up with a shapeless bundle under his arm and stood with the lantern while Bayard stripped the saddle and bridle off.

"How you manage to git so fur fum home dis time o' night, whitefolks?" he asked curiously.

"Lost," Bayard answered briefly. "Where can I put my horse?"

The negro swung the lantern into a stall. Perry stepped carefully over the sill and turned into the lantern light, his eyes rolling in phosphorescent gleams; Bayard followed and rubbed him down with the dry side of the saddle blanket. The negro vanished and reappeared with a few ears of corn and shucked them into Perry's manger beside the pony's eager nuzzling. "You gwine be keerful about fire, aint you, whitefolks?" he asked.

"Sure. I wont strike any matches at all."

"I got all my stock and tools and feed in here," the negro explained. "I cant affo'd to git burnt out. Insu'ance dont reach dis fur."

"Sure," Bayard repeated. He shut Perry's stall and while the negro watched him he drew the sack forth from where he had set it against the wall, and produced the jug. "Got a cup here?" The negro vanished again and Bayard could see the lantern through the cracks in the crib in the wall opposite, then he emerged with a rusty can, from which he blew a bursting puff of chaff. They drank. Behind them Perry crunched his corn. The negro showed him the ladder to the loft.

"You wont fergit about dat fire, whitefolks?" he repeated anxiously.

"Sure," Bayard said. "Goodnight." He laid his hand on the ladder, and the negro stopped him and handed him the shapeless bundle he had brought out with him.

"Aint got but one to spare, but hit'll help some. You gwine sleep cole, tonight." It was a quilt, ragged and filthy to the touch, and impregnated with that unmistakable odor of negroes.

"Thanks," Bayard answered. "Much obliged to you. Goodnight."

"Goodnight, whitefolks."

The lantern winked away, to the criss-crossing of the negro's legs, and Bayard mounted into darkness and the dry, pungent scent of hay. Here, in the darkness, he made himself a nest of it and crawled into it and rolled himself into the quilt, filth and odor and all, and thrust his icy hands inside his shirt, against his flinching chest. After a time and slowly his hands began to warm, tingling a little, but still his body lay shivering and jerking with weariness and with cold. Below him Perry munched steadily and peacefully in the darkness, occasionally he stamped, and gradually the jerking of his body ceased. Before he slept he uncovered his arm and looked at the luminous dial on his wrist. One oclock. It was already Christmas.

The sun waked him, falling in red bars through the cracks in the wall, and he lay for a time in his hard bed, with chill bright air on his face like icy water, wondering where he was. Then he remembered, and moving, found that he was stiff with stale cold and that his blood began to move through his limbs in small pellets like bird-shot. He dragged his legs from his odorous bed, but within his boots his feet were dead, and he sat flexing his knees and ankles for some time before his feet waked as with stinging needles. His movements were stiff and awkward, and he descended the ladder slowly and gingerly into the red sun that fell like a blare of trumpets into the hallway. The sun was just above the horizon, huge and red; and house-top, fenceposts, the casual farming tools rusting about the barnyard and the dead cotton stalks where the negro had farmed his land right up to his back door, were dusted over with frost which the sun changed to a scintillant rosy icing like that on a festive cake. Perry thrust his slender muzzle across the stall door and whinnied at his master with vaporous salutation, and Bayard spoke to him and touched his cold nose. Then he untied the sack and drank from the jug. The negro with a milk pail appeared in the door.

"Chris'mus gif', whitefolks," he said, eying the jug. Bayard gave him a drink. "Thanky, suh. You g'awn to de house to de

fire. I'll feed yo' hawss. De ole woman got yo' breakfus' ready."
Bayard picked up the sack; at the well behind the cabin he
drew a pail of icy water and splashed his face.

A fire burned on the broken hearth, amid ashes and
charred wood-ends and a litter of cooking vessels. Bayard shut
the door behind him, upon the bright cold, and warmth and
rich, stale rankness enveloped him like a drug. A woman bent
over the hearth replied to his greeting diffidently. Three pickaninnies became utterly still in a corner and watched him with
rolling eyes. One of them was a girl, in greasy, nondescript garments, her wool twisted into tight knots of soiled wisps of colored cloth. The second one might have been either or
anything. The third one was practically helpless in a garment
made from a man's suit of wool underclothes. It was too small
to walk and it crawled about the floor in a sort of intense pur-
poselessness, a glazed path running from either nostril to its
chin, as though snails had crawled there.

The woman placed a chair before the fire with a dark,
effacing gesture. Bayard seated himself and thrust his chilled
feet to the fire. "Had your Christmas dram yet, aunty?" he
asked.

"Naw, suh. Aint got none, dis year," she answered from
somewhere behind him.

He swung the sack toward her voice. "Help yourself.
Plenty there." The three children squatted against the wall,
watching him steadily, without movement and without sound.
"Christmas come yet, chillen?" he asked them. But they only
stared at him with the watchful gravity of animals until the
woman returned and spoke to them in a chiding tone.

"Show de whitefolks yo' Sandy Claus," she prompted.
"Thanky, suh," she added, putting a tin plate on his knees and
setting a cracked china cup on the hearth at his feet. "Show

'im," she repeated. "You want folks to think Sandy Claus dont know whar you lives at?"

The children moved then, and from the shadow behind them, where they had hidden them when he entered, they produced a small tin automobile, a string of colored wooden beads, a small mirror and a huge stick of peppermint candy to which trash adhered and which they immediately fell to licking solemnly, turn and turn about. The woman filled the cup from the coffee pot set among the embers, and she uncovered an iron skillet and forked a thick slab of sizzling meat onto his plate, and raked a grayish object from the ashes and broke it in two and dusted it off and put that too on the plate. Bayard ate his side meat and hoecake and drank the thin, tasteless liquid. The children now played quietly with their Christmas, but from time to time he found them watching him steadily and covertly. The man entered with his pail of milk.

"Ole 'oman give you a snack?" he asked.

"Yes. What's the nearest town on the railroad?" The other told him—eight miles away. "Can you drive me over there this morning, and take my horse back to Mr MacCallum's some day this week?"

"My brudder-in-law bor'd my mules," the negro replied readily. "I aint got but de one span, and he done bor'd dem."

"I'll pay you five dollars."

The negro set the pail down, and the woman came and got it. He scratched his head slowly. "Five dollars," Bayard repeated.

"You's in a pow'ful rush, fer Chris'mus, whitefolks."

"Ten dollars," Bayard said impatiently. "Cant you get your mules back from your brother-in-law?"

"I reckon so. I reckon he'll bring 'em back by dinner time. We kin go den."

"Why cant you get 'em now? Take my horse and go get 'em. I want to catch a train."

"I aint had no Chris'mus yit, whitefolks. Feller workin' ev'y day of de year wants a little Chris'mus."

Bayard swore shortly and bleakly, but he said: "All right, then. Right after dinner. But you see your brother-in-law has 'em back here in plenty of time."

"Dey'll be here: dont you worry about dat."

"All right. You and aunty help yourselves to the jug."

"Thanky, suh."

The stale, airtight room dulled him; the warmth was insidious to his bones wearied and stiff after the chill night. The negroes moved about the single room, the woman busy at the hearth with her cooking, the pickaninnies with their frugal and sorry gewgaws and filthy candy. Bayard sat in his hard chair and dozed the morning away. Not asleep, but time was lost in a timeless region where he lingered unawake and into which he realized after a long while that something was trying to penetrate; watched its vain attempts with peaceful detachment. But at last it succeeded and reached him: a voice. "Dinner ready."

The negroes drank with him again, amicably, a little diffidently—two opposed concepts antipathetic by race, blood, nature and environment, touching for a moment and fused within an illusion—humankind forgetting its lust and cowardice and greed for a day. "Chris'mus," the woman murmured shyly. "Thanky, suh." Then dinner: 'possum with yams, more gray ashcake, the dead and tasteless liquid in the coffee pot; a dozen bananas and jagged shards of cocoanut, the children crawling about his feet like animals scenting food. He realized at last that they were holding back until he had done, but he overrode them and they dined together; and at last (the mules having been miraculously returned by a yet uncorporeal brother-in-law) with his depleted jug between his feet in the wagon bed, he looked once back at the cabin, at the woman standing in the door and a pale windless drift of smoke above its chimney.

Against the mules' gaunt ribs the broken harness rattled and jingled. The air was warm, yet laced too with a thin distillation of chill that darkness would increase. The road went on across the bright land. From time to time across the shining sedge or from beyond brown and leafless woods, came the flat reports of guns; occasionally they passed other teams or horsemen or pedestrians, who lifted dark restful hands to the negro buttoned into an army overcoat, with brief covert glances for the white man on the seat beside him. "Heyo, Chris'mus!" Beyond the yellow sedge and brown ridges the ultimate hills stood bluely against the plumbless sky. "Heyo."

They stopped and drank, and Bayard gave his companion a cigarette. The sun behind them now; no cloud, no wind, no bird in the serene pale cobalt. "Shawt days! Fo' mile mo'. Come up, mules." Between motionless willows, stubbornly green, a dry clatter of loose planks above water in murmurous flashes. The road lifted redly; pines stood against the sky in jagged bastions. They crested this, and a plateau rolled away before them with its pattern of burnished sedge and fallow dark fields and brown woodland, and now and then a house, on into a shimmering azure haze, and low down on the horizon, smoke. "Two mile, now." Behind them the sun was a copper balloon tethered an hour up the sky. They drank again.

It had touched the horizon when they looked down into the final valley where the railroad's shining threads vanished among roofs and trees, and along the air to them distantly came a slow, heavy explosion. "Still celebratin'," the negro said.

Out of the sun they descended into violet shadow where windows gleamed behind wreaths and paper bells, across stoops littered with spent firecrackers. Along the streets children in bright sweaters and jackets sped on shiny coasters and skates and wagons. Again a heavy explosion in the dusk ahead, and they debouched into the square with its Sabbath calm, littered too with shattered scraps of paper. It looked the same way at home, he knew, with men and youths he had known from boyhood lounging the holiday away, drinking a little and shooting fireworks, giving nickels and dimes and quarters to negro lads who shouted Chris'mus gif'! Chris'mus gif'! as they passed. And out home the tree in the parlor and the bowl of eggnog before the fire, and Simon entering his and Johnny's room on tense and clumsy tiptoe and holding his breath above the bed where they lay feigning sleep until his tenseness relaxed, whereupon they both roared "Christmas gift!" at him, to his pained disgust. "Well, I'll de-clare, ef dey aint done caught me ag'in!" But by mid morning he would be recovered, by dinnertime he would be in a state of affable and useless loquacity, and by nightfall completely *hors de combat*, with Aunt Jenny storming about the house and swearing that never again should it be turned into a barroom for trifling niggers as long as she had her strength, so help her Jupiter. And after dark, somewhere a dance, with holly and mistletoe and paper streamers, and the girls he had always known with their new bracelets and watches and fans amid lights and music and glittering laughter. . . .

A small group stood on a corner, and as the wagon passed and preceded by an abrupt scurrying, yellow flame was stenciled on the twilight and the heavy explosion reverberated in sluggish echoes between the silent walls. The mules quickened against the collars and the wagon rattled on. Through the dusk now, from lighted doorways where bells and wreaths hung, voices called with mellow insistence; children's voices replied, expostulant, reluctantly regretful. Then the station, where a 'bus and four or five cars stood, and Bayard descended and the negro lifted down the sack.

"Much obliged," Bayard said. "Goodbye."

"Goodbye, whitefolks."

In the waiting room a stove glowed red hot and about the room stood cheerful groups, in sleek furs and overcoats, but he did not enter. He set the sack against the wall and tramped up and down the platform, warming his blood again. In both directions along the tracks green switch lights were steady in the dusk; a hands-breadth above the western trees the evening star was like an electric bulb in a glass wall. He tramped back and forth, glancing into the ruddy windows, into the waiting room where the cheerful groups in their furs and overcoats gesticulated with festive though soundless animation, and into the colored waiting room, whose occupants sat patiently and murmurously about the stove in the dingy light. As he turned here a voice spoke diffidently from the shadow beside the door. "Chris'mus gif', boss." He took a coin from his pocket without stopping. Again from the square a firecracker exploded heavily, and above the trees a rocket arced, hung for a moment, then opened like a fist, spreading its golden and fading fingers upon the tranquil indigo sky without a sound.

Then the train came and brought its lighted windows to a jarring halt, and he picked up his sack again. And in the midst of a cheerful throng shouting goodbyes and holiday greetings and messages to absent ones, he got aboard, unshaven, in his scarred boots and stained khaki pants, and his shabby, smoke-colored tweed jacket and his disreputable felt hat, and found a vacant seat and stowed the jug away beneath his legs.

Five

1

"

. . . and since the essence of spring is loneliness and a little sadness and a sense of mild frustration, I suppose you do get a keener purifaction when a little nostalgia is thrown in for good measure. At home I always found myself remembering apple trees or green lanes or the color of the sea in other places, and I'd be sad that I couldn't be everywhere at once, or that all the spring couldn't be one spring, like Byron's ladies' mouths. But now I seem to be unified and projected upon one single and very definite object, which is something to be said for me, after all." Horace's pen ceased and he gazed at the sheet scrawled over with his practically illegible script, while the words he had just written echoed yet in his mind with a little gallant and whimsical sadness, and for the time being he had quitted the desk and the room and the town and all the crude and blatant newness into which his destiny had brought him, and again that wild and fantastic futility of his roamed unchallenged through the lonely region into which it had at last concentrated its conflicting parts. Already the thick cables along the veranda eaves would be budding into small lilac matchpoints, and with no effort at all he could see the lawn below the cedars, splashed with random narcissi among random jonquils and gladioli waiting to bloom in turn.

But his body sat motionless, its hand with the arrested pen lying upon the scrawled sheet, the paper lying upon the yellow varnished surface of his new desk. The chair in which he sat was new too, as was the room with its dead white walls and imitation oak woodwork. All day long the sun fell upon it, untempered by any shade. In the days of early spring it had been pleasant, falling as it now did through his western window and across the desk where a white hyacinth bloomed in a bowl of glazed maroon pottery. But as he sat musing, gazing out the window where, beyond a tarred roof that drank heat like a sponge and radiated it, against a brick wall a clump of ragged heaven trees lifted shabby, diffident bloom, he dreaded the long hot summer days of sunlight upon the roof directly above him, remembered his dim and musty office at home, in which a breeze seemed always to move, with its serried rows of books dusty and undisturbed that seemed to emanate coolness and quietude even on the hottest days. And thinking of this, he was again lost from the harsh newness in which his body sat. The pen moved again.

"Perhaps fortitude is a sorry imitation of something worth while, after all. To the so many who burrow along like moles in the dark, or like owls, to whom a candle-flame is a surfeit. But not those who carry peace along with them as the candle-flame carries light. I have always been ordered by words, but it seems that I can even restore assurance to my own cowardice by cozening it a little. I dare say you cannot read this as usual, or reading it, it will not mean anything to you. But you will have served your purpose anyway, thou still unravished bride of quietude." Thou wast happier in thy cage, happier? Horace thought, reading the words he had written and in which, as usual, he was washing one woman's linen in the house of another. A thin breeze blew suddenly into the room; there was locust upon it, faintly sweet, and beneath it the paper stirred upon the desk, rousing him; and suddenly, as a man waking, he looked at his watch and replaced it and wrote rapidly:

"We are glad to have little Belle with us. She likes it here: there is a whole family of little girls next door: stair steps of tow pigtails before whom, it must be confessed that little Belle preens just a little; patronizes them, as is her birthright. Children make all the difference in the world about a house. Too bad agents are not wise enough to provide rented houses with them. Particularly one like little Belle, so grave and shining and sort of irrelevantly and intensely mature, you know. But then, you dont know her very well, do you? But we both are very glad to have her with us. I believe that Harry   " The pen ceased, and still poised, he sought the words that so rarely eluded him, realizing as he did so that, though one can lie about others with ready and extemporaneous promptitude, to lie about oneself requires deliberation and a careful choice of expression. Then he glanced again at his watch and crossed that out and wrote: "Belle sends love, O Serene." and blotted it and folded it swiftly into an envelope and addressed and stamped it, and rose and took his hat. By running he could get it on the four oclock train.

Thou wast happier in thy cage, happier. . . . . . . The corridor, with its rubber mat and identical closed doors expensively and importantly discrete; the stairway with its brass-bound steps and at each turning, a heavy brass receptacle in which cigarette butts and scraps of paper reposed upon tobacco-stained sand, all new, all smelling of recent varnish. There was a foyer of imitation oak and imitation marble; the street in an untempered glare of spring sunlight. The building too was new and an imitation of something else, or maybe a skillful and even more durable imitation of that, as was the whole town, the very spirit, the essence of which was crystallized in the courthouse building—an edifice imposing as a theatre drop, flamboyant and cheap and shoddy; obviously built without any definite plan by men without honesty or taste. It was a standing joke that it had cost $60,000, and the people who had paid for it retailed the story without anger, but on the contrary with a little frankly envious admiration.

Ten years ago the town was a hamlet, twelve miles from the railroad. Then a hardwood lumber concern had bought up the cypress swamps nearby and established a factory in the town. It was financed by eastern capital and operated by as plausible and affable a set of brigands as ever stole a county. They robbed the stockholders and the timber owners and one another and spent the money among the local merchants, who promptly caught the enthusiasm, and presently widows and orphans in New York and New England were buying Stutz cars and imported caviar and silk dresses and diamond watches at three prices, and the town bootleggers and the moonshiners in the adjacent swamps waxed rich, and every fourth year the sheriff's office sold at public auction for the price of a Hollywood bungalow. People in the neighboring counties learned of all this and moved there and chopped all the trees down and built themselves mile after mile of identical frame houses with garage to match: the very air smelled of affluence and burning gasoline. Yes, there was money there, how much, no two estimates ever agreed; whose, at any one given time, God Himself could not have said. But it was there, like that afflatus of rank fecundity above a foul and stagnant pool on which bugs dart spawning, die, are replaced in mid-darting; in the air, in men's voices and gestures, seemingly to be had for the taking. That was why Belle had chosen it.

But for the time being Horace was utterly oblivious of its tarnished fury as he walked along the street toward the new, ugly yellow station, carrying his letter the words of which yet echoed derisively in his mind Belle sends love Belle sends love. He had made acquaintances "In spite of yourself," Belle told him harshly. "Thinking you are better than other people." Yes, he had answered. Yes, with a weariness too spent to argue with its own sense of integrity. But he had made a few, some of whom he now passed, was greeted, replied: merchants, another lawyer, his barber; a young man who was trying to sell him an automobile. Naturally Belle would Belle sends love Belle sends He still carried his letter in his hand and glancing at the bulletin board on the station wall he saw that the train was a little late, and he went on down the platform to where the mail car would stop and gave the letter to the mail carrier—a lank, goose-necked man with a huge pistol strapped to his thigh Thou wast happier   The express agent came along, dragging his truck in thy cage, happier   "Got another 'un today?" he asked, greeting Horace.

"What?" Horace said. "Oh, good afternoon."

"Got another 'un today?" the other repeated.

"Yes," Horace answered, watching the other swing the truck skillfully into position beside the rails Happier The sun was warm; already there was something of summer's rankness in it—a quality which, at home where among green and ancient trees and graver and more constant surroundings, dwelt quietude and the soul's annealment, it had not even in July. Soon, soon, he said, and again he went voyaging alone from where his body leaned against a strange wall in a brief hiatus of the new harsh compulsions it now suffered. This will not last always: I have made too little effort to change my fellow man's actions and beliefs to have won a place in anyone's plan of infinity In thy cage, happier?

The locomotive slid past, rousing him: he had not heard it, and the cars on rasping wheels, and from the door of the express car the clerk with a pencil stuck jauntily beneath his cap, flipped his hand at him. "Here you are, Professor," he said, handing down first to the agent a small wooden crate from which moisture dripped. "Smelling a little stout, today, but the fish wont mind that, will they?" Horace approached, his nostrils tightening a little. The clerk in the car door was watching him with friendly curiosity. "Say," he asked, "what kind of city fish you got around here, that have to have mail-order bait?"

"It's shrimp," Horace explained.

"Shrimp?" the other repeated. "Eat 'em yourself, do you?" he asked with interest.

"Yes. My wife's very fond of them."

"Well, I'll be damned," the clerk said heartily, "I thought it was some kind of patent fish-bait you were getting every Tuesday. Well, every man to his taste, I reckon. But I'll take steak, myself. All right, Bud; grab it."

Horace signed the agent's receipt and lifted the crate from the truck, holding it carefully away from himself. The smell invariably roused in him a faint but definite repulsion which he was not able to overcome, though Belle preferred shrimp above all foods. And it always seemed to him for hours afterward that the smell clung about his clothing, despite the fact that he knew better, knew that he had carried the package well clear of himself. He carried it so now, his elbow against his side and his forearm at a slight, tense angle with the dripping weight.

Behind him the bell rang, and with the bitten, deep snorts of starting, the train moved. He looked back and saw the cars slide past, gaining speed, carrying his letter away and the quiet, the intimacy the writing and the touching of it, had brought him. But day after tomorrow he could write again Belle sends love Belle sends Ah, well, we all respond to strings. And She would understand, it and the necessity for it, the dreadful need; She in her serene aloofness partaking of gods Belle sends

The street from curb to curb was uptorn. It was in the throes of being paved. Along it lines of negroes labored with pick and shovel, swinging their tools in a languid rhythm. Steadily and with a lazy unhaste that seemed to spend itself in snatches of plaintive minor chanting punctuated by short grunting ejaculations which died upon the sunny air and ebbed away from the languid rhythm of picks that struck not; shovels that did not dig. Further up the street a huge misshapen machine like an antediluvian nightmare clattered and groaned. It dominated the scene with its noisy and measured fury, but against this as against a heroic frieze, the negroes labored on, their chanting and their motions more soporific than a measured tolling of far away bells.

His arm was becoming numb, but the first mark—a water plug—where he changed hands for the first time, was still a hundred yards away; and when he reached it and swapped the crate to the other hand, his fingers were dead of all sensation and his biceps was jumping a little within his sleeve. Which goes to prove the fallacy of all theories of physical training. According to that, every succeeding Tuesday he should be able to go a little further without changing, until by Christmas he would be able to carry the package all the way home without changing hands; and by Christmas ten years, all the way back to Gulfport, where they came from. Prize, maybe. More letters behind his name, anyway. C.S. Carrier of Shrimp. H. Benbow, M.A., Ll.D., C.S. Thou wast happier

The next mark was the corner where he turned, and he went on along the treeless street, between smug rows of houses identical one with another. Cheap frame houses, patently new, each with a garage and a car, usually a car that cost as much again as the house did. He reached the corner and changed hands again and turned into a smaller street, trailing spaced drops of melting ice behind him.

He lived on this street, and it was still open: motors could run on it, and he went on, dripping his trailing moisture along the sidewalk. With a motor car now, he could have Soon; perhaps next year; then things But naturally Belle would miss her car, after having had one always, a new one every year. Harry, and his passion for shiny wheels. . . . . . . which some would call generosity. . . . . . . "You lied to me. You told me you had plenty of money." Lied Lied took me away from my Well, it would be better now, with little Belle. And Harry would find . . . who functioned in movie subtitles, harshly: "What else do you want of mine? My dam blood?"

Man's life. No apparent explanation for it save as an opportunity for doing things he'd spend the rest of it not being very proud of. Well, she had her child again, anyway, he told himself, thinking how women never forgive the men who permit them to do the things which they later have any cause to regret; and remembering that day when, with little Belle's awkwardly packed suitcase in the rack overhead and little Belle primly beside him in a state of demure and shining excitement at the prospect of moving suddenly to a new town, he had shrunk into his corner like a felon until the familiar station and that picture of Harry's ugly dogged head and his eyes like those of a stricken ox, were left behind, he wondered if little Belle too would someday. . . . . . . But that last picture of Harry's face had a way of returning. It's only injured vanity, he argued with himself; he's hurt in his own estimation because he couldn't keep the female he had chosen in the world's sight. But still his eyes and their patient bloodshot bewilderment, to be exorcised somehow. He's a fool, anyway, he told himself savagely, And who has time to pity fools? Then he said God help us, God help us all, and then at last humor saved him and he thought with a fine whimsical flash of it that probably Belle would send him to Harry next for a motor car.

Man's very tragedies flout him. He has invented a masque for tragedy, given it the austerity which he believes the spectacle of himself warrants, and the thing makes faces behind his back; dead alone, he is not ridiculous, and even then only in his own eyes Thou wast happier A voice piped with thin familiarity from beyond a fence. It was little Belle playing with the little girls next door, to whom she had already divulged with the bland naiveté of children that Horace was not her real daddy: he was just the one that lived with them now, because her real daddy's name was Daddy and he lived in another town. It was a prettier town than this, while the little girls listened with respect coldly concealed: little Belle had gained a sort of grudging cosmopolitanish glamor, what with her uniquely diversified family.

At the next gate he paused, and opened it and entered his rented lawn where his rented garage stared its empty door at him like an accusing eye, and still carrying his package carefully away from him he went on between the two spindling poplars he had set out and approached his rented frame house with its yellow paint and its naked veranda, knowing that from behind a shade somewhere, Belle was watching him. In negligee, the heavy mass of her hair caught up with studied carelessness, and her hot, suspicious eyes and the rich and sullen discontent of her mouth Lied lied took me away from my husband: what is to keep The wild bronze flame of her hair Her Injury, yes. Inexcusable because of the utter lack of necessity or reason for it. Giving him nothing, taking nothing away from him. Obscene. Yes, obscene: a deliberate breaking of the rhythm of things for no reason; to both Belle and himself an insult; to Narcissa, in her home where her serenity lingered grave and constant and steadfast as a diffused and sourceless light, it was an adolescent scribbling on the walls of a temple. Reason in itself confounded If what parts can so remain. . . . "I didn't lie. I told you; did what she would not have had the cowardice to do." What is to keep Ay, obscene if you will, but there was about her a sort of gallantry, like a swordsman who asks no quarter and gives none; slays or is slain with a fine gesture or no gesture at all; tragic and austere and fine, with the wild bronze flame of her hair. And he, he not only hadn't made a good battle; he hadn't even made a decent ghost. Thou wast happier in thy cage, happier? Nor oceans and seas. . . . . . .

"She had ghosts in her bed," Horace said, mounting the steps.

2

In January his aunt received a post card from Bayard mailed at Tampico; a month later, from Mexico City, a wire for money. And that was the last intimation he gave that he contemplated being at any given place long enough for a communication to reach him, although from time to time he indicated by gaudy postals where he had been, after the bleak and brutal way of him. In April the card came from Rio, followed by an interval during which he seemed to have completely vanished and which Miss Jenny and Narcissa passed quietly at home, their days centered placidly about the expected child, which Miss Jenny had already named John. Miss Jenny felt that old Bayard had somehow flouted them all, had committed lese majesty toward his ancestors and the lusty glamor of the family doom by dying, as she put it, practically from the "inside out." Thus he was in something like bad odor with her, and as young Bayard was in more or less abeyance, neither flesh nor fowl, she fell to talking more and more of John. Soon after old Bayard's death, in a sudden burst of rummaging and prowling which she called winter cleaning, she had found among his mother's relics a miniature of John done by a New Orleans painter when John and Bayard were about eight. Miss Jenny remembered that there had been one of each and it seemed to her that she could remember putting them both away together when their mother died. But the other she could not find. So she left Simon to gather up the litter she had made and brought the miniature downstairs to where Narcissa sat in the "office" and together they examined it.

The hair even at that early time was of a rich tawny shade, and rather long. "I remember that first day," Miss Jenny said, "when they came home from school. Bloody as hogs, both of 'em, from fighting other boys who said they looked like girls. Their mother washed 'em and petted 'em, but they were too busy bragging to Simon and Bayard about the slaughter they had done to mind it much. 'You ought to seen the others,' Johnny kept saying. Bayard blew up, of course; said it was a damn shame to send a boy out on the street with curls down his back, and finally he bullied the poor woman into agreeing to let Simon barber 'em. And do you know what? Neither of 'em would let his hair be touched. It seems there were still a few they hadn't licked yet, and they were going to make the whole school admit that they could wear hair down to their heels, if they wanted to. And I reckon they did, because after two or three more bloody days they came home once without any fresh wounds and then they let Simon cut it off while their mother sat behind the piano in the parlor and cried. And that was the last of it as long as they were in school here. I dont know what they kept on fighting folks about after they went away to school, but they found some reason. That was why we finally had to separate 'em while they were at Virginia and send Johnny to Princeton. They shot dice or something to see which one would be expelled, I think, and when Johnny lost they used to meet in New York every month or so. I found some letters in Bayard's desk that the chief of police in New York wrote to the professors at Princeton and Virginia, asking 'em not to let Bayard and Johnny come back there any more, that the professors sent on to us. And one time Bayard had to pay fifteen hundred dollars for something they did to a policeman or a waiter or something."

Miss Jenny talked on, but Narcissa was not listening. She was examining the painted face in the miniature. It was a child's face that looked at her, and it was Bayard's too, yet there was already in it, not that bleak arrogance she had come to know in Bayard's, but a sort of frank spontaneity, warm and ready and generous; and as Narcissa held the small oval in her hand while the steady blue eyes looked quietly back at her and from the whole face among its tawny curls, with its smooth skin and child's mouth, there shone like a warm radiance something sweet and merry and wild, she realized as she never had before the blind tragedy of human events. And while she sat motionless with the medallion in her hand and Miss Jenny thought she was looking at it, she was cherishing the child under her own heart with all the aroused constancy of her nature: it was as though already she could discern the dark silver shape of that doom which she had incurred, standing beside her chair, waiting and biding its time. No, No she whispered with passionate protest, surrounding her child with wave after wave of that strength which welled so abundantly within her as the days accumulated, manning her walls with invincible garrisons. She was even glad Miss Jenny had shown her the thing: she was now forewarned as well as forearmed.

Meanwhile Miss Jenny continued to talk about the child as Johnny and to recall anecdotes of that other John's childhood, until at last Narcissa realized that Miss Jenny was getting the two confused; and with a sort of shock she knew that Miss Jenny was getting old, that at last even her indomitable old heart was growing a little tired. It was a shock, for she had never associated senility with Miss Jenny, who was so spare and erect and brusque and uncompromising and kind, looking after the place which was not hers and to which she had been transplanted when her own alien roots in a far away place where customs and manners and even the very climate itself, were different, had been severed violently; running it with tireless efficiency and with the assistance of only a doddering old negro as irresponsible as a child.

But run the place she did, just as though old Bayard and young Bayard were there. But at night when they sat before the fire in the office as the year drew on and the night air drifted in heavy again with locust and with the song of mockingbirds and with all the renewed and timeless mischief of spring and at last even Miss Jenny admitted that they no longer needed a fire; when at these times she talked, Narcissa noticed that she no longer talked of her far off girlhood and of Jeb Stuart with his crimson sash and his garlanded bay and his mandolin, but always of a time no further back than Bayard's and John's childhood. As though her life were closing, not into the future, but out of the past, like a spool being rewound.

And Narcissa would sit, serene again behind her forewarned bastions, listening, admiring more than ever that indomitable spirit that, born with a woman's body into a heritage of rash and heedless men and seemingly for the sole purpose of cherishing those men to their early and violent ends, and this over a period of history which had seen brothers and husband slain in the same useless mischancing of human affairs, had seen, as in a nightmare not to be healed by either waking or sleep, the foundations of her life swept away and had her roots torn bodily from that soil where her forefathers slept trusting in the integrity of mankind;—a period at which the men themselves, for all their headlong and scornful rashness, would have quailed had their parts been passive parts and their doom been waiting. And she thought how much finer that gallantry which never lowered blade to foes no sword could find, that uncomplaining steadfastness of those unsung (ay, unwept, too) women than the fustian and useless glamor of the men that obscured it. And now she is trying to make me one of them; to make of my child just another rocket to glare for a moment in the sky, then die away.

But she was serene again, and her days centered more and more as her time drew nearer, and Miss Jenny's voice was only a sound, comforting but without significance. Each week she received a whimsical, gallantly humorous letter from Horace: these she read too with tranquil detachment—what she could decipher, that is. She had always found Horace's writing difficult, and parts that she could decipher meant nothing. But she knew that he expected that.

Then it was definitely spring again. Miss Jenny's and Isom's annual vernal altercation began, pursued its violent but harmless course in the garden beneath her window. They brought the tulip bulbs up from the cellar and set them out, Narcissa helping, and spaded up the other beds and unswaddled the roses and the transplanted jasmine. Narcissa drove into town, saw the first jonquils on the deserted lawn, blooming as though she and Horace were still there, and she sent Horace a box of them, and later, the narcissi. But when the gladioli bloomed she was not going out any more save in the late afternoon or early evening, when with Miss Jenny she walked in the garden among burgeoning bloom and mockingbirds and belated thrushes where the long avenues of gloaming twilight reluctant leaned, Miss Jenny still talking of Johnny, confusing the unborn with the dead.

———

Early in June they received a request for money from Bayard in San Francisco, where he had at last succeeded in being robbed. Miss Jenny sent it. "You come on home?" she wired him, not telling Narcissa. "He'll come home, now," she did tell her. "You see if he dont. If for nothing else than to worry us for a while."

But a week later he still had not come home, and Miss Jenny wired him again, a night letter. But when the wire was dispatched he was in Chicago, and when it reached San Francisco he was sitting among saxophones and painted ladies and middle aged husbands at a table littered with soiled glasses and stained with cigarette ash and spilt liquor, accompanied by a girl and two men. One of the men wore whipcord, with an army pilot's wings on his breast. The other was a stocky man in shabby serge, with gray temples and intense, visionary eyes. The girl was a slim long thing, mostly legs apparently, with a bold red mouth and cold eyes, in an ultra smart dancing frock, and when the other two men came across the room and spoke to Bayard she was cajoling him to drink with thinly-concealed insistence. She and the aviator now danced together, and from time to time she looked back to where Bayard sat drinking steadily while the shabby man talked to him. She was saying: "I'm scared of him."

The shabby man was talking with leashed excitability, using two napkins folded lengthwise into narrow strips to illustrate something, his voice hoarse and importunate against the meaningless pandemonium of horns and drums. For a while Bayard had half listened, staring at the man with his cold eyes, but now he was watching something or some one across the room, letting the man talk on, unheeded. He was drinking whisky and soda steadily, with the bottle beside him. His hand was steady enough, but his face was dead white and he was quite drunk; and looking across at him from time to time, the girl was saying to her partner: "I'm scared, I tell you. God, I didn't know what to do, when you and your friend came over. Promise you wont go and leave us."

"You scared?" the aviator repeated in a jeering tone, but he too glanced back at Bayard's white arrogant face. "I bet you dont even need a horse."

"You dont know him," the girl rejoined, and she clutched his hand and struck her body shivering against his, and though his arm tightened and his hand slid down her back a little, it was under cover of the shuffling throng into which they were wedged, and a little warily, and he said quickly:

"Ease off, Sister: he's looking this way. I saw him knock two teeth out of an Australian captain that just tried to speak to a girl he was with in a London dive two years ago." They moved on until the band was across the floor from them. "What're you scared of? He's not an Indian: he wont hurt you as long as you mind your step. He's all right. I've known him a long time, in places where you had to be good, believe me."

"You dont know," she repeated. "I——" The music crashed to a stop; in the sudden silence the shabby man's voice rose from the nearby table:

"——could just get one of these damn yellow-livered pilots to——" His voice was drowned again in a surge of noise, drunken voices and shrill woman-laughter and scraping chairs, but as they approached the table the shabby man still talked with leashed insistent gestures while Bayard stared across the room at whatever it was he watched, lifting his glass steadily to his lips. The girl clutched her partner's arm.

"You've got to help me pass him out," she begged swiftly. "I'm scared to leave with him, I tell you."

"Pass Sartoris out? The man dont wear hair, nor the woman neither. Run back to kindergarden, Sister." Then, struck with her utter sincerity, he said: "Say, what's he done to you, anyway?"

"I dont know. He'll do anything. He threw an empty bottle at a traffic cop as we were driving out here. You've got—— "

"Hush it," he commanded. The shabby man ceased talking and looked up impatiently. Bayard still gazed across the room.

"Brother-in-law over there," he said, speaking slowly and carefully. "Dont speak to family. Mad at us. Beat him out of his wife." They turned and looked.

"Where?" the aviator asked. He beckoned a waiter. "Here, Jack."

"Man with diamond headlight," Bayard said. "Brave man. Cant speak to him, though. Might hit me. Friend with him, anyhow."

The aviator looked again. "Looks like his grandmother," he said. He called the waiter again, then to the girl: "Another cocktail?" He picked up the bottle and filled his glass and Bayard's, and turned to the shabby man. "Where's yours?"

The shabby man waved it impatiently aside. "Look," he picked up the napkins again. "Dihedral increases in ratio to air pressure. By speed up to a certain point, see? Now, what I want to find out—— "

"Tell it to the Marines, buddy," the aviator interrupted. "I heard a couple of years ago they got a airyplane. Here, waiter!" Bayard was now watching the shabby man bleakly.

"You aren't drinking," the girl said. She touched the aviator beneath the table.

"No," Bayard agreed. "Why dont you fly his coffin for him, Monaghan?"

"Me?" The aviator set his glass down. "Like hell. My leave

comes due next month." He raised his glass again. "Here's to wind-up," he said, "and no heel-taps."

"Yes," Bayard agreed, not touching his glass. His face was pale and rigid, a metal mask again.

"I tell you there's no danger at all, as long as you keep the speed below the point I'll give you," the shabby man said with heat. "I've tested the wings with weights, and proved the lift and checked all my figures; all you have to——"

"Wont you drink with us?" the girl insisted.

"Sure he will," the aviator said. "Say, you remember that night in Amiens when that big Irish devil, Comyn, wrecked the Cloche-Clos by blowing that A.P.M.'s whistle at the door?" The shabby man sat smoothing the folded napkins on the table before him. Then he burst forth again, his voice hoarse and mad with the intensity of his frustrated dream:

"I've worked and slaved, and begged and borrowed, and now when I've got the machine and a government inspector, I cant get a test because you damn yellow-livered pilots wont take it up. A service full of you, drawing flying pay for sitting on hotel roofs, swilling alcohol. You overseas pilots talking about your guts! No wonder the Germans——"

"Shut up," Bayard told him without heat, in his cold, careful voice.

"You're not drinking," the girl repeated. "Wont you?" She picked up his glass and touched her lips to it and extended it to him. Taking it, he caught her hand too and held her so. But again he was staring across the room.

"Not brother-in-law," he said. "Husband-in-law. No. Wife's brother's husband-in-law. Wife used to be wife's brother's girl. Married, now. Fat woman. He's lucky."

"What're you talking about?" the aviator demanded. "Come on, let's have a drink."

The girl leaned away from him at the length of her arm.

With her other hand she lifted her glass and smiled at him with brief and terrified coquetry. But he held her wrist in his hard fingers, and while she stared at him wildly he drew her steadily toward him. "Turn me loose," she whispered. "Dont," and she set her glass down and with the other hand she tried to unclasp his fingers. The shabby man was brooding over his folded napkins; the aviator was carefully occupied with his drink. "Dont," she whispered again. Her body was twisted in her chair and she put her hand out quickly, lest she be dragged out of it, and for a moment they stared at one another—she with wide and mute terror; he bleakly with the cold mask of his face. Then he released her and rose and thrust his chair back.

"Come on, you," he said to the shabby man. He drew a wad of bills from his pocket and laid one beside her on the table. "That'll get you home," he said. But she sat nursing the wrist he had held, watching him without a sound. The aviator was discreetly interested in the bottom of his glass. "Come on," Bayard repeated to the shabby man, and the other rose and followed him.

In a small alcove Harry Mitchell sat. On his table too were bottles and glasses, and he now sat slumped in his chair, his eyes closed and his bald head rosy with perspiration in the glow of an electric candle. Beside him was a woman who turned and looked at Bayard with blazing and harried desperation; above them stood a waiter with a head like a monk's, and as Bayard passed he saw that the diamond was missing from Harry's tie and he heard their bitter suppressed voices as their hands struggled over something on the table beyond the discreet shelter of their bodies, and as he and his companion reached the exit the woman's voice rose with a burst of filthy rage into a shrill hysterical scream cut sharply off, as if someone had clapped a hand over her mouth.

———

The next day Miss Jenny drove into town and wired him again. But when this wire was dispatched, Bayard was sitting in an aeroplane on the tarmac of the government field at Dayton, while the shabby man hovered and darted here and there in a frenzied manner and a group of army pilots stood nearby, soberly noncommittal. The machine looked like any other bi-plane, save that there were no visible cables between the planes, which were braced from within by wires on a system of springs; hence, motionless on the ground, dihedral was nega-tive. The theory was that while in level flight dihedral would be eliminated for speed, and when the machine was banked, side pressure would automatically increase dihedral for manoeuver-ability. The cockpit was set well back toward the fin. "So you can see the wings when they buckle," the man who lent him a helmet and goggles, said drily. "It's an old pair," he added. Bayard glanced at him, coldly humorless. "Look here, Sar-toris," the other said. "Let that crate alone. These birds show up here every week with something that will revolutionize flying, some new kind of mantrap that flies fine — on paper. If the C.O. wont give him a pilot (and you know we try anything here that has a prop on it) you can gamble it's a washout."

But Bayard took the helmet and goggles and went on toward the hangar. The group followed him and stood quietly about with their bleak, wind-gnawed faces while the engine was warming up. But when Bayard got in and settled his gog-gles, the man who had lent them to him approached and put something in his lap. "Here," he said brusquely. "Take this." It was a woman's garter, and Bayard picked it up and gave it back to him.

"I wont need it," he said. "Thanks just the same."

"Well. You know your own business. But if you ever let her get her nose down, you're going to lose everything but the wheels."

"I know," Bayard answered. "I'll keep her up." The shabby man rushed up again, still talking. "Yes, yes," Bayard replied impatiently. "You told me all that before. Contact." A mechanic spun the propeller over, and as the machine moved out toward midfield the shabby man still clung to the cockpit rim and shouted at him. Soon he was running to keep up and still shouting, and Bayard lifted his hands off the cowling and opened the throttle. But when he reached the end of the field and turned into the wind the man was running toward him and waving his arms. Bayard opened the throttle full and the machine lurched forward and when he passed the shabby man in midfield the tail was high and the plane rushed on in long bounds, and he had a fleeting glimpse of the man's wild arms and his open mouth as the bounding ceased.

From the V strut out each wing tipped and swayed, and he jockeyed the thing carefully on, gaining height. He realized that there was a certain point beyond which his own speed was likely to rob him of lifting surface. He had about two thousand feet now, and he turned, and in doing so he found that aileron pressure utterly negatived the inner plane's dihedral and doubled that of the outer one, and he found himself in the wildest skid he had seen since his hun days. The machine not only skidded: it flung its tail up like a diving whale and the air speed indicator leaped thirty miles past the dead line the inventor had given him. He was headed back toward the field now, in a shallow dive, and he pulled the stick back.

The wingtips buckled sharply; he flung the stick forward just before they ripped completely off, and he knew that only the speed of the dive kept him from falling like an inside out umbrella. And the speed was increasing: already he had overshot the field, under a thousand feet high. He pulled the stick back again; again the wingtips buckled and he slapped the stick over and kicked again into that wild skid, to check his speed. Again the machine swung its tail in a soaring arc, but this time the wings came off and he ducked his head automatically as one of them slapped viciously past it and crashed into the tail, shearing it too away.

3

That day Narcissa's child was born, and the following day Simon drove Miss Jenny into town and set her down before the telegraph office and held the horses champing and tossing with gallant restiveness by a slight and surreptitious tightening of the reins, while beneath the tophat and the voluminous duster, he contrived by some means to actually strut sitting down. So Dr Peabody found him when he came along the street in the June sunlight, in his slovenly alpaca coat, carrying a newspaper.

"You look like a frog, Simon," he said. "Where's Miss Jenny?"

"Yessuh," Simon agreed. "Yessuh. Dey's swellin' en rejoicin' now. De little marster done arrive'. Yessuh, de little marster done arrive' and de ole times comin' back."

"Where's Miss Jenny?" Dr Peabody repeated impatiently.

"She in dar, tellygraftin' dat boy ter come on back hyer whar he belong at." Dr Peabody turned away and Simon watched him, a little fretted at his apathy in the face of the event. "Takes it jes' like trash," Simon mused aloud, with annoyed disparagement. "Nummine; we gwine wake 'um all up, now. Yessuh, de olden times comin' back ergain, sho'. Like in Mars' John's time, when de Cunnel wuz de young marster en de niggers fum de quawtuhs gethered on de front lawn, wishin' Mistis en de little marster well." And he watched Dr Peabody enter the door and through the plate glass window he saw him approach Miss Jenny as she stood at the counter with her message.

"Come home you fool and see your family or I will have you arrested" the message read in her firm, lucid script. "It's more than ten words," she told the operator, "but that dont matter this time. He'll come now: you watch. Or I'll send the sheriff after him, sure as his name's Sartoris."

"Yes, ma'am," the operator said. He was apparently having trouble reading it, and he looked up after a moment and was about to speak when Miss Jenny remarked his distraction and repeated the message briskly.

"And make it stronger than that, if you want to," she added.

"Yes, ma'am," he said again, and he ducked down behind his desk, and presently and with a little mounting curiosity and impatience Miss Jenny leaned across the counter with a silver dollar in her fingers and watched him count the words three times in a sort of painful flurry.

"What's the matter, young man?" she demanded. "The government dont forbid the mentioning of a day old child in a telegram, does it?"

The operator looked up. "Yes, ma'am, it's all right," he said at last, and she gave him the dollar, and as he sat holding it and Miss Jenny watched him with yet more impatience, Dr Peabody came in and touched her arm.

"Come away, Jenny," he said.

"Good morning," she said, turning at his voice. "Well, it's about time you took notice. This is the first Sartoris you've been a day late on in how many years, Loosh? And soon as I get that fool boy home, it'll be like old times again, as Simon says."

"Yes. Simon told me. Come along here."

"Let me get my change." She turned to the counter, where

the operator stood with the message in one hand and the coin in the other. "Well, young man? Aint a dollar enough?"

"Yes, ma'am," he repeated, turning upon Dr Peabody his dumb, distracted eyes. Dr Peabody reached fatly and took the message and the coin from him.

"Come along, Jenny," he said again. Miss Jenny stood motionless for a moment, in her black silk dress and her black bonnet set squarely on her head, staring at him with her piercing old eyes that saw so much and so truly. Then she walked steadily to the door and stepped into the street and waited until he joined her, and her hand was steady too as she took the folded paper he offered. MISSISSIPPI AVIATOR it said in discreet capitals, and she returned it to him immediately and from her waist she took a small sheer handkerchief and wiped her fingers lightly.

"I dont have to read it," she said. "They never get into the papers but one way. And I know that he was somewhere he had no business being, doing something that wasn't any affair of his."

"Yes," Dr Peabody said. He followed her to the carriage and put his hands clumsily upon her as she mounted.

"Dont paw me, Loosh," she snapped. "I'm not a cripple." But he supported her elbow with his huge, gentle hand until she was seated, then he stood with his hat off while Simon laid the linen robe across her knees.

"Here," he said, and extended her the silver dollar and she returned it to her bag and clicked it shut and wiped her fingers again on her handkerchief.

"Well," she said. Then: "Thank God that's the last one. For a while, anyway. Home, Simon."

Simon sat magnificently, but under the occasion he unbent a little. "When you gwine come out en see de young marster, Doctuh?"

"Soon, Simon," he answered, and Simon clucked to the horses and wheeled away with a flourish, his hat tilted and the whip caught smartly back. Dr Peabody stood in the street, a shapeless hogshead of a man in a shabby alpaca coat, his hat in one hand and the folded newspaper and the yellow unsent message in the other, until Miss Jenny's straight slender back and the squarely indomitable angle of her bonnet had passed from sight.

But that was not the last one. One morning a week later, Simon was found in a negro cabin in town, his grizzled head crushed in by a blunt instrument anonymously wielded.

"In whose house?" Miss Jenny demanded into the telephone. In that of a woman named Meloney Harris, the voice told her. Meloney   Me   Belle Mitchell's face flashed before her mind, and she remembered: the mulatto girl whose smart apron and cap and lean shining shanks had lent such an air to Belle's parties, and who had quit Belle in order to set up a beauty parlor. Miss Jenny thanked the voice and hung up the receiver.

"The old grayheaded reprobate," she said, and she went into old Bayard's office and sat down. "So that's where that church money went that he 'put out.' I wondered. . . . . . . " She sat stiffly and uncompromisingly erect in her chair, her hands idle on her lap. Well, that *is* the last one of 'em, she thought. But no, he was hardly a Sartoris: he had at least some shadow of a reason, while the others. . . . . . . "I think," Miss Jenny said, who had not spent a day in bed since she was forty years old, "that I'll be sick for a while."

And she did just exactly that. Went to bed, where she lay propped on pillows in a frivolous lace cap, and would permit no doctor to see her save Dr Peabody who called once informally and sat sheepishly for thirty minutes while Miss Jenny vented her invalid's spleen and the recurred anger of the salve fiasco upon him. And here she held daily councils with Isom and Elnora, and at the most unexpected moments she would storm with unimpaired vigor from her window at Isom and Caspey in the yard beneath.

The child and the placid, gaily turbaned mountain who superintended his hours, spent most of the day in this room, and presently Narcissa herself; and the three of them would sit for rapt murmurous hours in a sort of choral debauch of abnegation while the object of it slept digesting, waked, stoked himself anew and slept again.

"He's a Sartoris, all right," Miss Jenny said, "but an improved model. He hasn't got that wild look of 'em. I believe it was the name. Bayard. We did well to name him Johnny."

"Yes," Narcissa said, watching her sleeping son with grave and tranquil serenity.

And there Miss Jenny stayed until her while was up. Three weeks it was. She set the date before she went to bed and held to it stubbornly, refusing even to rise and attend the christening. That day fell on Sunday. It was late in June and jasmine drifted into the house in steady waves. Narcissa and the nurse, in an even more gaudy turban, had brought the baby, bathed and garnished and scented in his ceremonial robes, in to her, and later she heard them drive away in the carriage, and then the house was still again. The curtains stirred peacefully at the windows, and all the peaceful scents of summer came up on the sunny breeze, and sounds—birds, somewhere a Sabbath bell, and Elnora's voice, chastened a little by her recent bereavement but still rich and mellow as she went about getting dinner. She sang sadly and endlessly and without words as she moved about the kitchen, but she broke off short when she looked around and saw Miss Jenny looking a little frail but dressed and erect as ever, in the door.

"Miss Jenny! Whut in de worl'! You git on back to yo' bed. Here, lemme he'p you back." But Miss Jenny came firmly on.

"Where's Isom?" she demanded.

"He at de barn. You come on back to bed. I'm gwine tell Miss Narcissa on you."

"Get away," Miss Jenny said. "I'm tired staying in the house. I'm going to town. Call Isom." Elnora protested still, but Miss Jenny insisted coldly, and Elnora went to the door and called Isom and returned, portentous with pessimistic warnings, and presently Isom entered.

"Here," Miss Jenny said, handing him the keys. "Get the car out." Isom departed and Miss Jenny followed more slowly, and Elnora would have followed too, darkly solicitous, but Miss Jenny sent her back to her kitchen; and she crossed the yard and got in beside Isom. "And you drive this thing careful, boy," she told him, "or I'll get over there and do it myself."

When they reached town, from slender spires rising among trees against the puffy clouds of summer, bells were ringing lazily. At the edge of town Miss Jenny bade Isom turn into a grassy lane and they followed this and stopped presently before the iron gates to the cemetery. "I want to see if they fixed Simon all right," she explained. "I'm not going to church today: I've been shut up between walls long enough." Just from the prospect she got a mild exhilaration, like that of a small boy playing out of school.

The negro ground lay beyond the cemetery proper, and Isom led her to Simon's grave. Simon's burying society had taken care of him, and after three weeks the mound was still heaped with floral designs from which the blooms had fallen, leaving a rank, lean mass of stems and peacefully rusting wire skeletons. Elnora, someone, had been before her, and the grave was bordered with tedious rows of broken gaudy bits of crockery and of colored glass. "I reckon he'll have to have a headstone, too," Miss Jenny said aloud, and turning, saw Isom hauling his overalled legs into a tree, about which two catbirds whirled and darted in scolding circles. "You, Isom."

"Yessum." Isom dropped obediently to the ground and the birds threatened him with a final burst of hysterical profanity. They entered the whitefolks' section and passed now between marble shapes bearing names that she knew well, and dates in a stark and peaceful simplicity in the impervious stone. Now and then they were surmounted by symbolical urns and doves and surrounded by clipped tended sward green against the blanched marble and the blue, dappled sky and the black cedars from amid which doves crooned endlessly reiterant. Here and there bright unfaded flowers lay in random bursts against the pattern of white and green; and presently John Sartoris lifted his stone back and his fulsome gesture amid a clump of cedars beyond which the bluff sheered sharply away into the valley.

Bayard's grave too was a shapeless mass of withered flowers, and Miss Jenny had Isom clear them off and carry them away. The masons were preparing to lay the curbing around it, and the headstone itself sat nearby beneath a canvas cover. She lifted the canvas and read the clean, new lettering: Bayard Sartoris. March 16, 1893–June 11, 1920. That was better. Simple: no Sartoris man to invent bombast to put on it. Cant even lie dead in the ground without strutting and swaggering. Beside the grave was a second headstone; like the other save for the inscription. But the Sartoris touch was there, despite the fact that there was no grave to accompany it, and the whole thing was like a boastful voice in an empty church. Yet withal there was something else, as though the merry wild spirit of him who had laughed away so much of his heritage of humorless and fustian vainglory, managed somehow even yet, though his bones lay in an anonymous grave beyond the seas, to soften the arrogant gesture with which they had said him farewell:

Lieut. John Sartoris, R.A.F.
Killed in action, July 5, 1918.
'I bare him on eagles' wings and brought him unto Me'

A faint breeze soughed in the cedars like a long sigh, and the branches moved gravely in it. Across the spaced tranquillity of the marble shapes the doves crooned their endless rising inflections. Isom returned for another armful of withered flowers and bore it away.

Old Bayard's headstone was simple too, having been born, as he had, too late for one war and too soon for the next, and she thought what a joke They had played on him: forbidding him opportunities for swashbuckling and then denying him the privilege of being buried by men who would have invented vainglory for him. The cedars had almost overgrown his son John's and John's wife's graves. Sunlight reached them only in splashes, dappling the weathered stone with fitful stipplings; only with difficulty could the inscription have been deciphered. But she knew what it would be, what with the virus, the inspiration and the example of that one which dominated them all, which gave to the whole place in which weary people were supposed to be resting, an orotund solemnity having no more to do with mortality than the bindings of books have to do with their characters, and beneath which the headstones of the wives whom they had dragged into their arrogant orbits were, despite their pompous genealogical references, modest and effacing as the song of thrushes beneath the eyrie of an eagle.

He stood on a stone pedestal, in his frock coat and bare-headed, one leg slightly advanced and one hand resting lightly on the stone pylon beside him. His head was lifted a little in that gesture of haughty pride which repeated itself generation after generation with a fateful fidelity, his back to the world and his carven eyes gazing out across the valley where his railroad ran and the blue changeless hills beyond, and beyond that, the ramparts of infinity itself. The pedestal and effigy were mottled with seasons of rain and sun and with drippings from the cedar branches, and the bold carving of the letters was bleared with mold, yet still decipherable:

Colonel John Sartoris, C.S.A.
1823   1876
Soldier, Statesman, Citizen of the World
For man's enlightenment he lived
By man's ingratitude he died

Pause here, son of sorrow; remember death.

This inscription had caused some furore on the part of the slayer's family, and a formal protest had followed. But in complying with popular opinion, old Bayard had had his revenge: he caused the line "by man's ingratitude he died" to be chiselled crudely out and added beneath it: "Fell at the hand of—Redlaw, Sept. 4, 1876."

Miss Jenny stood for a time, musing, a slender, erect figure in black silk and a small uncompromising black bonnet. The wind drew among the cedars in long sighs, and steadily as pulses the sad hopeless reiteration of the doves came along the sunny air. Isom returned for the last armful of dead flowers, and looking out across the marble vistas where shadows of noon moved, she watched a group of children playing quietly and a little stiffly in their bright Sunday finery, among the tranquil dead. Well, it was the last one, at last, gathered in solemn conclave about the dying reverberation of their arrogant lusts, their dust moldering quietly beneath the pagan symbols of their vainglory and the carven gestures of it in enduring stone; and she remembered something Narcissa had said once, about a world without men, and wondered if therein lay peaceful avenues and dwellings thatched with quiet; and she didn't know.

Isom returned, and as they moved away Dr Peabody called her name. He was dressed as usual in his shabby broadcloth trousers and his shiny alpaca coat and a floppy panama hat, and his son was with him.

"Well, boy," Miss Jenny said, giving young Loosh her hand. His face was big-boned and roughly molded. He had a thatch of straight, stiff black hair and his eyes were steady and brown and his mouth was large; and in all his ugly face there was reliability and gentleness and humor. He was rawboned and he wore his clothing awkwardly, and his hands were large and bony and with them he performed delicate surgical operations with the deftness of a hunter skinning a squirrel and with the celerity of a prestidigitator. He lived in New York, where he was associated with a surgeon whose name was a household word, and once a year and sometimes twice he rode thirty six hours on the train, spent twenty hours with his father (which they passed walking about town or riding about the countryside in the sagging buckboard all day, and sitting on the veranda or before the fire all night talking) and took the train again and ninety two hours later, was back at his clinic. He was thirty years old, only child of the woman Dr Peabody had courted for fourteen years before he was able to marry her. The courtship was during the days when he physicked and amputated the whole county by buckboard; often after a year's separation he would drive forty miles to see her, to be intercepted on the way and deflected to a childbed or a mangled limb, with only a scribbled message to assuage the interval of another year. "So you're home again, are you?" Miss Jenny asked.

"Yes, ma'am. And find you as spry and handsome as ever."

"Jenny's too bad-tempered to ever do anything but dry up and blow away," Dr Peabody said.

"You'll remember I never let you wait on me, when I'm not well," she retorted. "I reckon you'll be tearing off again on the next train, wont you?" she asked young Loosh.

"Yessum, I'm afraid so. My vacation hasn't come due, yet."

"Well, at this rate you'll spend it at an old men's home somewhere. Why dont you all come out and have dinner, so he can see the boy?"

"I'd like to," young Loosh answered, "but I dont have time to do all the things I want to, so I just make up my mind not to do any of 'em. Besides, I'll have to spend this afternoon fishing," he added.

"Yes," his father put in, "and choppin' up good fish with a pocket knife just to see what makes 'em go. Lemme tell you what he did this mawnin': he grabbed up that dawg that Abe shot last winter and laid its leg open and untangled them ligaments so quick that Abe not only didn't know what he was up to, but even the dawg didn't know it till it was too late to holler. Only you forgot to dig a little further for his soul," he added to his son.

"You dont know if he hasn't got one," young Loosh said, unruffled. "Dr Straud has been experimenting with electricity; he says he believes the soul——"

"Fiddlesticks," Miss Jenny interrupted. "You'd better get him a jar of Will Falls' salve to carry back to his doctor, Loosh. Well—" she glanced at the sun "—I'd better be going. If you wont come out to dinner——?"

"Thank you, ma'am," young Loosh answered. His father said:

"I brought him in to show him that collection of yours. We didn't know we looked that underfed."

"Help yourself," Miss Jenny answered. She went on, and they stood and watched her trim back until she passed out of sight beyond the cedars.

"And now there's another one," young Loosh said musingly. "Another one to grow up and keep his folks in a stew until he finally succeeds in doing what they all expect him to do. Well, maybe that Benbow blood will sort of hold him down. They're quiet folks, that girl; and Horace sort of. . . . . . and just women to raise him. . . . . . ."

His father grunted. "He's got Sartoris blood in him, too."

All of Narcissa's instincts had been antipathetic to him; his idea was a threat and his presence a violation of the very depths of her nature: in the headlong violence of him she had been like a lily in a gale which rocked it to its roots in a sort of vacuum, without any actual laying-on of hands. And now the gale had gone on; the lily had forgotten it as its fury died away into fading vibrations of old terrors and dreads, and the stalk recovered and the bell itself was untarnished save by the friction of its own petals. The gale is gone, and though the lily is sad a little vibration of ancient fears, it is not sorry.

Miss Jenny had arrived home, looking a little spent, and Narcissa had scolded her and at last prevailed on her to lie down after dinner. And here she had dozed while the drowsy afternoon wore away, and waked to lengthening shadows and a sound of piano keys touched softly below stairs. I've slept all afternoon, she told herself in a sort of consternation; yet she lay for a time yet while the curtains stirred faintly at the windows and the sound of the piano came up mingled with the jasmine from the garden and with the garrulous evensong of sparrows from the mulberry trees in the back yard. She rose and crossed the hall and entered Narcissa's room, where the child slept in its crib; beside him the nurse dozed placidly. Miss Jenny tiptoed out and descended the stairs and entered the parlor and drew her chair out from behind the piano. Narcissa stopped playing.

"Do you feel rested?" she asked. "You shouldn't have done that this morning."

"Fiddlesticks," Miss Jenny rejoined. "It always does me good to see all those fool pompous men lying there with their marble mottoes and things. Thank the Lord, none of 'em will have a chance at me. I reckon the Lord knows His business, but I declare, sometimes. . . . . . . Play something." Narcissa obeyed, touching the keys softly, and Miss Jenny sat listening for a while. The evening drew subtly onward; the shadows in the room grew more and more palpable. Outside the sparrows gossiped in shrill clouds. From the garden jasmine came in to them steady as breathing, and presently Miss Jenny roused and began to talk of the child. Narcissa played quietly on, her white dress with its black ribbon at the waist vaguely luminous in the dusk, with a hushed sheen like wax. Jasmine drifted and drifted; the sparrows were still now, and Miss Jenny talked on in the twilight about little Johnny while Narcissa played with rapt inattention, as though she were not listening. Then, without ceasing and without turning her head, she said:

"He isn't John. He's Benbow Sartoris."

"What?"

"His name is Benbow Sartoris," she repeated.

Miss Jenny sat quite still for a moment. In the next room Elnora moved about, laying the table for supper. "And do you think that'll do any good?" Miss Jenny demanded. "Do you think you can change one of 'em with a name?"

The music went on in the dusk softly; the dusk was peopled with ghosts of glamorous and old disastrous things. And if they were just glamorous enough, there was sure to be a Sartoris in them, and then they were sure to be disastrous. Pawns. But the Player and the game He plays. . . .   He must have a name for His pawns, though, but perhaps Sartoris is the game itself—a game outmoded and played with pawns shaped too late and to an old dead pattern, and of which the Player Himself is a little wearied. For there is death in the sound of it, and a glamorous fatality, like silver pennons downrushing at sunset, or a dying fall of horns along the road to Roncevaux.

"Do you think," Miss Jenny repeated, "that because his name is Benbow, he'll be any less a Sartoris and a scoundrel and a fool?"

Narcissa played on as though she were not listening. Then she turned her head and without stopping her hands, she smiled at Miss Jenny quietly, a little dreamily, with serene fond detachment. Beyond Miss Jenny's trim fading head the maroon curtains hung motionless; beyond the window evening was a windless lilac dream, foster-dam of quietude and peace.

EDITORS' NOTE

In the autumn of 1926 Faulkner began writing *Flags in the Dust*, the first of his novels to be set in what he later called "my own little postage stamp of native soil," and in October 1927 he submitted a typescript to Boni & Liveright. This typescript, dated "Oxford, Miss / 29 September 1927," is a composite of several different typings of portions of the novel, done on more than one typewriter and by at least two different typists. Numerous pages bear two or more page numbers; many pages contain revised versions of passages crossed out on previous pages; and there are numerous revisions made by Faulkner in ink throughout the typescript. The novel was rejected by Horace Liveright, who described it in a letter to Faulkner as "diffuse and non-integral with neither very much plot development nor character development. . . . The story really doesn't get anywhere and has a thousand loose ends." After making further revisions, Faulkner sent *Flags in the Dust* to his friend and agent Ben Wasson, who later said that he showed the novel to eleven publishers before Harcourt, Brace accepted it in September 1928 on the condition that it be shortened to about 110,000 words. Faulkner agreed and traveled to New York, where he worked on *The Sound and the Fury* while Wasson did most, if not all, of the cutting; much of the deleted material was excised from episodes involving Horace and Narcissa Benbow.

Sartoris was published by Harcourt, Brace on January 21, 1929 (the new title was chosen by Harcourt). Neither the typescript Faulkner sent to Wasson in 1928, nor any of the typescripts or proofs used by Harcourt in the publication of *Sartoris*, are known to survive. In 1973 Random House published an edition of *Flags in the Dust* edited by Douglas Day, who used the typescript dated "29 September 1927" as his text, although he made some editorial alterations and interpolated into his text one passage from *Sartoris* that does not appear in the typescript and which seems clearly to have been written by Faulkner. The result is a conflated text that aims to be as close as possible to the typescript that Faulkner sent to Wasson in 1928.

By preserving Faulkner's spelling, punctuation, and wording, even when inconsistent or irregular, the Polk text strives to be as faithful to Faulkner's usage as surviving evidence permits.

The following notes were prepared by Joseph Blotner and are reprinted with permission from *Novels 1942–1954* (1994) in the edition of Faulkner's collected works published by The Library of America. Numbers refer to page and line of the present volume (the line count includes chapter headings). No note is made for material included in the eleventh edition of *Merriam-Webster's Collegiate Dictionary*. For more detailed notes, references to other studies, and further biographical background, see: Joseph Blotner, *Faulkner, A Biography*, 2 vols. (New York: Random House, 1974); Joseph Blotner, *Faulkner, A Biography, One-Volume Edition* (New York: Random House, 1984); *Selected Letters of William Faulkner* (New York: Random House, 1977), edited by Joseph Blotner; Calvin S. Brown,

A Glossary of Faulkner's South (New Haven: Yale University Press, 1976); and George Hayhoe, "A Critical and Textual Study of William Faulkner's *Flags in the Dust*" (Ann Arbor: University Microfilms International, 1979).

11.10　Fort Moultrie fell]　The fort, one of a series guarding Charleston harbor, was evacuated on the night of December 26, 1860, by its federal garrison, which then moved to Fort Sumter.

19.1　shaled]　Fell.

34.21　net]　Hunting pattern.

42.28　Ak. W.]　Armstrong-Whitworth F.K.8, a two-seat British biplane bomber and reconnaissance aircraft.

43.15　Camel]　Sopwith Camel, a single-seat British biplane fighter aircraft.

43.17　Fokkers]　German single-seat fighter aircraft, including the DR.I triplane and D.VII biplane.

43.33　Richthofen's]　Captain Manfred von Richthofen (1892–1918), the top German fighter ace of World War I, was credited with 80 aerial victories before his death in combat.

59.3　dog-robber]　Orderly.

62.27　Senator Vardaman]　James K. Vardaman (1861–1930), a Democrat, served in the Mississippi house of representatives, 1890–96; as governor, 1904–8; and in the U.S. Senate, 1913–19, where he warned that the conscription of African-Americans during World War I would threaten white supremacy.

72.28　S.O.S.]　Service of Supply.

85.5　quoilin']　Quarreling.

118.18　Liberty Loan]　U.S. government bonds sold to finance World War I.

158.28　triangle]　Signifying non-combatant status.

161.2　o.d.]　Olive drab.

167.3　peanut parcher]　Movable appliance for roasting peanuts.

170.33　Arlens and Sabatinis]　Popular novelists Michael Arlen (1895–1956), author of *The Green Hat*, and Rafael Sabatini (1875–1950), author of *Scaramouche* and *Captain Blood*.

180.30　Ahenobarbus]　A powerful Roman family whose members included the Emperor Nero.

229.11　Van Dorn]　Earl Van Dorn (1820–1863) was a Confederate general from June 1861 to May 1863, when he was killed by a jealous husband in Tennessee.

267.4　peanut parcher]　See note 167.3.

308.32　toll]　Bribe or entice.

352.32　sulled]　Acted sullen.

354.25　Raphael Semmes]　Semmes (1809–1877), a Confederate naval officer, commanded the commerce raider *Alabama* from 1862 to 1864.

387.12　A.P.M.'s]　Assistant Provost Marshal.

Printed in the United States
by Baker & Taylor Publisher Services